D1170661

"Marianna, may I make love to you? Please say yes..."

No one had ever talked to her like this.

She made no resistance as he pulled her to him; the gentleness of his voice, the kindness of his words, disarmed her as no threat or show of strength would have done. It was so nice to yield, willingly to be pulled against his bare, warm chest; to feel his fingers tangle in her hair as he drew her face to his; to feel his lips upon hers, so gentle, so soft, so loving; and then, not so gentle, not so soft, but still loving, and asking, asking something of her, something that she had not realized she would be happy to give . . .

Patricia Matthews

This is a story only America's First Lady of Love could write. She has stirred the hearts of millions of women around the world with her enthralling stories of passion set in the romantic past. Her record of ten consecutive bestselling romances is unsurpassed.

Tides of Love

by Patricia Matthews

BANTAM BOOKS
Toronto / New York / London

TIDES OF LOVE
A Bantam Trade Book / June 1981

All rights reserved.
Copyright © 1981 by Patricia Matthews,
Cover art copyright © 1981 by Bantam Books, Inc.
Book designed by Cathy Marinaccio
This book may not be reproduced in whole or in part, by
mimeograph or any other means, without permission.
For information address: Bantam Books, Inc.

ISBN 0-553-01328-9

Published simultaneously in the United States and Canada

Bantam Books are published by Bantam Books, Inc. Its trademark, consisting of the words "Bantam Books" and the por-
trayal of a bantam, is Registered in U.S. Patent and Trademark
Office and in other countries. Marca Registrada. Bantam
Books, Inc., 666 Fifth Avenue, New York, New York 10103.

PRINTED IN THE UNITED STATES OF AMERICA

0 9 8 7 6 5 4 3 2 1

SEA-STORM

by
Patricia Matthews

The swell and soar and tumble of waves,
The rumble of waves on the rocky shore.
A smooth expanse of warm white sand,
Shrill cry of birds.

The wind-brushed sky, a sullen blue,
Incites the sea,
Until they join together
In rebellious mood,
To birth a storm of foam and spray,
Then darken, blend and fade to gray,
While gulls seek sanctuary
On the salt-damp rocks.

And a part of the soul long hushed, flies free,
Till it finds surcease in the violent sea,
While the heart cries wild,
The throat draws tight,
Excitement flares.

Then the waves grow soft
And the sea birds fly,
While the mind grows calm
With the clearing sky.
The sun sinks low,
And the soul once more seeks a quiet place.

Tides of Love

Part One

1840:

The Outer Banks and Boston

Chapter One

THE wind, carrying a burden of cold salt spray, cut viciously through the dark night, and Marianna Harper, lowering her chin into the wide collar of the man's coat she wore, turned her face away from the blow.

Her hands, deep in the coat pockets, were already numb, and despite the gum boots, her feet ached from the chill and the wet.

The storm had been raging since late afternoon, whipping the waves into huge, jagged combers that tore at the Outer Banks as if to destroy them. The wind was at least sixty knots and howled along the sandy beaches with a terrible frenzy.

Inside the hut it had been uncomfortable enough—with the leaking roof dripping sour, cold water and the wind blustering through every chink to chill one's flesh and make one's bones ache—but now, in the roiling dark, at the water's edge, it was sheer torture, and only Marianna's fear of Ezekial Throag and the others kept her at her post.

From the direction of the roaring sea, she could hear the sound of a ship's bell tolling wildly. It had the shocking sound of a cry for help.

For a moment Marianna felt a stab of pity for the poor souls on the ship that was about to be bilged on the shoals. She usually tried not to think of such things, for these thoughts brought her only confusion and discontent; but sometimes, like now, while she was waiting and her mind was not occupied with her tasks, she couldn't help but think of the people out there, about to be drowned; or, if they were spared by the sea, to be bludgeoned by Ezekial Throag and the others. After all, they were people like herself, and she could not help but wonder how they must feel, how afraid they must be, as the ship's back broke beneath them.

Marianna knew well enough what Ezekial Throag and the others would say to such thoughts. They would say that she had gone soft, and they would tease and torment her. But just the same, she often felt that what they did, what they were doing, was very wrong.

She also often puzzled over how Ezekial Throag seemed to know when a ship was due; he was almost never wrong. It was a shivery thing—almost as if he possessed some frightening mystic sense that informed him of ships passing close to the Banks.

Marianna peered out from behind the rock behind which she was crouching for shelter against the biting wind. About two hundred feet south along the beach, she could see the yellow glow of the huge, whale-oil lantern flickering in the windblown sand and spray.

It was this light that the ship would be heading away from, thinking it a lighthouse warning. As they steered away to avoid the light, the ship would run aground on the treacherous shoals, the bottom would be ripped out of the vessel, and passengers and cargo would be spilled out into the icy waters.

Then Marianna and the others would go to work. All of them—men, women, and children—would wade into the surf and pull to shore that which they had destroyed and killed for. It was the way they made their living. They were wreckers.

Suddenly the ship's bell sounded startlingly near, the sound borne on a gust of wind, and then, even through the storm's roar, Marianna thought she heard the final death cry of the ship, a moaning, roaring sound of rending metal and tearing wood.

Along the beach great fires suddenly blazed, springing up at Throag's thundering bellow. It was the signal. She must now go to work.

Closing her mind to all thought save that of the task

ahead, Marianna took her hands from the comparative warmth of her pockets and plodded toward the water's edge, peering through the gloom for the sight of floating chests, crates, or other goods.

The water was icy, and she dared not go too close to the surf, or she risked being sucked into the sea herself.

There! A keg bobbed toward her, rolling on the white foam of a comber.

Deftly Marianna snagged it with her pike, grasped it, and wrestled it upon the beach to a spot where it would not be reclaimed by the waves. She could see the dim forms of the other wreckers along the beach as they all scurried about their tasks.

As she left the keg on the sand, Marianna sighed softly to herself. When it was all over, when they had gathered all that they could for the time being, they would return to the huts, and she knew what would happen then.

After a wrecking Jude Throag was always randy as a goat. He would want to have her, tired and wet though she might be. Of course, he took her almost every night, anyway, but after a wrecking—which seemed to excite him in some mysterious way beyond her understanding—he was always insatiable, taking her three or four times, pummeling her body and bruising her flesh until she felt that she simply could not endure it.

Sometimes Marianna wished that she could have remained a child. Things had been so much simpler then. She had had only to do her duties and mind her tongue, and she had been left alone.

But now—now that had all changed. Last year she had turned fourteen, and her body had begun to alter. Her bosom had swelled, fine fuzz had appeared on areas that had been bare and neat before, and her bottom had grown fat.

When that had happened, the men had started to notice her. Their attitude toward her had changed; no longer did they call her child and shoo her off, but made ugly, vulgar jests when she was near and pinched her. How she hated the pinching!

And then she was fifteen, and Jude—Ezekial Throag's

son and second in command—had singled her out for his. With no fancy flourishes, Marianna's mother had told her on her fifteenth birthday that she was to be Jude's woman.

The idea had frightened and repelled her. Jude was old, at least thirty, and big and swaggering and rough-talking. Besides, he already had a woman, redheaded Jenny, who had been with him for several years.

But her mother had shaken her head. "Jenny's to go," she said firmly. "Jude told me himself. He wants you, girl. You should be glad. He's the leader's son. He's strong, and when Ezekial goes, Jude will take his place. You will be the leader's woman."

Her mother's lips had spread in an awful smile, and Marianna knew that there was nothing she could do.

And so, she had been given to Jude Throag, and he had casually and brutally deflowered her in the bedroom of her mother's hut, while the others drank and laughed in the other room. It had hurt, and Marianna had not liked it. She could not understand why redheaded Jenny had cried and looked at her, Marianna, with venom in her eyes. Surely, Jenny should be glad to be let off, to have someone else take her place.

Later Marianna had tried to talk to Jenny, but Jenny left the mark of her hand on Marianna's face and stalked away. One of the other women, Old Mary, had finally explained to Marianna that Jenny was jealous and unhappy at losing Jude to another woman.

Marianna could not understand it then, and she could not understand it now. Of course she had known about sex—you couldn't live the way they did and not see everything that went on—but somehow, this knowledge had never really touched her. Somehow, she had never thought that she would be involved in it herself. And it was so awful! She was so small, still not much taller than she had been as a child, and Jude was so huge, particularly that part of him that she had begun to think of as his weapon—for that was the way he used it, like a ram, to batter her down, like a club, to pound away at her. She was always sore, always tender, there below.

Now she drove her iron hook into a small crate that the

6

waves had just tossed up onto the beach and pulled it shore-
ward, grunting, thinking of the further punishment her
small body would absorb that wild night.

The wind had quieted, only occasionally making a lunge
at the hut, and the rain had all but stopped.

Inside the main room of the Throag hut, a fire roared,
sending warmth and cheer around the room and into the
cold bones of those assembled around it. The air in the
room was rank, but Marianna, being accustomed to it, did
not notice it particularly. She drank her tot of rum, like the
rest, and prayed silently that Jude would consume so much
that he would be rendered incapable of performing his will
upon her.

The other Bankers were laughing and singing rough songs,
telling tales, discussing how it had been out there tonight
for them, gloating over the catch they had made.

Marianna sat as quietly as she could, hoping to go
unnoticed, hoping to be left alone. She was deadly tired
and, despite the fire, still chilled to the bone.

Sitting pressed between the malodorous bodies of Old
Mary and her own mother, Marianna tried to make herself
as small as possible so that it would be easy for Jude to
overlook her.

Jude waxed expansive under the influence of the rum
and was talking in an animated fashion to his father.

They looked so much alike, Marianna thought, Ezekial
and Jude Throag. Despite the fact that they were father
and son, they seemed not much apart in age. Ezekial, like
his son, was a huge man, with a barrel chest and heavy,
muscular arms. His coal-black hair was still not touched
with gray, despite the fact that he must be well over fifty
years of age, and his eyes showed a feral cunning and more
fire than did those of his son.

Marianna both feared and hated Ezekial Throag. He ruled
the little band of wreckers with a heavy and awesome hand,
taking the best of everything for himself and his son, cowing
the others with his great strength and brutal temper.

The men said that he was a good organizer and that
without him, they would not fare nearly so well as they did.

He was clever, was Ezekial Throag, and always scheming new ways to lure the ships onto the shoals and new ways to salvage the loot from the wrecks.

So, although the men grumbled among themselves, they did his bidding. They did better under his leadership than did many of the Bankers, and so they were willing to put up with a certain amount of abuse.

Marianna, almost dozing from the effects of the rum and the fire, suddenly felt her arm seized. Before she was completely alert, she found herself on her feet and then clasped in a pair of hard-muscled arms.

She opened her eyes to see Jude's face grinning down at her in drunken lust. She shut her eyes again and sighed. Jude laughed and lifted her high.

"Well, it's good night to you all, mates. I'd love to stay up with you, but you know how it is when a man has a new woman," he said crudely. "With a new woman, a man's appetite grows apace!"

Marianna heard the coarse laughter and ribald remarks as Jude turned with her in his arms.

She opened her eyes slightly to see Jenny glaring at her and turned her head away, only to meet the gaze of Ezekial Throag. He was looking at her with his strange, gray-green eyes, and he was smiling slightly through his thick black beard.

Marianna felt herself shiver. He was staring at her in much the same way that Jude looked at her, and this recognition shook her to the core. In their society the strong took what they wanted, and Ezekial Throag was the strongest man of all. Still, Jude was his son; and if he had a soft spot at all, it was for Jude. Surely he would not take his own son's woman!

But the thought of Ezekial's smile remained with Marianna and made her unusually subdued as Jude strode with her into the small inner room that held their pallet.

Without ceremony he dumped her onto the rumpled pallet and fell down beside her, reaching for her and pulling her close to him.

Marianna felt her flesh shrink away from his touch, as his

drink-thickened fingers fumbled at her bodice, pulling the material away from her breasts.

It was cold in the room, and Marianna could feel her skin goose-bump as the damp air touched her. At that, she thought, it touched her with more tenderness than Jude did.

She lay, resigned and unresisting, as he hoisted her skirt, then pulled open his breeches to expose his huge member.

She closed her eyes and turned her head aside, not wanting to see it. It was an ugly thing and only capable of causing pain. It was obvious to her that men obtained considerable pleasure from this act that he was performing—that is, if anything that caused a man to rise to uncontrollable levels of excitement and made him gasp and moan so, could be called pleasure—and yet she couldn't understand why certain women seemed to enjoy it, also.

Jenny, for example. Marianna would have thought she would welcome the rest from the rough embraces of Jude Throag; but no, Jenny had hurried into another, just as unsavory, liaison with Ben Thomas, a hulking-shouldered, bad-tempered man, as if she couldn't wait to mate with a man again. It was incomprehensible to Marianna.

Jude was grunting as he thrust his swollen member repeatedly into Marianna's tender parts. She bit back a groan and clenched her fists as he began to move faster, humping and jerking like a great, beached whale, all the while muttering and moaning.

Mercifully he was quick about it and soon spasmed noisily, nearly crushing her beneath his great, lax weight.

He had no sooner stopped moving than he began snoring, a sound Marianna heard with gratitude, for it meant that there would be no repeat performance this night. He hadn't drunk enough to make him incapable, but at least he had consumed enough to put him into a sound sleep, from which she knew he would not awaken before late morning.

Thankfully she squirmed from beneath him—he weighed a ton, relaxed like this—and inched away from him to the edge of the pallet, where she finally sank into sleep, the one place to which she could escape.

It was a thin, pale light that greeted Marianna's eyes in the morning, seeping slowly in through the small, grimy window set high in the wall, and she knew that the storm had been followed by fog.

Jude was snoring open-mouthed beside her. He stank of semen, rum, and sweat.

She wrinkled her nose in disgust and throwing the covers back, stepped gingerly out onto the ragged rug. It was bone-chilling cold and damp, and she shivered convulsively and dressed quickly, then reached for the heavy coat that hung on a peg on the wall. The fabric was damp from the night air, but after she had had it on for a few moments, it started to trap her body heat, and she began to feel warmer. She still had on the heavy stockings she had worn the night before, and she thrust her feet into the gum boots she had left beside the pallet.

Thus attired, she stood ready to face the day.

There was a slice of cracked mirror hanging on the wall, and as she reached for the door latch, she caught a glimpse of herself—wild-haired and brown, her hair a dark mop of tangled curls, her naturally olive skin tone deepened by the sun. Her mother had once told Marianna that she was pretty, but the only thing Marianna liked about herself were her eyes. "Gypsy eyes," Ezekial Throag had once remarked, meaning it as an insult. But *she* liked her eyes. They were large and very dark, with thick, fringing lashes and well-defined brows. But was she pretty? Well, it didn't seem to matter much. Banker women didn't keep their bloom long. The harsh sun of summer, the sea winds, the dank fogs of winter, all seemed to take their toll; they scoured away a woman's beauty, as the sea and wind scoured the rocks and sand, leaving only the bare bones, as it were. Strong was the thing to be on the Banks; beauty was of little consequence. You had to be strong to survive.

Turning away from the mirror, Marianna raised the latch and slid out into the outer room. A chorus of snores greeted her. Most of last night's revelers were sprawled where sleep had overtaken them. Averting her gaze, Marianna left the hut, shutting the door quietly behind her. Once outside, she drew a deep breath. The air was damp and cold, but it was clean and full of the live smell of the sea.

Her stomach rumbled, and she remembered the small keg she had secreted the night before. She was hopeful that it contained food, maybe ship's biscuits, or perhaps something even tastier.

Ezekial Throag strongly discouraged his followers from keeping any plunder for their personal use; but in truth, all of the band did so when the opportunity presented itself.

The men, particularly those who went out in the long-boats, had the best chance at any valuable cargo, and all kept aside what they could; and the women and children on shore felt no guilt about secreting away a keg, or a crate or two, if no one was watching.

The small keg that Marianna had buried in the sand proved to contain not plain ship's biscuits, but sweet biscuits, which had no doubt been, for the captain's table. Hidden by the thick fog, she wolfed down the unaccustomed sweets by the handfuls until she felt bloated, uncomfortable, and very thirsty.

She reburied the keg and returned to the hut where she drank several dippers of water. The weary revelers were thankfully still sleeping. Good! It would give her the first chance at any salvage that had washed ashore after they had left the beach.

Experiencing the excitement of the hunt, Marianna headed toward the now peaceful whispering of the sea, still not discernible through the smothering bank of fog. At the water's edge it was a bit clearer, but she realized in exasperation that it was going to be hard to see anything that had washed up unless she practically fell over it.

She started along the beach and in short order found another small keg like the one she had discovered last night, a large crate that she could not budge by herself, and a beautiful amethyst flacon, sealed, and, miraculously, unbroken.

She turned the flacon back and forth between her hands, feeling its smoothness; seeing, even in the fog, the light that seemed captured in the brilliant glass. She had never seen anything so lovely and had never imagined having something of such beauty for her very own.

Gazing around to see if she was observed, she quickly put the flacon into the inner pocket of her coat. She would have to hurry now, the others would be stirring soon. She would see if there were any other small or manageable items, and if not, she would return to the large crate with a crowbar and see what was inside. Once there had been a chest with women's clothing, beautiful goods, which the women had fought over and then parceled out, piece by piece, among themselves.

Marianna had been too small then to have been awarded a share, but she remembered still a swatch of blue velvet, bluer than the summer sky and softer than the down on a baby gull.

Patting the bulge the flacon made in the coat pocket, she moved on, squinting through the swirling fog. Suddenly she tripped over something low and yielding on the sand.

Swearing under her breath, she caught her balance and looked down. A long, dark form lay sprawled at her feet, shrouded in seaweed and flotsam.

Leaning closer, Marianna let out a soft cry. It was a man, she could see his face now, pale through the kelp.

At that moment the fog thinned, and a pale wash of light showed the figure more clearly. No, not a man, but a youth. Not much older than herself, and beautiful as a woman.

Shocked, Marianna stared down at him, a great and sudden sadness washing over her. So young he was, and so beautiful! Had he died in the storm, drowned, or had Ezekial Throag, Jude, or one of the other men, bashed him with their great clubs? It was no matter, Marianna supposed, but she hoped that he had drowned. It somehow seemed more fitting.

Still, it was a pity that he was dead. She would have liked to see the color of his eyes. . . .

The youth stirred. His head raised slightly, and his eyelids fluttered.

Marianna felt her heart begin to hammer with fear and excitement. She felt a mixture of emotions difficult to sort out: delight that this beautiful youth was not dead, and dismay that he was alive. Throag would not like the fact that there had been a survivor of the wreck, and he would remedy that oversight at the first opportunity.

Marianna stood poised for flight, uncertain as to what she should do. Then the youth groaned, and she stopped thinking as instinct took over.

She dropped to her knees on the sand. Brushing the kelp away from his face, she put her arm under his shoulders and raised him. His eyelids quivered again and then opened, leaving her looking down into the bluest eyes she had ever seen, bluer even than the scrap of velvet she had long admired. He stared at her uncomprehendingly, then opened his lips, as if to speak.

Marianna parted her own lips, as if in response. Oh, what a pretty mouth he had! She had never seen such a mouth on a man.

His eyes began to show awareness, and she found herself talking to him as she might a child, words of comfort and kindness. "There, there. 'Tis all right now. You're alive. You'll be fine, you will. There now."

He swallowed, and the movement caused him to wince in pain. "Where?" he croaked in a dry voice.

Marianna glanced quickly back over her shoulder, hoping that none of the others would happen upon them, and then back at the young man. She whispered, "Your ship sank. You've been washed ashore on the Outer Banks."

He stared at her, confusion mirrored in his eyes. "The Outer Banks?"

"Shh-h—yes. Just off the Carolina coast. The islands."

The youth closed his eyes and grimaced as if a sudden pain had seized him, and Marianna, concerned, brushed the damp hair away from his forehead. It was smooth and cold to her touch, and she shook her head in dismay. He had lost his body heat, and the cold might very well take him, particularly if he stayed out here in the wet.

But *what* was she to do with him? The sensible thing, of course, would be to tell Jude or his father. She shuddered, for she knew what they would do—club him once or twice, smashing that beautiful face to a bloody pulp, and then toss him back into the sea. Somehow, she knew that she could not let that happen. But where could she take him? She would have to hide him, and on the barren, windswept Banks, hiding places were in short supply. Also, every man, woman, and child knew one another. There were no outsiders. It seemed an impossible task.

And then she thought of Old Jack's hut. Stuck away it was, in a tiny cove, away from the main settlement, for Old Jack had been a sour and uncooperative man, who liked to be off by himself. Old Jack had died last week, of old age and old rum; but the shack was still there and unoccupied, for none of the others wished to live that far from the main group. She would take him there, make him as comfortable as she could, and see what happened. Marianna knew that she was taking a grave risk. But she had no love for either Jude or his father, and she felt something, even if she couldn't put a name to it, for this lad.

"Can you move?" she asked. "Do you think you can walk?"

The youth's eyelids fluttered open. What thick lashes he had, she thought, almost as thick as her own.

He swallowed. "I don't know," he said in a shaky voice. "I'll try."

He kept on staring at her in the most curious way, a strange expression on his face, until Marianna began to feel uncomfortable.

"C'mon now," she said sharply. "Let's try it then."

He smiled, a slow, weak smile, but one that sparked his features with a sudden light and charm that took her breath away. "You're beautiful!" he said in hushed wonder. "So beautiful. Like a sea princess."

Marianna felt herself blushing furiously, the heat tightening her face. "C'mon now," she said again, "there's no time for such talk. We must get you up and away from here, if you're to stay alive."

His expression changed to one of puzzlement. "Why? What do you mean?"

"There's no time to explain. Just believe what I say and *do* what I say."

He nodded and with an effort raised his upper body.

14

"That's a good fellow," said Marianna, putting her hands under his arms. "On your feet now."

This took a bit more effort to accomplish, but in a few moments the youth was standing, leaning on Marianna for support; and although he was very shaky, she thought that she could get him to Old Jack's hut.

Slowly they moved off. The youth's weakened condition made him uncoordinated, and it was like walking a great baby, Marianna thought.

The fog had not lifted, but Marianna was sure that she could detect sounds of life from the direction of the cluster of huts. The others were up and about now, and soon they would be coming down to the water's edge to search for salvage.

The walk seemed to take an interminable time, and the young man grew heavier and heavier as they drew nearer to the shack. But despite her small stature, Marianna was both strong and tough. She managed to get the much taller and heavier youth to the gray, wind-scoured shack and inside, where she had him lie down on the rough pallet that had belonged to Old Jack.

There were no covers or quilts—Old Jack's few belongings had been scavenged by the wreckers—so she removed her heavy man's coat and placed it over the stranger, tucking it around him.

His face was very pale, and his eyelids looked thin and blue, almost transparent. "Are you all right?"

"I—I'm not sure," he said through chattering teeth. "So cold, I'm so cold." He shivered. "My wet clothes . . ." The words trailed off.

Of course, she thought. They must come off. Why hadn't she thought of that already?

She removed the greatcoat and began to take off the wet clothing that was plastered to his slender frame. It was fine material, she could see. Gentleman's clothing—a velvet vest, a fine linen shirt. Carefully she peeled the garments off one by one, feeling a vague embarrassment as she did so, although why she should was a mystery, since the sight of the nude male body was no novelty to her. The Bankers were far from a modest lot, and they lived a communal sort of life. Long before Jude had taken her, Marianna knew what the male form looked like; yet somehow this was different. Perhaps it was because this young man was so alien a creature, so different from the men she had seen and known.

His shoulders were broad and well formed, she saw as she lifted the shirt over his head, but his chest was smooth and hairless as a girl's. Dropping the shirt onto the dirt floor, she tentatively moved her palm over the skin; so smooth—and so cold that it was amazing that there was life within. Quickly she covered his chest with her coat, arranging the heavy garment so that it only covered the upper body, and then bent to the task of removing his breeches.

Gentlemen's breeches they were, too, of fine fabric and excellent fit. With a rising sense of curiosity, Marianna undid the waist and began to pull them down. He was so different from the other men, would he be different there, as well? Or would that part of him be as ugly as Jude's weapon?

The breeches slowly peeled away, showing linen drawers, an item she found a wonderment. A leather purse fell onto the ground with a jangle. The catch opened, and Marianna glimpsed the glitter of gold coins. If Jude or his father saw those coins! Hastily she snapped the purse closed and returned it to the breeches.

Then the underdrawers joined the pile of clothing on the ground, and his lower body lay pale and exposed to her gaze. She knew that she should cover him, yet she hesitated, fascinated by the sight of his thighs, muscular, and larger than she would have thought, and his well-formed legs and well-developed calves. Here also he lacked much body hair, except at the joining of his thighs, where a bright, golden patch of wiry hair nested his male organs, which were drawn up and shriveled from the cold. They appeared pale and harmless, nothing like the dark, threatening dangle that was Jude's, even in repose.

Somewhat reassured, Marianna pulled the greatcoat over him, again tucking it around his cold body.

He tossed his head. "So cold," he muttered. "So cold.

16

Help me!" His eyes flew open and stared into her eyes. "I'm going to die, aren't I?"

The question was voiced calmly enough, but Marianna felt an unaccustomed lump in her throat. The coat was not enough, she realized. Covering would keep in body heat, but this youth had no body heat to keep in. She must not lose him now. What *was* she to do?

And then she knew. She must give him her own warmth. She had seen it done before. Quickly she climbed onto the pallet next to him, placing her body close to his, touching him from shoulder almost to toe, spreading the greatcoat over both of them.

As she snuggled close, he groaned and turned to her, instinctively seeking her warmth. Her arms went around him, and she felt the cold smoothness of his back under her hands. The only thing warm about him was his soft breath on the top of her head.

Marianna lay there stiffly, holding the strange youth tightly, feeling awkward and chilled. But slowly, very slowly, warmth began to creep over her, coming from her body, through her clothing, and going out to the young man. She could feel it, she thought; like an ocean current, moving gradually outward from her body to his. Gradually his body warmed under her hands, and his breathing slowed until she knew he was asleep.

Marianna lay next to him for a long time, feeling something that she had never before known or experienced— tenderness.

Chapter Two

MARIANNA awoke abruptly, for a moment unaware of her surroundings. She could hear in her mind the echo of the faint shout that had awakened her.

Startled, she became aware of the warmth of human skin beneath her hands and of the fact that she was lying next to the body of a man, a strange man, not Jude; and then full remembrance returned, and her heartbeat slowed to normal.

The others were up and about now. She could hear the distant sound of their voices raised in shouts as they called to one another. They must be finding good pickings along the beach.

Carefully she inched away from the young man's sleeping form, wondering at the fact that there was no unpleasant odor about him. He smelled as fresh and clean as the sea.

He was warmed now and seemed to be in a healthy sleep. She hoped that he would remain so until she could return with some kind of proper covering, food, and fresh water. It was going to be a chore, keeping him alive, but Marianna did not regret her decision. He was the most beautiful human being she had ever seen; and although she did not completely understand her own feelings toward him, she knew that he had brought her pleasure merely by the act of being, and that she did not want to lose him.

As she slipped off the pallet, he cried out softly and opened his eyes.

"Don't go," he said, his voice soft and furry with sleep. "Please, don't leave me."

"Sh-h," she whispered. "I must. I must find you some covering, some clothes and food."

He frowned. "I have clothing."

She shook her head in exasperation. "You can't wear your own clothing. They would recognize you for a stranger on sight."

"They?" he said in the same puzzled manner.

"The others. Ezekial Throag and his son, Jude."

"I don't understand."

"That's damned clear enough," she said, sighing. "The others, the men, they would kill you if they learn you are here, that you came from the wrecked ship."

He frowned. "Kill a man whose only sin is that he is alive? What kind of men are as ruthless and uncaring as that?"

"Damn and blast, you're dimwitted!" She shook her head again. "You don't seem to understand. We're wreckers. Throag and the others, they *made* the wreck happen. They lured your ship onto the shoals, as they have so many others. It is their custom to kill anyone that the sea leaves alive. *Now* do you understand?"

His face had gone pale, although he still looked disbelieving. "You have done me a great service, so I can do nothing else but believe you. Still, it is a hard thing to understand."

"Well, you had better understand! I didn't go to all of this trouble just to have them club you to death and toss you back into the sea!"

The young man's face went whiter still, and he slumped back onto the pallet. Despite herself, Marianna's heart went out to him, but she had no time for sympathy. She must get back to the village before Jude came looking for her.

"Look now," she said sternly, "you must do what I say. You must stay here, quietly, and not go outside where you might be seen. If you hear anything, anyone outside the hut, hide in that cupboard." She pointed to a delapidated wooden affair leaning against one wall.

"I'll be back as soon as I can, but it may be some time. I must not make them suspicious. Do you understand that much?"

He nodded weakly, staring at her with a strange light in

his blue eyes. Feeling oddly self-conscious, Marianna leaned over and pulled the greatcoat up to his chin. "There now. You do as I say and rest, and I'll be back before you know it."

He smiled again and closed his eyes, and she tiptoed out of the shack, feeling a strange warmth deep inside her, and not knowing the reason for it.

The hut where Marianna and Jude lived was empty, and as far as Marianna could tell, most of the other huts were as well.

The sound of voices, of cries and shouts, came from the direction of the beach, and Marianna knew that the others were busy with their salvaging. She breathed a sigh of relief. She should have time to obtain the items she must take back to the young man; but she would have to make an appearance on the beach before too long so that Jude would not come looking for her.

Quickly she bundled up two ragged coverlets, some bread and cheese, a jug of fresh water, and a bottle of wine, then began looking for some clothing that would fit her young man—for so had she begun to think of him. He was, after all, *her* salvage.

Jude's clothing was out of the question, much too big. She tried to think of any of the men who were near the youth's size, and finally thought of Luther Martin, Nan Martin's twenty-year-old son, who was of medium height and slender. But how to get some of his clothing?

Outside, Marianna stowed her bundle under the corner of the hut, which was raised up away from the sand and tide on wooden pillars. When she was sure that the items were not easily to be seen, she headed for the Martin hut, not far distant.

To her dismay, when she arrived there, Marianna found Nan Martin at home. In answer to Marianna's question, Nan said that she was feeling poorly and had stayed home. "Besides," she added, "I'm getting on now, and the others push me aside and take me share. I figure there's little use in busting me hump just to have some greedy ones take me goods. I'd just as leave stay here and nurse me poor head."

Marianna forced herself to smile sympathetically. "You're probably right," she said, gazing covertly around the small, one-room hut, much smaller than the one she occupied with Jude. She saw a pair of breeches discarded on the floor near the crude hearth and a heavy, woolen jersey carelessly thrown across a bench near the door.

"But it is a shame that you won't be there to share in the goods from the big crate they're just breaking open."

Nan looked up, a spark in her usually lackluster eyes. "What do you suppose is in it?"

Marianna smiled. "Why, choice viands, they say. Salted ham and the like."

The woman reached for a soiled shawl hanging over the edge of the table. "Well now, maybe I'll be wandering down to the beach for a mite. A bit of ham would go nice. Be a right fair change from that everlasting fish we been eating."

She was hurrying now, so concerned with getting to the beach before the mythical crate was opened and the goods distributed that she was barely aware of Marianna's presence.

"You go on along, Nan," Marianna called after her as the old woman scurried down the path to the beach. "And don't let them do you out of your share now!"

Smiling to herself, Marianna watched the woman disappear, then hurried to gather up the breeches and the jersey. Near the fireplace, she found a worn pair of boots and picked them up as well. Laden, she beat a nervous retreat back to her own hut, where she concealed the purloined objects with the bundle she had already hidden under the building.

She had just finished the task and had started around the side of the hut when she felt a touch on her shoulder. So nervous was she, from her furtive activities, that she jumped and cried out, causing Jude Throag to grunt in annoyance.

"Where you been, girl?" he demanded accusingly. "I been looking for you all over the beach. Look here!" He held up a bottle of wine and a chunk of salted beef. "We found a big'un, meant for the cap's table, doubtless. We'll sup well tonight."

Marianna, inwardly laughing at this turn of fate that had

21

turned her subterfuge into the truth, relaxed. Jude didn't seem in the least suspicious.

"I came back for a sip of water," she said, giving him what she hoped was an innocent look. "Hauling salvage from the surf is thirsty work." She wiped perspiration from her forehead with her hand and hoped that he would mistake it for the sweat of her labors, and not apprehension.

He grinned, showing a missing tooth. "Well, I guess it works out well enough, me finding you here like this. I mean, we could both do with a bit of a lay-down, don't you think?"

Marianna's smile froze. She well recognized the look in his eyes, but considering the situation, she had little choice but to smile back. "You'll be wanting a bit of a tumble, then?"

He laughed and tucked the wine and beef under one arm in order to embrace her with the other. "You catch my meaning, wench. They'll never miss us for the bit of time it will take to satisfy one of the other hungers, heh?"

Marianna resigned herself, girding her body for what was to follow. After meeting the young man from the ship, after touching his clean, white form and appreciating the beauty of it, Jude's smelly, hairy person seemed more repugnant than ever.

But she let herself be led into the hut and into the room where they slept. She could only pray that the young man tossed up by the sea was worth all the trouble she was undergoing in his behalf.

Jude had been right about one thing. It did not take him longer than "a bit of time" to satisfy himself, and when he was finished, he drank most of the bottle of wine, slapped her bottom, and took himself off to the beach, leaving her, as Marianna put it, to "clean myself up."

As she cleansed herself of the stains of Jude's lust, she could not help but notice that her own body was not as clean as it might be. Cleanliness was not a virtue of the Bankers.

She compared herself to the young man. She had not noticed a soiled spot on his person, neither soot nor grime. True, he had been in the sea, but she knew from experience that sea water alone would not remove the ground-in grime that darkened the skin of most of the Bankers.

What would this young man think of her if he were to view her body as she had seen his? Probably turn away in disgust, she thought, grimacing.

In addition to the bit of mirror by the door, there was a cracked pier glass propped against one wall of the hut, a relic from a long-ago wreck. The glass was yellow and spotted, and Marianna seldom spared a glance into it, yet it was clear enough to show her from head to toe.

She went to it and with her sleeve wiped off the accumulated dust. Then, mentally steeling herself, she looked into the glass, staring deep into her own eyes, in an attempt to see herself as the young man might see her.

It was not an encouraging sight: a tangle of dark hair; a brown, pointed-chinned face; large, shadowy eyes; and a shapeless drape of rags covering the rest of her.

Marianna knew that she should be hurrying, she had much to do, but she stood nonetheless, studying her reflection, her mind a battlefield of conflicting emotions and conjectures.

All of a sudden, she began to remove her clothing. Off came her waist and jacket, down came the ragged skirt, off came the gum boots and woolen stockings, until she finally stood nude and shivering in front of the hazy glass.

Hesitantly she stepped back, trying to view all of her body, yet afraid of what she would see.

The smoky glass showed a small female figure, rounded and curved, with few harsh lines. The feet were grimy, but small and well formed; the legs straight, the thighs plump and rounded, the hips more rounded still, with only a sparse triangle of hair below the slightly rounded belly. The waist was small, making the plump breasts above appear even larger than they were, an incongruity under the rather childish face above.

Marianna was far from pleased with the image she saw. She was too short. Her legs were too short. Her face was not womanly enough. She recalled thinking that beauty did not matter much in a Banker woman. Now she had to deny it; she wanted to be beautiful for the young man. *He* was

23

beautiful. Could she be less so, and remain happy in his presence?

She gazed down at her breasts and touched one, watching it change shape slightly beneath the pressure. A great lot of bother these objects were, yet they were what attracted Jude and caused the other men to gaze upon her with hot eyes. Also, they were tender and vulnerable and got in the way when doing hard work, such as hauling kegs and crates up out of the surf. She wondered if her young man would like them. He was so different from any other man she had ever known that she as yet had no idea of how he would react to any given situation.

She held out one slender arm and examined the skin closely. Dirt. Definitely dirt, ground into the skin. She lifted the arm higher and tentatively sniffed at her exposed armpit. Wrinkling her nose, she turned her head away. Yes, she smelled, too, not as badly as Jude perhaps, but she stank, just like everyone else. She supposed a person noticed it less when the smell was his or her own. Looking down at her legs, she saw that they also wore signs of infrequent bathing.

Turning away from the pier glass, without really thinking of the precious time she was wasting in such a vain activity, Marianna rummaged in the leaning cupboard for the chipped enamel basin that she knew was there.

Still naked, she hurried into the larger room, to the water keg, and drew a pitcher full, which she poured into the wash basin. It took her a bit longer to find a clean cloth, but she finally came across a bit of gray flannel that had been hidden under a piece of salvage in one corner of the sleeping room. And last of all, the soap—yellow, strong-smelling, and waxy in her hand.

Shivering and uncomfortable, she began to scrub, starting with her face, ears, and neck, down her torso, then legs, arms, and feet. The soap stung, its odor pungent in her nostrils, and her flesh pimpled with goose bumps from the cold, yet she kept doggedly at it until all of her body had been soaped and scrubbed; then she went into the other room for more water, to wash away the soap.

Finished at last, she stood up straight and stared again

into the pier glass, feeling that, strangely, more than the dirt had washed away in that chipped basin. Much, much more.

Looking at the pile of clothing she had shed, Marianna shook her head, unable to face the thought of putting the soiled garments next to her newly clean body.

She searched through the clothes cupboard and finally found a skirt and waist that were less soiled than the rest, and some reasonably clean woolen stockings. They would have to do.

Quickly she put the garments on, then found a broken-toothed comb that she occasionally used and pulled it through her tangle of curls until some order had been achieved.

Much refreshed and feeling very pleased with herself, she wondered briefly about why she felt this way. Did bathing have some sort of restorative power above and beyond mere cleanliness? It was an interesting thought, but she did not have time to ponder it now. She must take the things she had gathered to the young man, then get back to the beach and mingle with the others.

Engrossed with her thoughts, she opened the front door of the hut and stepped down onto the block of wood that served as a stoop. Watching her step carefully, she did not see the tall figure just in front of her, until she looked up into the face of Ezekial Throag.

In an instant her high spirits and confidence were dashed. One look into Ezekial Throag's cold green eyes was all that she was ever able to face. There were not many things that truly frightened her: Jude—though she could usually handle him; drowning—she'd had a terrible fright when she was very young; and Ezekial Throag.

The elder Throag, it seemed to Marianna, was in fact much like the act of drowning—unpredictable, uncontrollable, a natural force upon which a mere human could have no effect.

Marianna could feel herself draw inward. "Good afternoon, Master Throag. I was just returning to the beach."

She cast her eyes downward, staring at the toes of the gum boots. She could feel his presence looming over her, tall and dark and forbidding, like a great storm cloud.

"Look up, girl," he commanded in his deep voice.

Marianna did so reluctantly, not wanting to meet his gaze again, but his sheer will forced her gaze up and up until his eyes were locked with hers, turning her into a spineless thing, like the small, helpless sea creatures washed up from the deep.

Ezekial Throag gazed down upon his son's woman, keeping his expression forbidding. He was well aware of the effect that his mere presence could evoke, and he enjoyed the feeling of power that came with such domination and the fear that he could thus arouse.

In this instance he particularly enjoyed it, as the woman, girl, actually, was a lovely thing, even under the shapeless clothes, and without any of the artifices that woman in better circumstances had access to.

It was a pity, really, that he had agreed to let his son have her; but, busy with more important matters, he had not really noticed the child until it was too late, and Jude had already spoken for her.

If it was any other man than his son, Throag would have no qualms about taking her from him, but his son was his son, and the only person in this life that he had ever really cared for, although the boy was at best disappointing, showing none of the intellectual sharpness, or leadership, of his father. Still Jude was his issue, his only living link with the world.

Throag's thoughts returned to the girl before him. Her small face seemed brighter than usual—cleaner, he finally decided—and her eyes had a bright shine. Was it fear of him? He knew that she feared him. Or was it something else? She seemed to be holding something in. She was too controlled.

He shrugged. Well, whatever it was, it couldn't be too important. He let his brooding gaze linger on her soft, slightly parted lips and wondered how it would feel to crush them beneath his own. He let the thought show in his eyes and was pleased to see the girl flush. How easy she was to intimidate, to manipulate!

Throag allowed himself a slight smile, thinking of how delightful it would be to manipulate her in other ways, and was gratified to see her begin to tremble. He knew she was wondering what he wanted with her, if he was going to berate her for something she had done or if he was merely going to pass the time of the day or give her some instructions. It was this feeling of always being slightly off balance that Throag tried to instill in his minions. It kept them afraid of him; and if they were afraid of him, they obeyed him without question. Power was really a very simple thing.

"You'd best hurry," he finally said coldly. "The sea is beginning to roughen up, and I want the rest of the salvage gathered in before it becomes impossible."

"Yes, Master Throag," Marianna said, ducking her head. "I'll go right away."

The girl scurried off, toward the beach, and Throag stood staring after her, the cold smile still on his lips. Yes, it was a damned shame that Jude had noticed the girl's budding first. But no matter, there were more important things to think on. The wreck last night had been a good one. There had been much salvage, aside from the main consideration, and the brothers in Northampton should be pleased. Yes, he was good at his job. Very good.

Throag continued to stare after Marianna's disappearing figure for a long time.

It was late that night before Marianna was able to return to the hut where she had hidden her young man. In an agony of impatience, she had forced herself to work alongside the others on the beach and then return with them to the huts. She did not dare do otherwise, for she had felt Throag's watchful gaze on her all the afternoon. Did he suspect something? But how could he? Still, Ezekial Throag was not an ordinary man, he seemed to know everything! It was as if he had an extra pair of eyes that never closed, watching day and night.

It was her duty to cook for Jude and his father. She cooked up some of the salt beef and made hearth bread, which they ate with some excellent jam, salvaged just that afternoon; but Marianna, though she loved sweets, tasted nothing as she put the sweet-coated bread into her mouth. She was thinking of her young man and how empty his belly must be and how parched his throat. She *must* get to him, or he would die.

She and Jude retired early, as was their custom, and, as was his custom, Jude took her roughly before he went to sleep.

Marianna suffered through it, feeling her newly clean body soiled by his touch and his body fluids. Afterward, she lay quietly, though it was sheer torture, until he was snoring heavily.

Jude was a deep sleeper, and once asleep, seldom woke for anything less than the tolling bell that summoned them when there was a wreck. Even then he had to be roused and poked into wakefulness, so Marianna was reasonably sure that once he was asleep, she would not be missed.

After enough time had passed and his snoring was regular and deep, she crept from her pallet and put on her clothing, finding another coat to replace the one that she had left to cover the young man.

The darkness outside was misted by a night fog, but Marianna had no trouble finding her way to Old Jack's hut.

Once there, she felt her heart stop for a moment with fear, for the hut, so dark and silent in the night, did not look as if it could possibly house a living body. Hesitantly she approached the entrance. Had he died, weakened as he was, with no water, no food? Had all her efforts been for nothing?

With a trembling hand she lifted the latch and peered into the darkness. "Boy?" she whispered. "Young master?" She held her breath, waiting for an answer.

"Is that you, my rescuer? I don't even know your name—"

Marianna sighed with relief. His voice was weak, but he was still alive. "Where are you? It's darker than the inside of a cat in here."

"Here," he said in a low voice. "I'm on the pallet, where you left me."

Marianna groped her way to the pallet and dropped to her knees. Her hand found his head. Suddenly shy, she snatched her hand back. "I've brought you food and drink and some dry clothes."

"Did you bring a light?"

She shook her head before realizing that he could not see her. "No, I feared to. A light might be seen from the village. Here"—she fumbled open her bundle and handed him a piece of bread and salt beef—"eat. You must be fair starved."

She felt his hands take the food eagerly. "Yes, but water first, if you please, or I won't be able to swallow."

She gave him the water jug. "There's wine, too, and a bit of jam."

"You're wonderful," he said, between gulps of water. "You thought of everything."

She felt herself grow pleasantly warm under these words of praise. In her life such words were rarely heard.

She fed him carefully, handing him bits of beef and bread, and the bottle of wine. When he had finished, Marianna wrapped the remaining food in the piece of cloth in which she had carried it, then put it on top of the clothes cupboard. "Twill make it harder for the rats to get at," she said practically.

He sighed. "Ah, yes, that's better. I feel stronger already—I must know your name. 'My rescuer' sounds very awkward."

Marianna smiled in the darkness and seated herself near him on the pallet. "My name is Marianna. Marianna Harper." Her smile widened, even though he could not see it. "Do you know what I called you? To myself, I mean?"

"No," he said, a hint of laughter in his voice.

"I called you 'my salvage,' " she said, not entirely truthfully, not wanting him to know that she had also thought of him as "my young man."

He laughed softly. "Well, I guess that's what I am, just another piece of flotsam washed up by the sea, but my real name is Phillip, Phillip Courtwright." His voice grew somber as he spoke the last words, and Marianna wondered if he was thinking of the others, those who had died in the wreck of his ship.

"What do we do now?" he asked, his voice still serious.

Marianna, not grasping his meaning, hesitated a moment before answering. "Do you mean right now?" she finally said.

"No, I mean what happens next. You can't keep me hidden here forever, you know. We have to devise some sort of a plan so that I can get away from here. I have important matters to pursue."

Marianna felt her spirits plummet. She had thought ahead no farther than this moment and had not faced the thought of his going away. Her voice was tart as she replied, "Well, I certainly haven't had time to be thinking of plans to get you away from here. I've been too hellfire busy just trying to keep you alive. It's been a goddamned deal of work, just trying to keep you alive and well. Right now, I'm tired to the death, and I still have to walk back to the village."

"Oh!" he said, contrite. "I'm terribly sorry, Marianna. I didn't think. I didn't mean to sound ungrateful. My God, if you hadn't found and cared for me—!"

She made no resistance as he pulled her to him; the gentleness of his voice, the kindness of his words, disarmed her as no threat or show of strength would have done. It was so nice to yield, willingly to be pulled against his bare, warm chest; to feel his fingers tangle in her hair as he drew her face to his; to feel his lips upon hers, so gentle, so soft, so loving; and then, not so gentle, not so soft, but still loving, and asking, asking something of her, something that she had not realized she would be happy to give.

Marianna was no longer thinking. It was as if she had turned off the reasoning part of her mind. She helped him remove her clothing, piece by piece, until she was as naked as he. His touch was a revelation to her, for she had never known a male touch that was not rough and brutal. She had not known that her skin, her flesh, could experience such pleasure from a touch. His fingers caressed her nipples, electrifying the pathways of her nerves, sending waves of indescribable pleasure and desire over her body. He was treating her as he might a treasure, not something to use, then toss aside. Her spirit, as well as her flesh, luxuriated in the feeling of skin against skin, and her body arched under his stroking hands.

"Marianna?" His voice had a tremor, and she shivered as she heard the plea in it. No one had ever talked to her like this. "Marianna, may I make love to you? Please say yes. I'm burning. I ache to be inside you."

She laughed softly. "This is a fine time to be asking. You've already half done so."

His breath was ragged and hot in her ear. "Then I may?"

"Yes, Phillip, yes!" she said breathlessly, wanting to know whether or not the rest of it would be as different from her experience as the preliminaries had been.

His need was great, she could tell by the trembling of his body and the size to which his member had grown; but he was still gentle and careful as he went into her, as if afraid he might hurt her. Marianna wondered at his control and felt an anxiety of her own, a desire to have the union consummated, for she was herself experiencing a feeling of great want, a desire for friction, for movement.

And then he was inside her, and it was the nicest feeling Marianna had ever known. The movement, the friction, for the first time brought her pleasure, a pleasure so intense that she wondered why she had not known of it before this.

So this is what they talk about, she thought; this is why women want men to bed them. For the first time, she was glad to be a woman.

And then all thought was washed away by a tide of sensation that caused her to moan and cry out in the throes of a pleasure that was almost pain.

When Marianna awakened sometime later, she knew that she had slept deeply. Her body was marvelously relaxed and languorous, and she was, for the first time that she could recall, truly happy.

She could feel Phillip's body next to hers and hear the sound of his regular breathing.

So this was what the man and woman relationship was all about! Yet, did they all feel this? Had red-haired Jenny felt this with Jude? Was that why she had been so jealous, and so angry at losing him? If this was true, why hadn't she, Marianna, experienced the same with Jude? Why had she experienced nothing but discomfort and repugnance? It was a subject she would have to ponder on.

Her mind jumped to Phillip's words: "I must get away from here." She couldn't let him go, not after what had just happened. She had to keep him here, with her. Hot tears

31

scalded her eyes. That was impossible, she knew. It would be putting both their lives in jeopardy. She could maintain the deceit for a few days, but no longer. Someone would be bound to become suspicious.

She wondered how long it was until dawn. She had best slip back to her own hut; it would not do for Jude to wake up and find her gone.

Carefully she eased off the pallet, but Phillip woke up and seized her around the waist. "No! Don't go, Marianna. Lovely, sweet Marianna! Don't go just yet."

"I must," she whispered. "If Jude finds me missing, it will be all up with you, and with me, as well. You stay here, keep hidden, and I will manage somehow to slip back to-morrow with more food and water."

"Thank you, dearest Marianna," he said, pulling her close and kissing her lips gently. "The food and water were much needed, but oh, Marianna, how I needed you! Have you any idea how wonderful you are?"

Marianna felt herself flush. Such extravagant words. She scarcely knew how to take them.

"Marianna, my ministering angel!"

He pulled her closer still, turning her about, and before she could frame an objection, she was swept away again, with the touching, the clinging, and the lovely, final pene-tration and the movement that brought them once more to that wonderful, soundless explosion.

When she finally climbed from the pallet, Marianna's legs were weak, and she felt tender and vulnerable. She was hardly conscious of the walk back to the village, and her happiness even managed to insulate her against the act of climbing onto the pallet beside Jude's gross, smelly bulk. Her dreams were restless and filled with erotic imag-ery.

During the next two days, Marianna existed in a dream world, performing her tasks by rote, with mindless effi-ciency, for her thoughts were always with Phillip and on the stolen time they spent together. She was so oblivious to her surroundings that she did not notice that she was the object of Ezekial Throag's suspicious scrutiny or that Jude was muttering darkly over her efforts to avoid his attentions in bed.

Being bedded by Jude now was more than unpleasant. Before she had known nothing else, yet still had found his brutish lovemaking repellent; now, after having experienced physical love with Phillip, it was almost unbearable.

Yet she was so deep in her dream world that she failed to recognize Jude's growing discontent. She was far too busy thinking of the things that Phillip had told her and wondering how to keep him here, on the Banks, and away from the others at the same time.

Phillip had told her that he had been on a mission, a journey to accomplish some undefined goal, when his ship had run aground on the shoals. He said that he must complete this mission, that he had sworn a solemn vow to do so. He told her that he must leave, that he must get away, and asked her to get him sufficient provisions to make his way to Charleston. However, in her anxiety not to lose him, Marianna had procrastinated, hoping that some other solution to their problem would present itself.

Now, it was the fourth day since Phillip had been washed ashore, and Marianna was on her way to Old Jack's hut, carrying her usual load of food and drink, intent only on thoughts of Phillip and herself together.

Phillip, when she entered the hut, was whittling on a piece of driftwood, with a knife that she had fetched for him. His eyes lighted when she entered the shack, but his expression was grave.

She ran into his arms, and they embraced passionately.

Finally he pulled away and gazed down into her glowing face. "Marianna, we *must* talk. I can't stay here much longer. I'm going mad for lack of anything to do, and I worry about what I've sworn to do, which is going undone. Also, if what you have told me is true, I am in constant danger of being discovered and killed by your people Marianna, I *must* go! I must leave this place."

"Hush now, love, hush. Not now," she whispered, stopping his words with her lips. "Look, I brought you some sweet biscuits and some fresh cod. You'll have a fine supper."

"Marianna," he said desperately, "you're not listening to me. I am quite serious. You have saved me, saved my life, and I love you for it, but you may yet be the cause of my losing it!"

Her arms fell away, and a great sadness washed over her. She knew that what he said was all too true, yet she did not want to face it. She could not, *would* not, let him go.

"Oh, Phillip!" she cried, throwing her arms around his neck again, hugging his face to hers. "We'll talk. We'll talk, I promise we will. But first, hold me. Kiss me!"

Giving a sigh of resignation, Phillip acquiesced. They were straining together in a fierce embrace when the door slammed open, striking the inside wall of the flimsy building with enough force to cause the hut to shake dangerously.

Startled, Marianna whipped around to see Jude Throag charge into the room, a knotted wooden bludgeon held high in his hands.

Chapter Three

JUDE'S figure loomed ominously in the faint moonlight spilling in through the doorway, causing Marianna to realize that night had fallen while she had been here. All she could think of in that first shocked instant was how frail she and Phillip were in comparison to Jude.

She heard the sound of her own voice crying out in fear and felt Phillip's body stiffen. What were they to do? What *could* they do?

"Bitch!" Jude spat the word, his voice so thick with fury that the word was almost incomprehensible. "So this is what you've been up to! Goddamnit, who is the filthy sneak? I'll have his head for this!"

Marianna jumped up, placing herself between the two men, thankful now for the darkness. Apparently Jude assumed that Phillip was one of the men from the village; and although she did not see how this fact would help them, she instinctively felt that it was better if Jude did not know that Phillip was an outsider.

"Jude, please!" Marianna pleaded, moving toward him. "Don't hurt him, please!"

Jude laughed, a harsh, grating sound. "Don't hurt him, you say? Don't hurt him, slut? What kind of a man is he, to need a woman to stand between him and a fair fight?"

"Not a fair fight," Marianna said in a trembling voice. "You have a club!"

Jude laughed again. "I need no club to take care of the likes of him. Let him stand forth and be seen!"

Marianna did not move. "Jude—"

35

"I said, let him be seen!" Jude roared. "Light the lantern, girl!"

"There is no—I have no lantern. Not even a candle."

"You lie."

"No, no, I speak the truth. I was afraid the light would be seen from the village."

Jude snarled, "Don't want to be seen, heh? Now who can it be that you are so fearful for him? Is it a lad? Is that it, wench? Well, I just happen to have a candle butt in my pocket, and a packet of lucifers, as well. So we'll soon see just who it is that is cuckolding me. I want to see his face when I bash his skull in for him!"

Marianna began to tremble. She could feel Phillip's breath in her ear. So far he had not spoken, and she wondered at his control. A fight between Banker men was always preceded by an exchange of crude insults and hot words.

A weak light began to burn, and Jude exclaimed, "There, that's better!"

Then, as the light grew, illuminating Jude's heavy face from below, Phillip moved unexpectedly, darting forward so quickly that Marianna was not quite certain what was happening.

Jude was totally taken by surprise. His lips parted, but he only had time to emit an explosive grunt before Phillip was upon him. The candle stub tumbled to the ground and went out. As it did, Jude uttered a guttural cry.

"Phillip!" Marianna shouted.

There was no answer save the noise of a violent scuffle, another grunt from Jude, and then the sound of a body hitting the ground. Marianna sucked in her breath. Was the body that of Jude, or Phillip?

"Phillip?" she called again, and then Phillip spoke, "It's all right, Marianna. Find the candle and light it. I want to see if he's dead."

After much hasty fumbling, Marianna managed to retrieve the candle and find the packet of lucifers in Jude's pocket. She lit the candle stub and held it out to Phillip. He knelt and felt for the artery in Jude's throat.

Marianna kept her gaze averted. The one glimpse of Jude had told her all she needed to know—eyes open and staring blindly, the knife handle sticking out of his left side. There was no doubt in her mind that he was dead.

She heard Phillip draw in his breath with a sigh, and then she felt his hand upon her shoulder. He was breathing heavily.

"Yes, he's dead. I was fortunate to get in the first blow with the knife. If he'd had time to set himself, I'd be dead instead of him. Marianna—I must go now. There is no alternative."

She heard his voice as if through heavy cotton. Although the words were clear enough, it was difficult for her to grasp his meaning.

"Marianna, are you listening to me?" He turned her to face him and gave her a hard shake. He had placed the stub of candle on the table, and in the dim light his face was pale and sweating. "If your people would have killed me before, what will they do to me when they find this man dead?"

What indeed? Marianna thought dully. Her thoughts turned to Jude's father. Shuddering, she imagined his blazing wrath. She began to tremble, and Phillip tightened his grip on her shoulders. "You must tell me which way to go from here, and you must tell me where they keep their boats so that I can get to the mainland. Do you hear me, Marianna?"

She was staring deep into his eyes, but was seeing nothing. Suddenly her senses seemed to come together, and she knew what she had to do. "That won't be needed," she said quietly.

He stared at her, an expression of puzzlement on his face. "What on earth do you mean?"

"I mean that I'm coming with you. I will show you the way and help you with the boat."

Phillip was shaking his head. "But that's—! I mean, it's not necessary. No one will connect you with his death. You can be safely back in your village and in your bed long before he's missed."

Marianna was thinking of Ezekial Throag. "You're wrong, Phillip. They will suspect me, or at least Jude's father will. He's been watching me. I should have known that I could not fool *him*. You don't suppose Jude had wits enough to think things out for himself, do you? No, his father must have told him that I was acting queerly. He must have told Jude to follow me. I have to go with you, Phillip. To remain behind will mean my death. Hellfire and spit, would you leave me here to face that?"

Phillip glanced away. "You know I wouldn't." He sighed. "All right, Marianna. I have to assume that what you say is true. We will go together, but it will be difficult. A man can travel without money or comfort, but for a woman it is a different matter."

Marianna smiled bitterly. "You forget that I am a Banker woman and not used to easy ways. I'll be able to keep up with you, have no fear."

As the bit of candle guttered, Marianna and Phillip scurried around the hut, collecting what food and water was left and then wrapping the victuals in the covers from the pallet. Phillip, who had been wearing the rough clothing Marianna had provided him, now changed back into his own clothes, and then reached for the heavy coat she had originally worn. As he did so, he felt in his pocket, his eyes widening in surprise as he brought forth a small amethyst flacon of the sort that ladies used to carry their perfumes.

"What's this?" he demanded.

"Oh!" Marianna darted forward and snatched the flacon from his hand. She said abashedly, "It's mine. I found it on the beach the same day that I found you. It will bring us good fortune."

"I certainly hope so," he said glumly, as she tucked the flacon into her bodice. "We will need all we can get. The bit of money I have in my purse won't take us far. I'm ready now, Marianna. Douse the candle."

Marianna blew out the candle and slipped the stub of wax into her pocket, along with Jude's lucifers. She was desperately frightened, and yet exhilarated. This was her chance, her one chance to get away from the Banks, from her mother, and most importantly, from Ezekial Throag. Still, it was a terrifying prospect; for this life was all she had ever known. Would it be much different out there in what she thought of as the "regular world"? At least, she would be with Phillip, and he would help her—they would help one another.

Her throat tight with the strength of her emotions, she whispered, "I'm ready."

Phillip took her hand, and following slightly behind him, she let him lead her through the door of the hut and into the damp darkness of the night.

In all the years that followed, Marianna never forgot that night: the struggling through the moist sand; the fear; the hope; the cold; the fatigue.

All the boats were pulled up onto the beach only a few yards from the village, and Phillip and Marianna were forced to pass close to the ragged collection of huts, so close that voices could be heard. A scrawny dog ran out, snarling at them. Marianna quickly stooped and petted him. Pacified, the animal trotted at their heels down to the boats.

Marianna now took the lead, showing Phillip one of the smaller dories, and together they struggled to get it into the water. It was a difficult, nearly impossible task for one slender youth and a small girl; but finally, spurred by desperation, they turned it upright and dragged it to the water's edge.

Phillip hurried back to the cluster of boats for the oars, and when he returned, they pushed off, wading deep into the channel to get the dory water-borne.

And then, at last, they were away, heading into the quiet channel between the Outer Banks and the Carolina coast, while Marianna mentally braced herself for a hue and cry behind them. Thankfully, none came.

Her skirts were wet and freezing cold against her legs, and her whole body felt numb. Huddled in the stern, she watched the dark shadow that was Phillip labor with the heavy oars. Finally she crawled up to sit beside him and relieved him of one of the oars. Quietly as possible, drawing on the last of their strength, they rowed together toward the mainland and, Marianna hoped, safety.

In the darkness of his hut, Ezekial Throag lay atop the mattress of the only real bed in the village and stared up at the blackness of his ceiling.

Beside him, her body not quite touching his, lay the sleeping form of Betsy Jones, whose husband, Luke, had been drowned in a heavy sea just last week. Betsy was young, plump, and fresh—for a Banker woman. She helped to relieve his tensions and warmed his bed at night; at least for as long as it pleased him to allow her to do so.

Although shortly before he and Betsy had joined in a furious and satisfying coupling, sleep would not come to Throag, for his mind was a tumble of pictures of violence.

Across the screen of his mind, he watched Jude enter Old Jack's hut and confront the guilty couple; Marianna, naked and round, as he imagined her, and the unknown man—Throag pictured him as young, for some reason—twined in a lascivious embrace. He imagined their terror when they saw Jude; imagined Jude with his great club beating the smaller man down; imagined Marianna's horrified gaze, her screams; imagined Jude striking the young man again and again, then throwing the club aside and coming to Marianna with the blood of her lover on his hands and clothing; imagined him taking her brutally there on the dirt floor. Throag saw it in sharp detail, saw every thrust and heard every cry; until it was he, not Jude, plunging into Marianna's tender flesh; he, not Jude, thrusting his strength, his maleness, into her yielding femininity, feeling her tight and moist around him.

Groaning, Throag turned, grasping Betsy's arm and pulling her to him. Still half asleep, she made no protest as he mounted her and entered her with hasty lust.

With Marianna's face before his inward eye, Throag drummed out the conclusion of his fantasy, crying aloud in his violent release. Again spent, he lay back, pushing Betsy to one side. Betsy, unspeaking, went back to sleep.

Yes, Throag thought, he had been right in relaying his suspicions to Jude, for it was Jude's duty, no, his due, to be the one to mete out justice.

Throag had been watching the girl ever since that time three days ago, when he had seen her coming out of the hut. He smiled to himself, feeling satisfied and powerful. He had noticed the girl caching food and drink and had observed her slipping from his son's hut in the dark of the night. He realized that the last wreck must have yielded up a survivor; there could no be no other reason that she

40

would take victuals, wine, and clothing to Old Jack's hut.

Also, there was the air of excitement about her, the glow of a young woman in love, a glow she had failed to show with Jude.

Well, it should have been taken care of by now. Jude should have accomplished the deed, punished the girl, and would soon be returning home.

Home. Throag dwelled on the word sardonically. Yes, to his son, this was the only home the boy had ever known. What would Jude think when Throag told him that they would soon be leaving the Outer Banks; that they would be going to Charleston, or perhaps New Orleans, where Throag would set himself up in a good business, perhaps as a ship's chandler, a business where there was good money to be made and the work was not hard. Despite his great physical strength, Throag had never been fond of hard work; it was too tedious.

Not that he wasn't making money where he was. Throag chuckled to himself, thinking of the hoard of gold buried beneath his shack. Wrecking had been good to him financially, but the years of rough living were taking their toll. He was tired of wearing seamen's rough clothing, tired of never being clean, tired of his own stench; and he was tired unto the death of the sorry lot he commanded.

A man of single purpose, Throag had been able to put these annoyances aside while concentrating on his chief aim in life—making his fortune. But now that he was growing older, the discomforts were making themselves known to his body, and he had begun to long for some pleasure and comfort from all the gold he had amassed, for after all, he had been born to better things.

Joseph Henderson Darter was from a well-to-do family, born to a ship's chandler, Ebenezer Wilton Darter, and his wife, Mirabelle Darter, nee Henderson, on March 31, 1785, in New York. He had been one of three children born to the couple, his birth being followed in rapid succession by that of a brother, Henry, and a sister, Louise.

Throag could still remember his anger and disgust at the births of his siblings. He had considered them intruders, small enemies who took from him attention and possessions rightly his; and he treated them accordingly, so that the two younger Darters cowered in terror of him and were continually tattling on him to their mother.

Since this invariably brought punishment, Throag quickly learned guile, to present an open, honest countenance that completely shielded his true nature. He was also very clever, and the two younger children were no match for his intricate plottings and small tortures, which made their lives a hell.

Since Throag always had an alibi for the time during which any unpleasantness occurred, the younger children soon gave up complaining to their parents and tried as best they could to avoid their brother.

Throag's face twisted in a grimace. The little weasels! How he hated them still. Henry, he supposed, now operated the family business; and Louise, no doubt, was wife to some smugly prosperous tradesman and mother to a half-dozen brats. They probably thought him dead, and rejoiced in the thought—although they would be far too mealy-mouthed and righteous to admit it, even to themselves.

Well, he would waste no more thought on them. He was not dead. No, indeed! In fact, in his own way, he had done very well. Yes, in his own way.

His own way had always been very important to Throag, even as a lad. Once, in a fit of anger, his mother had accused him of being born lacking. "You are bright," she said. "God help you, mayhap too bright, and you are good enough to look upon and can be well-mannered when you so choose. But you are lacking, Joseph. Lacking some human quality that the rest of us possess. You seem to have no sense of right or wrong, no conscience. Sometimes, I think you have no soul!"

After speaking this last, his mother clapped her hand to her cheek, as if overcome by the awful import of her words; but he only looked at her with contempt. He was, as far as he could tell, lacking nothing that he wanted, and was, in fact, rather intrigued by her statement that he had no soul, for such a thing would set him apart from the others, whom he generally despised.

Later, Throag gave some thought to her charge and examined himself in the light of what he knew of other people. He *was* different, he concluded, in that when there was something he wanted to do, or something he wanted to get or to have, he did not agonize over the right or wrong of it, but simply did what he had to do to accomplish his aim. It seemed to him that other people wasted far too much time in decision-making, in agonizing over morality. He was bothered by no such weakness. His reasoning was very simple: if he wanted it, he took it; if he was angered, he struck out. And afterward, he suffered no remorse, no guilt, for his actions. Others, he noticed, did; and although he was not certain just *what* it was they felt, it seemed to cause them to feel bad, taking away any pleasure in the act that had preceded it. If that was what he lacked, Throag felt that it was to his ultimate benefit. He felt that he was much more efficient and superior than they.

So, with cleverness and deceit, Throag made his way through his early years more or less smoothly, learning to disguise his special nature and to take advantage of it without causing an uproar, which would get back to his parents, who, he felt, were also a little afraid of him, or at least of his nature.

However, as Throag grew older, he found life in his parents' house increasingly boring and confining.

When he was seventeen, he finally did something so heinous, so unforgivable, that it could not be concealed even by someone as clever as he. It involved a young woman, a girl, really, near his own age, a friend of the family. Her name was Anne Roberts, and her father, president of a large bank, was a close friend of Ebenezer Darter. Anne and Throag had known one another since childhood, and for most of that time Throag had considered her a silly milksop of a girl, pallid and uninteresting in the extreme.

But then, in her sixteenth year, the pallor suddenly became attractive, and her yielding ways sexually appealing, for she had blossomed into a tall, slender girl with full breasts, rounded hips, and a tiny waist. Anne had delicate, mysterious features, and her normal reticence now seemed romantic. Thus it was that an unpopular child grew into a desirable young woman, surrounded by hopeful young swains, one of whom was Ezekial Throag.

Yet it would be incorrect to imply that Throag hovered near or around her, like the others, for since his family was close to the Roberts family, he had the inside track, so to speak; and in any event, he would not have lowered himself to mingle with the other young bucks in a group courtship.

Throag, at age sixteen, was not a novice in the sexual arena. The brothels and cribs knew him as a familiar face, as did the gambling casinos and saloons. Of course, his parents knew nothing of this, and he was careful that this state of ignorance should continue.

Usually he left the nice girls alone, considering them too much bother for too little reward. Virgins, he had found, were not to his liking. They wasted far too much time in weeping, vaporing, and protesting, and were much inclined to expect marriage in return for what they had given up to the male.

But in the case of Anne Roberts, Throag felt differently. It was not that he felt tenderness for her, for he readily admitted that he felt tenderness for no living creature; but for some unfathomable reason, he wanted her, desired her with a hot lust that disturbed his dreams and threatened to embarrass him in her presence.

Used to having what he wanted, Throag had little patience with the games she—and every other *nice* girl—insisted on playing: the fluttering of the eyelids over the top of a fan; the delicate touch—accidental, of course—on the hand; the soulful looks; the swooning sighs. Such a lot of nonsense! It was with great difficulty that he restrained himself, when they were alone in the garden, from throwing her onto her back and having her there. However, although he might have no scruples, Throag was not stupid, and he well realized what would be the consequences of such rashness. So, he bided his time.

He knew that Anne was attracted to him—her soulful glances and rosy blushes gave her away—and he suspected her of passions she did not herself realize that she possessed.

His plan was simple and brutally direct. One day they would be alone together, really alone. He would play her game for a bit. He would woo her, whisper soft compliments into her ear, titillate and tease her, and then he would offer her tea, or some other seemingly harmless drink, which he would dose liberally with the pale liquid that Butgers, the lascivious neighborhood pharmacist, had assured him would render her relaxed and incapable of resistance, yet not unconscious. After the deed was done, Throag was counting on her sense of guilt and shame to keep her silent. Also, if the potion worked as promised, it should induce a condition not unsimilar to deep intoxication, which should leave her in such a befuddled state that she might not even remember the act that had taken place. He thought it not a perfect plan, but workable.

And eventually, his patience paid dividends. In July, when the Roberts family was packing for their annual vacation trip, Anne became ill. Throag's mother, knowing how much the Roberts were looking forward to their trip, offered to look after their daughter until she was well, and then would send her on to join them.

Anne's illness, a chest ailment, kept her in bed for a full week, and the convalescent period lasted much longer. Even after she had stopped having pains in her chest and the coughing had lessened, she was still weak and very pale, and Mirabelle Darter fussed over her like a brood hen, plying the girl with teas and custards, while Henry and Louise hung about constantly, pestering her to tell them stories and playing childish games, until Throag thought he could stand it no longer.

But his chance finally came. One afternoon, near the end of Anne's convalescence, his mother had to make her monthly visit to her elderly, ailing aunt, who lived a half day's journey away. It was his mother's custom to take the younger children with her, but this time she hesitated, not wishing to leave Anne alone with only the servants in attendance.

Throag, with a sincerity that even a mother could not question, urged her to go, pointing out piously that the children had not been on an outing for weeks and how much Aunt Ariadne looked forward to the visits. His mother, reassured by his show of good sense and calm manner, arranged for the journey, accompanied as usual by the younger children.

And so, finally Throag and Anne Roberts were alone in the house, or almost alone, for Jonas, the coachman, had accompanied Mrs. Darter; Martha, the middle-aged housekeeper, was having her usual weekday off, leaving only Sally, the witless maid.

Of course, Throag devised a plan to get Sally out of the way; he told her that she did not look well and suggested that she have a few nips of sherry and take a nap. He even fetched the sherry bottle for her. He knew that it was a weakness of hers and that she would now sleep the afternoon away.

All obstacles cleared away, he entered Anne's room to put the rest of his plan into action.

In the beginning it all went as planned. The boring confinement of her illness had rendered Anne all the more susceptible to Throag's blandishments, and she unhesitatingly drank the cup of tea he so thoughtfully brought her.

Throag, too, had a cup of tea, although his was liberally laced with brandy, instead of the potion he had put into hers. After draining her cup, Anne lay back against the chaise, where she had been reclining. "My goodness, I feel so drowsy all of a sudden."

Throag watched her with avid interest and a quickening pulse as her eyelids drooped closed and her body slowly relaxed. When he thought she was sufficiently drowsy for his purpose to be accomplished, he sat down beside her and began removing her clothing. Butgers had been correct concerning the efficacy of the concoction—Anne did not object, but only made a soft sound in her throat. She was relaxed and pliant, yet seemed to be partially conscious.

He took a few minutes to gloat over her apparently willing body, ravaging her with his eyes. He reveled in the feeling of power that filled him, until his urgency compelled him to unsheathe his swollen member, the symbol of his power, and do with it what he had so long planned to do.

The sensation of taking the helpless girl was delicious,

and he was driving toward what he knew would be an exquisite burst of pleasure when Anne began to stir, to toss her body from side to side, and at last she cried out and attempted to strike him.

Startled, he gazed down into her wide-open, blue eyes. They were filled with loathing and fear. Throag swore under his breath and mentally damned Butgers, but did not desist from what he was doing.

Anne began to struggle now in earnest, bucking under him like an unbroken mare, but Throag only gripped her tighter, further inflamed by her writhings.

In a state of physical transport, Throag closed his eyes, only to open them immediately as pain shot up his arm. Anne had fastened her teeth into his left wrist.

He was almost at the moment of climax, and although the bite was painful, it did not deter him. Hips still moving frantically, he tore his wrist from her teeth. Snarling, he locked both hands around the girl's neck. Her own hands clawed at his, her nails gouging his flesh, yet her efforts had little effect as his body and limbs jerked in the spasms of rapture, his hands contracting at the same time.

When it was all over and he lay spent and limp upon her, Anne was motionless. After he rolled from atop her, Throag bent down to her, thinking that she was simply swooning and hoping that she would remain in the swoon until he could remove himself from her accusing presence. The whole thing had gone awry. He would thump Butgers's head for him!

But after a close inspection, Throag realized that the girl was not just unconscious, but dead. His mind raced, searching for a story that would be acceptable. He could say that an intruder had broken into the house, bent on robbery; that he and the robber had fought and that he had been bested, knocked unconscious. The intruder had then gone upstairs to Anne's room and attacked her. Or, Anne had asked him, Throag, to go to the pharmacy, to fetch her rose water for her face or some sal volatile; and in his absence an intruder had broken in and killed Anne.

The possibility of his story being accepted was never put

to the test, for while he was standing there, over Anne's body, Sally came hurrying into the room. She skidded to a stop, staring at him with huge, frightened eyes.

"What's the matter with you, you silly twit! What are you gawking at?" Throag snarled. "I just came in this very moment and found poor Anne like this. Someone must have broken into the house!"

There was disbelief in Sally's eyes, and something else. Surely there was no reason that she should suspect him? Still, she was staring at him, her gaze fixed on his waist. Following the direction of her stare, Throag saw, to his dismay, that his breeches were still undone, his linen showing in the gaping opening.

For a moment he considered killing Sally as well. An intruder could just as well have killed both her and Anne. But just then he heard the sound of footsteps in the hall. Someone else was coming!

There was nothing to do but flee. He shoved Sally aside as he rushed through the doorway, and in the hall he careened into the returning housekeeper, knocking her to the floor.

Behind him, both women began to scream; but, granted a few moments' grace before they recovered their wits, Throag had time to race into his room, grab his coat, hat, and purse, and then hurry into his parents' room, where he went directly to the drawer where he knew his father kept a cache of money. In less than five minutes Throag was out of the house and moving swiftly down the street. He never went back.

In the broken-backed bed in the hut on the Banks, Ezekial Throag stretched and smiled grimly to himself. That had been the beginning of his adventures, the beginning of his life, really.

Knowing that he would be pursued, he had put as much distance as possible between himself and New York. Finally, he ended up in Charleston, South Carolina, where he had become friendly with a man who told him that he made a good business out of luring rich-cargoed ships onto the shoals of the Outer Banks and then salvaging the cargo. This man had introduced him to two other men, the brothers Barth, from Northampton, Long Island. The brothers owned a small shipping firm, but they had grand plans for expansion and had use for a man like Ezekial Throag.

Thus it was that he had come to the Outer Banks, where, through his cold intelligence, cruel cunning, and total lack of scruples, he eventually became the leader of one of the motley bands of wreckers who inhabited the low, sandy islands. He changed his name, picking Ezekial Throag for its forceful, intimidating sound, and took a woman, who died some years later giving birth to his son, whom he named Jude, after Judas Iscariot.

Thinking of Jude now, Throag realized that it was almost morning. He should get some sleep, so he would be fresh to hear Jude tell of how he had dealt with the girl and her lover. It would make a good start for the new day.

It was rather late, by Throag's standards, when he again awoke. Betsy had left his bed, and he was alone.

He breakfasted off the remains of last night's supper, washing down the stale food with a draft of strong wine.

Wiping his mouth with his sleeve, he strolled from his hut in the direction of Jude's place, anticipating his son's pleasure at the events of last night.

But when he arrived at the rickety, wooden structure, Throag found it empty, the door open, and the house still. He frowned. Where were they? When there was no salvaging to be done, most of the wreckers stayed close to their huts, working on the boats or just passing the time of day in their doorways or on the stoops.

Not really concerned yet, he walked over to the nearest hut and found the man of the house smoking a pipe in the shade of the house wall. "Have you seen my son?" Throag demanded. "Have you seen Jude?"

The man looked up at him, a trace of fear in his dull eyes. He shook his head. "No, that I haven't, Mr. Throag. Haven't seen hide nor hair of either him or that woman of his. Been here since early on, too."

Throag scowled and without another word, stalked off to the next house, where he asked the same question.

Finally convinced that no one had seen either Jude or the girl, the only alternative was that they were still at Old Jack's hut, and why that should be was a mystery.

During the walk to the distant shack, Throag felt the first prickles of apprehension. There was something wrong here, he could feel it in his bones. Surely, Jude wouldn't elect to stay here, in this isolated place, so late in the day. Food and drink were at his house, and he must know that his father anxiously awaited to hear the full story.

The sun was now high, and it was growing hot, despite the wind that blew in from the sea. Throag began to feel uncomfortable in his heavy coat and removed it.

A gull cried, a lonely, piercing sound, and circled over him. Throag hunched his shoulders. He was not a superstitious man, but suddenly he viewed the gull as a bad omen. Angry anxiety began to gnaw at him as he hurried on toward the shack, which was only a few yards distant.

The interior of the hut was dark, for the entrance faced away from the sun, and it was a few moments before Throag's vision adjusted and he could make out the figure of a man on the dirt floor. His eyes narrowed, and his fists clenched by his sides as he approached the dark sprawl, which he already knew in his heart was his son.

He gazed sorrowfully down into the open eyes that stared unseeingly upward. He swallowed once, as a taste like bile filled his throat and mouth.

Jude was dead! His only son was dead. Killed by that bit of a girl and her paramour.

A cold, deadly anger began to course through his bloodstream. A keening sound of grief came from him, and he made a fist and raised it, shaking it at the invisible sky.

"I swear," he said thickly and furiously, "I, Ezekial Throag, who once was Joseph Darter, do swear by my own blood that I will avenge this, the murder of my only son!"

He lowered his head and looked down once again at Jude's body. "I will punish the wench, my son," he said conversationally. "I will follow her, to the ends of the earth if necessary, and I will make her pay for what she has done. I will make *them* pay! I will think of nothing else until you are revenged. This I swear!"

Chapter Four

THE farm cottage was small and low, blending into the countryside around it like a natural growth.

Next to the cottage was a wooden barn and a roughly fenced pen, which contained three large pigs. A small kitchen garden grew behind the back door.

Marianna, squatting behind the low stone fence, peered hungrily over the top at a ragged chicken scratching in the front yard. She was numb with cold, clear to the bone, and her half-wet clothing clung to her shivering body like a garment of ice.

Teeth chattering, trembling uncontrollably, she watched as Phillip crouched low, then crept toward the clothesline, moving stealthily in the early morning chill.

They had arrived at the mainland only an hour ago and had left the dory on the beach, hiding it as best they could among the rocks along the shore.

Marianna had only a vague idea in which direction the town of Charleston lay, but Phillip, once he had reached shore, seemed to know about such things and had directed them in a southerly direction. Chilled, weak, and empty with hunger, they set out along the dirt track winding through the low vegetation of the savannas of the Carolina coast. They hurried, realizing that they must be well away from their landing spot when Ezekial Throag came after them. Even with a hoped-for headstart, Marianna kept glancing back over her shoulder, expecting to see him any second.

It was Phillip who had first seen the farmhouse and

Marianna who had urged that they approach it in the hope of finding something to eat.

And now Phillip, instead of trying to catch one of the chickens, was trying to steal *clothing!* Marianna shook her head in vexation. True, her clothing was wet, but it would soon be dry, for the day promised to be clear. When she had told Phillip this, he had grimaced and said, "Well, they may get dry, but they'll never be presentable. We've got to find you something that will make you decently attired. I mean, we can't go traveling about the countryside with you dressed like *that*."

Marianna looked down at her ragged skirt, man's jacket, and heavy gum boots, and shrugged. This was the way she had always dressed, and it was no different, no better or worse, than the clothing of the other women she had lived with on the Banks. But when she struggled to explain this to Phillip, he would not listen.

Now, she watched grumpily as he stalked the clothesline, laden with clothes flapping in the breeze.

Fortunately there was no dog, and Phillip managed to approach the line and make his choices without being seen. Still in a crouch, he hastened back behind the wall. Face flushed, he handed the garments to Marianna. "I have no sisters, and I'm afraid that I know little of women's clothing, but I'm sure you'll find these better than the ones you've been wearing."

Annoyed anew, and cold and hungry, she snatched the clothes from him. "And where am I to dress? Will you damned well tell me that?"

He pointed to a small copse of trees, off to their left. "There, in those bushes. And when you're done, hide or bury the clothes you're wearing."

"All right," she said grudgingly. "But you had best see about filling our bellies, or we'll not make it much farther. It seems to me that right now food would be more important than any damn dresses!" She glared contemptuously at the armload of clothing.

His lips thinned. "Marianna, must you swear so much? It's not ladylike."

She snapped, "And who said I was a lady?"

He sighed and gave her a strained smile. "You don't understand, do you?" He touched her hand gently and then, appalled at its coldness, chafed it between his. "Marianna, I don't mean to sneer at the way you dress. It's just that it would be out of place where we are going. Charleston is a large town, and people dress in a different way. Your own clothing would signal you out as different, and we don't want to be noticed. Above all, we don't wish to attract attention. Now, do you understand?"

She nodded and lifted her chin, firming her small jaw. "I may not know much of how the city ladies dress, or act, but I'm not stupid. I can understand what I'm told, right enough. But I also understand that I'm damned weak with hunger, and if I don't get something in my belly soon, I'm not going to be able to walk much farther!"

He shook his head in amusement and released her hand. "I'll get us something to eat. You just go on over there and change your clothing. I'll be along soon, with food, I promise."

"And something to drink."

He nodded. "And drink."

She hesitated. "And just how do you plan to get it?"

He grinned. "Never you mind. Just go to the trees. I'll take care of the rest."

Marianna obeyed, going over to the copse of shrubbery, not much higher than her waist. Crouching down slightly, she stripped off the heavy, wet garments. Oddly enough, she felt warmer without them and realized that they must have been damper than she thought.

Sifting through the pile of clothing provided by Phillip, she found a thick, linsey-woolsey skirt, in a soft gray; a fitted bodice, with long, straight sleeves, in the same material; a cotton petticoat; and a pair of undertrousers. There was also a cotton shirt, with very short sleeves.

She slipped her arms into the cotton shirt, which felt soft and warm against her skin. Then she put on the petticoat and tied it at the waist. It reached clear to the ground, and she thought the outfit, just as it was, very attractive.

Reaching for the skirt, she put it on, fastened it, and then donned the bodice and laced it up the front. The skirt dragged the ground, and the bodice was long in the waist and tight across the bosom, yet it was not a bad fit, considering the circumstances under which everything had been acquired.

Thus attired, Marianna stared dubiously at the cotton underdrawers. She knew what they were, for she had seen some once in a chest of clothing salvaged from a wreck, and her mother had explained their purpose to her. But none of the Banker women wore any underclothing at all, and they seemed an unnecessary bother to Marianna. Still, Phillip had stolen them for her, and she might as well go the whole way, to please him, if nothing else.

Hoisting up the skirts, she put on the peculiar garment, smiling at the slit between the legs, which she quickly divined the purpose of. She nodded approvingly. If you had to wear the damned things, the slit was certainly a good idea. It would be difficult enough to heed the calls of nature while wearing such a long, full skirt, and it would be even more difficult if each time this occurred the trousers had to be lowered.

She tied the strings at the knees and the waist, and feeling a little overdressed but much warmer, she turned to the task of picking up her old clothing and disposing of it, as Phillip had instructed.

She had just finished when Phillip appeared, a broad grin on his face, carrying a fair-sized cloth bag, which bulged promisingly.

He held it up as he stopped before her. "You see? I told you I would take care of things. Now we will have breakfast!"

Marianna felt herself answering his smile. Warm now, and with the promise of food, she felt much more hopeful and was able to throw off the dark doubts that had plagued her since they had fled the Banks, especially the thought of Ezekial Throag's anger when he learned what had happened to his son.

"And there's something to drink as well," Phillip was saying, waving a jug, which he held in his other hand. "Cider. You can't ask for better than that to wash good food down with, now can you?"

Marianna reached out for the sack. She could smell fresh, warm bread. "How did you get it? Did you steal it?"

He laughed and dropped down to sit with his back against a small tree. "No," he said, smiling wryly. "I thought that stealing the lady of the house's clothing was enough to risk. I bought it."

In a grumbling voice Marianna said, "You could have stolen a chicken. It would have saved you money."

He laughed and ruffled her hair. She was already busy digging into the mysteries of the sack. "Yes, I might have done that," he said, "but then I might have been caught. At any rate, a chicken would have required cooking. No, since I had already robbed them once, I figured that it was time to make an honest purchase. I explained to the lady of the house that my wife and I were traveling, on foot, and were badly in need of food, for which I would be glad to pay. The husband, I learned, is away. With only a slight suspicion, she asked me where my wife was, and I told her that you were resting up from the long journey. I was nice and polite, and the woman finally agreed to let me buy food and drink for my weary bride, whom, I told her pitifully, was with child. I do believe that was what balanced the scales in my favor. Fortunately, she didn't come out of the house or look at her clothesline."

He broke into laughter at the expression on Marianna's face. "She even added a jar of milk for the expectant mother."

Marianna had the food out now—a fresh loaf of bread, crusty and fragrant; a great wedge of cheese; a few onions; and the jar of milk.

Eagerly she tore off a chunk of bread and another of cheese and began to eat. The cheese was mild and faintly salty, the bread hearty and rich with the taste of coarse grain. She had never in her life tasted anything so delicious.

Phillip followed her example, and soon there was no sound in the little glade, save the everyday sounds of their eating. When they had eaten and drunk their fill, Phillip, sighing in contentment, lay back against the tree. "I feel better now." He looked at Marianna, his face serious. "This has been a hard beginning, and the days to come will be harder still. Do you regret coming with me?"

She shook her head. "If I hadn't, I would be dead now, lying beside Jude in that hut. I know it."

"You could still go back. . . ."

She jumped to her feet. "Never! I am *never* going back. I will never set foot on that place again. You don't believe me, I know. You think that I could tell them that you killed Jude and they wouldn't harm me. But I tell you that you are wrong. You do not know Ezekial Throag. He does not forget, and he does not forgive. If our paths ever cross again, it will mean my life!"

"Hush now, little one, hush." He stood to take her into his arms. Lifting her chin with one hand, he gazed down into her eyes. "I'm sorry, Marianna. I just had to be certain that you were committed. I did not want to take you away if you were not sure."

"I'm sure," she said, placing her head against his chest. "Nothing that could happen to us, to you or to me, would be as bad as what Ezekial Throag would do to me. I will go on."

The journey to Charleston took Phillip and Marianna a wearying number of days, most of it traveled by foot, although there were occasional, short cart and wagon rides offered by kindly countrymen.

The food bought at the first farm lasted until the second day. From then on fresh supplies were purchased, and occasionally stolen, as they needed them.

The nights were usually spent out in the open. Once in a while, a friendly farmer would let them use his barn.

Although the traveling was arduous and Marianna welcomed each night with gratitude for the rest it provided, she was happy. She was with Phillip, she was getting enough food, and she was seeing the country. The only really bad moments were at night, when she often dreamed of Jude's death, and of Ezekial Throag. When this happened, she would be awakened by the sound of her own voice crying out and would turn to Phillip's open arms for comfort and forgetfulness.

Phillip's small store of coins held out until they were only a short distance from Charleston. He spent the last of his money for bread, meat, and some apples, which he purchased from a small country store. He held his purse upside down and shook it dolefully. "Well, that's the last of it, little one. It's a good thing we are almost to our destination."

Marianna took one of the apples and sank her teeth into the firm, rosy flesh. "And just what do we do in Charleston?" she demanded. "You have never told me."

Phillip polished an apple on his sleeve. "I know a man there, a shipping agent. He once worked for my father, and my father once did him a kindness, which I hope he has not forgotten. My hope is that he will arrange free passage to Boston."

Marianna finished the apple and wiped the juice from her chin with her sleeve.

"You shouldn't do that, Marianna," said Phillip gently. "You will soil your sleeve."

Marianna shrugged. "What else will I wipe my chin with?"

Phillip looked embarrassed. "With your kerchief, if you have one. If not, well, on a handful of leaves or dried grass."

She looked at him curiously. "It seems a damnable lot of bother to go to, when my sleeve is so handy."

"Nonetheless," he said firmly, "you must do as I say. As I told you, Marianna, things will be different where you are going. You will have to learn different ways."

Marianna shrugged again. All his talk of "different ways" bored and irritated her, but if it pleased Phillip, she would try. "All right," she said, smiling into his eyes. "I'll try to do what pleases you. I truly will."

Phillip, looking into those deep-fringed, dark eyes, forgot what it was he had been saying. He touched the thick lashes gently with his finger tips. "Does your mother have such long lashes? Did you get your eyes from her?"

Marianna made a face and shook her head. "My mother has pale eyes, the color of a gray sea. She's a cold woman, my mother."

"Then it must be your father. What was he like?"

Marianna's smile faded, and she looked away. "I never knew my father. Mother would not speak of him, except to say that he was a seafaring man. A man from the southern countries. I used to think of him, when I was little, and dream that some day he would come for me and take me away to some happy place." She smiled bitterly. "But he never did. There was only my mother." She changed the subject abruptly. "Now, Phillip, what will we do in Boston?"

Phillip took both her hands in his. "I have an aunt there. My father's sister, a wonderful woman. I am going to ask her to look after you, to take care of you, and make you into a proper lady. Will you like that?"

Truthfully, Marianna doubted very much that she would, but since it seemed to be what Phillip wanted of her, she nodded obediently. After all, no matter what happened, she would always be with him, and that was all that mattered now—that she should not be separated from this wonderful young man who was like no other she had ever known.

Charleston was much larger, noisier, and more frightening than Marianna would ever have imagined. A practical girl, she was not used to thinking far ahead, but took events one at a time and dealt with them as they came.

But this. . . . This confusion of people and horses and carriages; the clatter of wheels on cobblestones; the cries of vendors; the bewildering multitude of buildings—all of it cowed her and made her feel helpless and small. And the people! She had never imagined so many people.

Ashamed of her cowardice, she clung to Phillip's arm, too confused to ask the questions that crowded into her mind. Phillip also seemed distracted, and his face was pale and intent. He had things on his mind, it was plain to see; so she did not bother him with her fears, only clung to his side more closely, fearful of being separated from him even for an instant.

Of all the wonders that Marianna saw, she was most impressed by the women. Phillip had been right when he had told her that town ways were different and that townspeople dressed differently than the Bankers.

The women's clothing was amazing and beautiful to see; full-skirted, laced, furbelowed. They made Marianna feel like a small, gray sandpiper in their midst as they sailed by, proud as frigates and graceful as clipper ships, ostrich plumes on bonnets nodding. They did not see her, or if they did, gave her a glance of disdain. She could never look like that. *Never!* Would Phillip expect her to, when they were living in Boston?

"This way," Phillip said suddenly, guiding her by the elbow down a rather narrow street lined with shops.

They were nearing the wharves now; Marianna could smell the ripe aroma that appears anywhere that man meets the sea.

The well-dressed ladies were no longer in evidence, and the clothing of the men had undergone a change as well. Now and then she saw a man dressed in gentleman's clothing, but most of the men were dressed in seamen's gear or work clothes; and Marianna began to feel more at home.

At last they arrived at their destination, a large wooden building that could have housed all the huts of Marianna's village.

"You must wait out here," Phillip told her. "Just outside the doorway so no one will be likely to notice you. If someone should accost you, just duck inside. I won't be but a moment. If we're fortunate, we'll soon be on our way to Boston."

Marianna nodded, so preoccupied with the sights, sounds, and smells that she almost did not mind that Phillip would be out of her sight.

She did not know how long Phillip was gone. She was kept busy watching the movement of the foot traffic, the horses, carts, and ragged children, nearly as dirty and ill-clothed as the children of her own village. In some ways, she thought, Charleston was no different than the Banks. It was just that here, only some of the people were poor and ill-clothed, and on the Banks, all were.

Quite pleased at herself for arriving at this conclusion, Marianna turned her back to the street and looked inside, through the glass windows set into the double doors of the building. Inside, clear at the rear of the large room, she could see Phillip talking to a tall, stoop-shouldered man with a gloomy face. Phillip was gesticulating angrily.

She turned back to the street again and noticed that it

was growing dark. She hoped that Phillip would finish his conversation soon so that they could find a place for the night. She also hoped that the man would give him some money for food, for her stomach was growling noisily, and she was tired.

The number of people on the narrow street had thinned out, and the air was growing chilly as a damp wind began to blow in from the sea. Marianna shivered. What was taking Phillip so long?

She had no sooner framed the thought than he barged through the heavy doors, his face set in a scowl and his fists clenched.

Marianna knew that he had been turned down. Mentally she shrugged. She had expected no better. It was Phillip who held the notion that this man would help them. It was Marianna's experience that little help was to be expected from anyone but immediate family, and then only if it did not deprive them of any time, comfort, or money.

"It's all right, Phillip," she said comfortingly, placing her hand on his arm. "We'll get to Boston without his help."

She saw his lips tighten. "The bloody, ungrateful bastard!" He swallowed. "My father helped him when he was in sore need of it, and asked for no thanks. Now he will not repay the debt in kind."

Marianna squeezed his arms. "It's all right. Really it is. We'll get to Boston on our own."

He looked down at her, his eyes softening. "You already knew he'd turn me down. How did you know?"

She shrugged. "It's the way of the world."

"The way of the world! I don't know whether to be amused or cry. Here you've been isolated on that spit of land all your life. Ignorant, many people would say, and yet so wise in many ways. Well, no matter. You are a brave girl, Marianna, and a good companion. But we have no more money, and Boston is many, many miles from here, much too far to walk." He sighed, looking around. "Now we have to find some place for shelter for the night. This is no area to be wandering around in after dark."

They had not gone far before Marianna understood what Phillip had been speaking of. The people on the streets now seemed to be of a different stripe than those who had frequented the area in the daylight hours. Rough-looking men, boisterous with drink and obviously looking for excitement, began to appear in groups of two or three, or more.

And there were women, not the fine town ladies, but painted women with gaudy clothing and manners as rough as those of the men. Unlike the grand ladies of the afternoon, these women swaggered instead of sailed, and their looks, instead of being distant, were hot and bold, particularly when they fastened upon Phillip.

Marianna, having no experience with strumpets, did not know just what they were, but her instincts told her clearly enough what they were after. She clamped Phillip's arm in a firm grip and raised her head as if to say, "Hands off, this one is mine."

One woman marched determinedly up to them. Marianna wanted to look away, yet was too fascinated to be able to do so.

The woman's hair was of a strange, unnatural shade of yellow, bright and stiff-looking, where it showed beneath her ruffled bonnet, which was of silk and dyed a shade of very bright blue.

Her gown was blue as well, and cut so low that her rather prominent white breasts threatened to spill out over the top. Despite the evening chill, the woman's shawl was draped low, so as to expose her bosom, which, Marianna saw as she drew nearer, had been powdered with a heavy, white substance.

But it was the woman's face that startled Marianna most of all, for it was painted, a phenomenon of which Marianna had heard but never seen. The face was very white, with round, red spots upon the cheeks, and the eyebrows were arched, dark lines over eyes, which were also rimmed with black.

The woman smiled with thickly painted red lips, showing discolored teeth. "How's about a little in-and-out, love? Only half price for a handsome lad like you."

She was looking directly at Phillip, and Marianna gasped as, in one quick motion, the woman made a grab for Phillip's privates. Phillip's face flamed in outrage and embarrassment. He took Marianna's arm in a firm grip, steered her around the woman, and up the dimly lit street. The woman's raucous laughter pursued them.

Marianna tried to pull back. "Are you going to let her get away with that?" She gave her arm a jerk. "Hellfire and spit, I'll make her sorry that she—"

"That's it, me girl!" a passerby shouted. "Give the wench what for! You gotta hang onto what's yours, I always say!"

"Come along, Marianna." Phillip hustled her along. "Don't talk to them. It will only make things worse."

Marianna, still sputtering in anger, held back.

In a low voice Phillip said, "Marianna, you're making a spectacle of yourself. Now, come along."

Reluctantly she complied, but she still seethed with fury. What kind of people were these? The Bankers were rough, but the women didn't behave like this! They might make a coarse remark or two, and most of them didn't object when the men were too free with their hands, but she had never seen one take the initiative in such a way.

It was growing quite dark now, and here and there along the streets a gaslight bloomed, a small oasis of light in the thick blackness of the moonless night.

Marianna shivered, "Phillip, I'm getting very tired, and my belly hurts, it's so empty!"

Phillip put his arm around her and pulled her against him. "I know, little one. We'll stop soon. There must be someplace where we can find shelter. But I don't know what I can do about food."

The street, in this particular area, was nearly deserted, and the gaslights, few and far between, did not illuminate much furhter than their immediate vicinity. Doorways loomed like gaping mouths, and Marianna found herself peering into them with apprehension.

At the mouth of one alleyway, Marianna heard a rustling sound that caused the hair on the back of her neck to stir in fright. "Phillip!" she whispered hoarsely, but he had already heard the sound.

"Run, Marianna!" he shouted, and gave her a hard shove.

But it was too late. The alley mouth spewed out two figures who were immediately upon them. Marianna felt herself seized brutally by the arms as a hard hand searched her body, and she heard Phillip's labored grunts as he battled against his own attacker.

Chapter Five

"*T*HIS one ain't got a penny on 'im! How about yours?" The voice, guttural and coarse, came from the figure grappling with Phillip.

Above her head, Marianna heard a voice answer, while the probing hand still roamed over her form. "Nah, this one neither. Looks like we picked a couple of poor'uns. But there's one bit of luck, Red." A shrill laugh, not unlike a horse's whinny, sounded close to Marianna's ear. "This one's female, and a fine, ripe, young one, by the feel of her. At least we can have us some sport!"

"Well now, that is a bit of luck, right enough. I'm randier than a billy goat, and a piece of prime will be right nice," shouted the other man. "I'll just whomp this one a nice tap on the skull so he won't be bothering us at our sport, and we'll have a go at her."

"No!" Marianna shouted into the night, anger and fear making her cry hoarse. "Leave him be!"

The man called Red laughed. "Don't worry none, girlie, I won't damage him permanent."

Marianna waited, her heart pounding, for the thud of some heavy object striking Phillip's head, but instead she heard a strange, challenging shout that shook her badly.

The man holding her started. "Bloody Christ! What was that?"

Out of nowhere, it seemed, sprang the form of another man. It was too dark to see more than a shadowy outline, but he was tremendously tall and broad of shoulder; he seemed to be everywhere at once. Marianna felt her arms released so suddenly that she staggered back against the wall as the tall stranger attacked the pair of thugs. Reaching out to catch her balance, she encountered an arm and recoiled in fear before she heard Phillip whisper, "It's me, Marianna." Then she was drawn into his arms, and they huddled together like two children, as the fight raged around them.

It was difficult to see, and the air rang with shouts, oaths, the sounds of scuffling feet, and, strangely, the sound of rollicking laughter from the man who had come to their rescue. It soon became clear to Marianna that the tall man, with the aid of a stout stick, was getting the better of the two ruffians. He danced in and out, plying the stick with great skill and gusto. Abruptly the thugs gave up, fleeing down the alley, leaving the tall man alone.

"I guess that does it for them! Aye, that it does." The deep voice came from the direction of the shadowy figure; and then the man was upon them, close in the darkness, and a match suddenly flared, revealing the upper portion of a tall, heavy-shouldered man in a sea captain's rig.

Marianna squinted up into a face with high cheekbones, a strong nose, a smiling, well-shaped mouth, and penetrating eyes. He had thick, chestnut hair, which curled beneath the captain's cap, and as his smile broadened, Marianna lost all fear of him.

"Now, what do I have here?" The deep voice fairly boomed in the narrow, dark street. "Two lost babes in the woods, it would seem. What on God's great earth are a pair of innocents such as you doing in this neighborhood in the dark of night?"

Marianna felt Phillip draw himself up to his full height. She could sense his indignation.

"I do indeed thank you for your help, sir," Phillip said formally, "but I have often been abroad in such neighborhoods and have usually managed to fend for myself. I am not so young as I might appear."

The match had gone out, and the captain struck another. Marianna could see the amusement reflected in his eyes. "Aye, of course not, sir, and I am indeed sorry if I implied any disrespect." He peered closely at Marianna. "I am certain that if you had not been trying desperately to protect the young lady here, you could have handled this unhappy affair yourself."

Marianna glanced around at Phillip and saw that his face was set. She knew very well that, with or without her, he could not have held off two such thugs. So why didn't he admit as much and be done with it? Men were a strange lot, full of odd pride and inflated with male vanity. It was clear to Marianna that Phillip was put out at being rescued by this man, and it was also clear that, compared to this man, Phillip was, indeed, a boy. But what did all that matter? What mattered was that they had been saved from harm, and if they were fortunate, this might also mean a meal, and even a bed for the night.

She spoke up. "We were here on business, sir. Phillip was supposed to meet a man who would get us to Boston, on board a ship. But it all went wrong, and now we have no place to stay the night and no money for food." She looked up at him with a woebegone expression, for although it had been her experience that while kindnesses from others were few and far between, she *had* learned that a female child, with sufficient coaxing and wheedling, might sometimes soften the nature of adult men, and she was not loath to use this slight advantage if it would gain them a full belly and a place to lie down for the night.

The second match went out now, and Marianna could not see the result of her stratagem, yet the stranger's voice had a touch of laughter in it when he again spoke. "Well, it so happens that I was on my way to have a bit of supper, and I would be delighted to have you both join me. Over a meat pie and a tankard of ale, we can discuss your problem at length, and perhaps I can offer a solution. What say you?"

"Yes, thank you," said Marianna.

"No, thank you," said Phillip.

Marianna turned her head to glare at Phillip. Annoyed, she gave his shin a sharp kick. "We'd be most happy to join you, sir," she said.

"Fine! And whom do I have the honor of taking to supper, may I inquire?"

"My name is Marianna Harper." She pulled at Phillip's sleeve.

"Phillip Courtwright, at your service, sir." Phillip's voice was cool.

"Happy to make your acquaintance. I am Adam Street, captain of the *Viking Queen*, the finest whaling vessel sailing out of Sag Harbor. Now, let's make haste to the Barnacle Inn. I must warn you, mates, that it doesn't look like much. Still, the food is good and ample, and later, after eight o'clock, they provide entertainment. A singer, who can warm the cold cockles of your heart. Come along now."

He strode on ahead, swinging the heavy walking stick, and Marianna and Phillip followed behind, arguing in furious whispers.

"We don't know what kind of a man he is," Phillip hissed in her ear. "It's foolish going off with him like this!"

"It's clear enough he means us no harm. He saved us, didn't he? Hellfire and spit, where else are we going to get a meal?"

"Very well, but if anything goes wrong, you will have only yourself to blame."

The Barnacle Inn proved to be a small, smoky establishment right on the waterfront, filled with billowing noise and the odor of food. The narrow room was already packed, but the owner, who seemed to know Captain Street, somehow found them a table, snug in one corner, with a good view of the rest of the tavern.

As they sat down, Marianna's gaze was drawn to the polished stick that had been the means of their rescue. It was thick and smooth, a pale ivory in color. She said curiously, "Captain Street, I have never seen a stick such as that. It is not wood, that much is clear."

Smiling proudly, Captain Street balanced the stick in his large hands. His eyes were a bright, penetrating blue. He said, "This walking stick is made of whalebone. A man in Sag Harbor is an artist at making these. This one was made for me from my very first whale and has come in handy in many rough ports around the world."

He placed the stick reverently on the table and turned to the proprietor to place an order for meat pie, ale, and a loaf of bread. Marianna studied him covertly. He was a handsome man, this Captain Street; in his early thirties, she judged. Young to be the captain of a whaler, but then there was an air of assurance about him.

As he glanced her way, Marianna looked away guiltily, her gaze going around the room. All of the customers seemed to be seafaring men; although here and there, Marianna could see one of the painted women of the streets. Mentally, she already felt much better. The prospect of a good meal had cheered her immensely, and she had high hopes that the captain would also be so kind as to provide them with a place to sleep.

Smiling, she squeezed Phillip's arm. "You see," she whispered, "everything is fine."

His scowl was dark, yet he did not take his arm away.

At that moment the proprietor arrived with a steaming meat pie and three immense tankards of ale. He placed these down on the table, along with a round, crusty loaf of bread, and bade them to eat and drink with good cheer.

Marianna needed no further prompting. She served herself generously from the pie, spilling gravy upon the table while doing so. Breaking off a great chunk of bread, she proceeded to eat. She noticed that the captain looked at her with a raised eyebrow and that Phillip's face flushed a dark red, but she was too hungry to be concerned about good manners now. If she was to be scolded, let it be after her hunger had been appeased.

"After you, captain," Phillip said politely, directing a pointed glance at Marianna, who merely shrugged and continued eating.

"No," Captain Street said, smiling. "You first, sir. You are my guest."

Marianna watched Phillip as he served himself with studied patience. It's all nonsense, she thought to herself. He must be fully as hungry as I am, yet he must pretend that he is not. Her way was a good deal more practical and direct.

After Phillip and the captain had served themselves, there was no conversation until the pie dish was wiped clean with the last crust of bread and more ale had been ordered.

Marianna felt replete, warm, and because of the ale,

more than a little lightheaded. She listened drowsily as Captain Street and Phillip conversed.

Being naturally talkative, Marianna would normally have been actively participating in the conversation; but now, feeling comfortable and relaxed, she did not interrupt as Phillip told of his adventures on the Outer Banks and of the events that had brought them to this place. He had, she noticed wryly, lost his initial animosity toward the captain, and now the two men acted toward one another as if they were old friends, or elder and younger brother.

Her attention sharpened when the captain began to relate his own story. His ship, it seemed, had come into Charleston for repairs before returning to his home port. Sag Harbor, Long Island. He had just completed an extremely successful whaling voyage, a voyage that would earn him enough money so that he would not have to worry for some time to come. Phillip congratulated him warmly.

Adam Street smiled. "Yes, Lady Luck was good to me this time out, and because of this, I calculate that I owe her a tribute, so to speak."

"What'dya mean?" Phillip was slurring his words a bit. The ale was having an effect on him, Marianna thought, smiling secretively.

"Well, you see, young Phillip, it seems to me that when a man receives great good fortune from the fates, he owes something in return. Aye, a debt, so to speak. And because of this, I would like to do something for the pair of you. I would like to offer you free passage aboard the *Viking* to Boston. What say you to that?"

Marianna looked at Phillip expectantly. Phillip was frowning down into his ale. "Why, I think that is amazingly kind of you, sir. Amazingly kind and exceedingly generous. And I further think that it was very fortunate that you came upon us there on that street, that *we* were the ones that met you, at such a fortuitous time. We accept, sir."

"Stout fellow!" Adam Street shouted, clapping Phillip on the shoulder with such force that the youth's body almost buckled.

"The repairs on my ship should be completed by the day

after tomorrow, at the latest," Adam went on, "and we shall sail then. Until that time, you shall be my guests aboard the *Viking*." He grinned at Marianna. "Will you like that, madam?"

Marianna smiled happily and forthwith slid from her stool to the sawdust-covered floor. She did not hear the men's laughter, did not feel herself being lifted gently onto a bench, and did not hear the rest of their conversation. Thus it was that she did not hear Phillip tell Captain Street that, although he would gladly take advantage of the offer of quarters aboard the *Viking Queen* until she sailed, he would not be making the voyage to Boston—Marianna would be going alone.

Marianna awakened to a gentle rocking motion and the sounds of creaking wood. For a moment she did not know where she was, and then, as memory returned, she smiled and stretched. Everything was going to be all right. It was going to be fine. The kind captain who had rescued them was going to give them passage to Boston, where they would take up residence with Phillip's aunt. There, they would be forever out of reach of Ezekial Throag.

She turned and reached, reached out for Phillip, but he was not beside her. For a minute she experienced panic, doubting her memories of last night; but then she saw the second pillow and the hollow made in the mattress by another body than her own, and she realized that Phillip had only wakened earlier than she.

Quickly she got out of the double bunk, her feet shrinking at the feel of the cold, damp floor, and hustled into her clothes. She found a basin and a pitcher of warmish water setting atop a sea chest, with a clean but well-worn linen towel and a square of flannel. She took some care in washing herself and in straightening her hair, for she knew that Phillip would wish her to make as good an impression as possible. When she had done all she could to groom herself, she mounted the ladder that led, she discovered, to the deck above.

Above decks, she noticed a strange, unpleasant odor, which seemed to hang over the ship like a pall. The deck was aswarm with men, all working busily at tasks she did not comprehend. She received many a curious glance, but the men kept on with their duties, despite the curiosity they obviously felt over her presence; and finally, after making her way the length of the ship, she found Phillip and Captain Street, supervising the placing of a patch on the ship's hull, on what she would learn was the port side.

Captain Adam Street, in the daylight, proved no less formidable a sight than he had in the night. A huge man, he loomed over Phillip as a full-grown oak towers over a sapling. His was an imposing figure, and Marianna, because of her diminutive stature, felt dwarfed by him. It was, she thought, a good thing that he was an easygoing and friendly man, for in anger he could be terrifying. Briefly she recalled with what glee he had entered into the fray last evening.

After greetings were exchanged, Marianna said, "Captain, what was that awful cry you gave last night?"

Phillip gazed at her uncomprehendingly, but Captain Street began to laugh, a deep, rumbling sound that shook him from head to toe. "That's my aborigine cry, lass," he said, when his laughter was under control. "Learned it from the natives in Australia."

Marianna nodded approvingly. "It works. It scared the bejesus out of those two bastards, that it did!"

Adam gave a shout of laughter, but Phillip whispered frantically, "Marianna! You mustn't talk like that. Ladies don't use such language, especially in public."

Marianna nodded. She was in too good spirits to take offense at his scolding; and besides, she wanted to please him. If ladies didn't talk like she did, but he wished her to be a lady, then she would *try* to speak as he wanted her to.

"I'll try, Phillip. I promise I will."

"You know, lass, you are something," Adam said, suddenly catching her under the arms and boosting her up onto the wide railing, where he could look into her face without bending his neck. "How old are you, girl?"

"Sixteen," she said, somewhat breathlessly.

He looked dubious. "Hmmm. I would have thought younger."

"She's small," Phillip said quickly. "It makes her look younger than her years."

"Well, you'll like it in Boston. Aye, that you will." He smiled and chucked her under the chin, as he would a child. "There are many grand shops, and a great deal of things to do. Boston's a large town. You'll be happy there, and the lad here tells me his aunt will make a fine lady of you. Of course," he added with a grave countenance, "I'm not sure that will be all to the good."

Marianna smiled, although she had mixed emotions concerning this conversation, and she was not too comfortable with the direction it was taking. She resented being talked to as if she were a child, and all this talk of how happy *she* would be and how *she* was being made into a lady . . .

Leaning toward Phillip, she balanced herself on his arm. "Yes," she said, in what she thought was a dignified manner. "*We* hope to be very happy in Boston, Phillip and me."

She saw Adam Street give Phillip a questioning look and saw Phillip bite his lip and look away. A cold feeling began to grow in Marianna.

"But then we always have a fine time when we are together," she plowed on, feeling that she must keep talking or something dreadful would happen.

"Haven't you told her?" Adam demanded of Phillip.

Phillip shook his head. "Not yet."

Marianna clutched Phillip's arm all the tighter. "Hasn't told me what? Phillip? Hellfire and spit, I'm getting quite cross with all this slant-wise talking! You two had better tell me what's up, straight out. I mean it. No fancy dancing around it."

Adam gave Phillip another searching look and then touched his cap. "I have to be about my business, lad, but I would suggest that you stay and explain the situation to the young lady. I'll see you both later, for supper."

As soon as he was out of hearing, Marianna slid down off the railing and confronted Phillip. "Phillip? What was he talking about? What did he mean? What is it you haven't told me?"

Phillip, face pale, raised a hand to stop her flood of questions. He said miserably, "I was going to tell you. Today, in fact. The only reason I did not do so sooner was because I feared that what I had to say would distress you."

Marianna clutched his arm tightly. "What *is* it, Phillip? Tell me right out, without all this dancing around the subject!"

Phillip disengaged her fingers from his arm and took both her hands in his. "Marianna," he said, sighing, "I will not be going with you to Boston. If you will think about it, you will recall that I never said that I was. That was something that you just took for granted."

Marianna stood rooted in dismay, not believing the words she had heard. "You're not going with me?" she repeated stupidly. "I am going alone?"

Phillip nodded and squeezed her hands. "It's not because I do not want to, little one. You know how I feel about you, how much I love you. But it is something that I must do. Something that I have sworn to do, on the body of my dead father. Do you understand?"

Marianna shook her head angrily. "No! Damnit, I don't understand! I thought that you were coming with me, that we would be together. I thought—" Her voice faltered, tears burning her eyes.

Phillip pulled her close, burying his face in the thick hair beside her throat. "Marianna, we *will* be together. When I have finished what I have to do. It won't be long, I promise you, and the time will pass quickly, for you will be busy, occupied with learning new things. It will all be for the best. Besides, you are so young now. When I return— well, by then you will have had a chance to learn something of life as it is lived in places other than the Banks."

"It's because I'm not a proper lady! It's because I'm un-educated, without fine manners!" She struggled to free herself from his arms. With surprising strength he held on to her.

When she had subsided somewhat, he said tenderly, "That's not true, little one, not a word of it. True, I want you to become a lady, but that is for your benefit, more than mine." He lifted her chin with his hand and looked into her eyes teasingly. "And when you become the proper lady, perhaps you will not want me then."

"I will never not want you. Never!" Marianna said fiercely.
She lowered her head and burrowed her face into his waistcoat. Her heart was cold and heavy as a stone, and she felt
as if all life and hope had been drained from her. Despite
her feeling for Phillip, she had no faith in his promises, no
real belief that he would return to her. How could he do
this to her, show her love, kindness, and passion, and then
just leave her? It was unthinkable!

"Don't go!" she pleaded. "Don't go. Stay with me. Aren't
you happy when you're with me? Don't I please you in
bed?"

His face twisted with pain, and he seized her wildly
waving hands. "Marianna, please! Don't speak such things.
I love you. You know that. But you should also know that
there are some things a man has to do, so that he can live at
peace with his own nature. I have to go, and there is nothing that you can do, much as you may hurt me, to keep
me."

Marianna gave a great sob that seemed to wrench her
small body. She tore free of his grasp and fled to the cabin
where they had spent the night.

Throwing herself across the double bunk, she burrowed
into the covers, as if to hide herself and her pain from
human view. It was all over, all the love and the joy, all the
new pleasures that Phillip had shown her. She hated him,
hated him for what he was doing to her. In reality, he was
no different than Jude. Oh, yes, he was fair of face and
form, and kind and gentle in his manner, but he was hurtful
nonetheless, perhaps more so, for Jude had made no promises, and so there had been none to be broken; he had
given no joy that could be turned into bitter disappointment; he had not lifted her up, only to dash her down.

Phillip came to her there, in the cabin, and sat on the
edge of the bunk, talking to her softly, his voice almost a
croon as he told her that he would return, that he would
come back to her. That he would write, whenever he could.

Finally her sobs ceased, not because she really believed
his promises, but because she had no tears left. He smoothed
her hair and spoke to her tenderly, and then she tumbled

into a deep sleep, from which she did not awaken until evening.

Phillip was gone. She knew, without being told, that he was gone from the ship, gone from her.

There was no trace of him, only two letters in white envelopes, atop a sea chest.

Adam Street read one letter to her—the other was addressed to Phillip's aunt in Boston. Marianna had been embarrassed to have to admit that she could not read, but she was too anxious to know the contents of the letter to let her embarrassment deter her from going to the captain for help.

Adam read:

Dear Marianna:

I was going to stay with you until tomorrow, when the ship sails, but since my going seems to upset you so, I believe that it is better that I leave now so that you may make peace with the existing circumstances. I will tell you again, in writing, that I love you, and will return to you, when my mission is done. I want you to believe this and cling to the thought.

I know that you feel alone now, and abandoned, but my dear aunt is a kind woman, and I think that you two will get on well together. I would not send you to her if I thought otherwise. Captain Street is a good man and will look after you until you reach your destination.

Take good care of yourself, little one, and do not forget me.

Yours sincerely,
Phillip Courtwright.

When Adam finished reading the letter, Marianna wept softly. Why had Phillip gone? They could have had one more night together. She had driven him away with her fears, with her angry tongue, and now perhaps she would never see him again. He might die before his mission was ended! It was her fault. Her sense of loss was now added to by feelings of guilt, and the flow of tears increased.

Adam patted her shoulder awkwardly. "There, there, child," he said, his deep voice gentle. "All will be well. The lad will return to you."

Abruptly Marianna felt a need to strike out, to hurt someone else as badly as she had been hurt. Besides, why did he insist on calling her *child?*

"I am not a child!" she flared. "I have been a woman to a man for the past year. To Jude Throag. And I have been a woman to Phillip. Does that make me a child?"

Adam Street recoiled, giving her an odd, appraising glance, and she could see shocked surprise on his countenance. The sight made her feel both better and worse.

"I am sorry," he said slowly. "I didn't mean to disparage you. And aye, it's true, you are a child no longer, and that is a pity, although I'm sure you do not think so. In any case, I only want to be your friend.

"We will be sailing on the morrow. If you wish to leave the *Viking,* you are, of course, free to do so. I will not hold you here. However, I most strongly advise you to go to Boston as Phillip has arranged. I will speak no more of it, but leave you to think upon what I have said."

With a slight dip of his head, Adam turned and stooped slightly so that he could exit through the cabin door.

With burning eyes Marianna watched him go. Her tears, it seemed, had all been shed. Angry, hurt, and ashamed of herself for lashing out at the captain, she threw herself upon the bunk and pounded the mattress with her fists until they began to ache.

Chapter Six

W HEN the *Viking Queen* sailed out of Charleston, Marianna was still on board.

Although not wholly resigned to going on to Boston, she did not know what else to do or where else to go. Without Phillip she felt alone and abandoned, ill at ease in an environment she was not familiar with, and worst of all, helpless, a feeling she was not used to experiencing.

However mean her life had been, and she was beginning to realize just how mean that was, Marianna had always felt that she had some degree of control over events. There had been many bad things in her life, but they had been factors with which she was familiar, things with which she could deal, in one way or another. Now it was different. This was another world, with different rules, rules that she did not know. The ship, and Captain Adam Street, gave her at least a base, an anchor, in this world beyond the Banks.

On this, the first day out, the seas were high, and Marianna, in the cabin, was dismayed by the rocking and pitching of the big ship.

Adam had visited her early in the morning and advised her that to come above decks would be unwise—they were encountering foul weather. He told her to make herself comfortable in "his" cabin and that he would dine there with her that evening.

That was the first inkling she had that the captain had given her and Phillip his own cabin, and now she looked around the room with a more curious eye.

Besides the wide, double bunk, the furnishings consisted

of a long trestle table, a large sea chest, a sturdy walnut desk, a padded easy chair with a footrest, and four plain, rounded, low-backed chairs for seating at the table. Curious as to why the furniture remained in place when the ship rolled, Marianna investigated and found everything bolted to the deck.

She had to admit that it was kind of the captain to give up his own private quarters. She wondered where he was sleeping. She supposed that wherever it was, it was not nearly so grand as this.

Marianna would have enjoyed the cabin, enjoyed the comfort of the bunk, the soft chair; she would have enjoyed the adventure of it, if only Phillip had been with her. But because he was not, because he was gone, it all meant nothing.

On the open sea now, the ship rolled heavily, and Marianna felt her stomach rebel. She had never been on a craft larger than a dory, and somehow found being enclosed in the belly of this great ship during this rough weather more frightening than being in an open boat. She *must* get some air.

There was a row of heavy brass hooks along one wall of the cabin, on which hung an assortment of coats and foul-weather gear. Taking down a heavy southwester, Marianna attempted to put it on but found that it was scaled to fit Captain Street; she could scarcely lift it, much less wear it. Looking around for something more appropriate, she saw nothing that would fit her, and feeling increasingly nauseated, she finally scrambled up the ladder wearing only the clothing she had on.

Above decks, a storm was pounding relentlessly at the ship. The air was alive with the sounds of creaking wood, snapping canvas, and the shouts of the crew. Marianna could see no land; in fact, all she could see was water—in the air and on all sides—and the ship appeared to be the only solid thing in a world of water and motion.

Clinging desperately to the railing, already drenched to the skin, she realized her foolishness in disobeying the captain's directions. Half-blinded, she turned about, trying to find her way back to the cabin. She took two steps and slipped on the deck, slippery as though greased, sliding down its inclined surface with frightening speed.

As she fell she cried out, but her feeble cry was lost in the furious cacophony of the storm.

Terrified and helpless, she slammed roughly up against the opposite railing and looked up to see a huge wave rising over the side of the ship, blotting out the whole world, a wave that she knew could sweep her overboard and into the churning sea.

As she tried to scramble to her feet, she screamed again, and then she felt a strong arm wrap around her, hauling her roughly to one side.

She heard the terrifying roar of the wall of water and felt herself sheltered as in a cave of living flesh, protected from the full force of the wave. Then all was water, icy cold against her skin, in her eyes and mouth, clawing at her with tremendous force, buffeting her against the other body sheltering her.

And then, when she thought she could hold her breath no longer, the water was gone, and she was crouching wet and gasping beneath the form of Adam Street, who had his hands locked around the railing, his body bent protectively over hers.

He straightened, and when Marianna had knuckled the sea water from her eyes, she had to face him.

She found him glaring at her in a fury. "What the hell are you doing above decks?" he shouted. "I told you it would be best to stay below!"

Angry at being caught in the wrong, Marianna shouted back, "You didn't say I *had* to!"

"I thought you had *some* sense. You told me how grown up you were. Only a child would be so foolish—" He sighed. "Oh, damnation! Here, I'll take you back."

Putting one arm around her, he hustled her, like a recalcitrant child, to the companionway and down. Feeling angrier by the minute, Marianna could do little but go along.

Back in the cabin, he shut the door, braced his hands on his hips, and scowled down at her. "You look like a drowned cat." He reached down to the bunk, pulled off the top blanket, and flung it at her. "Here, wrap yourself in this, *after* you get out of those wet things."

Almost crying in her anger and frustration, Marianna caught the flung blanket. "And just where am I supposed to change?"

He shook his head. "Right here. I'll turn my back." After he had turned around, he added, "You're perfectly safe, you know. I'm not in the habit of molesting children."

Hellfire and spit, he was insufferable! Teeth chattering, she stripped off her wet things and wrapped herself in the warm blanket.

"There," she said. "I'm finished."

He faced around and nodded. "Good."

Gathering up her wet clothes, Adam wrung them out over the wash basin, then spread them to dry over the backs of the chairs.

"These are soaked. They'll take hours to dry in this weather. I'll see if I can find you something else." He flung back the lid of the large sea chest.

Marianna, her anger somewhat diluted by curiosity, wondered what kind of clothing he could have in the chest that she could possibly wear. She was even more curious when she saw him take from the chest a long-sleeved, high-necked cotton dress and hold it up, as if to measure its size. "I was afraid of that," he mused. "It's far too long for you. Can you sew, lass?"

Marianna pulled the blanket more tightly around her. "Of course I can sew."

"Then you can take a large hem in this." He tossed the garment to her. "You will find sewing materials in my desk."

Marianna, instinctively reaching for the dress, dropped one edge of the blanket, then snatched it back before it fell away, exposing her nudity. The dress fell to the deck.

A smile tugged at the corners of Adam's mouth. "I'm sorry," he said, his voice kinder now. "Here, let me show you how to wrap that blanket around you so that it will stay on."

Then he was next to her, his big hands gentle as he began to rearrange the blanket.

Marianna stepped quickly back and squinted at him suspiciously. "I'll do it myself," she said stiffly.

Inexplicably, his face flamed. "Suit yourself. I told you, I don't molest children."

Marianna felt tight and mean inside. She knew what men were like. First Jude and his brutal demands, and then Phillip, with all his pretty ways, who had still hurt her in the end. Her mother was right. All men wanted from a woman was the use of her body. That was all a woman was to them, a bit of pleasure. Well, no man was going to have pleasure with her ever again! She would not be used, and she would not be hurt. A kind man Adam Street might be, but he was still a man, and she had seen something in his eyes that she recognized—something that put the lie to him calling her a child.

"I'm no child, Captain Street, and I think you know it well enough," she said boldly.

His face still flaming, he spun away. "You are a thorny wench, and I'll be damned glad to see the last of you!" And then, more gently: "I only wanted to help, you know."

Marianna, somehow sensing that she now had the upper hand, did not relent. "I thank you, sir, for all that you have done, but I like to do for myself."

Adam said no more, merely shook his head, gave a put-upon sigh, and left the cabin, slamming the door rather loudly after him.

Adam Street charged up the companionway, almost welcoming the storm outside. It could be no worse, he thought, than that slip of a girl down below. She was surely a difficult creature.

And yet, why was he so incensed? He knew of her circumstances, knew that she was little better than a savage, raised without proper schooling or care; and despite her insistence otherwise, she *was* young, little more than a child. So why, knowing all this, did he allow her to infuriate him so?

Normally, he would have shown more forbearance. Being a man who was much given to examining his own motives, it bothered him that she was able to annoy him so easily. And, being a truthful man as well, even with himself, he had to admit that her taunt had some merit, for he *did*, God help him, desire the girl. Despite his good intentions, he wanted her. He would do nothing about it, of course. He might not have any control over his desires, but he did, thank the Lord, have control over his actions. It had been an integral part of his heritage, his upbringing. . . .

Adam Street was the second son in a family of five children born to Captain William Henry Street and his wife, of Gloucester, Massachusetts.

The males in the Street family had been seafaring men for five generations. It was expected that William's eldest son, Caleb, would follow in his father's footsteps, and he had done so, although it was more from a desire to please his father than from any innate love of the sea.

However, Adam loved the sea with an abiding passion, as did his three younger sisters, who all eventually married seafaring men.

William Street, a strict, stern man, placed all his hopes and dreams on the shoulders of his eldest son, seeing Adam only peripherally, as if he were but a pale shadow of his elder brother. Still, Adam respected his father and longed to follow in his footsteps.

When Caleb was seventeen, Captain William Street took him aboard his ship, the *Nancy June*, as an apprentice seaman. Adam, then fifteen, begged to be allowed to go along, but his father was adamant. Adam must wait until he was older.

At that time there was a ship in port named the *Mary Rose*. The *Mary Rose* was notorious because of her captain, Jonas Bender; Captain Bender was a cruel and willful master, given to fits of madness when his ship was at sea for long periods. During these spells, he behaved irrationally, and often sadistically, toward his crew.

If William Street had been at home, he would have warned Adam of this, but his father was at sea, and Adam gave no thought to consulting any older and wiser person.

On an afternoon when his mother was out with his sisters, Adam stuffed a few items into a sea bag and presented himself to the second mate of the *Mary Rose*, applying for a job as apprentice seaman.

It so happened that the *Mary Rose* had lost several sailors in a bad storm during the last voyage, and since her captain's savage nature was so well-known, he was having difficulty filling out his crew.

The second mate accepted Adam readily enough, and Adam went proudly aboard, thinking that at long last he was going to sea.

The *Mary Rose* was a large brig, square-rigged and serviceable. She was carrying a cargo of wool and cotton bound for the Orient and would return with a load of rice, tea, fine silks, china, and opium.

It was going to be a long voyage, but Adam, blithely unaware of the unsavory reputation of the ship and her captain, did not mind. By the time the voyage was completed, he would be a seaman, one of the cherished fraternity, and then, surely, his father would not refuse to let him ship aboard his own vessel.

So, high in spirits and expectations, Adam stowed his sea bag under the small bunk he had been given and wondered briefly how he was going to arrange his six-foot, one-inch body so as to get most of it upon that narrow shelf.

Even the dank, dark crewmen's quarters, with its unpleasant odors, failed to dismay him. He looked upon the unkempt, evil-looking crew with positive good will, and did not seem to notice the dark looks bent his way. Adam was familiar with ships and with sailors, but he had never consorted with a crew of this stripe and did not realize that a green hand was looked upon as fair game by the more experienced crew members. Voyages were long, and often dull and boring. The crew looked forward to any diversion, and a new hand, fresh and green, offered limitless possibilities.

It started off in a relatively harmless way, when the older sailors began sending Adam on errands to fetch nonexistent items. Since he was as familiar with ships as they, he knew what they were about, but he took this well enough, for there was no real harm done, except the wasting of his time.

But then the pranks became more serious and more physical: he would be tripped while carrying full slop pails or kept occupied passing things at the mess table so that he did not have time to eat his own food.

The first mate, a wiry, sour man named Croft, seemed deaf and blind to this harassment, which extended to other new sailors as well as Adam; and indeed, if the expression on his face was any indication of his feelings, the first mate seemed to enjoy the small brutalities as much as the other men did.

Adam's duties aboard the ship were rigorous and demeaning, as they were for all new men. He was able to accept this as a price to be paid for his apprenticeship, yet the constant hazing soon began to wear at his nerves.

The captain was seldom seen during this time. He was little more than an aloof figure upon the bridge, stout and imposing, a voice of command filtering down through the first and second mates to the members of the crew.

The weather held, and the *Mary Rose* made good time toward her first stop in port, where she would take on fresh provisions and water. Adam, naively, looked forward to going ashore, but was soon disabused of this notion by Jim Hanks, one of the older sailors, a man who did not participate in the brutal treatment of the new members. "Nay, lad. You'll not set foot upon yonder island. The captain will send only small boats ashore, with trusted officers aboard."

Adam looked at him in some confusion. "But why?"

The older man laughed. "Desertion, laddy. Captain Bender's afraid if he lets the crew ashore, they won't come back. The longer we're at sea, the more likely it is the men will desert. On the return voyage, nearer to home port, he won't much care."

Adam was now thoroughly confused. "I don't understand."

Hanks chuckled again. "Fewer to share, lad, more money for the captain." He became serious. "And this'un is a hellship, Adam. You'll rue the day you ever signed on."

So their first port of call was seen only from the ship, longingly, by the crew, and was soon behind them as the *Mary Rose* made again for the open sea.

The weeks went by, weeks of searing sun, hard work, and bad food, for despite the fresh fruits and water taken on board, the food was growing increasingly foul. There were maggots in the meal, and the salt beef and pork were rancid and inhabited by an occasional maggot as well. Adam gagged at the sight of his supper upon his plate, but he was a growing lad and had to fill his belly.

By now the main cabin stank of the accumulation of odors and fluids excreted by the male body, and a rank and sickening smell it was.

The hazing by the older crew members had not lessened, but had in fact increased as the tedium of the long voyage set in and they grew ill-tempered and surly. It caused Adam to wonder if the sea was such a noble calling, after all. All he saw about him was injustice—men required to work with only bad food to sustain them; cruelty practiced by the strong upon the weak; unfair, often brutal treatment by the mates, apparently condoned by the captain.

Adam began to reflect that the common seaman's life was no better than that of a cur's.

And then came the first flogging.

Adam had made three good friends aboard the *Mary Rose*, the old sailor, Jim Hanks, and two new sailors, Martin and Brill.

Martin was a big, stout lad of Adam's own age, well-coordinated and well capable of handling himself, but Brill was a rather soft, plump boy, not accustomed to hard work or rough ways, and Adam was surprised that he had chosen to go to sea at all. Still, Brill was a bright youth, with good thoughts in his head and a handy way with words. He had a journal with him, in which he would write every evening after mess. As far as Adam knew, no one had ever seen what Brill wrote in this book, and Brill kept it hidden away when he was not writing in it.

The ship had been in the doldrums for several days. The sea, flat as a blue plate, reflected a blistering sun, and no air stirred the limp sails. Food was becoming short—they were due in port soon for fresh supplies—and tempers were even shorter.

Adam had noticed that Brill, in particular, was looking unhealthy; his usual high color had faded to a dingy gray, and his eyes mirrored a look of suffering.

Adam, concerned, questioned him, but the other boy merely shook his head and refused to talk about it. Adam kept an eye on him, worried for his friend's well-being, and he soon noticed that Brill disappeared every afternoon. He could not be found at work, in the forecastle, or in any of the places where he would usually be present.

Adam discussed the matter with Martin, but Martin could add no light to the matter. The only thing they could be certain of was that almost every afternoon Brill disappeared, only to return in time for mess, pale of face and looking sick; and he was growing thinner day by day.

On one hot, windless afternoon, Adam and Martin decided to follow Brill, one or the other shadowing him wherever he went. Adam was following him when part of the mystery was solved, for Brill went to the captain's cabin. Adam waited, and it was a long, hot wait in the broiling sun. Two hours went by, and then Brill reappeared, quite clearly shaken, walking on weak legs past Adam's hiding place.

Adam and Martin were afire with curiosity. What was Brill doing in Captain Bender's cabin every afternoon? Obviously it was with the captain's consent, or insistence, but whatever could the captain want with Brill?

At a loss, they went to Jim Hanks with their question. When it was asked, Hanks's face turned dour, and he looked at them closely. "You don't know about Captain Bender?"

The boys shook their heads. Hanks frowned. "Don't you know what some men do to lads, young lads like you two?"

Adam and Martin exchanged curious looks and again shook their heads.

Hanks sighed heavily. "Well then, I'm afraid that I can't be the one to tell you, for it fair turns my stomach just to consider it. But mark this, lads, and mark it well. Stay away from Captain Bender. When he paces the decks, keep out of his sight. Draw no undue attention to yourselves."

Hanks refused to say more and walked away, leaving the boys staring at one another in puzzlement and some apprehension.

"What do you suppose he's on about?" Martin asked, his voice low. "What's the captain doing to Brill?"

Adam shook his head. He had heard dark, furtive whispers, whispers he had not believed, about a certain kind of man who did not love women, but boys; yet, he had no clear concept of what was involved or what went on. He was feeling quite upset, and uneasy in his stomach, remembering the look on Brill's face when he left the captain's cabin. He said, "Maybe we should ask Brill?"

And this they did, at mess that very night. The result was startling. Brill dropped his fork, and his face turned a greenish pale. He stared at his two friends in horror, then leaped up and fled the mess cabin.

Adam and Martin sat on, more confused than ever. Brill did not occupy his bunk that night. The next morning they looked for him, but did not find him.

The new day had dawned as hot and windless as the three days past. Lethargy and depression hung over the great ship, and the sails remained as limp as death, waiting for a freshening wind that never came.

That afternoon Adam again stole to his vantage point from where he could observe the captain's cabin. Eventually Brill appeared, feet dragging, head low. Adam did not call out to him, but watched him go into the cabin and waited.

But this time there was no lengthy wait. This time, only a few minutes had passed when a terrible, primal howl issued from the cabin, a howl that sent a shiver down Adam's back.

The howl was followed by the sound of crashing furniture and a man's voice raised in fury and pain—the captain's voice, Adam felt sure.

His fists tightened. Should he go to Brill's aid? What was happening?

And then the voice grew louder, and the cabin door crashed open. The captain stood there, holding Brill by the scruff of his jersey, shaking him violently, cursing vilely all the while.

The captain was attired only in his underclothing, and his face was a flaming red.

Drawn by the uproar, the second mate came running and at the captain's bellowed order, took Brill into custody. Brill was led away, shaking and weeping openly, as Captain Bender stood, legs braced, arms akimbo, face still red with his wrath, his gaze raking the deck, as if looking for a witness to the scene.

Adam, his stomach a knot, crouched in his hiding place, making himself as small as possible. He knew that something terrible was going to happen, but he did not know what.

It happened that afternoon. Brill, obviously terrified, was led to the main mast, while the rest of the crew gathered, at the captain's command, to watch.

Adam, Martin, and Jim Hanks stood together and watched in horror. Martin asked in a low voice, "What's going to happen to him, Hanks?"

"They're going to flog him," Hanks said bitterly.

Martin stared at him with round eyes. "But for God's sake, *why?*"

Hanks had an expression of disgust on his face. "For flagrant disobedience, the captain claims. He says Brill disobeyed a direct order and struck him in anger." He shook his head dolefully. "I can imagine what that direct order was. Poor, poor lad."

In silence they watched the rest of it, watched as Brill was lashed to the mast, hands tied above his head. He was shirtless, his soft, white body sweating in the sun. They watched as the second mate, a slight smile on his face, raised high the great whip, the cat-o'-nine tails, and brought it whistling down upon the boy's back.

As the whip struck home, with a sound that caused Adam to cringe, Brill let out a shrill scream, and a collective sigh issued from the throats of the waiting men. Adam began to feel sick.

Again and again, the whip was brought down across Brill's back until his flesh ran red with blood, like so much fresh meat. Brill's screams ceased, and he slumped, held upright only by the bonds around his wrists. Adam knew that he had fainted.

Still, the whip came down across his back.

Adam glanced up to where the captain watched from the

bridge, a cruel smile on his porcine face. Adam had never hated anyone in his life as he hated the captain in that moment. Watching the man gloat over the beaten body of his friend, Adam vowed that if ever he became a captain, he would be the opposite of this man—if such a depraved creature could be called a man—and he also vowed that if the opportunity arose, he would kill Captain Bender, after first causing him as much agony as the captain had caused Brill.

When it was finally over, Adam and Martin were allowed to cut Brill down and to treat his wounded back with salt-water and a healing salve. They both became almost ill while trying to tend the lacerated flesh, but Jim Hanks, who had seen many a flogging, took over the chore, sending both boys to their bunks.

It was the last time Adam saw Brill. Both he and Martin were asleep when Hanks and one of the other seamen brought Brill below to his bunk, and when they awoke in the morning, their friend was gone. There was blood on his blanket and a trail of blood leading up the companionway to the deck. It soon became clear that sometime during the night, Brill, delirious with pain and fever, and with God only knew what kind of emotions preying on his mind, had dragged himself up onto the deck and then thrown himself overboard.

That morning the wind freshened, and with the sails at last full, the *Mary Rose* moved out at a good clip.

The change in weather, and the fact that they were moving, put the men in good spirits, and it appeared that few of them except Adam, Martin, and Jim Hanks gave much thought to a clumsy boy who was with them no longer.

Later that day, while gathering up Brill's meager belongings, Adam and Martin found Brill's journal. Adam thought briefly of flinging it into the sea unread, but his curiosity, and Martin's, was too great. They read the journal entries, written in Brill's neat, almost delicate script, and then flung the journal overboard, for in the reading they had learned a great deal more than they had bargained for about the depravity of man and the abuse of power.

There were other floggings aboard the *Mary Rose*, some for little provocation, some for none at all, as far as the crew could ascertain, but to Adam, none were as bad as that first flogging of his friend.

The voyage went on, interminably it seemed to Adam, yet he was toughened now, and growing up as well. He was determined that Captain Bender would not get the better of him and that finally he would have his revenge upon this man whom he considered the blackest of villains.

Heeding Hanks's advice, he stayed out of the captain's sight, did his work, and did not complain when he was abused or harassed by the older crew members.

In this manner he earned a measure of respect, and gradually they stopped tormenting him, and he began to be treated as one of the crew. Some of the newer sailors were not so fortunate, and many of them fell victim to the captain's depravity, while others deserted ship or fell ill and died.

It was on the return voyage that matters finally came to a shattering resolution. Adam could have jumped ship in Hong Kong—in fact, he gave the idea considerable thought—but he finally made the decision to see the voyage through, partially because he had as yet found no way to make Captain Bender pay for Brill's fate. Also, one character trait had already firmed up in Adam, one that would remain with him for the rest of his life. When he started something, he would follow through until the end. Shipping out on the *Mary Rose* had been a grave error, but to give up before the voyage was concluded would make him a quitter, at least in his own mind.

Many crew members *had* opted to remain behind in the Orient, and one of them was Martin; but Jim Hanks was still aboard, for this was to be his last trip. He was growing too old, he said, for life at sea, and with his share of the profits from this voyage, added to what he had saved over the years, he intended to buy a little farm in his home town.

And so, the voyage home commenced, with many new men, and fresh supplies, on board; and now Adam was left pretty much alone, for there were other, younger lads to torment.

Captain Bender, about halfway through the return voyage, reverted to his old ways, and Adam was sickened to see the pattern beginning anew. His resolve to revenge Brill grew daily, but still no opportunity arose to achieve his purpose. He felt that the voyage would be a failure if he did not keep his vow to his dead shipmate.

The chance he had been waiting for finally came. The captain had been in an unusually bad temper for a week or more, and he prowled the decks day and night. One afternoon, while he was stalking the deck, his gaze fell upon Adam, who was busy splicing rope.

Jim Hanks, who was working with Adam, saw the captain pause and stare at Adam in speculation. Adam did not notice Captain Bender until the man tapped him on the shoulder with the knobby walking stick that he always carried.

"You, there!" The captain's voice was rather nasal and harsh. "Young man!"

Adam straightened up and turned, saw the captain, and his heart began to beat fast. This was the chance he had been waiting for! He might die for it, but he *would* have the captain's life.

He glanced over at Hanks and saw the expression of dismay on the older man's face. He looked back at the captain. "Yes, sir!" he said, snapping to attention.

A smile tugged at the corners of the captain's too-full lips. "My, my, how well trained you young men are becoming. That pleases me. Tell me, young man, what is your name?"

The captain leaned close as he spoke, and Adam recoiled slightly from the man's sickly sweet breath. "Adam Street," he said clearly. "Sir."

Captain Bender nodded ponderously. "A fine name. Your father would not happen to be Captain William Street, by any chance?"

"Yes, sir. He is, sir."

The captain tapped his lips with a finger as fat as a sausage. "Well, well. I have owed your father a debt for some time. Now might just be the time to repay it. Come to my cabin, Adam Street, in an hour. Be prompt, mind."

Captain Bender turned away as Adam saluted and said briskly, "Yes, sir." When the captain was out of earshot, Adam turned to Hanks. "I know what you're thinking, Jim. But I mean to kill him. I swore an oath on poor Brill's dead body."

"You'll hang for it, you know," Hanks said, sighing.

Adam shook his head stubbornly. "About that, I don't know. But I *must* do it. The man's a disgrace to the captain's rank, an utter blackguard. He's unfit to live."

Hanks nodded slowly. "I agree with you, lad, about the captain, but have you thought it through? Have you thought what your death, or imprisonment, will do to your parents? Your mother?"

Adam tightened his lips. He had not thought of his family, true, but it was too late to back out now. He had told Hanks what he was going to do, and do it he must, whatever the consequences.

Hanks saw his expression and sighed again. "Foolish, foolish! All of your life ahead of you, and you're ready to fling it away over one injustice. It will be a difficult world for you, my young friend, *if* you live to face it."

"I don't care," Adam said, his voice ringing with anger and bravado. "I *must* do it."

"So be it then," Jim Hanks said.

The captain's cabin was, after the fetid, uncomfortable quarters Adam had lived in for so long, the ultimate in luxury. There was a rich satin cloth covering a large bunk, an ornately carved dresser, a huge, padded easy chair, an elaborately ornamented wash basin and water pitcher, with fine linen towels hung above it, and a fine crystal lamp hanging from the ceiling in the center of the cabin.

The air was pungent with some kind of Oriental incense, and Adam coughed behind his hand as he entered the cabin. He was carrying a knife tucked into the waistband of his breeches, at the small of his back; he had purchased the knife in Hong Kong for just this moment. His heart was pounding furiously, and his head felt light.

Captain Bender, attired in a heavily embroidered kimono, was sprawled in the padded easy chair, an anticipatory smile on his lips. "Ah, there you are, lad. Just on time. I do so admire promptness in my crew members."

He laughed, a high-pitched giggle, and Adam felt his stomach turn as he remembered the look on Brill's face as he had stumbled out of the captain's cabin.

"Yes, sir," Adam said, saluting briskly. "Reporting as ordered, sir."

Captain Bender waved a languid hand. "You may dispense with the formalities in here, my boy. Just be certain you do not forget it on deck. Now come here. Approach closer. I want to view you properly."

Adam, his legs feeling like lead pipes, edged cautiously closer.

"Closer, my boy. Much, much closer."

Adam took another step. His stomach was a tight knot, and he could scarcely swallow.

"I said closer, boy!"

The captain's deceptively plump arm shot out, and his hand closed painfully around Adam's forearm. He was surprised at the strength of the man; he did not look as if he could defend himself against a child.

"Now, down! Down on your knees so that I don't have to stare up at you."

With a deft twist of his arm, Captain Bender put cruel pressure on Adam's arm, and Adam went awkwardly down upon his knees. Adam was now directly in front of the captain, close enough to be able to see the small black hairs sprouting from the man's nostrils. The captain had Adam's left arm upraised, in a firm grip, and all that Adam could think of was the knife in his waistband. Should he grab for it now, or wait until he was in a better position? Or would he ever *be* in a better position?

Captain Bender was breathing hard and seemed to be extremely agitated. Adam's mind examined and then discarded the notion that the captain was in the grip of much the same emotion that he, Adam, experienced when in the company of a girl.

The captain grinned wolfishly. "You're a handsome lad, aren't you? A fine, strong, brawny boy, but your skin is silken, and soft as a girl's." One pudgy hand came out, and he lightly stroked Adam's cheek. "I'll wager you're that way all over, eh?"

Adam felt the taste of bile in his mouth. Every word this man spoke was an affront, an insult, and an abomination. He must do it now!

Twisting his body about, he reached for the knife concealed behind his back, just as the cabin door burst open with a crash.

The next few minutes were never to become clear in his mind. He glimpsed several figures, one of whom he recognized as Jim Hanks, pour through the door, and then all was confusion. Adam was pushed or jerked away from the captain and then was hustled by Hanks through the cabin door, his protests going unheeded. He could hear the sounds of a great commotion from the cabin, but Hanks led him quickly away and in a short while pushed him down onto his bunk in the forecastle, then stood staring down at him, breathing heavily from exertion.

Adam was confused and angry. "Why did you interfere? I was ready to do it, just one moment more and—"

He tried to get up, but Hanks shoved him back, hard. "Yes, lad. Just a few minutes more, and you would have ruined your future and your life."

"But the captain—!" Adam's voice broke in frustration. "He can't be allowed to continue!"

"He won't continue, Adam, upon my word." Hanks dropped down onto the bunk across from Adam's. "He is being properly taken care of, be sure of that. Tomorrow morning, the ship's log will read that Captain Bender, poor sod, fell overboard during the night. His fits of madness are known to all, and the log will show that he had been growing increasingly erratic and depressed of late."

"I don't understand. That's mutiny! The first mate—"

"Exactly," Hanks said, smiling grimly. "The mate hates the captain with a passion and has long been anxious for a ship of his own to command. When we went to him with our plan, some days ago, he was more than pleased to go along with it. Not only will he have his own command, but a captain's share as well."

Hanks tilted his head for a moment and listened, but no unusual sound could be heard. He smiled tightly. "Well, Captain Bender should now be disposed of. Only those of us involved will ever know of this, and that means you keep your mouth shut about it, lad. Brill is avenged, and you, my young friend, will live to fight another day, as they say."

Adam swallowed hard. His emotions were mixed, a mixture of disappointment and relief. "But I wanted to do it. I made a solemn vow."

Hanks said wearily, "Lad, there are vows, and there are vows. A grown man makes a vow, realizing full well the consequences, but he is using the judgment of a man. You're a strapping lad, Adam, and a fine one, but although your heart is good, your reasoning powers have yet to ripen. You act with the rashness of youth. Don't be angry at yourself for failing to make good this vow. It was a good vow, but not for you, at this time. There will be other vows, lad, and other deeds in the future. Now then, you just forget what has happened this day, and tomorrow the rest of the crew will receive the sad tidings that Captain Bender vanished."

And that was what Adam did. The rest of the voyage was uneventful, except for boredom, and Adam returned home with his small share of the profits—an older, wiser, and somewhat subdued young man.

Now, guiding his own ship through the storm, Captain Adam Street dismissed thoughts of that time and of his friend, Jim Hanks, who had been so kind and so tolerant of his youth on that long voyage.

That girl below, Adam thought, was no older than he had been at the time. Couldn't *he* practice the same patience and understanding with her that Jim Hanks had shown with him?

Turning his face into the howling wind, Adam promised himself that he would be more patient with Marianna during the rest of the way to Boston.

And he resolved that he would keep a tight rein on any lustful thoughts he might entertain of her.

The wind, shrieking through the rigging, seemed to jeer at him.

Chapter Seven

MARIANNA stood on tiptoe at the porthole of the captain's cabin and stared out at the bustle of Boston Harbor.

She was wearing the dress Adam had taken from the sea chest, hemmed now; and her unruly curls had been tamed by a brush and tied back with a bit of ribbon. All in all, she would have been neatly dressed, except for her feet, which were bare.

Adam had taken one look at her worn gum boots and had shaken his head in despair. Finally he had sent one of the mates ashore to purchase stockings and ladies' walking boots for Marianna to wear. When the man returned, Adam was going to personally deliver her—like so much excess cargo—to Miss Prudence Courtwright, Phillip's aunt. Well, the captain might be surprised to know that he might well deliver her, but that didn't mean that she would stay. Marianna had yet to make up her mind about that. There must be *some* way an intelligent girl could earn a living in a city such as this.

It *was* a grand city, beyond her imagining. Charleston had intimidated her, yet it was nothing compared to Boston. The harbor was crammed with all manner of ships, predominantly merchantmen and whalers; the docks were swarming with workers, like ants, loading and unloading the newly arrived ships.

Oh, if only Phillip were with her! How wonderful it would be to share it with him.

A fat tear oozed out beneath one eyelid and ran down her cheek. Determinedly, she blinked back the others that threatened to follow. Phillip wasn't here, and nothing could be done about that, but she would never, absolutely *never*, let herself care for a man again. It hurt too much.

Marianna saw the returning mate hurrying up the gang-plank, carrying a paper-wrapped bundle. She moved away from the porthole so as not to appear too anxious. Although still angry at what she considered Phillip's desertion, and smarting from Adam's condescending attitude, she was also excited about seeing the city. She had, after all, wanted to get away from the Outer Banks, and all that life there implied; and this seemed about as far away as she could get in terms of differences in surroundings. She was a bright girl, Marianna knew that about herself, and she learned quickly. Surely, there would be something here for her to do. She could walk the streets, if necessary; and then she thought of the painted strumpets on the waterfront streets of Charleston and made a face. No! She was giving up men altogether, so that was definitely out. First, just to find out what the woman was like, she would go to Phillip's aunt.

After that, she would see.

The house was small, tidy, and made of brick. It sat neatly in a well-tended garden, giving off an aura of respectability and order. Marianna thought it was beautiful but refused to admit this to Adam, who stood, somewhat uncomfortably, by her side.

"Well, here we are," he said heartily.

"Yes, here we are," she said dully.

Adam said, "I'm sure you'll be happy here."

Marianna snorted vigorously. Even though the house was very attractive, she knew that she would never be happy here. Phillip's aunt would no doubt disapprove of her and be ready with rules and orders. And how could she be happy any place without Phillip?

"I'll probably never be happy again," she said, "but you needn't concern yourself, Captain Street. I'm not used to happiness, anyway."

She was pleased to see his face darken and his expression become sorrowful. She had no idea why this should please her; she only knew that it did.

"You will be happy, Marianna. You have most of your life ahead of you. Someday you will meet a young man who will teach you how to be happy."

She looked at him with scorn. "I have already met such a man—Phillip. He abandoned me."

Adam shook his head in exasperation. "Marianna, that's not what I understood. Phillip told me that he would come back for you. He loves you."

For some obscure reason this only made Marianna angrier than ever. "Hellfire and spit! Words! When you want to use us, you men are all easy with fine words and promises, but later, after you've had what you want—" She turned her face away.

"Damnation! You *are* an aggravating wench, Marianna," he said explosively. "As far as I can see, both Phillip and I have done you nothing but kindness, and yet you have but harsh words for us. Didn't you ever hear of the word gratitude?"

"No, I don't think that I have," she retorted. "But then I'm only an ignorant Banker girl, without proper schooling. At any rate, I think that we'd better be getting to the door, because there is an old lady with just her head poked out between the curtains, looking at us and no doubt wondering what the hell we're doing standing here yammering on her front walk."

He said grimly, "And another thing—a lady doesn't swear."

"I'm no lady, didn't Phillip tell you?"

With that, Marianna flounced up the walkway, trying to walk in a dignified manner in her new boots and succeeding only in appearing both comical and vulnerable.

Adam Street found himself smiling at her retreating back. She *was* a little spitfire, but she was funny and bright as well. Heaven help poor Miss Courtwright!

Prudence Courtwright turned out to be not quite what Marianna, or Adam, had expected.

True, she did have white hair, beautiful white hair, soft and waving and of a peculiarly luminous color, drawn back into a simple knot at the back of her neck; and true, she was no longer young. Yet the word old seemed inappropriate to describe her, for her slender figure was still that of a young woman, and her eyes, almost as blue as her nephew's, were still bright and full of energy and intelligence.

At their knock she opened her door and with frank and open curiosity, observed the unlikely couple. "Yes?" she said. Her voice was low and pleasing.

Adam, cap in his hand, bowed slightly. "Ma'am, I am Captain Adam Street, of the *Viking Queen*, and I come to you at the request of your nephew, Phillip Courtwright."

Prudence Courtwright's face flushed, and her eyes brightened. "Phillip? He's alive and well?"

"Yes, madam. At least he was a few days ago, when we left Charleston."

Prudence Courtwright brushed back a wisp of hair with a slender, well-tended hand. "Oh, do come in! Where are my manners?"

She stepped back and motioned them inside. Marianna entered reluctantly, feeling, irrationally, that if she stepped one foot inside the house she would be trapped.

Adam, right behind her, urged her gently forward by nudging her from behind. Marianna turned her head and glared at him angrily. Adam noticed that Prudence Courtwright did not miss the byplay. It would be difficult to put anything past this lady, he thought; she would be a match for this girl, if anyone would be. The thought reassured him.

Prudence Courtwright motioned to a well-upholstered, blue settee and a high-backed chair. "Do make yourselves comfortable. I shall go put on the teakettle, and then you may tell me all about Phillip."

"Yes, madam," said Adam, settling his bulk upon the settee, leaving the high-backed chair for Marianna.

As the older woman bustled out, Adam said to Marianna, "She seems like a lovely woman, sensitive and intelligent. You could be doing a lot worse than staying with her."

Marianna said grudgingly, "Maybe."

She seemed uncomfortable, and Adam had to wonder if she had ever been in a house as fine as this one.

The truth was that she had not. Marianna looked furtively

about, with secret delight and some dismay. Everything was so grand! How could she ever adjust to living in a house like this? She touched the fabric of the chair, thinking how easily it would soil. It *would* be nice, staying here, with all these lovely things, but frightening also; for Phillip's aunt was a kind of woman Marianna had never known before, intimidating in her patent physical and mental superiority. The woman would hate her, Marianna was sure, especially when she read Phillip's letter and learned that her nephew had been—well, had been "associated" with the likes of a Banker woman. Marianna did not even hear the next comment Adam directed at her, for Prudence Courtwright was back in the room, seating herself decorously on a low, brocaded chair and looking at them expectantly.

"Now, I know who you are, Captain Street, but who is this young lady?"

Adam Street felt in his inner pocket, brought out Phillip's letter, and handed it to the woman. "This is Marianna Harper, Miss Courtwright, and I think that this letter from your nephew will explain the rest better than I might."

Prudence Courtwright took the letter and placed it in her lap. She stared down at it for a moment before opening it. She needed a moment to compose herself.

The sight of the girl with Captain Street had come as a considerable shock to her; but she was too much of a lady, and too kind, to show the surprise and consternation she felt. She was not a snob, at least she did not consider herself one, and had no patience with those who accepted others only on the basis of a faultless pedigree. Still, this ragged urchin with the huge, defiant eyes was definitely not the sort of person she would have expected to find on her doorstep. And, as Prudence had led the captain and the young girl into her parlor and bade them seat themselves, she had worried, privately, over the fabric of the chair where the girl seated herself.

The girl appeared to be little more than a child, and yet the small, slight figure had a certain ripeness and a considerable bosom for a figure so small. The hair was a wild tangle of curls, and it framed a face that was probably pretty, underneath the layer of grime that covered it. She definitely needed a good wash, and Prudence found herself sniffing disapprovingly.

So, it was with some misgivings that she opened Phillip's letter and read it. She was not pleased by what she read. Accept this ragamuffin into her home? How could she ever do that?

Covertly, still pretending to read Phillip's letter, she studied the girl and saw the vulnerability and fear behind the defiant eyes, saw the trembling of the full lips, and the nervousness expressed by the clenching of the small hands.

But it was the stoicism that finally undid Prudence, the look in the girl's eyes and the set to the mouth that seemed to say that hardship was expected and kindness was too much to hope for. The girl was prepared for, no, *expecting* Prudence to turn her away; and she confronted this apparent fact with a kind of stubborn courage that Prudence could not help but admire.

When Prudence Courtwright had finished reading Phillip's letter, her expression was grave, and Marianna's heart plummeted. She was displeased; Marianna had known that it would be so. Suddenly she felt much let down, and depressed. Of course, she hadn't really intended to stay, but still it was such a *nice* place. . . .

To her dismay she felt the beginning of a tear starting in her left eye and blinked fiercely, just as Prudence Courtwright looked directly into her face. Marianna steeled herself for rejection.

"Phillip's not coming home," the older woman said pensively. "Not just yet." Her glance went to Adam. "But he was in good health and spirits, when last you saw him?"

Adam nodded vigorously. "Aye, he was in fine shape, partially due to the fact that this young lady"—he nodded to Marianna—"saved his life. He wanted me to assure you, madam, that he owes her a great deal, more than he can ever repay."

Marianna's face flamed, and she felt a strong urge to crawl under the nearby window table with the long, floor-length cloth.

Prudence Courtwright smiled over at Marianna. "Yes, he says as much in his letter. I appreciate what you have done, my dear, more than you can ever know. I will be both pleased and happy to have you abide with me. You are most welcome. It has been far too long since there has been a young person in this old house, and I will welcome the chance to practice my old craft. I am, I *was*, a teacher, my dear," she added, seeing Marianna's confusion. "Phillip means a great deal to me, for he is my only living relative, and all that I have of my dead brother and his dear wife."

Prudence paused for a moment, looking away in sorrow. When she had agreed to let the girl stay with her, she found herself accepting it, quite calmly, as if it were the most ordinary thing in the world. But as soon as she had spoken, misgivings again crowded in upon her. The girl was clearly a near savage: what were her morals like? Would she steal? Would she cause trouble with the neighbors? It was true that Prudence desperately needed some physical help, for her arthritis sometimes made even the most simple tasks painfully difficult. But would this girl be willing to work, to learn?

Then her gaze met the girl's huge eyes, and she could not look away. There was an intelligence there, a strong will, and a certain quality, a quality that belied the unkempt appearance and dress. Prudence had to admit it, her heart went out to the child. Yes, she should have her chance. She *would* have her chance!

She got to her feet, smiling. "I have a lovely spare room, my dear, just at the top of the stairs, which will do nicely for you. Come, let me show it to you."

Marianna stood, not quite knowing what to do. Things seemed to be moving fast, too fast. She had not yet made up her mind whether or not she *wanted* to stay here; and yet, it appeared to be settled, and the captain, the captain would be leaving—

She looked at Adam in sudden panic. Despite her moments of anger at him, he represented a kind of safety to her, and now she was loath to see him go.

"Captain," she said hesitatingly, "Captain Street, I—"

Adam smiled gently. "Goodbye, Marianna. I hope things go well for you, and for Phillip. If I ever make port here, I shall look in and see how you are doing."

He turned, cap in hand, nodded to Prudence Courtwright, and started out. Marianna could find no words to stay him. He was her last link with Phillip, and he was going.

And then, as he reached the door, he turned back, taking something from his pocket. "By the way, one of the sailors found this in the pocket of your old coat when he was going through it before throwing it away. I believe it belongs to you."

He held out the small amethyst flacon, and the lovely color glowed warmly in the sunlight streaming through the window.

The sight of it made Marianna's throat ache. With a glad cry she reached out for it, and Adam placed it in her hand. She closed her fingers around its cool smoothness.

"Thank you, captain," she said. "Thank you for everything."

It was his turn to hesitate. He stared down at her, a strange look in his eyes. He opened his mouth to speak, then closed it, nodded formally to Prudence Courtwright, set his cap at a slant on his head, and strode from the room.

"Come along, dear," Prudence Courtwright said kindly. "Let me show you to your room."

Silently Marianna trudged behind the older woman up the steep wooden staircase—to the room that would be hers for the next two years.

It was a fine spring day, and Marianna, looking out of the open doorway, wished that she was finished with her studies so that she might enjoy the garden.

The smell of the flowers—snapdragons, roses, peonies— all blended into a lovely bouquet that fairly ravished the senses.

Marianna sighed and looked down at the book she held in her hand, a history of England, and resignedly raised it to her eyes. Prudence Courtwright was a stern taskmaster and a demanding teacher. She asked for Marianna's best, and usually received it.

In the two years since she had been brought to this house by Adam Street, Marianna had learned many new things, but undoubtedly the most important was love and respect for the elderly woman who had so generously taken her in.

It had not all been easy, by any means; not for either of them. Marianna smiled to herself now, thinking of how she had been at first, how ignorant and willful, how ill-prepared for the civilized world.

And now? Well, she knew that she was far from perfect—in fact doubted that she would ever be—but she was much improved. Prudence herself had often said so.

She could hear the older woman stirring in the kitchen and hoped that she was not overdoing. One of the things Marianna had discovered was that Prudence, despite her appearance, was not strong. She had a weak heart, and the doctor had forbidden her to exert herself too much.

Strangely enough, this was one of the reasons Marianna had stayed on. At first her prickly Banker pride had made her resentful of accepting what she considered nothing more than charity from Phillip's aunt, but the fact that Prudence needed help with the physical tasks of the house, needed someone to stay with her, made it that much easier for Marianna to accept the terms of what had come to be their unspoken agreement.

Marianna let the book fall to her lap again. Phillip. Where was he now? Did he ever think of her? There had been one letter, a year ago, written to both Marianna and his aunt, telling them that he was in good health and very busy, and that he would return. Marianna had scanned the pages in vain for a personal message—pleased that she was able to read it herself now—but there had been only the most general of closing phrases, "Your loving nephew, and friend," nothing to her directly, no word to her alone.

Marianna kept the letter in a small wooden box, which Prudence had given her for her special things. So far there were only three such items—the amethyst flacon, the letter, and the bit of ribbon with which Captain Street had tied back her hair.

If only she could see Phillip again! Sometimes her heart

literally ached for him, and her fingers longed for the touch of him. Her treacherous body often throbbed for him during the long nights, but she closed her mind to her body's yearnings, for if Phillip was gone for good, which she suspected was the case, she had sworn never to experience physical love again.

She colored now, thinking of her life before; of the time spent as Jude's woman and of the nights in Phillip's arms. It had become clear to her, early on, that such things were not in the experience of "nice" Boston women and girls. Being bright, it had not taken long for her to realize that female virginity was highly praised and much prized by genteel young ladies. No wonder Phillip had gone away from her! What must he think of her? No doubt he felt in her debt, for she had saved his life, but she had long realized that he would never marry her. He couldn't possibly, knowing what he did about her.

Still, she longed for him, and in the dark, alone, she fantasized his return and their happy reunion.

Marianna had never spoken of this to Prudence, yet it was constantly on her mind, and she worried about it during odd moments. If Phillip *did* return, just how would she face him?

But she had been happy here, despite her original misgivings. She had studied hard, learned, even made friends. Wouldn't *they* be shocked if they knew about her past, for they were all proper young Boston ladies of good families, who, after Marianna's hard edges had been softened somewhat, and upon the recommendation of Prudence Courtwright, had accepted her as a bright and entertaining addition to their number.

Marianna sighed pensively. Things were so changed for her, so much better, and yet something was missing. . . .

Wistfully she gazed again out of the open door, down the flower-lined walkway, and her body stiffened.

There was a man coming down the walk, a sea bag thrown over his shoulder, the sun behind him casting his face into shadow; a slight man, whose hair, haloed by the bright sunlight, shone like gold.

Her heart leaped and then seemed to stop. It couldn't

be! He had been in her thoughts, and now she was imagining things. She felt weak. She attempted to speak his name, but the word would not pass her lips. And then he was at the doorway, squinting inside, which must be dim to his sun-dazzled eyes.

When he spoke, his voice was as familiar to Marianna as the sound of her own heartbeat. "Aunt Prudence? Marianna?"

"Phillip!" Marianna said in a papery whisper; and then, louder: "Phillip!"

His laugh was her answer, and in the next instant, forgetting her fears about what he would think of her, forgetting everything but his miraculous appearance, she was flinging herself against him, and his arms were around her. She was crying, laughing, and trying to speak, all at once.

Gently he held her away from him to look into her face. "Marianna," he said in wonder. "You look so grown up, little one. Has it only been two years?"

"It's been forever!" she exclaimed, weeping still. She threw her arms around his neck again, pulling him close.

He squeezed her once and then gently disengaged her arms. "Aunt Prudence!"

Marianna stepped aside as he went to greet his aunt, who had just come into the room. Marianna groped for her handkerchief and wiped her eyes and flushed cheeks. She was whipsawed by several emotions—elation at seeing Phillip; anger at herself for not greeting him in a more ladylike manner; and worry that his own greeting had seemed somewhat more reserved than she hoped for.

Prudence's greeting was only a little less demonstrative than Marianna's. Holding Phillip's hands, gazing up into his face, she smiled, tears swimming in her eyes. "Phillip! My dear boy, it has been so long! We've worried so about you, but everything is fine, now that you're here."

She looked from Phillip to Marianna. "And thank you for sending Marianna to me. She's given me something to do and has proved a good friend and companion, as well. She is like a daughter to me. Now, sit down, put your feet up, and I'll put on the tea. I have some of that plum cake that you love so. Then, you can tell us all about what you have been doing. No, no, Marianna, you stay here and keep him company." She motioned to Marianna, who had moved to accompany her to the kitchen. "Besides, I know you two want to be alone."

But when they were alone, a rather strange silence descended upon them. Marianna, longing to go to him, to hold him, hug him, kiss him, held back, and Phillip, for what reason she could not guess, did likewise.

Phillip, she noted, looked thinner and older. He was a man now, the boy in him erased by time and, she assumed, troubled circumstances.

"You are more lovely than ever, Marianna," he said unexpectedly, looking at her with something of the loving expression that she so well remembered.

"Thank you, Phillip," she said primly. Why didn't he sweep her into his arms and forget all this silly talk? "You look well, too, although you are thinner than I remember."

A great many questions boiled up in her, but there seemed to be this strange kind of wall between them, invisible, yet prohibiting.

Phillip cleared his throat. "Have you been happy here, Marianna?"

"Oh, yes!" She nodded rapidly. "At first I was certain that I wouldn't be, but your aunt is such a wonderful woman. I—" Then, in a rush: "Phillip, I've missed you!"

He leaned forward intently. "I've missed you, too, little one, more than you'll ever know. I'm sorry that I wasn't able to write more often, but I've been traveling a great deal—"

Marianna's heart leaped when he spoke of missing her. Perhaps if they just talked for a little, making idle conversation, the strangeness would go away. "What have you been doing, Phillip? Why are you traveling so much?"

He placed his forearms on his knees and clasped his hands together. "It's a long story, Marianna. I suppose I should have told you before. I did tell you that my parents are dead, didn't I? My father died in disgrace, by his own hand, and the shock of it killed my mother. The thing is, the disgrace was not really my father's doing, but was brought about by the actions of two brothers, both unscrupulous, ruthless men. The Barth brothers brought financial ruin upon my father.

"You see, they are involved in the wrecking of ships, merchant vessels loaded with valuable goods. They have connection with certain wreckers, like your group on the Outer Banks, who lure ships to their destruction and then salvage the cargo. But the cargo is not the Barths' main concern. My father, for instance, had so many of his ships wrecked that he went bankrupt and lost his shipping company to the Barth brothers.

"I have good cause to believe that the Barth brothers also ordered the wrecking of the ship that I was on, when it was wrecked off the Banks. You see, I was not loath to make it known that not only did I believe them responsible for my father's bankruptcy, but that I intended to expose them for the blackguards they are. By wrecking the ship I was on, they hoped to silence me. But for you, they would have succeeded."

Marianna was appalled. She did not doubt him, for his story made clear much of what had been mysterious about Ezekial Throag's almost magical knowledge of when ships would be off the Banks.

"Ezekial Throag," she whispered.

Phillip nodded. "That had occurred to me. It is quite possible that Throag is in cahoots with the Barth brothers. In any event, Marianna, I shall never rest until the villainous brothers are made to pay—"

At that moment Prudence returned to the room, pushing a well-laden tea cart. "Here we are," she said cheerfully, "and I imagine you are starving, nephew. You are entirely too thin. But then, I shall have the pleasure of fattening you up."

Phillip smiled at her; uncomfortably, Marianna thought, and wondered why.

"Thank you, Aunt Prudence. I *am* hungry. We made port early this morning, and I didn't wait for breakfast, and was too busy at noon to eat."

He's been in Boston all day, Marianna thought in dismay, and has only now come to see us. The thought made her heart ache, but she said nothing.

Prudence, however, did. "You mean you've been in the city since morning, and just now got around to us? I'm hurt, nephew. You must have known how much we wanted to see you."

Phillip smiled sheepishly. "Yes, Aunt Prudence, I knew that, but there were things that I had to do, affairs I had to see to first." He reached for the cup of tea and plate of cake his aunt offered him. "I've just been telling Marianna about father, and of why I am committed to this course of action."

Prudence sighed, her glance going to Marianna. "My brother's unnecessary end was a great blow to me. He was a good man, a fine husband and father. We were very close. I shall not say that I agree with Phillip's dedication toward clearing his father's good name, for I fear for *his* life as well. Still, I understand his need and desire to do so. I only pray that it will not destroy him in the end." She reached again for the teapot. "Milk or lemon, dear?"

Marianna was too upset to think of food or drink. "You mean that is what you have been doing these two years past, Phillip? Trying to expose these men?"

"Yes. I mean to clear father's name, no matter what it may cost me in time or effort, or even bodily harm."

"You aren't finished yet? I mean, you aren't going to remain with us, but will be leaving again?"

He said unhappily, "I must, Marianna. I am close, but—" He smiled palely. "I'm like a hunting dog. I'm on the scent of the fox, but not yet close enough. I hoped you'd understand."

For a moment Marianna forgot all that she had learned during the past two years. The only thing she knew was that she was angry; she was absolutely furious. Here was Phillip, here she was, and Prudence as well, and all three could be happy, very happy together. But was Phillip going to stay? Oh, no! He was about to go running off on some mad chase to avenge his father. What could it matter now? His father was dead, but *they* were alive. If Phillip continued with this foolishness, he very well might die also, and that would certainly accomplish nothing.

"You are a foolish man, Phillip Courtwright!" she said angrily. "Life is too precious to waste it thinking only of a dead man, even if he was your father. Hellfire and spit, it's all a lot of noble nonsense!"

The expressions on their faces drew her up short, and she realized that she had been shouting.

"My dear Marianna, wherever did you learn such language?" Prudence said in a shocked voice.

"I suppose it was too much to expect you to understand," Phillip said tightly.

"You mean, because I'm just an ignorant Banker woman?" Marianna retorted. "You're right, Phillip. That's what I am. A Banker woman might not be much, but at least we know what is sensible and what is not!"

Leaping up from her chair, Marianna stormed up the stairs to her room, leaving aunt and nephew dumbfounded, staring after her.

That night at supper, the atmosphere was cool and very formal. Marianna was heartsore. She regretted her rash words, regretted even her anger, although a residue of it still lingered. Obviously, avenging his father's fate and clearing the man's name meant more to Phillip than she did. It was a hard thought to face, but face it she must.

But after supper, after sherry and polite, strained conversation, Marianna allowed herself to be persuaded to walk in the garden with Phillip, where the scent of the flowers, the moon, and the gentle warmth of the summer night all did their magic.

Prudence Courtwright, peeking anxiously through the parlor curtains, was pleased to note that within only a few minutes of walking up and down the narrow walkway, they were in each other's arms.

Feeling that what she did not know would not hurt her, Prudence went quietly upstairs to her bedroom. But once abed, she lay awake for a long time, thinking back over the past two years.

When she had realized the depth of Marianna's ignorance, how truly close she was to savagery, she had been appalled, a reaction she had successfully concealed from the girl.

Yet, for all her ignorance and thorny pride, there had

been a sweetness, an innocence, about Marianna, and her mind was bright and quick. Prudence had accepted the challenge.

Now she was glad that she had. The change in Marianna verged on a miracle. Prudence knew, without vanity, that she was an excellent teacher, but most of the credit belonged to Marianna. She soaked up knowledge like a sponge and had learned as much in two years as most people would have in twice that length of time. In addition, she had blossomed into a beautiful woman, with a loving nature. Withal, she was still high-spirited, with a flashing temper and touchy pride.

Prudence had, indeed, come to love the girl. How nice it would be if Marianna and her nephew came to love one another. They could live here, giving a sense of purpose to an old woman's last years.

She knew that Marianna adored Phillip, that had become evident early on. But Phillip, Phillip was the problem. Even if he loved Marianna, or came to love her, would he give up this obsession of his and settle down into wedded bliss?

Prudence closed her eyes and said a silent prayer. She went to sleep, a dreaming smile on her lips, before the prayer was completed.

"Marianna—little one, I *have* missed you terribly," Phillip said huskily.

They were in her room, on her narrow bed, and Marianna, almost witless with the pleasure of holding him close to her again, could only murmur an endearment in answer. Greedily she kissed his throat, his shoulder, his cheek.

"I do love you, you know," he whispered, and the joy she felt was beyond expressing.

"Stay then," she said, tracing the outline of his abdomen with a soft finger. "Don't go away again. Stay here with me. Oh, we'd be so happy, Phillip. So happy!"

He groaned and pulled her tightly to him, pressing her small body against him, as if to memorize it. "Oh, God, Marianna! You make it so difficult. don't you know that I want to stay?"

"Then stay, my love," she urged, moving her body against him, delighting in the sweet friction of their flesh. She felt him swell against her and experienced a surge of love and power. He was like a young god to her; and yet she could evoke this response in him, which gave her power over him.

With what was almost a sob, Phillip moved and thrust into her with a strong movement that brought her intense pleasure.

"Say you'll stay," she whispered as he moved in her. "Promise."

Instead of speaking, he moved with a raging frenzy that swept her up in its driving rhythm, until they experienced together an explosion of rapture.

As he lay atop her, his heaving breath stirring the hairs at the side of her neck, Marianna said again, "Promise me you'll stay."

Phillip pulled away from her, onto his side of the narrow bed. "I cannot, Marianna. Not and live with myself. You must accept that."

Marianna, feeling betrayed, turned her face to the wall. Already she could feel the pain of his leaving, aching in her like an old wound; again doubting his love, sure that once gone again, he would not return; again feeling used and forsaken.

Why had she been so foolish as to let him make love to her? She had learned about how ladies and gentlemen felt about such things before marriage. Why had she not remained distant and cool so that he would want her enough to stay, to wed her? That was the way it should have been. That was the way her new lady friends would have handled it. Instead, she had again fallen into his arms and into his bed, so to speak. He had used her, he had taken his pleasure with her, and now he would leave again.

"Marianna?"

Phillip made his voice and touch tender and loving, yet his finger on her cheek encountered the warm moisture of her tears.

As Phillip turned the corner at dawn, heading away from his aunt's house, he gave it one final, backward glance. The small house looked inviting and safe, and everything that he loved was there, within its four walls.

Although he could not see her from where he was, he knew that Marianna was watching him from her window.

His body still pleasantly fatigued from the night of love with Marianna, he thought sorrowfully of what he was giving up by leaving. He had never felt about another woman the way he felt about this bit of a girl. Beside her, all other women faded into pallid shadows. Being absent from her caused him acute, physical pain; for once having known that small, ripe, giving body, it seemed impossible to do without it; and yet she doubted his love, he realized. He had spent a good portion of the night trying to reassure her, trying to make her understand how much he cared, doing his best to make her believe that he would come back to her. He had failed miserably.

If he could only remain with her, he could, in time, make her feel secure and certain of his love, but he could not do that. He had to go, to follow the course he had set for himself. He dearly wished that he could have departed with Marianna's assurances that she would wait for him, for he was afraid that she, without a commitment from him, would turn to another man. Certainly men would flock around her, they could not fail to see in her what he himself saw. He tried not to dwell on this—he had other, more immediate matters to consider—yet the thought remained like an irritant in the back of his mind, and he kept touching it experimentally from time to time.

He took out his gold turnip watch, one of a few precious mementos of his father, and looked at the time. It was six o'clock. His ship, the *Excalibur*, was sailing at eight. His trunk was already on board; there was plenty of time to get settled in before the ship left the dock.

At this hour the tradesmen were not yet about, but the wharf would be busy, Phillip knew, as various ships prepared to sail. The familiar, ripe smell of the waterfront assailed his nostrils, as the early morning mist began to thin and pale sunlight started to touch the damp alleyways, evaporating the pearls of moisture with which the night fog had decorated the buildings and docks.

Phillip loved the sea, loved the smells, the excitement of it; but his wearying travels were eroding his original sense of adventure. Now, he was shipping out again, following one more tenuous clue, journeying to yet another port city. Sometimes he wondered where and when it would end. Still, he was getting close now, he could feel it. If only he would be allowed enough time to complete his investigation; for he was well aware that he had drawn the attention of the Barth brothers, and he was also aware that they wielded considerable power and influence. He was not certain what or how they might decide to deal with him; he only knew that they had the power and cunning to do so.

As the wind freshened, blowing the odors of saltwater, rotting fruit, and fish into his nostrils, Phillip allowed himself one last thought of Marianna. Marianna, he said in silent communication, I will come back to you. I promise. You must not doubt me.

He smiled wryly to himself. Was it a thought, or a prayer? He made the last turn down a narrow street toward where his ship was berthed.

As he headed down the street, he passed a narrow opening between two warehouse buildings. Two burly figures exploded from the dark maw and were quickly upon him.

He had only time to see two grim faces before he received a blow on the head from a cudgel. Dazed, he found himself, arms twisted up behind him, pulled into the dim recess between the buildings.

It had all happened so quickly, and in absolute silence, that Phillip was unable to react until he was deep within the reeking alley, and by that time, he was too late.

The largest of the pair grinned at him cruelly and raised high a hand in which he held a belaying pin. Phillip saw the weapon and opened his mouth to shout. Surely someone would hear and come to his assistance. Then the pin descended, and his thoughts were swallowed up in an explosion of pain and blackness.

When he regained a measure of consciousness, Phillip realized he was being carried onto a deck of a ship—*not* the

Excalibur—and he dimly recognized the faces of the men who carried him.

One man let loose of him, while the other held him upright. Phillip's feet striking the deck started a blaze of agony in his head.

Through a fog of pain he saw the one man lifting a hatch cover. In a barely audible voice Phillip croaked, "What is this about? What's to happen to me?"

The man straightened up, throwing the hatch cover back. He grinned unpleasantly. "Why, you're going on a nice sea voyage, matey. All around the Horn to Hong Kong. Now, what could be nicer than that?"

Hands were laid roughly on him, and Phillip was swung over the open hatch.

The same voice said, "Down we go, matey! Happy, happy sailing!"

As he fell Phillip thought despairingly, dear God, I've been shanghaied.

Part Two

1843:
Sag Harbor

Chapter Eight

THE house was empty. The pieces of furniture still stood in their accustomed places; curtains still hung, crisp and white, at the windows; the garden still bloomed; but the house was empty, for the spirit that had given it life was dead.

Marianna stood in the small, neat room that had been hers for more than two years and gazed at the trunk that contained all her worldly goods. It was certainly more than she had brought with her when she first came to this house; and she would be taking with her far more than the items packed inside the trunk, for she would be taking the love and devotion that Prudence Courtwright had given her; the skills the woman had taught her; an appreciation for the better things of life; and the ethical and intellectual values instilled in her by Prudence—all of which had changed her life for the better.

Slowly Marianna picked up her bonnet and tied it securely under her chin, thinking of the day, just a week ago, when Prudence had purchased it for her.

Tears blurred Marianna's vision, and she blinked them away. She must not give in to the waves of sorrow and loss that buffeted her, for she knew that if she did, she would do naught else but weep, and she could not allow herself that luxury. She had to leave here, this very day, and she needed all her wits about her to be able to cope with what was to come. She was embarking on another journey. On the journey from the Outer Banks to Charleston, Phillip had been with her. On the journey from Charleston to Boston, she had been in Captain Street's charge. This time, she was wholly on her own.

Resolutely she drapped her shawl around her shoulders and picked up her reticule.

Prudence had told her, during those last hours, to be strong, and not to mourn her. "I am going to a better place, my dear," she had said, taking Marianna's hand in hers. "I have had a full life, and a satisfactory one, and I bless you for making these past two and a half years the happiest that I have ever known. It has pleased me greatly to watch you flower, to see your thirsty mind soaking up knowledge."

Her voice had faded then, and her eyelids had closed, as she had slipped into a shallow slumber.

With a feeling of despair, Marianna had watched her. She had grown to love Prudence dearly, casting her in the role of mother, a position her real mother had filled inadequately.

At that time she had not thought of the future, of what would happen to *her*, when Prudence died. It was only later, at the reading of the will, that Marianna realized that she had lost her home, as well as her friend.

The little house, it seemed, was to be sold to pay Prudence's debts. Prudence had never seemed to worry about money, but Marianna now realized that there had been much that Prudence had kept from her, out of a desire to shelter her. Whatever money was left after the debtors were satisfied was to go to Marianna.

Plans to sell the house had moved with dispatch, and Prudence was scarcely buried when a sale was consummated. When the debts were all paid, Marianna received a small sum of money. Still, she had no idea of where she should go, or what she should do. She was better mannered, and certainly better schooled, than she had been when she came to Boston, yet she still had no real skills with which to earn a living. Her inheritance would not last long if she did not find a way to earn more.

She had not heard from Phillip since he had left, and in her practical, Banker mind, she did not expect to; still, in her secret heart, she had hoped that he would return to her.

Up until the last moment, when it was time for her to

leave the house, Marianna hoped that he would show up at the door, slender and handsome as he had been the last time she had seen him. But now she was ready to go; and there was no knock on the door, no footsteps on the garden path.

She sighed and left the room, going down the narrow stairs for the last time and out into the garden.

The nip of autumn was in the air, and many of the flowers were fading, as if in mourning for Prudence's death. However, their perfume still filled the air, and the late afternoon sunlight, deep and golden, shone upon the garden, bringing to it a peculiar, deep beauty that made Marianna's heart swell.

Once more, she thought of Phillip, and of the night they had walked here, and she felt as if her heart were breaking. She had to face up to the truth. It was clear that he had forgotten her, despite his fine promises. She was on her own and must act accordingly.

The slow, rhythmic clip-clop of a horse's hoofs roused Marianna from her reverie, and she glanced up to see Mr. Thornton approaching, sitting high upon the seat of his dray, behind the broad rump of his old draft horse, Ned.

Taking a deep breath, Marianna waved to him and smiled. Leaning down, she plucked a deep red rose from the bush that grew beside the walkway and breathed of it deeply as she spoke her silent goodbye to the house and garden—and a final farewell to dear Prudence.

It took only a few minutes for Mr. Thornton to bring down her trunk and place it on the dray; and then she was seated beside him on the high seat, and they were heading toward the dock.

Despite her melancholy at leaving, Marianna felt a stir of excitement. There was a whole world out there waiting for her, a world she had so far seen little of, yet this prospect brought with it a sense of trepidation, along with the excitement.

Mr. Thornton, looking at her out of the corner of his faded blue eyes, spat around a wad of snuff in his mouth. "Where is it you're heading, Miss Harper?"

She smiled brightly. "I'm going to Sag Harbor, on upper Long Island."

"Ayuh, Sag Harbor." Mr. Thornton spat again. "A whaling town, ain't it? You got relations there?"

Marianna shook her head. "No, but I know someone there."

The old man shook his head dolefully. "Them whaling towns is rough, I hear. Don't know that it's the right sort of place for a young lady like yourself to be going."

Marianna cupped a hand around her mouth to conceal a smile of pride. Prudence had done a good job on her, no doubt of that.

"What do you expect to do there?" the driver asked.

"I don't really know," she answered truthfully, not minding the old man's curiosity, for it distracted her from her own worries. "I guess I hope to find work of some kind."

Mr. Thornton snorted and flicked his whip idly over the back of the plodding horse. "Don't expect that there's much work for a lady of your sort, although I expect there's work for *some* kinds of women. Say again, why you going there?"

Marianna hesitated, for she could not answer the question satisfactorily, even to herself. "As I said, I know someone there. This person said that it's a beautiful town, and very prosperous."

"So's Boston," the old man grumbled, "and Boston's probably a heap more civilized. Them whaling towns is rough, like I said." He scowled over at her, as if in disapproval of her intentions, and Marianna felt herself flush.

Why *was* she going to Sag Harbor?

There were any number of places where she could go; after all, they were all equally alien to her. She could even remain in Boston, in the hope that Phillip would eventually return. So, why had she decided upon Sag Harbor?

When she had made up her mind to leave Boston, she recalled Captain Street's speaking of Sag Harbor in glowing terms and saying that his home was there. Of course, being a whaler, he would likely be at sea, so that she could not go to him for help, not that she would, anyway.

In any event, that was not the reason she chose Sag Harbor. Perhaps it was because it was the only other city, besides Boston and Charleston, that seemed real to her. All of the others were just names in history and geography books. And for some reason she did not fully understand, she felt that she was finished with Boston, that it was time for her to move on. Also she instinctively felt that if she remained there, she would not be able to "get on" with her life, for she would always be biding time, waiting for Phillip to return.

No, she had to leave Boston.

She turned to Mr. Thornton and gave him a dazzling smile. "Anyway, it will be an adventure, sir."

He blinked, started to speak, then broke off as they approached the dock and he got busy jockeying Ned into a position near the gangplank.

As Marianna climbed down from the dray, her glance went to the ship she was to board, and her thoughts swung to Captain Adam Street. Would he be there when she reached Sag Harbor?

It was a pretty little house, set well back from the street amidst a flower garden, but Ezekial Throag saw none of its beauty, for he saw it only as a hiding place, a lair that concealed the murderess who had killed his son.

Clad all in black, from head to toe, in well-cut and excellently tailored clothing, clean shaven and well shod, Throag bore little resemblance to the man who had led the band of wreckers on the Outer Banks.

Taking his tall hat in his hand, he paused at the gate in the picket fence, gazing at the little house, his expression malevolent.

On that night over two years ago, when his henchmen had returned emptyhanded from the search for the girl and her lover, Throag had vowed that he would never rest until he had found the girl and destroyed her.

A few weeks later, after digging up his accumulated treasure from the spot where he had hidden it, he cleaned himself up, left the Banks for the mainland in the middle of the night, and then journeyed to Charleston, where he changed his gold and other assets into cash and deposited it in his regular account, which he had maintained for several years. The total sum was enormous, enough to let him do whatever he chose, without the need of ever having to work again. He was a wealthy man, and he intended to spend that wealth—all of it, if necessary—to avenge the death of his son.

At the time he had not thought that it would take long to trace the ignorant girl and her accomplice, but in this he had been proven wrong. Although he had employed man-hunters, they had been unable to find the slightest clue as to the couple's whereabouts. If they only knew the name of the man, they told Throag, that might be a starting point, but there were so many cities, so many places—how were they to find a nameless youth and a girl among the multi-tude?

But at long last, just a month ago, the latest manhunter Throag had hired had managed the seemingly impossible and traced the wench to Boston. Considerable investigation had been necessary to make absolutely certain that the young woman living with one Prudence Courtwright was Marianna Harper, but now it was established beyond a doubt, and Ezekial Throag had come to claim his vengeance.

He could, of course, have hired someone to kill the girl—for the right price the manhunter would have done the job—but Throag knew that this would not satisfy him. He must do it himself, he must see her die, see the terror in her eyes; he must know that she knew *why* she was dying. Only then, would he be content. Only then, would he be able to go ahead with his own life.

The little house seemed unduly quiet, but there was a light somewhere inside, which had to mean that someone was there.

Slowly, savoring the thought of what was to come, Throag walked down the flower-lined walkway. For him, the flow-ers spread their fragrance in vain, and the birdsongs went unheard. He saw only the broad, white door that concealed his prey.

Throag lifted his great fist and brought it down upon the door, once, then once again. There was no response. Frowning, he thumped the door again without result.

Finally, he walked down the side of the house to where

low windows gave him a view inside the parlor. All was neat and well arranged within, but there was no sign of life. Perhaps they, the woman and the girl, had gone out, to attend to shopping or some other female business.

As Throag turned away from the windows, he saw a small, thin man in a dark suit coming up the path toward the house. Throag moved to intercept him, and they met just as the man reached the steps to the porch.

Throag nodded to the little man. "Do you happen to know, sir, whether this is the house of Prudence Courtwright?"

The man nodded, eyeing Throag with some misgivings. "Yes, sir, it is. Or I should say, was. Miss Courtwright passed on recently, and the house and its contents have been sold to satisfy her creditors."

Throag experienced a lurch of dismay. "And the young woman, Miss Courtwright's ward, I believe—she is no longer living here?"

"She is not." The man shook his head. "By the bye, sir, I am Alexander Stimson, solicitor. I handled the sale of the property. You are, sir?" He waited expectantly.

For a moment Throag thought that he would go mad. After all this time, to be so close and to be frustrated at the last moment. It was intolerable! With a supreme effort he kept his anger under control. "I am Ezekial Throag, a family friend of the young woman in question. I have an urgent message from her family, and it is most important that I contact her. But you say she no longer resides here?"

Stimson bobbed his head. "That's right. I felt very bad about being the cause of her having to leave." Through nearsighted eyes, he peered at Throag suspiciously. "I thought she had no family, nowhere to go. That is what she led us to believe."

Throag made himself smile. "A most unfortunate affair. The young lady is estranged from her family. She denies them completely. The reason I am here is to attempt a reconciliation. You understand, I'm sure?"

Stimson nodded. "Indeed I do, sir. Young people these days—" He let the phrase dangle. "Well, at any rate, the girl is gone. She left two days ago, I believe. We hated to see her go. I cannot understand why she didn't want to remain here, in Boston. She and my daughter were friends, you know."

"How charming," Throag said through gritted teeth. "Now, could you possibly be so kind as to tell me just where Miss Harper went, and then I will trouble you no further."

"Oh, it's no trouble at all, sir. No trouble at all," Stimson said, rocking back and forth on the balls of his feet, smiling slightly. "It's no trouble, sir, because I don't know. You see, she was very undecided as to what she was going to do. Quite broken up she was, about Miss Courtwright's passing. They had been very close, you see."

"I see," Throag said, not really listening now. His rage was so great that he could hardly restrain himself from locking his hands around the man's throat and throttling him as a bearer of bad news.

"We tried to get her to stay, of course," Stimson rambled on, "but she seemed determined to leave, while at the same time she wasn't certain where she wanted to go.

"Must have made up her mind all of a sudden, for the next thing I knew, she was gone, bag and baggage, without a word of farewell or a message stating where she might be reached, in the event the need arose. A most unusual and spirited young lady, if I may say so."

"Spirited, indeed," Throag said in a thick voice. Damn the wench! Found her and lost her, all in the same day. He would track her down eventually, Throag knew, but the taste of this failure was bitter as wormwood in his mouth, and he wanted very much to grab Stimson and choke the life out of him. He was a handy target for his, Throag's, frustration. But Stimson was a lawyer, and such an action would not be wise. Afraid to trust his voice, Throag tipped his hat to the man, turned on his heel, and strode away.

Halfway up the block, a small dog chanced to cross his path. Throag broke step, and one swing of his size twelve boot broke the creature's spine. It yelped pitifully and lay quivering in death throes on the cobblestones.

Throag grinned wolfishly and strode on, some of his black anger dissipating.

So the girl had escaped him once again. He would find her in the end. He would contact his manhunters and send them on the scent again. The next time they ran their quarry to earth, Throag decided, he would not dally until they were absolutely sure of her identity. He would move, and quickly.

But meanwhile, what was he to do?

Inactivity was beginning to bore him, and also it was time he was engaged in some lucrative endeavor. He still had ample funds at his disposal, but everything was going out and nothing coming in.

Then he thought of the Barth brothers, and his grin became that of a predator's.

The village of Sag Harbor was, as Adam Street had promised, a bustling town. In the sheltering arms of a deep and well-protected harbor lay more ships than in New York Harbor, for not only were the citizens of Sag Harbor engaged in whaling, but they were also trading in rum, sugar, and molasses with the West Indies—the famous "Triangle Trade." In addition to the protection afforded by the snug harbor, the town was shielded from the fury of the Atlantic by Long Island itself.

Ships entered the harbor so frequently that the cry of "ship in the bay!" was almost continuous. Atop the tall white houses, the captains' wives could be seen squinting out to sea, hoping that each new arriving vessel would be "their" ship. Sag Harbor ships traveled to every ocean and continent, and most Sag Harbor residents were familiar with strange and exotic ports. When all the berths at the Long Wharf were occupied, the streets of the town played host to a polyglot crowd of all races and nationalities.

And so it was, when Marianna arrived.

She loved the town on sight. She admired the green parks, the neatly planned streets, and the beautiful houses. Far smaller than Boston, Sag Harbor appeared to her to be of a much more manageable size, and yet it contained homes just as impressive as the finest in Boston, and all of the amenities to which she had become accustomed over the past two and a half years.

As she gazed out the window of her second-story room, which she had taken in a respectable boardinghouse, Marianna felt a great surge of excitement. She had been right to come here. It *felt* right. Surely, in all this hustle and bustle, there must be some work that she could do, something she could do to earn a living. She felt full of hope and much improved in spirits.

Her first priority had been to search out Captain Adam Street, but she learned at once that he had sailed some months before, and was not expected to return for some time.

So, she was on her own. She must now look over the town and seek some employment. Sighing, she turned away from the window.

Attiring herself in her best "sensible" dress and comfortable walking boots, Marianna left the rooming house and struck off for Main Street, which her landlady had advised her to see. "Some of the grandest houses in all of Sag Harbor are there, miss. Homes of the shipowners and captains. They are quite grand, and well worth seeing."

And the houses were indeed grand, as was the day itself. A fresh wind blew in from the sea, and the sky was cloud-dotted and a sharp, clear blue.

For a moment Marianna thought of Phillip's eyes and then resolutely pushed the thought out of her mind. There must be none of that. She had far more important matters to think about.

As she passed by a huge white house pillared in the Greek style, she wondered how it would feel to live in such splendor. It was almost beyong her imagining.

Soon the fine homes gave way to business establishments, and Marianna was walking amid a crowd of busy people, all intent upon their business. The sight of so many people made her aware of how alone she was, and for a moment she felt very vulnerable.

Main Street led directly down to the waterfront and to the Long Wharf, where ships were tied up three and four deep. Along the waterfront, and the streets leading to it, were scores of establishments catering to the seagoing trade—carpenters, coopers, caulkers, sailmakers, ship's chandlers, all with their individual signs hanging out front speaking of their wares and services. Even closer to the

Long Wharf were the warehouses and workshops, running along each side of the dock. Marianna had to pick her way between whaleboats, casks, and piles of whalebone, stacked in almost every open space. The area was smelly, crowded, and noisy, but she found it tremendously exciting. Although Marianna was almost the only woman present, everyone seemed too busy to notice her, and she reveled in the noises and the bustle.

But she saw no opportunity for gainful employment here, so she reluctantly left the Long Wharf, and turned again into the town, looking for the newspaper office, which her landlady had told her was on Main Street.

At last she found it and purchased a copy of the daily paper, which she took to a nearby restaurant. She ordered a noon meal and read the advertisements as she ate. The light meal she had ordered, along with a pot of tea, was excellent, yet she was disappointed to find that advertisements for positions for women were very scarce. If she were a man, she could have found work aplenty, but there were only three positions listed for women—two for housemaids, and one for a governess.

Her spirits dashed, Marianna put the paper down. She knew that, after only two years of tutoring by Prudence Courtwright, she was not qualified to work as a governess; and the thought of working as a maid galled her pride. Anyway, from listening to her friends in Boston, she knew how little serving girls and maids were paid.

Irritated, she poured the rest of the tea into her cup. What were women alone supposed to do? How were they expected to live? On the Banks there had never been any problem; a woman was simply a part of the community; and she did her share of the work, even if she belonged to a man. Out here in the world, men did all the important work; and when they took a woman, they put her upon a pedestal and looked after her every need, if they had the necessary money. If they did not, if they were tradesmen or laborers, their wives worked, well enough, yet it was still the men who earned the money to buy their daily necessities. There seemed to be no provision at all made for women alone.

Marianna set her cup down with considerable force, feeling angry and impotent. "Hellfire and spit, it's unfair! she said, unaware that she had spoken aloud.

"There's a lot of things in this world unfair, lovey," said an amused voice behind her. "Which particular thing did you have in mind?"

Marianna stiffened and then slowly turned. She saw a large, red-faced woman overflowing a chair at the next table.

The woman was wearing a purple, ruffled gown. The small, shovel-shaped bonnet on top of her rigid, sausagelike curls made her vast cheeks look larger. She was a formidable sight, and yet her smile was sweet and her blue eyes merry.

She smiled now and lifted her full cup in salute. "I'm Meg Mundy, lovey. I couldn't very well help overhearing. Unless I'm very much mistaken, I've not seen your pretty face before, now have I?"

The high, musical voice was utterly incongruous coming as it did from such a large person, but Marianna found the woman disarming and pleasant. She could not help smiling. "I'm Marianna Harper, and I just arrived in Sag Harbor two days ago. It is a charming place."

The woman nodded. "Right enough. It is that, and flourishing, too. Good for business." She winked. "Lovey, come and join me at my table, and I'll order another pot of tea and some of their jam tarts." She leaned forward conspiratorially. "That's the real reason I come here, you know. I can get tea at my own place, and good enough fare, but I like to come here for a bit of a change, meaning the jam tarts."

She smiled benignly, and Marianna could do nothing but smile back. The woman's good humor was contagious. Taking her cup, Marianna moved to Meg Mundy's table, leaving her paper behind.

Meg gestured to it. "Don't forget your newspaper."

Marianna shrugged. "It doesn't matter. There's nothing in it for me, anyway."

Meg, gazing at her shrewdly, reached over and patted Marianna's hand. "There now, lovey. I can see that something's troubling you. Why don't you just tell old Meg about it?" She patted Marianna's hand again, meanwhile motioning to the waiter.

And so Marianna told her story, breaking off only long enough to sip her tea and to consume two of the jam tarts, which were indeed delicious. "And so what are women supposed to do?" she finished plaintively. "Why are all the good-paying positions for men?"

Meg wiped the last crumb from her lips, sighed, and nodded. "Because it's the men, bless their souls, who make all the rules, lovey. It's a man's world, and always has been, and they have it set up so that it suits them just fine. The only jobs they leave for women are whoring and serving, for they figure that such jobs keep women in their places."

She shifted her bulk in the chair. "I can sympathize with what you're feeling, my girl. Many's the time I've felt much the same way myself. But now I'm a woman of great substance," she patted her ample middle and laughed, "as you can plainly see. I'd like to be able to tell you that I earned my establishment through hard work and thrift, but such is not the case. My place came to me through Mr. Mundy, as sorry a representative of the male sex as you might ever come across, but he did have the grace to do me one kindness in his life. By dying, he left me the owner of Mundy's Tavern, a flourishing establishment across Main Street there."

She looked at Marianna intently. "Tell me straight, lovey, you wear the clothes and manners of a lady, but I sense something else in you, something tough and bright. Do you really need a paying position?"

Marianna bobbed her head, her heartbeat suddenly speeding up.

"Are you too proud to serve in a common tavern, then?"

Marianna did not answer immediately. Prudence Courtwright would turn over in her grave, after working so hard to make her, Marianna, a lady. Yet the idea appealed to her. A tavern would be rough, she knew, but she had been used to a rough life, until Boston.

"It ain't ladylike work," Meg said, shrugging, "but a clever girl can pick up a nice bit of cash if she plays her cards right. And by that, I *don't* mean on her back. No, I'd keep the randy ones off you. I don't let men plague my girls. Of course, there are some that want to make a little money on the side, and I figure that's their business, so long as they do it away from Mundy's Tavern. But if a girl doesn't want that sort of thing, she has nothing to fear in my place. What do you say, lovey?"

Marianna looked across the table into Meg's beaming face and nodded. "Thank you, Meg. I accept. I'll work hard. You won't be sorry you hired me."

Meg grinned. "Oh, I'm not afraid of that, lovey. I'm wagering that I gain many a new customer that will come in just to see your pretty face. No, I don't figure to lose. I like to lend a helping hand, but I'm not in business for my health."

She stretched across the table a hand that looked like a white glove filled with air. Marianna took it in her own, and the bargain was made.

Chapter Nine

THE *Viking Queen* was rolling heavily through choppy seas, and Adam Street steadied the log with his left hand as he wrote with his right:

November 15, 1843: Log of the ship Viking Queen. *These twenty-four hours commence with choppy seas. Spoke with ship* Maria *out of Boston. Have seen no whales these past six days. First mate, Mr. Karnes, took a large sunfish, three hundred days out.*

Adam put the pen down and braced himself against the roll of the ship.

They had run into bad weather two days ago, and the seas had been rough and the sky overcast ever since. Adam hoped that tomorrow would dawn fair and that they would soon sight whales. The men were growing restive, as he was himself.

The ship rolled again but righted itself immediately.

Adam smiled proudly to himself. The *Viking Queen* was a stout vessel, built, like all Sag Harbor whalers, for strength and endurance, rather than speed. At three hundred and fifty tons, she was a solid, untemperamental combination of ship, try works, and living quarters for the men aboard her.

Square-rigged, she could withstand the wildest storms and the heaviest seas, and Adam Street loved her, as he would a woman.

He glanced down at the calendar on his desk. November,

already. If they could only take a few more whales, they could be home in time for Christmas. Christmas at sea was always bad for the men—boys really, for most of the crew averaged only twenty or twenty-two years of age. Yes, it would be good if they could be home by Christmas.

Well, he had best go above decks and see if the lookout had spotted anything.

The sea had calmed a bit by the time Adam reached the deck, and a pale veil of sunlight was beginning to filter through the high ceiling of clouds. Adam tilted his head back and gazed aloft to the lookout. Even as he did so, the man pointed excitedly and called out, "There she blows!"

Immediately all action on the deck stopped as the men all looked to see, trying to spot the spout.

"Three degrees off the starboard bow!" shouted the lookout. "Sperm!"

Adam smiled, pleased. Of all the whales that were sought and killed, the sperm whale was the most valuable, for it alone was the source of the valuable spermaceti, which was much in demand for medicinal purposes and fine candles; the sperm whale also yielded a fine quality oil and, occasionally, ambergris. Sperm oil was used in lighthouses and other sites in which a bright light was needed, and the rare ambergris was popular for use in perfumes and as an aphrodisiac.

As soon as the school of whales was located, the members of the crew hurried to their assigned places. The three thirty-foot whaleboats on the port side were quickly filled and lowered. Adam and his two mates, each in their places in the front of one of the boats, ordered the men to cast off.

With the boat steerer/harpooner in the rear and the captain or one of the mates in the bow, the four other men in each boat began to row, propelling the heavy whaleboats through the still choppy sea at an amazing speed.

As always, Adam felt the excitement of the chase, the hope of a good catch, and the small thrill of danger that always crept along his spine; for many a good man had gone out never to come back, and this possibility was always present.

When he spotted the broad, dark backs rising out of the water ahead of them, Adam motioned the oarsmen to slow their pace. Quietly they moved up on the great leviathans of the deep.

Adam always experienced a feeling of awe at this moment. They were so huge, so magnificent, and he and the others were so small. Killing the huge beasts was his livelihood, and yet he always felt a sadness when it came time to set the lance. Like the Indians who had hunted the whale before him, he asked the whale's forgiveness for killing him.

The sea was calmer now, and the great, barnacled backs were only a few feet in front of them as the whales rolled gently near the surface. Adam's boat inched forward, for the steerer was trying to get "wood to black skin"—attempting to guide the boat up onto the whale's back.

Then they were there, nudging the vast, dark hide, and the steerer was peaking his oar and readying his eleven-foot harpooning iron. Quickly he moved forward to the front of the whaleboat and raised the iron in his right hand. Steadying himself, he flung it, with all his practiced strength, into the whale's neck, then hastened back to take his place again in the stern, where he would tend the towline and the steering oar while the captain killed the whale with the hand lance.

Since the whale was a huge one, at least eighty meters in length, a second boat had come up on it from the other side, and a moment after Adam's harpooner had set his iron, yet another iron was driven deep into the whale's back.

At that instant the giant back heaved, as the whale boiled up. With one motion of its mighty flukes, the leviathan moved out from under them, leaving the whaleboat rocking as the twelve hundred feet of rope whipped out of the tub with so great a speed that it smoked.

Adam prayed that the rope was long enough and that the huge animal would not sound. He had no desire for a "Nantucket sleigh ride," and he hoped for a quick and merciful kill.

Fortunately the great beast did not sound, but plunged through the sea in a straight line. About the time Adam began really worrying about the length of the rope, the whale stopped and lay listlessly in the water. The choppy waves churned pink with its blood.

"Heave to, men!" Adam shouted, and the whalers began to haul in the line, pulling themselves and their boat up to the floating hulk.

When they were again close to the whale, Adam set himself and poised his fifteen-foot lance with its razor-sharp head. Summoning his strength, bracing against the rocking of the small boat, he threw it straight and true, and it pierced the flesh of the whale to a depth of almost the full length of the lance head.

As the lance struck home, the great bulk quivered, and a spout of air and water issued from its blowhole. A deep, moaning sound seemed to come from somewhere inside the animal, and its flesh quivered again. Then, without another sound, the whale began to turn in the water until it lay belly up, like any dead fish.

The men worked with skill and efficiency. A hole was cut in the lip, and a rope fastened therein, to tow the whale to the ship. Great gouts of blood had stained the water now, and Adam, realizing that sharks would soon be drawn by the scent, exhorted his men to hurry with their task.

It took some time to maneuver the great whale to the side of the *Viking Queen,* and when this was finally done, Adam clambered aboard, where he watched the rest of the familiar procedure.

Using the tall masts of the *Viking Queen* as leverage, the crew hoisted the huge carcass up, nearly out of the water and about level with the main deck. Next, the flensing stages were lowered until they rested just above the body of the whale.

Using blubber spades and flensing irons, the men cut and peeled huge strips of blubber, which were lifted to the deck and put into the try pots. The first incision released the blubber around the jawbone, which was raised aboard with a block and tackle. The head was then loosened and divided into two parts, to make the lifting easier. This stage of the operation, Adam always thought of as the "dirty work."

Since this was a sperm whale, the case, or upper part of the head, was brought on board first so that the valuable spermaceti could be dipped out; then the junk, or lower part of the head, was taken out, and its high quality oil barreled separately from that produced by the body of the whale.

It was a stinking, messy task, and one that Adam never cared to watch for too long.

With all the smoke and the high odor, thousands of birds and flies were soon hovering over the decks, and Adam could see the sharks beginning to gather.

Anxiously he scanned the water for the other whaleboats. One was returning empty, and the other, with a small sail raised, was towing a fair-sized whale. He made quick calculations. With the oil and whalebone from this whale, and if the sharks didn't get too much of the one the other boat was bringing in, the *Viking Queen* should be well-laden; and he would have accomplished a whaling captain's main objective—a "short and greasy voyage."

Adam smiled to himself. It looked as if they might be home by Christmas, after all. It would be good to be on land again. A year at sea was a long time, although a year's voyage was not considered a particularly lengthy one.

He had his little house in Sag Harbor, which was looked after in his absences by an elderly couple, the Horners, and he had at least two women who were usually willing to warm his bed. He looked forward to seeing them—Mary, with her pale hair and generous bosom; and Gerta, red-haired and freckled, but with a body shaped like a Grecian urn.

Turning away from the grisly activity on the flensing platform, Adam went below to begin plotting the return voyage.

It was a roaring night in Mundy's Tavern, and the rooms were filled to capacity with roistering seamen of every color and nationality.

Marianna—as was every serving girl working for Meg Mundy—was being kept busy taking orders for, and serving, huge trays of ale and rum.

Pausing for breath at the bar, as she waited for an order to be filled, Marianna straightened her hair, looking into the mirror behind the long bar. Even though her face was flushed from the heat and a few wild curls had escaped from their confinement, she was rather pleased with her reflection. She was nineteen now. A woman grown, and she was happy to think she looked it.

In her neat white spencer and dark skirt, with her hair parted in the center and pulled back into a large bun behind her ears, she liked to believe that she looked ladylike and dignified. She wore this dress partly because of her job and partly through choice.

Although Meg had been true to her word, fending the drunks and rampantly aggressive men away from her girls, she could not be everywhere at once, and Marianna had realized early on that she would have to take steps to defend herself.

In her observations of men, Marianna had come to a conclusion. Most men seemed to think of women as belonging to one of two categories: good women or whores. The good women they cherished, protected, and admired as they would their mothers or sisters. The other kind they considered fair game.

Marianna recognized that, by the very fact of her working in a tavern, she would be cast, at least in some men's eyes, in the latter role; and so, to contradict this, she dressed in as ladylike a fashion as possible. And it worked—at least much of the time. When it did not, when a customer was too drunk or too dense, or simply too crass to care, she was not above using whatever was handy to dampen their ardor. Many a randy sailor had found himself doused with a pitcher of ale or, in extreme cases, given a stout rap on the head with a belaying pin, which Meg kept ready behind the bar for emergencies and which Marianna occasionally borrowed.

It had taken awhile, but when the men finally learned that Marianna was not interested in sexual advances and that she was quite capable of defending herself, they became protective of her and discouraged any stranger who might not know where the pretty little barmaid stood on such matters.

Yes, all in all, Marianna thought, she was quite content with her life in Sag Harbor. Meg was a fair and generous employer, and there were extra gratuities given by seamen coming off a profitable voyage, with plenty of money in their pockets.

Marianna's nest egg was small, but growing steadily, and she looked forward to the day when she would have enough to open some sort of establishment of her own; for she well recognized that although the regulars at Mundy's Tavern considered her a lady, the townspeople did not. To the proper ladies of Sag Harbor, she was simply a "tavern wench," and so definitely was not their equal.

Once this would not have bothered Marianna a whit, but after the time spent with Prudence Courtwright, she thought of herself as being as good as anyone, and the high-nosed treatment rankled.

"Here you go, Mari." Ted, the middle-aged bartender, slid six large schooners of ale onto her tray, and Marianna smiled at him and picked up the heavy wooden tray.

Deftly she threaded her way among the close-packed tables, evading the attempted pinches and pats, and placed her tray, with a flourish, upon the table she was serving.

"That's my girl," said Big Red Hanrahan, slapping the scarred wooden table top with one huge hand. "The best little barmaid, and the prettiest, this side of the world."

Marianna smiled sweetly at the big man and took the coins he offered in payment for the ale. She picked up the empty tray and was turning to leave the table when a tall man at the next table suddenly shoved his chair back, catching her across the upper thigh and causing her to stumble.

The man turned about and gazed into her face. A sudden tightness gripped her throat, and she almost cried out. For a long moment she did not move, waiting for Captain Adam Street to recognize her; but although a look of speculative interest and appreciation filled his eyes, there was not the slightest spark of recognition.

Her heart began to hammer, and a vast disappointment seized her. How *could* he have forgotten her? True, it had been close to three years, but even so, he should recognize her. The fact that he clearly did not, made her less, in her own eyes, for despite the way she had treated him, she had considered Adam her friend.

Adam Street had strolled into Mundy's Tavern with the pleasant sense of returning home. It had been a good voyage, no, an excellent voyage, and he had been awarded the attention and respect that any successful hunter receives when he returns home to his own people.

As was the custom, most of the town had turned out to greet the arriving *Viking Queen*—to hear an account of the voyage and to receive the news from far places.

The ship was being unloaded now, under the supervision of the first mate, a man Adam would trust with his life; and Adam had retired to the tavern, with a group of friends.

Mundy's Tavern never changed, he thought; no matter if you were gone one year or two. A few of the faces might be different, but there was still the same familiar look and smell to it, to make a man feel at home.

Meg had cleared a table for them, and he had ordered mugs of ale for himself and his friends. After a round or two, and some pleasant conversation, he would slip away to visit Mary. She had been at the dock to meet him and had whispered to him that she would be home and waiting for him, if he should care to come by.

At the thought of her, Adam became uncomfortably aware of his growing desire; he'd not had a woman in many long months. He turned his thoughts away from Mary, so as not to disgrace himself in public.

He relaxed, leaning back in his chair, ale mug in his hand, and let the sound of talking voices wash over him. It was good to be home. One thing about the life of a seafaring man had always mystified Adam. Ashore, a sailor always itched to be at sea again, and yet, a month or so under sail, and a longing for shore set in—

A voice interrupted his reverie. "How long do you plan to stay in port this time, Adam?" It was Jack Hammond, captain of the *Lark*.

Adam, in the act of leaning forward to answer his friend's question, inadvertently pushed his chair back and felt it strike something. He turned and looked up into a pair of huge, dark eyes, flashing with annoyance. Godalmighty, he thought, where had Meg found this little beauty? And a beauty she was—small, but very nicely rounded both above and below a waist that a man could span with one hand; and she had the look of a real lady about her as well, which was not what a man expected to find in Mundy's Tavern. There was something hauntingly familiar about her that somehow made her all the more desirable.

"Well!" he said, grasping her small, firm arm just below the elbow and finding his hand wrapping all the way around it. "And who are you, madam? You're a new face at Meg's, I'll be bound, for I would be certain to remember anyone as pretty as you."

The girl's eyes blazed, and she jerked her arm away.

Somewhat taken aback, Adam stood up, thinking to soothe her obviously ruffled feelings, wondering why she should take offense to such a small incident. "I didn't mean to bump you, madam, if that is what's annoying you."

She stood glaring at him, her eyes growing darker by the second. The feeling Adam had, that she was somehow familiar, increased. At somewhat of a loss, but reluctant to show it before his friends, Adam turned to them and smiled wryly. "I ask you, now, isn't this the prettiest face you fellows have seen in many a day? If any of you know this charming young lady, I'd be pleased if you would introduce me and explain to her that I am not the awkward clod that I appear to be?"

He waited for the usual male response to such byplay and was surprised to see that they were not smiling. Jack Hammond made a rueful face and motioned for Adam to resume his seat.

"I'd be happy to do that, Adam," Hammond said, "if the young lady is willing, but I should warn you that you had best tread gently around her, for she is a wee bit special to all of us, and any man here, who knows her, will fight to protect her."

Adam frowned at Hammond in astonishment. This was sure as hell not the reaction he had expected!

"Never mind, Captain Hammond," the girl said icily. "I have no desire to be introduced to this man. I pick my friends carefully, thank you."

With this, she whirled away and disappeared into the crowd, leaving Adam staring open-mouthed after her.

When he turned a questioning look on his friends, the conversation had skipped on to other matters—deliberately, Adam felt. He sat down and sipped at his ale, thinking about it, every once in a while scanning the room for sight of the barmaid.

When a lull occurred in the conversation, he said, "All right, mates. I may, occasionally, be an ill-mannered lout, but I'm not stupid. Now, just what is this all about?"

Captain Hammond said innocently, "What is what all about, Adam?"

Adam shook his head in exasperation and banged his mug down. "You know damned well what I'm talking about, Jack! The girl! Why are you all so protective of her? She's a barmaid, for God's sake! I have nothing against barmaids, but hell!"

Hammond's face darkened. "Now just a moment, my friend. You and I go back a long way, but I won't have you talking about Marianna that way. I—"

The rest of his words were lost to Adam, for he heard nothing after the name Marianna.

Godalmighty! That was why she looked so tantalizingly familiar! It was the girl, the little rag-tag savage that he had rescued, along with her friend, nearly three years ago. It had to be her, but Godalmighty, how she had changed! Then, he had called her a child, and a child she had been, wild and untamed as a woods colt; and now here she was, a grown woman, self-assured and beautiful. His mind again focused on Hammond's words.

"She may work in a tavern, but Marianna's a decent girl, and we respect her as such. I suppose that many of the older men look upon her as a daughter of sorts, and woe betide the young buck who gets too free with her, and that includes you, old friend."

"Aye," Adam said absently. "I'll bear that in mind, Jack. Do you know where she comes from?"

Jack nodded, but one of the other men at the table, Rob Hill, spoke first. "She comes from Boston, Adam. She had an aunt there, we hear, an elderly invalid who died, leaving the poor girl with no money and no way to make her way in the world. That's why Meg hired her. It's hard for a woman, that it is, and she has to eat and have a roof over her head, the same as you and me."

"She could wed," Adam said, wondering what these men would think of the girl if they knew of her history.

Rob shook his head. "Waiting for her lover, I understand, a lad who's away on a long trip of some kind. The common feeling, among us, that is, is that he won't be coming back. That he's been killed or has died from more or less natural causes, but of course we don't let on to Marianna about that."

Rob Hill looked sad. "It's pitiful, the way she waits for the lad. If I was a younger man, I'd try to wed her myself. She needs looking after, that she does."

The other men, all sober of face, nodded solemn agreement, and it was all Adam could do to keep from laughing in their faces. The little wildcat certainly had them fooled. They thought she was a sweet, unsullied young thing, unknowing of men. He shook his head in admiration of her, and the men nodded, assuming that he was agreeing with Rob's sentiments.

"Aye, it's a sad tale," Adam said, and drained his mug. "I'll remember it well, if I ever have occasion to speak to the young lady again. Now, if you gentlemen will excuse me, I'd best return to the *Viking* and see how the unloading is progressing."

But Adam did not return to the wharf, at least not immediately. Instead, he slipped around to the rear of the tavern and took up a post by the rear exit, watching for his chance to catch Marianna alone. Eventually his patience was rewarded, as Marianna stepped out into the alleyway for some fresh air. The only light came through the open door.

As Adam walked up behind her, he again wondered at how much of a lady she had become—at least on the surface. Her gestures, her manner, were nothing like those of the girl he remembered; indeed, it was hard to believe that she was the same person.

"Marianna?" he said softly, looming over her and touching her elbow.

She jumped, letting out a small cry. She turned, looked up, and saw him, and her eyes widened, then narrowed in anger.

She stepped away from him, her small body held rigidly, shoulders thrown back. All at once, Adam felt a great tenderness toward her; she looked so small and so brave. He smiled down at her. "Marianna, do you remember me?"

She said crisply, "Oh, *I* remember you well enough, but it would appear that I have a much better memory than you. So you have finally remembered *me?*"

He nodded. "Of course, Marianna. How could I forget?"

"Easy enough, if what happened inside was any indication!"

He shook his head. "The temper certainly appears to be the same, at least. In all fairness, Marianna, you've changed a great deal, and it *has* been three years. You've grown up, you know."

"But you're still talking to me as if I were a child! Well, I wasn't a child then, and I'm less of one now, and I'll thank you not to talk down to me." Marianna flushed as she said the last few words, suddenly aware of the incongruity of the statement she was making to this giant of a man, who, of necessity, literally had to talk down to almost everyone.

Adam, off-balance by her attack, tried to keep smiling despite his rising annoyance. "Look here now, lass, try to keep a civil tongue, if you please. Maybe you have fooled others with your proper airs and ladylike ways, but I knew you back when. Remember?"

"You mean, remember when I was a poor Banker girl, with only rags on her back? Oh, yes, Captain Street, I remember."

"That wasn't all that was on your back," Adam said, more sharply than he had intended. "You've got all those dunces convinced that you're a virtuous and inexperienced girl, and they're determined to protect you. What kind of a game are you playing at? Are you setting them up for—?"

Without warning, Marianna stood on tiptoe and delivered

a stinging slap to his cheek. Her face was very red, and her eyes blazed with fury. "That's quite enough, Captain Street. I don't think that we have anything further to say to one another!"

She raised her eyes to his, and he saw a flicker of pain reflected there. "And to think I remembered you as a *kind* man," she said in a choked voice, then whirled and ran back into the building.

Adam felt chastened and full of regret. Why had he said those things? He didn't really want to hurt her. If only she hadn't been so damned thorny and disagreeable! Even so, it was not something that a gentleman would say.

He sighed, annoyed with himself and with her. Damn the girl, why did she always seem to bring out the worst in him? What was it about her that prodded his temper? It was a shame that she had grown up to be so desirable, for she was doomed to bring trouble to any male who crossed her path. Well, from now on he would try to see to it that he was not one of them. Let her keep her sharp temper and harsh words for some other man; he would not make himself a handy target again.

He strode angrily away from Mundy's Tavern, heading toward Mary Timms's little house on Howard Street. The house, almost smothered in climbing roses, looked inviting and cozy, and Adam began to feel better simply at the sight of it.

Mary Timms welcomed him warmly, clad only in a wrapper, with her long, pale hair unbound, smelling sweetly of lavender soap. Now here was a woman who knew how to please a man, Adam thought, as he folded her into his arms.

Little time was wasted in talking, for they had been apart for many months, and Mary, for all her demure look and gentle air, was a passionate woman.

She took to his embrace as eagerly as he took to hers, and soon her flowered wrapper lay discarded upon the polished wooden floor next to his clothing, and they lay together upon her four-poster bed.

Her body was as smooth and sweet as a ripe peach, and Adam, feeling as a man might who sights water after miles

of arid desert, paid homage to it, running his rough seaman's hands over her satiny skin, over her full breasts,
down across her stomach, and along her flanks, until she
arched like a cat.

"Adam, darling, I've missed you so," she whispered softly,
then pressed his face into the soft skin of her throat.

"And I you," he answered, inhaling her sweet scent. He
brushed his hand gently down across the soft puff of pubic
hair—a touch that caused her to tremble and press against
him.

"Now, Adam!" she said urgently. "Now!"

At the sound of the excitement in her voice, Adam readied
himself, his own passion mounting until he feared he would
go out of control. Quickly he rose above her, and she opened
herself to him, surging to meet him joyously. And then he
was drowned in the soft warmth of her, his reasoning powers ceased to function, and rapture seized him as their
bodies clashed repeatedly together, until he felt his juices
boil and erupt and Mary cried out her pleasure.

It would have been a perfect moment, except for the fact
that even as he spent his accumulated passion in her body,
the memory of Marianna's face flickered across Adam's mind,
causing him to groan aloud in mingled pleasure and disgust
with himself.

Southampton was, by any standards, a cut above the
towns situated on upper Long Island. Several shipping com-
panies had headquarters there, and yet the rough element
usually present in most towns in the area was not so preva-
lent.

Southampton was a town of many fine homes, two-storied,
with cupolas, stately trees, and fine lawns. It was the
wealthiest community in the area. Many whaling captains
and shipowners operating out of Sag Harbor had homes
there, since it was only a long carriage ride to and from Sag
Harbor.

Ezekial Throag, coming to Southampton for the first time,
did not feel out of place, but then he prided himself that he
would not feel out of place anywhere. He had adapted

himself to the customs and mores of the Bankers, had he not, and Southampton was more his natural milieu.

Throag felt at home the moment he disembarked from the passenger boat from New York. At fifty-four Throag was still a man to be reckoned with. The only sign of age was the iron-gray in his hair. Dressed in a black broadcloth suit, expensively tailored, he was an imposing figure as he strode along the dock, a porter trailing him, pulling three trunks on a cart. One thing about Throag's life had definitely changed. All those years spent on the Outer Banks, wearing rough, usually filthy garments, had given him an inclination for fine clothing. His wardrobe was now extensive; many men would consider the money he had invested in clothing a small fortune. In fact, he had become something of a dandy. He found something almost sexual about the caress of fine linen against his skin.

Since he intended to make Southampton his permanent address, at least until he received news of Marianna Harper's whereabouts, he wished to stay in a good place; not for him the transiency of a hotel. The porter had recommended the Inn of the Rose, which was actually a boardinghouse belonging to a widow by the name of Rose Lake. According to the porter, the inn offered most comfortable accommodations and set the finest table in all of Southampton.

The Inn of the Rose was situated on the edge of the commercial district, with most business establishments within walking distance, and Throag was impressed by his first view of it.

It was a two-story brick building, setting on a small rise with a fine view of the ocean. Great trees provided shade, and a stretch of green lawn was in front of it; scattered wrought-iron benches gave it the appearance of a small park.

He strode up the walk and to the veranda, which was lined with comfortable chairs. Two of the chairs were occupied by an elderly couple. Throag tipped his hat to them and smiled genially.

Rose Lake was a woman of about thirty-five, with red hair, a fine bosom, and saucy brown eyes. Her eyes widened when Throag introduced himself. "My goodness!" she said in a breathless voice. "You stand tall, sir!"

Throag felt a stirring of sexual desire. He had the feeling that he was going to bed Rose Lake, and from the speculative look in her eyes, he was confident that she was measuring him with just such a thought in mind.

He said boldly, "And you, madam, are a fine figure of a woman."

She blushed and curtsied. "Thank you, sir."

A few minutes later he was shown into a spacious bedroom upstairs, with heavy furniture and a large four-poster bed.

"You'll notice that the bed is larger than usual," Rose said. "That was for my Sam. He was a big fellow, like you." She smiled. "I've always had a liking for substantial men."

"Thank you, Rose. I may become a permanent resident, if everything works out to my satisfaction. Will that be agreeable to you?"

"I can think of nothing that would pleasure me more. It will be nice to have a real man around the house again," she said archly.

The weathered wooden sign over the doorway said simply: Barth & Barth, Shipping. The building had a rundown look, but Throag knew for a fact that Barth & Barth would have to be rated as one of the wealthiest shipping firms in the country. But then, the Barths were never ones for frills.

Dressed in his best, Throag paused a moment to adjust his hat to the proper angle and to straighten his flowing black tie before he pushed open the door. The interior was dim as a cave, albeit a scene of much activity. Behind a long counter more than a dozen men were bent over desks, working furiously over bills of lading, shipping schedules, and the like.

A scrawny individual bustled up to the counter as Throag approached. Throag had already noted a flight of stairs leading up to the second floor, off to his right.

At the sight of Throag's prosperous air, the clerk behind the counter rubbed his hands, fawning. "Yes, sir. How may I help you?"

"You may inform me where I might find the brothers."

The man's glance darted to the stairs, then back to Throag. "May I inquire as to your business with them, sir?"

"No, you may not. But you have already told me what I wish to know."

He started for the stairs. The clerk bleated, scooting around the counter to block his way. "You can't go up there, sir! I have my instructions. All visitors must first state their business and be announced."

"My business is private, and I will announce myself, thank you. Out of my way, little man."

Throag placed one big hand flat on the clerk's scrawny chest and gave a mighty shove. The man flew backward, hands windmilling, and struck the counter, then slithered to the floor. All the clerks behind the counter glanced up and stared at Throag in astonishment. He ignored them and made his way up the stairs.

There were four doors opening off the narrow hallway at the top of the stairs. Only one door stood open, and Throag saw a man bent over a set of ledgers, squinting nearsightedly at them. Throag passed on to the last door, marked private.

He opened the door and went in without knocking. Two men sat together behind a desk, stacks of money before them. They looked up at his entrance, eyes wide.

The Barth brothers were five years apart in age, yet they looked remarkably alike. They were small, mean men, with pinched faces, avaricious eyes of a muddy brown, and mouths like slits. In all the years Throag had known them, he had never caught a smile on the face of either. They always reminded him of moles, blinking fearfully at the light of day, content to dwell in murkiness, and truly happy only when counting their money.

Silas and Enoch Barth, a fine pair. Throag wouldn't trust them as far as he could spit. But they did have a talent for making money.

Silas Barth was the first to speak. Coming to his feet, he hovered over the stacks of money protectively and snarled, "What do you mean by busting in here unannounced, stranger! This is a private office."

"Stranger, Silas? Your eyesight failing in your old age?"

149

Throag said genially. "Don't you recognize an old chum?"

"Old chum?" Enoch Barth demanded. "We don't know you from Adam."

Throag stroked his clean-shaven chin and stepped closer to the desk. "Must be the absence of the beard. I reckon if you two don't recognize me right off, nobody else is likely to, either."

Silas Barth gasped. "Throag! Ezekial Throag!" He dropped back into his chair.

Throag beamed at the brothers. "Now that's more like it."

Enoch Barth placed a hand over his heart, as if it pained him. "What are you doing here? We thought you were—"

"Dead? Not hardly. I'm alive and well, as you can plainly see."

"But it's been almost three years since you left the Banks," Silas Barth said. "Where have you been all this time?"

"I've been looking for the persons who murdered my son," Throag said, his voice suddenly harsh.

Enoch Barth said cautiously, "If you're thinking of going back to the Banks, we've got someone else in charge down there now. You taking off like that, not a word to us—"

Genial again, Throag batted a hand at them. "No, no, I've had my fill of that kind of life. No, gentlemen, the way I figure it, I've been kind of a silent partner to the Barth brothers all these years, so now it's time I was taken in as a partner, before all the world."

"You must be daft, man!" Silas Barth gaped at him. "You think you can come in here and demand something as outrageous as that, and we'll agree?"

"Oh, I think you'll see it my way, gentlemen. How do you think the fine people of Southampton, and the people of the shipping community, would react to the fact that the pair of you have been behind the wrecking of ships for all these years, off the Outer Banks?"

"You can't prove a word of it!" Enoch Barth said instantly.

"Now can't I? I don't know if you gentlemen are poker players, but all you have to do to prove me wrong or right is to call my bluff."

The brothers fell silent, studying him through narrowed

eyes. Finally Silas Barth said thoughtfully, "You have nothing on paper. Nothing between us was ever put on paper."

"True. But there are other ways," Throag said amiably.

Enoch Barth got a crafty look. "What other ways?"

"People. People know about what went on, and I can get them to testify."

"Not Phillip Courtwright," Silas Barth said smugly. "We had him shanghaied on a ship bound for the Orient. We've seen the last of him." He leaned forward, his weasel face accusing. "If you'd done your job right, Throag, he'd've been killed with the rest in that last wreck off the Banks, and not been around to plague us."

Throag kept his face impassive, careful not to give away the fact that he had never heard the name Phillip Courtwright. He still did not know who Courtwright was, but in an intuitive leap, he knew that this was the man he was seeking, this was the girl's paramour and Jude's co-murderer, and no doubt a relative of the woman with whom Marianna had been living in Boston. He filed the name away in his mind; now he had another person for his manhunter to seek out.

He said casually, "I would say you mucked up, as well. Just because he's on board a ship for a spell doesn't mean that he won't come back to haunt you. Besides, I don't need Phillip Courtwright. There are others—my crew on the Banks," he lied. "They know what went on, your connection with the wreckers. They know you sent word down when a particular ship was due to sail past."

Enoch Barth sneered. "You're no longer their leader, Throag. They don't take commands from you any more."

Throag said steadily, "Are you two willing to wager your lives, not to speak of your good names, on that? I put the fear of the Almighty into that scurvy bunch on the Banks. They'll do what I tell them, say whatever I command them to say, depend on it." Of course, not a soul on the Banks knew of the Barths' connection with the wreckings, but this pair across the desk had no way of knowing that. For the first time Throag saw uncertainty on their faces and a shadow of dread in their eyes.

He decided that it was time to press home his advantage, but at the same time to ease up on them a little. "I am entitled to a share in your firm, after all. Your present prosperity is partly due to me. And I am entitled to some respectability after all those years of doing your dirty work." Suddenly Throag knew this was true. He yearned for respectability. His only son was dead, so there was nothing else left to him in life—except his consuming desire for vengeance. "I am willing to invest a reasonable sum in your firm, in exchange for Barth & Barth, Shipping being changed to Barth, Barth, & Throag, Shipping. I'll wager that I know shipping as well as the pair of you. Now, is that too much to ask?"

The brothers exchanged glances, and Throag could see their cunning brains at work. Promises were easy enough to make, but they had henchmen, Throag was certain, who would gladly slit his throat on command. He had little fear of that; Ezekial Throag could well take care of himself.

He said, "There is no great hurry. Why don't the pair of you think on it, talk it over, for a few days? I'm sure you'll come to the conclusion that this way is best for all concerned." He tipped his hat politely. "Good day to you, gentlemen. I am staying at the Inn of the Rose, should you have need to contact me."

He left them without another word. Let them mull his proposition over for a day or so. He knew that they would be devising various schemes to thwart him, undoubtedly with thoughts of killing him predominate.

Throag was confident that he could cope with any effort to kill him, and he was equally confident that in the end they would make him a partner in the firm. Grudgingly, to be sure, but for all their cunning and ruthlessness, the brothers were frightened little men. They would not dare risk any chance that he could besmirch their good name in Southampton.

After all, what could they lose by taking him in as a partner? They had long been familiar with his abilities; he would definitely be an asset to their company, and since he had offered to pay for a partnership, it would cost them nothing.

Throag was smiling as he approached the Inn of the Rose. How would it fit him to be in a legitimate enterprise after his long career of criminality? He knew himself well enough to realize that he would not have been content with it in the earlier years; he would have found it tedious and boring. But now, now he was older, and he no longer needed the thrill of danger to spice his life.

No, the role of respectability would fit him like a glove now. Only one other criminal act would he ever consider again—the deaths of Marianna Harper and Phillip Courtwright. And that act, to his way of thinking, was not criminal, no matter how the law might view it.

As he started up the steps to the inn, he saw Rose Lake waiting on the veranda. Seeing him, she got to her feet and moved to the top of the steps. She had donned a new dress and added color to her cheeks.

As his glance came to rest on her, Rose smiled in bold invitation and smoothed her dress down over the saucy outthrust of her breasts.

Throag read the invitation right, and his blood quickened. Then a thought crossed his mind, and he paused with one foot on the bottom step. He was going to bed this wench, probably within the next few minutes. She was a fine figure of a woman, in her prime, and still of child-bearing age. Why not use her? Why not sire a son by her? A son to take Jude's place?

Throag felt a twist of amusement. Such a thought had not once occurred to him since Jude's death. Why should it now, on this day? Because he had suddenly embraced the concept of becoming respectable?

Whatever the reason behind it, he knew that he was going to pursue the thought.

Rose arched an eyebrow. "Mr. Throag?"

"Yes, madam," Throag said gravely. "I was momentarily dazed by your charm and beauty."

Rose colored prettily, and Ezekial Throag moved rapidly up the steps—to a possible rejuvenation of himself and a hoped-for continuation of his bloodline.

Chapter Ten

CAPTAIN Jack Hammond and his wife were giving a party, and Marianna had been invited. She stood, fully dressed, in front of her bedroom mirror and examined the dress she had purchased for the occasion.

It had cost her more than she could afford, but since this was the first such party she had been invited to, she had deemed the price worth paying. Mrs. Beedle, the dressmaker, had made it up for her, and had assured her that it was in the latest fashion.

Critically Marianna examined herself in the glass and decided that it would do. Her gown was a brown gauze over light blue satin, with a modest décolletage. The bodice was made with a deep point, the waist tightly cinched, and the skirt was very full, over a crinoline. There was also a wreath of brown velvet leaves and blue forget-me-nots in her hair, which was styled with short curls in front, the back braided and coiled into a large knot at the back of her neck. She did indeed, she thought, look quite splendid.

Meg Mundy had lent her a lovely shoulder cape of embroidered muslin and lace, and she now tied it over her shoulders, pirouetting in front of the glass, so that her skirt swirled about her. Well! Just let Captain Adam Street see her now!

She tried smiling at herself, but the right expression would not quite form. Adam would be there, she knew, for Captain Hammond had mentioned his name, with a list of others he was inviting. Marianna knew that she had received her invitation only because of Captain Hammond's fondness for her, and she strongly suspected that he had invited her over his wife's objections. She was determined to show Mrs. Hammond that she was as much of a lady as any of them; and she would show Adam Street as well.

To think that she had come to Sag Harbor because of him; because she had remembered him as a kind man. To have him talk to her in such a manner! If only Phillip had been there. . . .

Marianna became still, and tears gathered in the corners of her eyes. Where was Phillip now? Was he alive or dead? Why hadn't he written, or sent word to her, before she left Boston?

Her throat felt tight, and all of her high spirits were gone. If only Phillip could see her like this, surely he would be proud of her.

She turned away from the mirror, remembering all the lonely nights she had gone to sleep imagining his body there beside her. He had promised to return, to come back to her, but she knew that he never would and that she would never again love any man or allow one to know her body intimately. So what did it matter what Adam Street thought of her? She had her own life now, and it was good enough in its own way. She did not need Adam Street, or his approval. Still, it would be soothing to her ego if he should apologize for his rudeness; if he should see how desirable she was to other men, and how popular; if he should recognize her as a person of some importance—if only in a small way.

These thoughts slipped across the surface of her mind, not fully formulated, but leaving behind a sense of pride and purpose. Yes, she would go to Captain Hammond's party, and she would be the belle of the ball; and Adam Street would be sorry that he had spoken to her in such a manner.

As she turned to leave the room, Marianna thought again briefly of Phillip and then put the thought sadly away. Would a time ever come when his memory would cease to plague her?

When Phillip Courtwright awoke in the forecastle of the brig, *Serena*, after being thrown down the hold by his two abductors, his first thought was that he was dead and in hell. A ghostly, yellow light flickered over the walls and the ceiling, cast by a smoking iron lantern hung from a beam in the center of the cabin. Moving wildly with the motion of the ship, it elongated shadows and illuminated the sprawling figures of recumbent men on either side of him.

The stench of vomit, rum, and human sweat and excrement fouled the air. The sound of retching came from somewhere in the darkness beyond the lantern light, and over all, there was the sound of a male voice cursing in regular cadence, like some kind of hellish accompaniment.

Phillip's head hurt abominably, and touching his temple, his fingers came away wet. In those first, awful moments, he did not know where he was or how he had gotten there, but in the minutes that followed he remembered his attackers, and he knew, in full despair, that he had been shanghaied and that they were already on the high seas. He did not know where the ship was heading, but whoever had arranged his abduction had probably made certain that she was embarking on a long voyage, for he felt certain that he had not been set upon by chance. It would be too much of a coincidence if that were so.

Trying to regain control of his roiling stomach and throbbing head, he sat up carefully.

The forecastle appeared to be full; all the bunks he could see were occupied, and most of the deck space around him was taken up by sprawled bodies.

Phillip swallowed convulsively, and his despair grew. He had been so close, so near to the end of his quest, to clearing his father's name. And Marianna! He had vowed to return to her. Now he would be delayed God only knew how many months, or even years.

He clenched his teeth against the need to give voice to his pain and despair. Could nothing go right for him? Was he doomed to always miss his chance, to be thwarted? No, by God! They would not defeat him. He would go on, no matter the obstacles or how long it took.

One fact became clear to Phillip within a very short time. If ever a ship was misnamed, it was the *Serena*, captained by Jonathan Ryker, a cold, hard man who cared only for profit, and nothing at all for the lives of his men.

Because Ryker refused to pay decent wages, he was always forced to impress most of his seamen, either through dishonest shipping agents, or by outright abduction. Of course, most of his crew deserted the ship when it made port, but that did not worry Captain Ryker, for he simply repeated the process for the return trip. Ryker, untroubled by such things as conscience or concern for his fellow men, thought that this method worked very well.

Phillip realized that it would do no good to complain to the captain about his situation, for he well knew that it would not matter to the man how he had gotten on board, Ryker's concern being that since he *was* on board he should do his work and keep his mouth shut. So Phillip tried to carry out his duties as well as he could, while remaining as unobtrusive as possible.

At first it was very difficult, for Phillip was not accustomed to hard physical labor, and the terrible food left him unsatisfied and often weak from hunger.

Also, the ship's company left much to be desired. Phillip's shipmates were drawn from the worst dregs of the waterfront. Altogether, it was a miserable existence, the worst months of Phillip's young life.

However, as time went on, he became used to the food and the backbreaking work, and he began to grow tough and hard, in mind as well as in body, for there was a flame inside that sustained him, a flame that he nourished toward that supreme moment when it would blaze up and consume the men who had destroyed his father.

When the *Serena* finally docked in Hong Kong, it was minus a third of the crew—dead of scurvy, pneumonia, or knife wounds—but Phillip had survived. Honed razor-thin and full of anger and purpose, he left the ship. But first, from the captain's cabin, he took several pieces of valuable jewelry, some three hundred pounds in cash, and a pair of heavy gold candlesticks. The deed was relatively easy to accomplish during the flurry of activity occasioned by making port. He calculated that since they had stolen his body, and services, for long months, he was entitled to some compensation. On shore, he quickly turned the stolen items into cash, which he used to purchase passage on the first ship sailing for Boston.

During the long voyage home, a paying passenger now, not a working one, he had time on his hands; yet he thought only of two things—his plans for exposing his father's murderers; and Marianna. He could not decide which obsessed him more, for although he worked during the day on his plans for revenge against the Barth brothers, at night his dreams were haunted by the memory of Marianna's face and body. In sleep she came to him, small and rounded, willing and warm; and his love-starved body answered with a response that shamed him in the morning, when he saw the evidence of his dream.

Even though his dreams brought relief of sorts, he felt a strong guilt, for it seemed to him that this meant that he was not paying full attention to his mission.

It was a long and wearying voyage, and when he finally arrived in Boston, over a year after his forced departure, Phillip was thinner than ever, and there were lines around his eyes that forever destroyed the boy, leaving only the man.

Phillip approached his aunt's house with mixed feelings. Thinking that he would be returning soon, successful in his quest, ready to take up a life with Marianna, he had made promises impossible to keep. Now he must tell his Aunt Prudence, and Marianna, that he must leave again, after the briefest of stays. He felt his pulse accelerate at the thought of Marianna. How could he ever bring himself to leave her again?

As he neared the house, Phillip noticed that it seemed different, changed, in ways that not even a long absence should have brought about. The lush flower garden had been trimmed and shaped into a formal arrangement, which, although orderly, lacked the warm and extravagant beauty of his aunt's old-fashioned garden. The house had been repainted, and the color of the window trim changed.

Phillip frowned and quickened his step, suddenly feeling that something was very wrong.

The woman who answered his knock was as neat and formal as the garden. Clad in sober gray, she looked at him coolly. "Yes? May I help you?"

Phillip felt suddenly disoriented. Something was certainly not right, and he was reluctant to inquire as to the reason. He had to force himself to speak. "I'm looking for my aunt, Prudence Courtwright, the owner of this house. I am Phillip Courtwright."

The woman's lips tightened. "This house no longer belongs to Prudence Courtwright," she said defensively. "My husband and I bought it some time ago."

Phillip's worst fears were confirmed. He said, as politely as he could, "Then could you tell me where I might find my aunt?"

The woman's stern face softened. "Oh, you poor man! You don't know, do you? I am sorry. Someone should have notified you. Your aunt is dead. I *am* sorry."

Phillip, drained of all strength and emotion, felt his body slump. It was what he had been unconsciously fearing since he had noticed the changes in the house. "And the young woman staying with her?" he asked in a low voice. "Miss Marianna Harper?"

The woman shook her head. "Again, I'm sorry. I know nothing of any young woman. I only knew of your aunt through what I've heard. She evidently was an exceptional woman."

Phillip sighed. "She was that, yes." Aunt Prudence dead! It was too much for his dazed mind to accept. And Marianna . . .

He was so tired, more so than he had realized; and now this, another puzzle to solve, another obstacle to overcome.

He glanced up as the woman in the doorway spoke. "Would you like to come in, sir? Have something cool to drink and rest for a bit?"

Phillip shook his head. It would be more than he could bear to see the inside of the house as it must be now, with different furnishings and with different people residing in it. "Thank you, just the same. I appreciate your kindness, but I must be about my business."

He bowed slightly, started to walk away, and then turned back. "Oh, could you possibly tell me the name of the solicitor who handled the sale of the house? Perhaps he would have some information as to Miss Harper's whereabouts."

The woman nodded. "Of course. The sale was handled by Alexander Stimson. Now that you mention him, I do recall his saying something about a nephew he wasn't able to locate and that we were to send you to him, in the event you came to the house."

She started to close the door and then opened it again. "I wish you good fortune, Mr. Courtwright. You seem a nice young man."

Phillip dredged up a smile. "Thank you, madam, for your good wishes. I shall certainly need all the good fortune that I can get."

As he turned away and retraced his steps down the walk, Phillip had to wonder if good fortune would be enough. What was he going to do? Of course, he had to press on with his plans to expose the Barth brothers for the villains they were—he was so close to that goal. And yet, he also had to find Marianna and let her know that he was alive and that he still loved her. Dear God, life was so difficult! Why must he be faced with such a choice? There was no way he could do both things at once.

When Phillip reached the street, he turned and looked back at the house. He stood there for a long moment, his eyes hooded in thought. When he moved away, he knew what he had to do.

Captain and Mrs. Hammond's party was a big event for the townspeople, and the ladies and gentlemen of Sag Harbor took full advantage of it.

The lawn before the Hammond house—a large expanse of green, dotted with trees and flowering bushes—was decorated with Japanese lanterns; and the house itself, a huge, white, Grecian-columned edifice, was brilliantly lit from within, and spills of golden light poured from every window and doorway.

The whole effect was one of great gaiety and beauty, and Marianna, on the arm of Billy Wilks, the young first mate who had been the first of many who had asked to escort her, could not help but feel her spirits rise as they approached the house. She looked at Billy and saw that he was smiling also.

"It's a grand house, isn't it?" he asked, squeezing her arm to his side.

"Yes," she said, nodding. "And it looks like everyone in town is here."

"Everyone who is anyone," he said cheerfully.

His words made Marianna feel even better. If that was true, then she was indeed somebody, at least to Captain Hammond, who had invited her. There were many, she knew, who would envy her this night; among them, the rest of the girls working in Meg's tavern. Well, she intended to make the most of it.

She smiled again at Billy, a pleasant young man, who would one day undoubtedly command one of his father's many ships. Although Billy was not tall, or particularly handsome, the young women of Sag Harbor considered him an excellent catch; and it was for this reason, as well as because he had been the first to ask, that Marianna had chosen him for her escort. Let Adam Street see firsthand just what caliber of man found her attractive!

They were climbing up the steps now, to be greeted by Captain Hammond and his lady in the doorway.

Marianna, looking as prim and modest as it was possible for her to do, curtsied slightly, her left arm still on that of her escort, and lowered her head demurely. Then she raised the full strength of her dark eyes to meet the gaze of her hostess. Smiling slightly, she murmured her greetings, adding, to Mrs. Hammond, how grateful she was for her kind invitation.

Mrs. Hammond, handing Marianna a dance card, appeared to be somewhat at a loss for words. She turned to her husband. "She's charming, Jack, utterly charming!"

The captain beamed. "I told you so, my love. Now you two just run along inside and sample some of my punch. Added a little something to it, I did, if you know what I mean."

He winked and chuckled, and Marianna and Billy moved on inside, making way for the next couple.

"She liked me!" Marianna said happily.

Billy grinned. "Why, of course. Why wouldn't she?" He pulled her to a stop. "There's the punch bowl. Shall I fetch you a cup?"

She nodded absently, her gaze busily taking in the large parlor and the assembled guests. Quickly she appraised the other women present and found, to her delight, that her dressmaker had not lied; no woman in the room wore a gown more attractive and stylish than hers.

Her gaze then went to the men. How fine they looked in their fitted breeches, cutaway coats, and vests, fitting partners for their wives and sweethearts. Of course, she was not really looking for Adam Street, but when she spied him—his great height made this a relatively simple task— Marianna's heart began to hammer. She wondered whom he had escorted to the party, and this unseemly curiosity made her angry at herself.

When Billy returned with a cup of Captain Hammond's punch, he found her pink-cheeked, with a strange glint in her eyes. He handed her the cup and studied her warily. "Are you all right, Marianna?"

Marianna tilted her chin, drank the punch in two unladylike swallows, and returned the empty cup. "Of course I'm all right, dear boy! Why shouldn't I be? Come, let's go over there, to the other side of the room." She pointed to the corner where Adam loomed over the others. "I see someone I wish to speak with."

Billy drained his own cup, placed the empty cups on a nearby table, and took Marianna's arm. He carefully steered her through the crowd of people, which seemed to grow denser by the minute.

They were only a few feet from Adam now, as Billy stopped. "Where did you say this person is you want to speak to?"

Marianna pressed close to him and peered around vaguely.

"Oh, dear, she seems to have disappeared." And then, as
the crowd's movement brought them close to Adam Street,
she looked up and flashed him her brightest, most winning
smile.

"For goodness sake, if it isn't Captain Street! What a
coincidence!"

Adam gave her a startled look, and his expression told
her better than words how taken he was by her appearance.
"Why, Miss Harper . . ." For a moment his smile was strained,
and then he visibly relaxed, and the smile became one of
pleasure. "This is a surprise, and a pleasant one, if I may
say so."

Marianna now tugged at Billy's arm, until he stood by
her side. "Captain Street, may I present Billy Wilks. Billy
is the first mate on the *Bridget*. But then, perhaps you
already know him? Billy's father is William Wilks, the shipowner."

Adam blinked, as if to collect himself, and turned his
smile on Billy. "Yes, as a matter of fact, I know Mr. Wilks
quite well. How are you, Billy?"

"Fine, sir, just fine." Billy grinned and bobbed his head,
reduced to boyhood again by Adam's presence.

Marianna's lips tightened in annoyance. Was it always
going to be this way? Was every man she brought near
Adam Street to be made less in some indefinable way by
this giant of a man?

"It's a lovely party, don't you think, captain?" she asked
sweetly, hiding her irritation.

"Aye, I do indeed. Here, may I introduce you to Mary
Timms? Miss Timms, Miss Marianna Harper."

As the slender but well-rounded Mary Timms stepped
forward from the group of people behind Adam, Marianna
felt her stomach tighten. She put out her hand gracefully
and smiled innocently, but her eyes were quite busy, going
over the other woman like a measuring tape.

If the other woman noticed, or took offense at Marianna's
scrutiny, she gave no evidence of it. Her eyes were steady
and gray, with a gentle-but-firm look, and her features were
even and serene. Her skin was good but showed a few
lines—Mary was older than *she* was, Marianna decided—

yet she was a good-looking woman, no denying that. She wore a pale pink gown of shot silk, with a tiered skirt, tight bodice, and a deep bertha that showed off fair, flawless shoulders.

"I'm very pleased to meet you, Miss Harper," Mary Timms said in a husky voice.

Marianna's smile was stiff and unnatural. Hellfire and spit! Even the woman's voice was attractive. "The pleasure is mine, I'm sure," she said as pleasantly as she could and was happy to note that nothing of what she was feeling showed in her voice.

"Well, we'd best mingle," she said brightly, "and I'm sure Billy wants some more of that punch."

She leaned against Billy, hoping that he would take the hint and move away, but he only stood there, smiling rather foolishly down at her.

Adam was speaking. "Wait, Marianna. First, let me have your dance card. When the dancing begins, I won't have a chance to claim one, I know."

Taken by surprise, Marianna handed over her card before she had a chance to think; it was as yet unmarked save for Billy's entries. Adam was smiling slightly as he wrote in his name. Was he laughing at her? Marianna could not be certain.

"There we are. The fifth dance is mine." As he returned the card to her, their hands lightly touched, and Marianna felt a tingle run up the nerves of her arm.

Hastily she pulled her hand back. "Thank you, captain." She urged Billy, with pressure on his arm, to move away.

For a time they mingled with the crowd downstairs, nibbling on tidbits and drinking punch. And then, above the clamor of talk and laughter, Marianna heard the sound of music and noticed that the crowd on the lower floor had begun to thin. She looked questioningly at Billy. "Where is the music coming from?"

He smiled down at her—he had a nice smile, though a little inane. "Upstairs. From the ballroom. The dancing is beginning."

Marianna nodded, as if she understood the procedure perfectly. The truth was that the parties she had attended back in Boston had all been rather small affairs, and although Prudence Courtwright had insisted that Marianna learn to dance, there had been scant opportunity for her to put this skill into practice.

"Shall we go up?" Billy asked.

She nodded again. Why not? She didn't see Adam Street or his lady friend among the people still in the parlor, which probably meant that they had already gone up to the ballroom. If she was going to show him how popular and sought after she was, she would have to be there, too. Of course, she first would have to get her dance card filled, but there should be no problem with that, should there?

Marianna was not quite prepared for the size and elegance of the ballroom, which stretched the entire length of the house. It was paneled with mirrors and crowned by three cut-glass chandeliers. A small orchestra, all elegantly dressed in fitted purple breeches, cutaway coats, and gleaming white, ruffled shirts with high stocks, played with controlled energy. The music was lively, and Marianna could not prevent her toes from keeping time to it.

She need not have worried about her dance card, for they had no sooner entered the ballroom than she was besieged by young men, all clamoring for the opportunity to dance with her.

Cheeks brightly flushed, she happily set about portioning out her dances and sweetly sympathizing with those left out when her card was filled. She hoped that Adam Street was watching; but when the flurry of signing was over and she gazed about the room, she saw that he was paying no heed to her at all. He was already on the dance floor, with Mary Timms, waiting for the first dance to begin.

Since the first dance, by custom, always went to a lady's escort, Marianna looked at Billy somewhat haughtily. "Your dance, I believe." She softened the words with a smile.

Without answering, Billy swept her out onto the floor. The orchestra was playing a brisk waltz, and soon Marianna forgot everything but the sound of the music and the breathtaking sweep of movement as she and Billy whirled expertly around the floor.

Although she had never before danced with Billy, he

proved to be an excellent dancer, nimble and graceful, and Marianna, who discovered that she had a natural aptitude for dance, followed his every motion, as if they had been partners for years.

Entranced as she was with the dance, Marianna still took note of the admiring glances that came her way, and again she hoped that Adam was taking notice also.

One after the other, her partners presented themselves to her, and soon her face was flushed, and damp with perspiration. Her partners kept her well supplied with punch, walked with her upon the terrace during the short waits between dances, and whispered complimentary words into her ear. She flirted with them all, sweetly, trying all the while to keep count of the dances. Had there been four yet? And then she saw Adam Street, looming tall over the surrounding men, coming toward her, a slight smile on his ruggedly handsome features.

Although she had been waiting for this dance, waiting for Adam, she was struck by a feeling of panic. Was her hair mussed? Were her cheeks too flushed? Had she consumed too much punch? Quickly she pulled out her linen handkerchief and touched the fabric to her forehead and cheeks.

Then he was there, in front of her, bowing slightly, and still wearing the smile. "This is my dance, I do believe."

She nodded with what she hoped was cool restraint. "I believe so, Captain Street."

The orchestra was striking up another waltz, a slow, romantic number, newly popular, and Marianna felt a lurch of dismay. If it were a lively number, there would be no need for talking.

Taking her right hand in his left and placing his long right arm around her waist, stooping slightly to do so, Adam swept Marianna onto the floor. She had an excellent view of his vest and watch fob. Her cheeks began to burn, for she suddenly realized what a ludicrous appearance they must make. She tried to make herself as tall as possible and then decided that would make it even more ridiculous. Adam was dancing in a sort of crouch, for it was the only way he could keep his arm around her, and even so, his arm on her back was nearer to her shoulders than her waist.

Craning her neck back, she looked up at him and caught on his face an expression of rueful amusement. She pulled away from his encircling arm. "I am afraid, sir, that we make an unsuitable couple," she said, as reasonably as she could manage, and began to walk away from the dance floor.

He strode after her and bent to take her arm, then settled for placing a hand on her shoulder. "For dancing, you mean," he said, a note of laughter in his voice.

"For anything, I should imagine," she said cuttingly, but did not attempt to move out from under his touch.

"Surely not," he said, his voice softer now. "And since this dance is still rightfully mine, I claim the right to your company until the music stops."

She shrugged indifferently. "If you insist, sir. It doesn't matter to me."

"Good! Then let's walk in the garden. It will be cooler there."

Marianna let him escort her down the stairs and out into the garden behind the house. It was indeed cooler, and the fragrant scent of summer flowers perfumed the air and made Marianna think of another garden in another city, and another man. Phillip, where was he now?

"You seem preoccupied," Adam commented.

"Yes." She resented his interrupting her reverie, melancholy though it had been.

"Marianna, I would like to apologize for my behavior in Mundy's Tavern the other day. It was ungentlemanly of me to speak so to you. My only defense is that you seem to have a particular ability to make me angry. Will you forgive me?"

This was what she had wanted, for Adam Street to apologize, for him to recognize her worth and desirability, but now, abruptly, her victory seemed like ashes, gray and worth nothing.

She nodded and said in a low voice, "Yes, if you will forgive me. My tongue, too, can be over sharp at times, I know. You were kind to me once, when I needed a friend. I have not forgotten that."

"Then I would like for us to be friends again," he said,

giving a heartfelt sigh. "May I call upon you some evening? Perhaps we could have supper?"

"That would be nice," she said dully. The memory of Phillip, it seemed, had deadened her capacity for feeling. All at once, she felt drained of all emotion. "I think we should go back now," she said, turning to go.

"Marianna, wait!"

There was an unexpected emotion in his voice that caused her to look up into his face, and then, so suddenly that she could not have stopped him if she had wanted to, his lips were on hers, firm and warm. Strangely, she felt nothing but surprise. His big hands were strong yet gentle on her shoulders, and she did not resist; but neither did she feel any response. But that's only natural, she found herself thinking; for I have vowed that I will belong to no man, ever again.

Adam finally took his lips from hers, but still she said nothing. What was there to say?

He said, "I'm sorry, Marianna. I don't really know why I did that. I don't usually seize young women until I'm certain that my advances will be well received. I hate to ask it of you again so soon, but will you forgive me?"

She shrugged. "If you promise not to repeat the act. You see, Captain Street, I'll be candid with you. I would like to be your friend, but I have vowed to give up all men, all physical love."

It was too dark to see his expression, but his voice expressed his astonishment. "You can't be serious! For God's sake, why?"

"I have been hurt too much," she answered firmly. "Love, and all that it means—it only brings a person pain in the end. I've already learned that." She gestured helplessly. "And so I've promised myself I'd never put myself in a position to be hurt again."

"So young for such vows! And you think you will have no difficulty holding to such a resolve?"

It seemed to Marianna that his voice showed a trace of amusement, and she tried to read his expression, but could not. "None at all," she answered strongly. "Of course, you may not wish to see me again, under those conditions. If you do not, I will understand."

When he spoke, his voice definitely had a slight bantering tone. "But I told you that I wanted to see you as a friend. Do you suspect me of harboring wicked designs on you?"

"Well, you did kiss me," she pointed out with perfect logic.

"Aye, I did," he said, and his voice was now serious. "But to answer your question, yes, I still wish to see you, my little friend, and I will make every attempt to control my baser nature."

Marianna touched his hand with hers. "I do believe that my first impression was right, Adam Street. You are a good, kind man."

Adam took that thought home with him, but it offered scant consolation. Her foolish vow annoyed him, yet he felt confused and off balance, made so by this girl who both captivated and irritated him. Why on earth had he kissed her? He had wanted to, he could not deny that, but he had also known that his timing was wrong. Usually his instinct was good in such matters, but not this time. And the way she had responded—or had not responded. What did it mean? She had not gotten angry and had not protested; on the other hand, she had not responded to his kiss. She had, in fact, seemed simply uncaring and cool toward him.

Well, at least he had apologized for his boorish behavior, which, under the circumstances, had been the proper thing to do. He realized that the best thing he could do was just forget about her, put her out of his mind completely, since it was obvious that she would bring him nothing but trouble. He had a well-ordered life; he was successful in his trade; and he had Mary Timms, and other agreeable ladies, with whom to pass his free time; so why should he complicate his life by getting involved with the unpredictable girl?

And yet he found himself doing so. In fact, he called on her the next day at her rooming house, where her landlady, a Mrs. Grodin, viewed him with a suspicious eye before she summoned Marianna down to meet him in the parlor.

Marianna looked refreshed and composed, and Adam was suddenly made conscious of the fact that he, on the contrary, suffered from the effects of a late and almost sleepless night.

Marianna was wearing a pale, beige house gown, high in the neck and long-sleeved, with neat, low collar and cuffs. She looked as prim and proper as a young schoolmistress, not at all like a tavern wench. Adam forced his thoughts back to the matter at hand and bowed slightly.

"I told you that I would call upon you," he said, and cursed himself for the uncertainty in his voice.

"You did, but I didn't expect you so soon," she said, smiling slightly. "Would you like to sit down, Captain Street?"

Adam sat uncomfortably on the horsehair sofa, and Marianna took the seat opposite him. Why on earth had he come here? Adam wondered. She didn't seem in the least glad to see him. He cleared his throat uneasily. "I wondered if you would like to go for a stroll. The afternoon is pleasant, and we might stop for a dish of cream at the hotel."

Marianna frowned prettily. "I suppose I would have time. I don't have to report to work until six this evening."

"That should give us plenty of time," he said gravely. Godalmighty, was the whole afternoon going to be this way, stilted and artificial, with them talking politely like two wary strangers?

"I'll just fetch my bonnet and parasol," she said primly, and then was gone in a flurry of skirts, leaving behind the gentle scent of lilac.

Adam waited impatiently, sitting stiff as a board, his hands upon his knees. Again, he wondered—why had he come here? He could be with Mary Timms, or with Greta, right now. Which reminded him—he had not even called on Greta yet; certainly her company would be less uncomfortable than that of Miss Rose Thorn upstairs. He sighed heavily.

And then Marianna came tripping back, and Adam forgot what he had been thinking. She was wearing a walking dress in a light but vivid shade of blue, with a matching bonnet and parasol. The lovely color enhanced her dark, vibrant beauty, and Adam felt his breath catch in his throat, his reservations about coming here gone in an instant. Prudence Courtwright had certainly done well with her. She was a beauty, no denying it.

"I'm ready," she said modestly, her eyes cast down. What a little actress she is, Adam thought; she knows instinctively the right role to play. He shook his head in admiration, stood, and gave her his arm. Very well, they would play the swain and his young lady, if that suited her fancy. He guided her through the door and out into the afternoon sunshine.

Once outdoors, they strolled seaward, down Madison Street, toward the point where it joined Main Street. They walked along slowly, and for a long while, neither of them spoke.

Adam felt a growing wonder. It was peaceful, really, and rather nice, just walking like this. When Marianna was quiet, a person could *almost* begin to think that she was agreeable. Still, they couldn't continue like this all afternoon; some sort of conversation, even if it was only superficial, seemed to be called for.

"There is a fine breeze," he said, gazing down—he couldn't see her face, only the top of her bonnet—until she looked up. "Don't you agree?"

Looking up at him, her lips barely curved in a slight smile. "Oh, yes. Definitely. A fine breeze."

Adam felt himself flushing. Admittedly, he had not made the wittiest remark of the year, but at least *he* was trying. Dammit, the next remark would have to come from her!

They kept walking, slowly, and Adam noticed that Marianna was the object of considerable interest to the other people on the street. The men, in particular, showed interest in her.

They had now reached the point where Madison Street and Main Street joined, and Adam could see the hotel up ahead. "Would you care to stop now for a dish of cream, or would you prefer to wait until we are heading back?"

Marianna raised her head. "Later, please, if you don't mind."

"Oh, I don't mind," he said, shrugging. "I don't mind at all. It's entirely up to you."

They strolled on, now having to avoid other foot traffic, for the center of Sag Harbor thronged with shoppers and tradespeople, with a number of sailors of every nationality mixed in, like exotic seasoning.

The loud clip-clop of shod horses, as their hoofs struck sparks from the cobblestones; the shouts of hawkers and vendors; the raucous cries of children at play; the barking of dogs; the murmur of conversation—all made a kind of music, to Adam, a music he enjoyed as a contrast to that other kind of music made far out at sea: the rustle and flap of canvas under full sail; the creaking of wood; the lonely mewing of gulls; and the roar of the wind through the rigging. These were lonely sounds, and Adam enjoyed the counterpoint that the city offered, as a change.

He felt a slight tug on his sleeve and looked down to find Marianna staring up at him inquisitively. "What on earth were you thinking about? You looked so far away."

Adam's first inclination was not to share his thoughts with her, or perhaps make up something to tell her, but somehow that seemed the wrong thing to do, so he finally told her the truth, feeling slightly foolish as he did so.

But to his astonishment, she smiled brilliantly and squeezed his arm. "Why, that's lovely! A lovely thought. And it's true, you know, when you think about it. Everything in life has its own kind of music."

They were in sight of the Long Wharf now, and the crowd had grown thicker and noisier; but despite this, Marianna was suddenly chattering away, like a brook just undammed.

Adam, delighted at the change in her, found her conversation stimulating. He took her on board the *Viking Queen*, where he checked on the repairs and refurbishing being done; and then they walked back to the hotel where they ate enormous dishes of frozen strawberry cream.

By the time he returned her to her rooming house, in time for her to change clothes for work, he considered the afternoon well spent. They had gotten along famously, without argument or heated words, for a whole afternoon, and he had definitely enjoyed himself. In addition, he now felt better both about himself and about his feelings for her. The possibility loomed that they might really become friends.

And become friends, they did. Their afternoon strolls became a daily occurrence, as well as early suppers at the hotel, when Marianna's hours permitted. Adam showed her his little house, which she found charming, and took her sailing on the bay in a small sloop belonging to a friend.

This new friendship became important to Marianna, giving her something she had not experienced in her life before—the undemanding attention and company of a male. Her relationship with Jude had been one of unwilling servitude, and her relationship with Phillip had been too physical and too intense to have been considered friendship; but with Adam, she learned what a more-or-less equal, give-and-take friendship between the sexes could be like.

It was not that there was no physical attraction; Marianna found the tall captain very handsome and, despite her resolve to remain aloof from intimacy with any man, desirable; and she had reason to believe that he wanted her, in the way that men want women. However, he never pressed the matter by word or deed, and she was content to have it remain that way.

She knew nothing of the concept of sexual tension between men and women, she only knew that there was an underlying feeling in their relationship that added a quality of excitement to their being together, and she liked it.

She also enjoyed the attention that Adam's company focused on her, and the envy in the eyes of the other women. Marianna knew that sometime in the not-too-distant future he would go back to sea again, but she tried to think of this as little as possible. In addition, she found that she was thinking of Phillip less and less as time passed, and was unable to decide whether this was good or bad.

Adam had been home for approximately a month, and in Marianna's company a goodly part of that time, when something happened that changed Marianna's life completely.

It was a chilly, fog-dampened evening—autumn was beginning its preview of winter weather—and Marianna had a rare evening off from Mundy's Tavern.

There was a magic lantern show and a pot-luck supper being held at the Methodist church, and Marianna and Adam had attended.

The show had been interesting—the subject had been India, which Marianna found immensely exotic—and the supper had been excellent. Replete with good food, her mind filled with the attractive images they had seen at the magic lantern show, Marianna leaned against Adam's comforting bulk as they wended their way slowly toward her rooming house.

The fog had crept in from the harbor until it filled all the empty spaces of the town, hiding the buildings, giving an eerie, other-worldly appearance to the usually familiar.

Out in the harbor a buoy was clanging. Even the sound of its bell seemed muffled by the fog.

They were walking very slowly—it was almost impossible to distinguish landmarks—when Adam stopped, turned, and guided Marianna through what proved to be a wrought-iron gate, for she could feel it beneath her hand as she touched it in passing. Her rooming house had no such gate.

"Where are we, Adam?" she asked, mystified. "Why are we stopping here?"

His touch on her shoulder was gentle but firm as he led her up a rise of stone steps. "It's impossible to see our way in this soup. We'll stop here until it clears up a bit. I'm damp and cold clear through, and I know you must be as well."

"But where are we?" she persisted.

"At my house. I recognized the iron fence when the fog shifted."

Marianna made no further comment, although there were questions boiling in her mind; however, they were questions that were not completely formulated, and difficult to voice. A sense of excitement began in her, and she was suddenly more conscious than ever of Adam's hand on her shoulder.

Adam said, "A nice hot toddy and a toast by the fire will take the chill out of our bones, and then we can go on to your rooming house."

She started to protest, then checked herself. Mrs. Grodin would be scandalized by such a late return, but if Marianna was fortunate, the old woman would be asleep and never know when she returned.

Inside the house Adam said, "Here, let me take your things."

She let Adam help her off with her heavy cape and woolen shawl, both damp from the fog.

In the small parlor logs had been stacked neatly in the brick fireplace, and after removing his own coat, Adam knelt and struck a match. Bright tongues of flame immediately licked upward from the pitch-fat kindling, and soon the logs were blazing. Marianna approached the fire and held her hands out to the warmth.

"It *does* feel good," she said, smiling at him shyly.

For some undefinable reason there was more than the usual tension between them, and she was acutely aware of his maleness, more than she had ever been. In the back of her mind the half-formed questions clamored to be asked, but she kept them at bay. She did not wish to examine the situation too closely; she did not want to think too clearly, too sharply. She had a feeling that something momentous was about to happen, and a part of her wanted it to come about naturally, with no prodding or poking about for reasons.

"Take the big chair, Marianna, near the fire. I'll fetch the mugs. Would you prefer rum, brandy, or mulled cider?"

"Cider, please," she said, sinking back into the soft depths of the big chair, which she felt sure was his favorite.

Adam returned shortly, with a tray bearing two large mugs filled with cider, cinnamon, and sugar. He placed the tray on the hearth and knelt to insert the poker into the flames. When the poker glowed red from the heat, he removed it and quickly plunged it into first one, then the other mug.

The rich odor of cinnamon scented the room, and Marianna

breathed it in happily. She felt very relaxed and content, yet, at the same time, expectant. It was an odd feeling, but nice.

She accepted the steaming mug, holding it between her hands to warm them. Adam, she noticed, did the same. They smiled at one another over the rims of the mugs as they sipped at the sweet, hot liquid, and Marianna felt her pulse begin to hammer.

Not a word passed between them until the cider was gone, and then Adam spoke Marianna's name as he stood and slowly drew her to her feet, his gaze fixed upon her all the while.

Looking up into his glowing eyes, it seemed to her that there was a power there, an electric force that traveled from his eyes to hers, drawing her very soul out of her, drawing her to him as a magnet draws iron filings. She had no will, no power to resist him. What was happening, what was going to happen, was inevitable.

His hands were on her shoulders, pulling her to him, until she was pressed against the material of his clothing; and then, abruptly, his hands were beneath her elbows, and she found herself placed upon the footstool in front of the big chair, and their faces were now more on a level. Adam smiled tenderly, and his mouth descended upon hers, gentle yet demanding, drawing, as his eyes had done, the essence of her, out through her lips. The experience was incredibly sweet and erotic. She had forgotten how wonderful sexual love between a man and a woman could be. How it had been with . . .

She gasped as Adam's hands gently moved down her back, and then up and over her breast, and she forgot everything else except the urges of her long-deprived body. It seemed as if she hungered for every touch, every caress, that Adam was lavishing upon her. Marianna wanted him, wanted him to make love to her; wanted him inside her; wanted . . .

Adam groaned aloud and then began to unbutton her bodice, his big seaman's hands awkward with the tiny buttons. Her own fingers moved blindly to his aid, undoing the buttons; her fingers were made wonderfully nimble by the desire to feel his body next to hers, that strong, broad-shouldered body that she had long known would be beautiful, even though she would have refused to admit to having such thoughts.

It seemed an eternity before all her clothing was unbuttoned and removed, and she stood nude before him.

When the last item was gone and she stood on the stool, with the warmth of the fire flickering over her skin, which suddenly seemed as alive and sensitive as an insect's antenna, Marianna felt like a statue upon a pedestal; an image that was heightened as Adam, groaning again, dropped to his knees and embraced her.

She trembled, quivering with desire and exaltation. He looked up the length of her body and whispered, "You're so beautiful," and then rose, stepped back, and began to strip away his own clothing.

His gaze never left her as he removed his clothes. His wide chest was brown and lightly covered with fine, curly, dark hair that glistened in the firelight. His arms were muscular and strong, his waist flat and lean. He was indeed as beautiful as she had imagined—not boyishly beautiful, like Phillip, but beautiful as only a grown man is beautiful. Her mind walled off any further thought of Phillip.

Now he unbuckled his belt and pulled down the tight breeches that clung to his legs.

Marianna, with a conscious effort, tore her gaze from his chest and looked at his waist—and then lower. The sight of his rampant manhood made her blush and draw in her breath sharply, for his member was already fully extended, and quite large.

For a long moment she wavered, experiencing a flash of fear, remembering Jude and his "weapon," which had caused her such discomfort and often pain. But Adam was not Jude, and his member was not ugly, but beautiful, straight, and perfect, though awesomely large.

She was given no more time to worry about it, for on the instant, she was plucked from the footstool into his strong arms and carried from the room.

Clinging to his neck, feeling light as a feather and incredibly precious, Marianna was carried up the stairs and into a room at the head of the stairwell.

She raised her head from his shoulder and the silken warmth of his skin to glance quickly at the room, which was lit by a flickering candle. It was a masculine room, but comfortable, in a plain way. She had time, before she was placed upon the coverlet of a high bed, to wonder if Adam had come up here to light the candle during the brief time he had absented himself for the cider. Then Adam was beside her, his body touching hers, his hands stroking her body; and she was close against him, like a second layer of his own skin—it seemed she could not get close enough.

And oh, it was a wonderful, sweet feeling, wilder and stronger than any she had ever known. She could feel her blood pumping in her veins; and all the secret parts of her body felt incredibly sensitive as he touched her tenderly, and then more demandingly, until she cried out in her eagerness to be one with him.

His need was great, she could tell, and passion had driven him to the final stages of savage abandon, yet he was incredibly gentle as he rose above her and poised there as if to question.

And with an eager moan, she gave permission. Lubricated by her own desire, entrance was still difficult, but not painfully so; or if it was, it was a pain that was also a pleasure, for he filled her as no other man ever had, plunging to the depths of her being, possessing her wholly.

And then, as he began the rhythms of love—oh, the exquisite rapture, the shattering ecstasy! Marianna felt that this was the first time she had really been possessed by a man, and there was intense delight in yielding to him, really yielding, for perhaps the first time in her life.

When her body finally climaxed, in shuddering pleasure, it was almost more than she could bear, and she cried out, hearing her voice like the voice of a stranger, harsh and joyous; and then Adam's body clenched, quivering in her, and he gave a mighty groan as his body throbbed in a long, violent paroxysm.

A few minutes later as Adam lay beside her, his breath

coming in gasps, Marianna drifted into a pleasant dream of kisses and touchings, awakening after a bit to find him sleeping quietly beside her, one arm thrown across her waist, his face close to hers.

Not wanting to wake him, she lay without moving, her mind clear now of thoughts of passion, wondering how this had come about. What would it mean to her, and to Adam, in the end? She was experiencing a strange mixture of feelings: relaxation and physical satisfaction—it was good to feel so thoroughly used, as if her body had performed a function for which it had been made, a function too long denied it; guilt, for she felt that her behavior had been, in a way, a betrayal of Phillip; and anger at herself for not being able to keep the vow of chastity she had made after Phillip's departure. Still, all in all, she had to admit that she felt good. In fact, she felt marvelous, she thought ruefully. Adam had been wonderful with her, and to her, and she was grateful.

Did she love him? Did she feel for him that emotion that people described as love? If what she felt toward Adam was love, then what was it that she still felt for Phillip?

Adam interrupted her reverie by muttering, then tightening his arm and pulling her close to the warmth of his body.

She snuggled against him, sighing. Secure in his arms, Marianna drifted off to sleep, her thoughts unfinished, having reached no conclusion.

Chapter Eleven

MARIANNA came awake slowly. Her habit was to awaken all at once, alert and ready to face the day, but this morning she felt lazy, rested, and wonderfully relaxed. She wondered what time it was and turned her face to look at the small enameled clock that she kept on the bedside table.

But there was no table, and when she turned back to the other side of the bed, she saw Adam, his face smooth and untroubled in sleep. The events of the night before came quickly back to her, and she gasped aloud, then covered her mouth so as not to awaken him. It was then that she noticed pale light spilling in through the window.

Dear God! She had spent the night in Adam's bed! She had not been home at all. Whatever would Mrs. Grodin think? Marianna had taken such pains to earn herself a spotless reputation in Sag Harbor, and in one night she had ruined it forever.

Adam sighed, turned over, and threw one leg across her thighs. She froze, and she felt heat surge to her face at the memory of their lovemaking, and for a moment she almost decided that it had been worth the loss of her good name. But that was wrong, wrong! That was the sort of thinking that kept women trapped in positions as tavern wenches. She had enjoyed last night, she could not deny that, but Adam would eventually put out to sea again, and *then* where would she be? What was she to do? Was there any lie that she could tell Mrs. Grodin that the woman would believe?

She glanced over at Adam and was startled to see that his eyes were open and that he was looking at her steadily, a musing smile on his lips.

"Why are you frowning, love?" he asked softly. "It was a wonderful night, for me. I thought it was for you, as well."

Marianna tried to smile back. He did look appealing lying there with his hair all tousled and those magnificent shoulders bare. She said sadly, "It's morning. I've been here all night."

"Aye, that you have." He reached across and pulled the covers down from her shoulders, exposing her breasts. "But why should that be the occasion for a sad face, my love?" His hand came to rest on her breast, and despite her agitation, she experienced a stir of response.

She knocked his hand away, but did not pull up the blanket. "Because I haven't been home! Hellfire and spit, Mrs. Grodin is bound to wonder why I didn't come home all night, and I can't very well tell her the truth, now can I?"

He shrugged. "You are a grown woman, Marianna. You can do what you wish."

"That's not quite true," she said crossly. "Perhaps you can do that, but a woman can never, really, do what she wishes, not if she wants other people to accept her. To women like Mrs. Grodin, a woman who stays out all night is no better than a whore."

She pushed herself up in bed and looked down at him sternly. "Despite what I once was, Prudence Courtwright taught me how to be a lady, and I've found that I like it. I've worked hard to build a good reputation in this town, and now it's all ruined, all gone."

Her shoulders slumped, and her lower lip began to tremble as she fought back tears.

"And all because of me," he said, stroking her shoulder.

She shrugged his hand off. "I didn't exactly fight you off, did I? No, I can't honestly blame it on you. I was weak. I know it."

"Well, then," he said cheerfully, grasping her about the waist and pulling her down to him, "I guess we'll just have to wed so that your reputation may be preserved."

Stunned, Marianna stared into his eyes, which had a devilish gleam in them.

"What are you saying, Adam Street? Hellfire and spit, you can't marry me for a reason like that!" Her eyes narrowed in anger. "You're joshing me, and it isn't very nice of you!"

He shook his head and then twisted about to place it in her lap. "No, I'm not joshing you, my beautiful Marianna, I am proposing to you. True, the words just sort of popped out, but I am completely serious. I want you to be Mrs. Adam Street, Captain Street's wife, and if anyone should then dare speak ill of your good name, I shall call him to task for it. So, what's your answer?"

Marianna still could not believe what she was hearing. Her wits could not have been more addled had he cuffed her alongside the head. What was this charming madman saying? Could he possibly be serious?

The questions tumbled through her mind so rapidly that she could not have thought of answers even if she had had any. What about Phillip? What about her vow of chastity? That question almost caused her to laugh aloud, in view of what had happened last night. But what about her plan for opening her own little shop? Did she love Adam? Did she love Phillip? Would she make a good wife?

She had often dreamed of being married to Phillip. During the time spent with Prudence Courtwright, she had dreamed of little else; but she was astute enough to realize that her visions of such a marriage had been pure fantasy—visions of eternal bliss in a rose-covered cottage in some never-never land, where such realities as money, work, and housekeeping were never given a thought.

Actually, she knew very little of real marriage, for her own mother had not only never been married but had been without a permanent man since Marianna could remember. Few, if any, of the wreckers on the Banks had been married, and her glimpses of the marriages of her friends' parents in Boston had been brief and superficial.

Would she even *like* being married? More to the point, would she like being married to Adam Street? Somehow, the possibility of becoming Mrs. Adam Street had never once entered her mind. She had thought of Adam, yes; he had intrigued her, even fascinated her; yet she had never in her wildest imaginings dreamed that he would ever propose marriage.

"Well?" He gently prodded her thigh with his thumb. "What do you say? Will you wed me?"

She looked at him distractedly. "I don't know what to say. I've never been so surprised at anything in my life. I have to think about it."

"Remember your reputation," he said in a chiding voice. "You had best decide soon so that we can take steps to squelch any rumors that Mrs. Grodin's tongue may start."

Marianna looked at him suspiciously. "What do you mean?"

"I mean that I have concocted a story that will seem, I should imagine, perfectly logical, and part of it is even the truth."

Marianna, staring down at his teasing smile had to smile back, her heart beating faster. Oh, he *was* a handsome thing, he did make love to her in a way that made her blaze with passion, and she did enjoy being with him. She had long ago made peace with the fact that Phillip was not going to return to her. So, why not?

She said, "I suppose this story you have thought up, to save my reputation—you won't tell me what it is unless I agree to marry you?"

"Of course not. That would weaken my bargaining position."

Marianna made a moue. "Well . . . in that case, I don't see that I have any choice, do you?"

"None at all, my love. But there is one thing—" He held up a cautioning finger.

She tensed. "What is that?"

"This vow of chastity, you have to recant on that, or I won't marry you." Without waiting for her answer, he gave a shout of laughter and swept her into his arms.

It was late afternoon before they emerged from his bedroom.

Mrs. Grodin evidently believed Adam's story—that Marianna, because of the fog, had been forced to spend the night in the small room in the back of Mundy's Tavern. At any rate, the announcement of the coming nuptials quite overshadowed the subject of Marianna's reputation.

Captain Jack Hammond had been one of the first people told, after Mrs. Grodin, and his wife generously offered the use of their home for the wedding reception, thus assuring Marianna of acceptance among the "better class" of families in Sag Harbor.

The wedding itself was held in the recently completed Whaler's Presbyterian Church, a magnificent edifice, designed by the noted architect, Minard Lafever, who had added a spire towering so high that returning mariners could catch sight of it as their ships rounded Montauk, on their journey toward home.

Such was Adam's reputation that the building could barely contain all of the guests who thronged there to witness him wed to the woman of his choice. And few could say that the choice was not an excellent one; for Marianna, although a relative newcomer, had made a good many friends of her own, and even those who did not know her, commented on her dark beauty.

For the wedding ceremony she chose a gown of white satin, ankle length, with short, puffed sleeves, over which were full, long sleeves of white gauze, fastened at the wrist. The bodice was ornamented with horizontal tucks and was pointed, showing off the full skirt, suspended over a very full crinoline.

On her feet were delicate white kid slippers, and her mittens were fashioned of Brussels lace, to match her veil, which was secured by a chaplet of white roses, around her dark curls.

Many were heard to say that a lovelier bride had never graced the town of Sag Harbor, and there were few to gainsay them. Only two guests were noticeably unhappy—Mary Timms and Greta.

Afterward, Marianna was never able to remember clearly all of the events of that day; it remained in her memory as a welter of confused images, pleasant, but chaotic.

She had been unable to eat breakfast, and her stomach churned with a mixture of apprehension and excitement.

The day seemed to pass in a hectic sort of daze, in which she drifted, totally bereft of any will of her own; for she had set this thing in motion by saying yes to Adam, and now it was moving toward its climax, and she was powerless to stop it, even if she had wished to do so.

She did pause briefly to wonder if Adam was experiencing the same emotional turmoil. Getting married, it seemed, was a very emotional business.

And then they were there, in the church. The building was so new that the clean smell of fresh paint mingled with the scent that rose from the banks of autumn flowers massed in front of the altar. The interior was lit by built-in, whale oil lamps, and their steady yellow glow reflected from the polished mahogany rails and flickered off the silver nameplates on the pews.

It was a beautiful church, with its balconies, graceful fluted columns, coffered ceilings, and decorated organ loft. Out of the day's confusions of images, Marianna would always remember that of the church, and of herself and Adam, standing before the Reverend Jacoby, reciting their vows, the vows that would bind them, one to the other.

At that instant panic descended upon her. She looked up at this giant of a man at her side. He was a stranger! She did not know him at all! What was she doing, binding herself forever to this man about whom she knew nothing?

But it was too late then, for Reverend Jacoby was asking if she, Marianna, would take this man, Adam Street, to be her lawfully wedded husband, to have and to hold, in sickness and in health, for so long as they both should live. And she heard her own voice speaking, saying yes firmly and clearly; and then Adam was lifting her veil and kissing her, and people were laughing and crying, and she knew that she was now married, for better or for worse.

The first two weeks of marriage were, somewhat to Marianna's surprise, not far different from her youthful dreams.

Her things were moved into Adam's small but well-appointed house, and Mr. and Mrs. Horner stayed on to take care of the house, leaving the newly married couple free to explore the town, the surrounding countryside, and each other.

Although the weather was turning increasingly cold, there were still some fine days, and during those days, they picnicked and sailed, sometimes landing at Shelter Island, to lunch upon the beach.

Marianna liked the island, with its stands of trees and sheltered beaches. Many shipowners and captains had fine homes and estates on Shelter Island, which had been settled in 1638, the first place in eastern Long Island to be inhabited by the white man.

But soon the weather became too severe to continue their ramblings, and they were forced indoors, where they roasted chestnuts over the coals in the fireplace and abandoned themselves to nights of intense lovemaking that left them both pleasantly exhausted.

Adam continued to venture out every day to check on the *Viking Queen*'s repairs and to conduct his business, but he was usually gone only a few hours.

One afternoon he did not return until dusk, and Marianna, nervously pacing the floor of the parlor, felt bitter words rise to her tongue when he finally did return, brushing snowflakes from his cape.

Marianna knew that she was being unreasonable but seemed powerless to stop it. "Where have you been? I've been alone all day!"

Adam frowned briefly at her, then smiled. Throwing aside his cape, he strode to her, taking her warm hands in his cold ones and looking down into her face. "That is something you will have to learn to endure, my love. I won't always be able to be with you, you know. I am a whaler by trade, and eventually I will put out to sea again. You know that."

Marianna was scowling, as much at herself as at him. Tugging at his hands, she pulled him close. "I know, Adam, I know," she said against the chill front of his waistcoat. "I don't like it, but I do understand. It's just that this is our honeymoon, and I hate to be separated from you for a single moment."

He tilted her chin up with a gentle finger and smiled tenderly. "I feel the same, but there was a reason why I was gone longer than usual today. I have a surprise for you!"

For some reason his words failed to cheer her; instead, she experienced a sinking sensation in her stomach. Things were going so well, they were so happy, just as they were. She had the strong feeling that this surprise was going to change their lives.

"I have bought us a new home," Adam was going on. "On Shelter Island. The Napier house."

Marianna could hardly credit her hearing. Adam had talked of eventually building them a home on the island, but she had thought of that as far in the future. Now, a home, already built, on the island?

"The Napier house?"

"Yes. I'd forgotten that you don't yet know all of the local history." He picked Marianna up and sat down with her on his lap in the large leather chair before the fireplace.

"Captain Louis Napier was one of Sag Harbor's most successful whalers. His ship, the *Emily*, was wrecked almost a year ago. All hands, including the captain, went down with her. His widow has decided to sell the house and return to her family in New York. It's a beautiful house, Marianna, well built and with plenty of room for children." He gave her a quick hug. "*This* house, with the Horners and us in it, is too small. We're forever falling over one another, and I know you love the island. We can move in at once, before the weather becomes too bad. We should be settled in before the heavy snows come."

He looked at her expectantly, and she dredged up a smile. True, she liked the island, to visit, for picnics; but it was somewhat isolated, cut off from the busy life of the harbor. When Adam was away at sea, what would there be for her to do? And why had he made this decision without consulting her? Didn't she have the right to share in a decision as important as this?

However, maybe that was the way things were supposed to be in a marriage—from what she had observed it would appear to be so. The men made the decisions, and the women supported their men's opinions. It was the duty of a good wife. Well, she wanted to be a good wife, didn't she?

"Aren't you happy about the house?" Adam asked in a puzzled voice. "You're so quiet."

Marianna forced herself to smile. He had meant well, and he must have spent a great deal of money, all just to make her happy. "Of course I'm happy! Why shouldn't I be? It's just that you surprised me. It's so sudden, Adam, it takes a little getting used to."

He grinned and hugged her tightly. "I *knew* you'd be pleased. Mrs. Horner can start packing in the morning."

Marianna's premonition that Adam's surprise would bring about a change in her life proved to be true.

Moving a whole household from Sag Harbor to Shelter Island was a time-consuming and rather complicated task, and it seemed to Marianna that she and Adam had little time now for themselves. He kept reassuring her that once they were settled into their new home it would be different, but she was far from convinced.

The last of their possessions was transported just before the heavy winter storms set in, as Adam had promised; but Marianna discovered that she felt rather like a prisoner in the new house—so strange, so different from their cozy nest in Sag Harbor.

The Napier house was a magnificent Italianate mansion, painted a dark red, with an ornate widow's walk, enclosing a cupola.

After the small house in Sag Harbor, it seemed embarrassingly large. Adam had said there was room for children. To fill these rooms, Marianna thought, she would have to be as fecund as a rabbit! The furniture they had brought from Sag Harbor did not even begin to fill the rooms, but Adam assured her that when he returned from his next whaling voyage, he would bring back furnishings and fabrics so that the house might be properly decorated and furnished.

The matter of Adam's next voyage was never far from her thoughts. Despite the confusion and hectic activity of moving, she could tell that he was growing restless. The *Viking Queen* was now ready to sail as soon as the weather permitted, and Marianna found that she resented his obvious yearning to be aboard her.

Others had told her—Adam himself had told her—that it was the way of seamen for them to long for their homes while at sea and to long for the sea when they were at home, but Marianna found his eagerness to be at sea highly unflattering and depressing.

He would be gone, probably, for at least a year. It was an interminable time. How could she get along without him during those endless months? What would she do with herself? The Horners, along with a new gardener hired by Adam for the new house, took care of the house and the yardwork. What would she do with her time?

Worried about his imminent departure, she thanked God for each day of the storm, for each new fall of snow, for it meant that he would be longer at home. Her lovemaking became almost savage in its intensity, as if by this alone she might keep him with her.

"Do you *have* to go?" she asked coaxingly. "Couldn't you let Mr. Karnes, your first mate, take the ship out?"

Adam reared back as if she had slapped him. "*My* ship? Godalmighty, Marianna, you just don't seem to understand about some things! Do you know how long it took me to get my own ship? To become a captain?" He got a reminiscent look on his face. "I came from a seafaring family, like many in this part of the country. My father was a sailor all his life, and I followed in his footsteps, shipping out at an early age. The sea is about all I've ever known, and all I ever wanted was my own ship.

"Aye, I worked hard, spending more time at sea than on land. But I studied when I had the time, by candlelight, until I thought my eyes would fall out of my head. I learned navigation and all else connected with ships and sailing. I was second mate by the time I was twenty-one and first mate on my first whaling vessel at the age of twenty-six.

"I was sailing with Captain Dortmund then. He was a hard captain, but scrupulously fair, and never tried to cheat his men when a voyage was prosperous. I saved every penny I could. Then we had an unusually bountiful voyage, my share of the profits being quite large. I was always a smooth talker," he grinned wryly, "and I was able to convince a shipbuilder here in Sag Harbor that I could pay him back if he'd sell me a ship on credit. I gave him what savings I had and sailed the ship on a shoestring. That was the *Viking Queen.* I had a stroke of good fortune on my side, of course. He had built the *Viking Queen* on consignment for a fellow who died bankrupt, and the shipbuilder was anxious to sell her. It took me several years of whaling with the *Queen* to finally turn the corner. But I did, on that voyage where I met you and Phillip Courtwright, in Charleston."

Adam sighed contentedly. "Now the *Viking Queen* is all mine, free and clear, but expenses continue, and buying this house cost me dearly, Marianna. I need another profitable voyage behind me. Whales are not as plentiful as they were when I started, and a whaler has to sail new waters."

Marianna stirred, about to protest that it had been *his* wish to buy the Napier house, not hers, but she subsided.

Adam went on, "Aye, Ben Karnes is a fine first mate, one of the best to ever sail the seas, but do you think I would let the *Viking Queen* sail without me? My entire life to date has gone into that ship. I love you, Marianna, but my love for you and my love for the *Queen* are two separate things, and must remain so. You must come to terms with that." He kissed her on the forehead. "So you see, my love, what you demand of me when you ask that I turn my ship over to another man to command?"

Marianna nodded reluctantly, although deep in her soul, she did not fully understand. The only thing clear to her was the fact that the ship came first, and it was a painful fact to face.

The ice in the coves had melted, and the first spring flowers were tentatively poking their heads through the ground in the meadows when Adam and the *Viking Queen* set sail from Sag Harbor.

Marianna had come to see him off; and she tried to smile and put on a brave face for his sake, although she felt depressed and abandoned. Even though Adam had said several times how he hated to leave her, how much he would miss her, and that he would hurry back to her as fast

as the whales allowed, he could not conceal the eagerness
and anticipation on his face and in his manner.

The *Viking Queen*, bright with new paint, with a fully
rested crew and sufficient stores for a long spell at sea,
seemed anxious, too. When she was towed out into the
channel and her sails unfurled, the ship caught the wind
eagerly, it seemed to Marianna, moving away slowly at first,
and then with increasing speed, as Marianna and the others
on the wharf waved until their arms grew tired.

It was not until the *Viking Queen*'s sails were only dots
on the horizon that Marianna finally turned away, shoulders
slumped.

"Will you be wanting to go back to the island now, missus?" asked Mr. Horner, who had rowed her and Adam
across from Shelter Island in the dinghy.

Marianna thought for a moment. It was early in the day,
and she had no desire to go back to that big, lonely house
on the island just yet. The isolation enforced by winter
weather had prevented her from making but few acquaintances there, and she longed to see and talk to her friends
in Sag Harbor.

Most of all, she wanted to see Meg Mundy; but realizing
that her new status in life made it inadvisable for her to
frequent the tavern, she sent Horner with a note requesting
that Meg meet her in the little restaurant where they had
first become acquainted.

After the isolation of the island, Sag Harbor seemed particularly busy and cheerful. Marianna took her time walking to the restaurant, enjoying the bustle of the streets,
conscious of the fact that she looked fetching in her new
redingote of blue and brown pekin, with its tightly fitted
bodice, high neck, and fitted sleeves with two folds of bias
silk at the top. She knew that the tight top showed off her
narrow waist to advantage, and the very full skirt, trimmed
with two bias folds down each side of the front, moved
gracefully as she walked with tiny steps along the walkway.

Her ensemble was completed by black shoes and gaiters,
a bonnet of rice straw, trimmed with pink ribbon, and apricot-
colored gloves and parasol.

Many were the admiring glances she collected, and what

with the pauses to exchange greetings with friends, she found Meg already there when she arrived at the restaurant.

The big woman looked larger than ever, her curls more golden, her cheeks pinker, and her face shone with delight when she saw Marianna coming through the doorway.

"Here, lovey, here I am!" she shouted in her tiny voice, as if Marianna could miss her.

Marianna felt her own face break into a smile as she hurried toward the big woman. Oh, it was good to see her! How Marianna had missed the noise and jovial atmosphere of the tavern—she realized that now.

"Meg," she said, kissing the older woman on her pink, perfumed cheek, "it's so good to see you!"

"And you," Meg said. "You're a sight for these tired old eyes, girl. How lovely you look. It seems marriage agrees with you, eh?"

Marianna nodded, but her smile wavered. "Oh, Meg! Adam just sailed. A new voyage . . ."

Meg nodded wisely and patted her hand. "There, there now, lovey. You ain't the first wife to have her man set out to sea, and you sure won't be the last. It's the way of things in a seaport town. That's how it is, when you're married to a whaling man."

Marianna took the wicker-bottomed chair across the table from Meg and sat down carefully, mindful of her full skirt. "I know, Meg. But we've just been married a few months. I know Adam loves me, but I swear he was eager to go, anxious to get back to hunting those great, smelly fish of his!"

Meg's eyes twinkled. "Those smelly fish, girl, as you call them, are what keep this town on its feet. They're what keep the lanterns burning, make you smell sweet, and stiffen your corsets. Don't ever sell them short, especially in a whaling village."

Marianna sighed pensively. "You're right, of course. I'm just being disagreeable, but I do hate having him go away. I don't know what I'll do with myself, out there on that island. I know hardly anyone yet, and from what I've seen and heard, the islanders are a clannish lot."

Meg patted her hand again. "Don't fret. You'll make friends. They can't help but like you. After all, a pretty young woman like yourself, all alone. They're bound to feel sorry for you, and even though the islanders do stick together, so do whalers' wives. They'll accept you, just give them time."

Marianna peeled off her gloves. "You *are* a tonic, Meg. I feel better already. Let's have some of those jam tarts you love so, a big pot of tea, and then you can tell me all the things that have happened here in town."

For the next hour Marianna and Meg chatted animatedly, drank tea, and ate tarts, as Meg told Marianna all of the latest gossip of Sag Harbor.

Marianna enjoyed herself thoroughly; and it was with reluctance that she looked at the small watch hanging from her neck and saw that it was time to go. "It's growing late, Meg," she said regretfully. "I really do have to go, if we're to get back to the island before dark."

Meg nodded. "It was good to see you, lovey. You must come into town more often."

"Oh, I intend to, Meg. I fear I'd go mad otherwise. I really don't know what I'd do with myself if I couldn't come into Sag Harbor now and then to see my friends."

Meg's round face turned serious. "Marianna, I usually don't hand out advice, but I think of you as a daughter, and I can't help but speak up when I see you heading for—well, let's just say, troubled waters."

Marianna frowned. "Whatever do you mean?"

Meg leaned forward and took both of Marianna's hands. "Lovey, you are not an ordinary young woman. You are spirited, intelligent, sometimes willful, and beautiful. It's going to be difficult for you, the life of a captain's wife, that is. The women here are used to it. They were raised with it, it's a way of life, difficult, but something that can be lived with. Their husbands are away a year or more, and the women are left behind to mind the children, the houses, and the property. They try to fill the time with quilting parties, church work, and good deeds, and they accept the life.

"But you, child, your husband is gone only a few hours,

and here you're already chafing. What will it be like for you in a few months?"

Marianna was both amused and irritated at Meg's concern. "What are you getting at, Meg? What are you trying to tell me?"

Meg squeezed her hands. "Only that you are going to have to make some changes in your thinking, Marianna, if you are going to make it through the months that Adam will be gone. You say you have no friends on the island—well, make some! The island is a little town in itself. They have churches, quilting groups, social events. Some of the best families in the area live there. Go to Captain Hammond's wife, have her give you letters of reference to her friends there."

Marianna nodded and pulled her hands gently away. "I will, Meg. I promise I will. You're right, I know. Now, is that all? Or are you going to scold me some more?"

Meg shook her head, her face serious. "I'm not scolding, child, only cautioning. There is one more thing. You're a very beautiful woman, lovey, and it'll soon be bruited about that your husband is away at sea. There may be some men who will attempt to take advantage of that. You mustn't do anything to encourage them. You don't want to dirty that reputation that you have been so careful to build."

Marianna stood up, impatient now. "Oh, Meg! How can you say such things? I'm not a fool about men, whatever else I might be. I know them well enough—what they are, what they can be. You need have no worry on that score."

"Do you now?" Meg's smile was wise. "Well, I just wanted to say my piece. I got my experience the hard way, lovey, and I would like to help prevent you from having to do the same."

Relenting, Marianna leaned down and kissed the other woman's cheek. "I know, Meg, and I thank you for caring. Now, I had best get myself down to the wharf. Mr. Horner will think I've been set upon by footpads. I'll see you soon."

"Soon," Meg echoed, her expression troubled.

The sun was low in the sky, and the early promise of spring now seemed false, for the day had turned chill again

194

by the time Marianna approached the wharf where Horner had moored the dinghy.

Pulling her shawl more closely about her shoulders and holding her deep bonnet to keep it secure in the brisk wind, she saw Horner standing on the wharf, smoking his old pipe.

She hurried to him. "I'm sorry that I was so long, Mr. Horner," she said breathlessly. "Meg Mundy is an old friend, and the time just slipped away."

The man's weathered face looked more melancholy than usual, as he said dourly, "It don't make a whole lot of difference, Mrs. Street. I'm afraid I have bad tidings."

Marianna frowned at his expression. "Bad tidings? What is it?"

"It's the boat. We shipped water all the way over from the island. The captain being in a hurry, I didn't tell him. But I checked her out after we landed, and there's a bad hole in her bottom."

Marianna sighed. The good feeling engendered by her visit with Meg evaporated, and the unhappiness she felt over Adam's departure was waiting, all too eagerly, to take its place. All at once, she felt tired and cross. "Well, did you repair it?" she demanded, knowing even as she spoke that if he had, he would not be telling her of the problem.

He shook his head morosely. "No, Mrs. Street. It wasn't something I could fix. I had to take her to a boatwright. He's putting a patch on her."

Marianna grabbed for her bonnet, as a particularly aggressive gust of wind attempted to lift it from her head. "How long will it take? Is it almost done?"

Horner shook his head, his long face more lugubrious than ever. "No, it ain't. Boatwright says he can't get to it before morning. I guess we'll have to spend the night here." He stood, looking at her forlornly, ready to take any harsh words of reprimand, resigned to the fact that such abuse was a servant's lot.

His servile manner annoyed Marianna, as it always did. "Oh, hellfire and spit!" she muttered under her breath. She had no toilet articles with her, and she knew that the inns were usually full. Perhaps she could stay the night with Meg.

"Excuse me, miss, but I could not help but overhear."

Marianna, startled, whirled around to see a stocky young man, dressed elegantly in a well-fitting afternoon suit, standing before her, hat in his hand.

"If you will forgive me, miss. My name is Stuart Brawley, and I just happen to be going to Shelter Island. I would be delighted to give you and your man passage, if you like."

He smiled, and Marianna could not help but return it. His smile was infectious, turning his rather serious, sharp-planed face into a visage of dimpled charm.

His deep gray eyes sparkled. "I assure you, young lady, that I am most respectable. I have a law practice here in Sag Harbor. What could be more respectable than that?" he said gravely, then made a small bow.

Marianna laughed aloud. "I am sure you are, Mr. Brawley, and we shall be most happy to accept your kind offer, and grateful, as well."

Horner spoke up. "If you please, missus. It'd be best if I stayed here, with the dinghy, so's I can bring her back in the morning, when she's fixed. I can sleep at the boat works. I know a fellow there."

Marianna hesitated, wondering if she should be alone with this young man. She recalled Meg's warning about men taking advantage of her. But this was different, this was an emergency, not a situation he had devised. It would be silly to refuse his offer because she was afraid of what he might do or of what people might think. It was clear that he *was* respectable, as he claimed, and she had the feeling that his company would be pleasant.

"I shall be pleased to accept your offer, sir," she said formally. "Mr. Horner, I shall see you tomorrow, when the boat is repaired. Tell the boatwright to send the bill to me at home."

Horner nodded. "Very well, madam."

Brawley stepped up and offered Marianna his arm. "My boat is just over there," he said, pointing to a large dinghy moored to a piling. "I am a good oarsman, quite competent, and I promise you a safe journey."

He gallantly helped her into the dinghy, and Marianna was impressed by his manners. It was obvious that he was a true gentleman, just like Phillip, she thought—and as always, when she thought of Phillip, a sharp, bitter twinge of sadness seemed to squeeze her heart.

When Marianna was settled into the boat, Stuart Brawley took his place at the oars and began to expertly maneuver the small craft out into the busy water traffic. For a few moments he was occupied in keeping them from colliding with any of the other craft, but when they were well underway, he was able to turn his attention to Marianna.

"Now then," he said firmly, in a deep, compelling voice. "I have told you who I am, may I have the pleasure of knowing the name of my beautiful passenger?"

Marianna felt herself blush. Where were her manners? She had quite forgotten to introduce herself. "I am Marianna Street. Mrs. Adam Street, to be exact."

Stuart Brawley elevated sandy eyebrows, which matched his thick, well-cut hair. "Captain Adam Street's wife? I know of Captain Street. He is well thought of."

Marianna nodded somewhat smugly. It was pleasant to hear such words from a stranger. "Yes, Captain Street is my husband."

"He sailed this morning, I was given to understand."

Stuart Brawley's expression was neutral, but Marianna sensed something behind his words, and Meg's cautionary advice again came back to her.

"You live on Shelter Island, I believe?"

"Yes, we live on the island. My husband and I bought the Napier house. Perhaps you know it?"

He nodded. "I do, indeed. In fact, I know the island quite well. My family has resided there for many years, and I usually know everything that goes on there."

Marianna raised her eyebrows. "Yet you don't seem to know that we purchased the Napier house."

"True." His smile was rueful. "My only excuse is that I've been away these past six months. I assure you, when I *am* home, I know everything that goes on in Shelter Island. As does everyone else, unfortunately," he added in a dry voice.

"Besides, I would never miss anyone as pretty as you, Mrs. Street."

He spoke in a conversational tone, yet Marianna felt herself stiffen. The words did not displease her, it was just that something told her they were not words that should be spoken by a man to another man's wife. Being a married woman is not easy, she thought; there are so many rules!

She pulled the coat tightly around her, as if its folds could give her protection from more than the chill. She made up her mind to keep the conversation on an impersonal plane. "You say you practice law, sir? In Sag Harbor?"

"Yes, I am just setting up practice," he answered in measured tones, pacing his speech to the sweep of the oars. "I found an office this very day. I hope that if you, and your husband, of course, should ever need legal help, you will avail yourselves of my services."

"Thank you, Mr. Brawley." Marianna could not imagine ever being in need of the services of a lawyer, yet it seemed the polite thing to say.

They were nearing the landing now, and Marianna could see that it was going to be a race between the dinghy and darkness, for the light was growing increasingly faint.

"Do you have transportation from the landing?" Stuart Brawley asked.

"Yes. We left a horse and carriage at the stable."

"Will you be able to manage it alone?"

She nodded. "It's a small rig, and the animal is gentle. I will be fine."

Abruptly he laughed. "Then may I prevail upon you to do *me* a good turn and deliver me to my door? My mother drove me to the landing this morning, and I had planned to walk home, thinking that I would be returning much earlier than this."

Marianna was anxious to get home. She was growing hungry and tired; yet she could hardly refuse this man a favor, in the face of his own generosity. "Of course. I would be happy to."

She only hoped that his home was not far out of her way, but she did not think it would be polite to inquire.

He seemed to read her thoughts. "Our house is not far from yours, Mrs. Street. It will not take you greatly out of your way. In fact, if I may be so bold, perhaps it would be best if I dropped you off at your home and drove your carriage on to mine, thus keeping you from being out alone on the roadway after dark. I could return the horse and vehicle to you on the morrow."

Marianna felt some misgivings about his suggestion, but it was so sensible that she could find no way of refusing.

They were at the landing now, and after securing the dinghy, Stuart Brawley carefully helped her from the boat. They were both greeted by name by the ferryman on the dock, and the fact that the man recognized Stuart Brawley set Marianna's doubts at rest. It would certainly be much simpler to let the lawyer do as he proposed.

"Well, Mrs. Street, is my suggestion agreeable? Will you let me drive you home and return your rig tomorrow?"

He was standing very near to her, and Marianna resisted an impulse to move away from him. It seemed somehow necessary for her to stand her ground. "Yes, Mr. Brawley, it sounds like a sensible plan. I accept your kind offer. To tell the truth, I'm not all that familiar with horses."

He smiled, teeth flashing in the dimness, and it seemed to her that there was a certain satisfaction in the curve of his lips. Well, it certainly could do no harm to allow him to drive her home. The only result would be that he would have to come to the house tomorrow, to return the rig; and all at once she found herself rather looking forward to that. Despite Meg's words of caution, Marianna was confident of her ability to fend off any man's advances—so long as the man was a gentleman. Besides, he had mentioned his mother; perhaps she should ask him to bring her when he came. Meg had said that she needed to make friends, had she not?

"You spoke of your mother," she said, as he helped her onto the seat of the carriage. "Do you suppose you could persuade her to call when you come to return the carriage tomorrow?"

He cocked an eyebrow at her, seemingly amused by her

question. "That is very thoughtful of you, Mrs. Street. I shall tender your invitation to mother."

"We could have luncheon in the arbor, if the weather permits. Mrs. Horner is a very fine cook." Marianna was glad she had thought of it. It *would* be nice to entertain someone.

The lawyer clucked to the horse, and in the gathering darkness they set off briskly down the road. "I don't know what mother's plans are for tomorrow, but I'm certain that she will be pleased by the invitation. The only reason she would not be able to accept, I'm sure, would be because of a prior engagement or sudden illness."

"Then it's all arranged," Marianna said, happy with the way she had handled the situation of this man's coming to her home.

Sighing, she relaxed against the back of the seat, pulling the traveling robe tightly around her knees as the evening chill crept up from the ground. It was going to be difficult, being apart from Adam, but she had made the first step toward making new friends and had averted what might have been a delicate situation.

The gentle motion of the carriage made her drowsy, and she closed her eyes. Face concealed by the deep sides of the bonnet, she dozed off, and so did not see the look on Stuart's face, a look that stated clearly that his interest in her was not that which one man should have for the wife of another.

Chapter Twelve

MARIANNA sat in the gazebo, comfortably ensconced in a wicker chair, and examined the neatly set table with admiration. It did look lovely.

The day had turned out fair and warm, and she had asked Mrs. Horner to prepare a luncheon suitable for eating out of doors. The woman had outdone herself, and there was a marvelously aromatic meat pie baking right now in the kitchen oven and a beautiful trifle setting in the cooler.

Marianna was looking forward to meeting Mrs. Brawley, for she had learned from Mrs. Horner that the Brawley family was an important one in the society of Shelter Island and Sag Harbor.

Mr. Brawley, Stuart's father, was dead, a heart condition having taken him five years before; but the money in the family came from Mrs. Brawley, nee Irania Stuart, and she controlled it with an iron hand—at least according to Mrs. Horner.

Stuart was the youngest of five children, of which only two were still living at home, Stuart and his sister, Lavinia. Marianna wished that she had known about the sister last night; she would have invited her to luncheon as well.

She sighed and straightened her bodice. She had dressed very carefully for the occasion, choosing a dress that she hoped would meet with Mrs. Brawley's approval. She was wearing a new bodice of lingerie, made of alternate puffings of thin muslin and embroidery, and a very full muslin skirt, in a shade called *pensée*, a kind of delicate violet. Atop her well-ordered curls she wore a cap of light, spotted lace,

201

decorated with roses. She looked, she hoped, ladylike and appealing. She intended to be very nice to Mrs. Brawley, win her over completely, and thus be introduced into the society of Shelter Island without the necessity of first going to call upon the individual ladies of the island.

A light breeze rustled the leaves of the vine that covered and shaded the small enclosure, bringing with it the fragrance of fresh grass, new leaves, and early spring flowers.

Marianna wished her guests would arrive. Despite her fears that she would not, she had slept well last night, as she had been thoroughly fatigued by her busy day in Sag Harbor; but this morning she had awakened with the knowledge that Adam was not with her, was, indeed, far away, and would remain so for a long period of time. This knowledge made her restless and discontented, and she knew that if she dwelt on it, it would only grow worse. She *needed* the Brawleys' presence to distract her, if nothing else.

Just when she was growing impatient, she heard the sound of a horse's hoofs in the distance. Hurriedly she touched her hands to her cap and her hair, then settled herself down to wait with as much composure as she could muster. She had told Mrs. Horner to escort them to the gazebo when they arrived.

In a moment she could see Mrs. Horner and Stuart Brawley coming toward her along the path that led to the main house. But where was his mother?

In the clear light of noon, Stuart Brawley, she could see, was even more attractive than he had appeared the evening before.

He was fashionably attired in a waistcoat of cream-colored cashmere, a coat of dark blue cloth, and white cascade necktie. His tall-crowned hat was in his hand.

The cream-colored breeches fitted tightly over his Wellington boots and were secured under the instep, showing that he had fine, muscular legs. Marianna blushed and returned her gaze to his face, which was smiling. His thick chestnut hair glinted in the sun, as if freshly washed. She had to admit that he made a fine appearance, but again, where was his mother?

She must have looked the question, for as soon as he was within speaking distance, he began to explain. "Mrs. Street, I am so sorry that mother was not able to accompany me, but it seems that she did have a prior engagement, after all. However, she asked me to thank you for your invitation and to say that she would be very pleased to come another time."

As he finished speaking, Stuart took her hand and bowed over it, touching it with his lips.

Marianna had to wonder if he was lying. She cast a quick glance at Mrs. Horner and found that worthy woman eyeing Stuart with approval. Evidently she accepted the story, even though Marianna was not certain that she herself did. Still, she had little choice but to pretend that she did, and she would have to ask him to partake of lunch, since the table was all set, obviously ready for guests.

So, she nodded graciously and motioned to the table. "Naturally, I'm sorry that your mother was unable to come today, but I do hope that you shall be able to stay for lunch, Mr. Brawley?"

His quick smile flashed, and again Marianna was struck by the way in which the expression changed his features. "I should be delighted. In fact, I'm famished, as I slept a bit late and did not have time for breakfast. Also"—he turned to Mrs. Horner—"I have heard about Mrs. Horner's cooking, and I would not dream of missing the chance to try it out for myself."

Mrs. Horner, blushing furiously, smiled—looking rather like a fat cat that had just eaten a mouse—and bustled away to attend to her culinary duties.

Well now, Marianna thought; he does have a way with the ladies. The thought put her on guard. She had no real reason to suspect that Stuart was dissembling when he told her that his mother had a prior engagement; yet instinct told her that his interest in her went beyond the gentlemanly. She would have to be extremely careful to keep all conversation between them on a nonpersonal level.

"Pray be seated," she said, gesturing to the chair opposite her. "Would you care for some wine? It is cool from the well house and very refreshing."

Stuart nodded and placed his hat on the extra chair. "Thank you, Mrs. Street. A good glass of wine would go down very well, I believe." He took the glass she poured and drank. "Excellent! Your husband has good taste in wines, as he does in women."

Marianna felt her face grow warm. There he went again! He *would* keep making personal remarks. Well, she would continue to ignore them.

She was saved from thinking of an innocuous reply by the arrival of Mrs. Horner, pushing the serving cart down the pathway from the house.

The aroma of the meat pie overpowered the scent of the garden, and Stuart raised his head and sniffed appreciatively. "Ah! That smells heavenly!"

Marianna considered his appreciation rather excessive, yet she did have to admit that the pie smelled delicious.

Mrs. Horner wheeled the cart into the gazebo and began serving, and for several minutes her busy clattering of dishes kept conversation at a minimum, for which Marianna was grateful.

But all too soon, Mrs. Horner was gone, and she and Stuart were alone with their meal. He was eating with good appetite. Marianna looked down at her own plate and felt a lurch of queasiness. Suddenly the attractive food seemed repugnant, and she feared that she might really be ill. What ailed her?

She swallowed convulsively and sought for some subject that they might discuss harmlessly, to keep her from thinking of the food upon her plate.

"How long have the Brawleys lived on Shelter Island?" she finally asked.

Stuart stopped eating and swallowed. "Almost since the island was first settled in 1638," he said, reaching for another piece of Mrs. Horner's white bread.

As the afternoon wore on, Marianna learned a great deal about the history of Shelter Island and found that she was entertained as well. Stuart Brawley was a witty conversationalist, and his view of life, it seemed, was slightly irreverent and unconventional, at least his view of Shelter Island and environs.

As she listened Marianna found that her strange nausea had subsided, and she was able to eat most of her lunch. Stuart finished off the rest of the pie, most of the sweet-smelling bread, and a good deal of the salad, then had a large helping of the trifle, which he pronounced excellent.

When their lunch was finished, Marianna realized that she was enjoying herself thoroughly. Stuart was good company; he was a man of many parts, and, she thought, he could be a good friend, as long as he kept things away from the personal. He was certainly the most interesting person she had met on the island, and she had a feeling that even after she made the acquaintance of her other neighbors, this would still prove to be the case.

"Now," he said expansively, removing a slender brown cigar from a silver case, "we must make plans to get you introduced to the social scene on the island, such as it is. Do you mind?" He waved the cigar, raising his eyebrows questioningly.

Marianna shook her head. Although she disliked the smell of tobacco smoke, it seemed ungracious to say no.

He lit the cheroot with a large wooden match and inhaled contentedly. "Mother is holding open house this coming Sunday, and you must come, of course. Three in the afternoon. Tea will be served, and you will meet many of the leading lights of our society. Then, on Wednesday evening, there is a meeting of the Columbian Temperance Society, at six. You should attend that, by all means. I will be happy to escort you, if you will be so kind as to accept my invitation." He looked at her intently and must have read the doubt in her face. "Or, perhaps it would be best if you attended with myself *and* my sister. Would you like that?"

"I should be most pleased to make your sister's acquaintance," Marianna said. A temperance society? *That* certainly sounded like a gay evening!

Stuart grinned. "I can tell from your expression that you are not overwhelmed by the prospect." He began to laugh. "I hope that you don't play at cards, Mrs. Street, for your face would certainly give you away."

Marianna could not help but laugh with him. He *was*

quick and discerning, traits that she found appealing. "Am I so transparent, then?"

"I'm afraid so, at least concerning certain things. With other things, you are a veritable sphinx of mystery."

Marianna's laughter stopped. He was also very cryptic, a trait she did not find endearing, since it made her uneasy.

"But put your mind at ease," he was going on. "Despite the forbidding title, the Columbian Temperance Society meetings are very interesting and well attended, for there you will hear music that will compare favorably to that performed anywhere in the world. The society was only founded in 1842, yet already the orchestra and choir are quite well-known. You will enjoy their performance, I assure you. You *do* like music, I trust?"

Marianna nodded vigorously. "Oh, yes. Indeed I do, and I would be pleased to attend the meeting with you and your sister."

"Good, then it's settled. You know it's nice to have a fresh new face on the island. You will give us a much-needed infusion of life."

Marianna smiled sweetly. She did hope so, for from what she had been able to see and hear so far, the islanders could use it.

Mrs. Brawley's open house proved to be a rather sedate affair, held at the elegant Brawley home, which was situated on a knoll overlooking the water. The house was quite large and well appointed, and Marianna could see that although life on the island might be a bit isolated, it need not lack for creature comforts.

She had prepared for the occasion carefully and while doing so, had again experienced the strange nausea and discomfort she had felt at the luncheon in the gazebo. But as before, it passed away, and by the time she reached the Brawley estate, she felt quite fit again.

Mrs. Brawley was very much as Marianna had expected, after listening to Mrs. Horner's descriptions of her. A tall, severe-looking woman with snowy white hair and an aristocratic face, she examined Marianna coolly and thoroughly as they were introduced.

This perusal triggered in Marianna a feeling of annoyance, and she returned the woman's appraisal with a cool disdain of her own. Who did the old dragon think she was? Marianna considered herself the woman's equal, as she was the equal of anyone. She refused to be intimidated by this woman, simply because she possessed power and money. And yet, in the back of Marianna's mind, a troubling thought arose. Did Mrs. Brawley know that she, Marianna, had been a serving girl in Mundy's Tavern a few short months ago?

Mrs. Brawley finally took Marianna's hand, in a gesture that seemed to grant grudging acceptance, and Marianna curtsied nicely but with dignity.

When Stuart took her arm to lead her away to meet the other guests, he chuckled. "Well, you handled mother very well, I must say. You continue to surprise me, Marianna."

She gave him a quick, sidewise glance. Another of his cryptic remarks! He always seemed to be hinting at something she did not understand.

"And here she is!" Stuart marched Marianna up to a slender young woman with striking green eyes and patrician features. "My sister, Lavinia. Lavinia, this is Mrs. Adam Street."

Lavinia extended a slender, long-fingered hand. Her eyes were friendly and warm, not cold like her mother's. "I'm pleased you could come, Mrs. Street."

Marianna took her hand and returned the smile. "Marianna, please."

Stuart beamed fondly at them, clearly pleased that they seemed to like one another. "There, I knew you would take to each other! Livy, I will leave Mrs. Street in your capable hands. Would you see to it that she meets our guests?"

Lavinia gave her brother an affectionate glance. "I shall be happy to, Stuart."

Gracefully she took Marianna's arm. She was considerably taller and had to lower her head to speak to Marianna. "I am certainly glad that there is another young woman living nearby. You have no idea how boring it can get on the island at times."

Marianna smiled cautiously. Didn't she, though!

"So many of the women here are older, and we simply have *nothing* in common," Lavinia rushed on. "I do hope we will become friends, Marianna."

"I'd like that, also."

Lavinia's smile turned teasing. "My brother seems quite taken with you. Last night at supper he talked of nothing else. Mother is quite up in the air about it."

Marianna frowned uneasily. "I do hope he isn't too taken," she said bluntly. "I *do* have a husband."

"Yes, I know." Lavinia's laughter trilled. "The dashing Captain Street! Everyone in Sag Harbor and the island knows of Captain Street! Why, ladies for miles around took to their beds in a swoon when they heard he had wed." She looked sidelong at Marianna for her reaction.

Marianna laughed somewhat smugly. "I gathered as much." Then her mood changed abruptly. "I do wish he hadn't had to go away. They stay away so long."

Lavinia's face grew serious. "Yes, whaling widows, all of you. Your husbands spend more time on the bosom of the sea than they do on yours, if you'll forgive my earthiness." She added vehemently, "That's why I'm never going to wed a seafaring man!"

Marianna glanced at her in surprise. Lavinia's attitude was unusual, for most young women in this area, Marianna had found, dreamed of marrying a handsome sea captain, since a captain's wife commanded prestige and respect.

"No," Lavinia was saying, "I shall marry a banker or a lawyer or perhaps even a doctor. Someone who stays upon land! Someone who will be there to hold my hand when I am ill. Someone who will be with me on the long winter nights. Someone who can be with me when I bear a child."

Her words caused Marianna's throat to close with the urge to cry. Oh, how she missed Adam. It was unfair, so unfair.

"Oh, Mrs. Partridge, I would like you to meet Mrs. Adam Street. She and her husband, the captain, recently purchased the Napier house."

Thus Marianna was introduced, and then introduced again, to countless women, mostly captains' and shipowners' wives, and to the few men who were in attendance. The men were few in number, since most of them were at sea.

So, Marianna thought; now I am a member of island society. However, the thought failed to cheer her as she would have believed, for Lavinia's remarks had brought to the forefront her own feelings of dissatisfaction and unhappiness.

In the days that followed the Brawley open house, Marianna was in exceedingly low spirits.

She had vowed to herself that she would busy herself in the garden and house, making it beautiful for Adam when he returned home, and that she would rebuff Stuart Brawley if he should come to call; she felt a danger in him, a threat that she could not exactly define. It was not that she did not like Stuart; it was just that it would not be seemly to be seen too much in his company. But for several days her good intentions were not put to the test, for he did not call on her.

She was having increasingly severe bouts of nausea, usually in the early morning, and she also found that her breasts were becoming tender and sore to the touch. What could be the matter with her? Had she contacted some illness?

She put off going to the village to Dr. Isaac White because she thought she would recover on her own. On the Banks, there had been no doctor, and you either recovered from a bout of sickness, or you died. Also, Marianna did not like the whiskery, unctuous old doctor; if she *was* ill, she did not want him to attend her. Well, it would probably pass. Worse things had.

And then, a week later, Stuart Brawley came to call, driving a new open carriage and a team of matching bays that pranced and stamped in harness before the house, as if anxious to be off.

"I've come to take you for a drive," he said, with his open, friendly smile. "As you can see, I have just acquired a new team and buggy, and I thought you might enjoy a brisk drive. We can stop at the village, if you'd care to visit the shops."

Marianna had been intending to help Mrs. Horner with a belated spring housecleaning, but a drive seemed much more attractive.

"I would be delighted, sir," she said, forgetting her resolve to keep him at a distance. "Just let me change my clothes. In the meantime Mrs. Horner will serve you some refreshments."

Stuart nodded and smiled, and Marianna, roused from her week-long lethargy, sped up the stairs to find a suitable outfit for a buggy ride.

She selected a dusty rose ensemble with a jacket top and smart bonnet. Getting into it, she found the skirt unaccountably tight. She must be getting fat, what with Mrs. Horner's cooking and lazing about as she had been. Starting tomorrow, she would start eating less and exercise more. She forced the waistband closed and buttoned it; it was a bit uncomfortable, but not unbearably so.

Marianna realized that she made a pretty picture as she swept down the staircase. She took care to pose prettily before she had fully descended. Now why had she done that, she scolded herself. She wanted to keep her relationship with Stuart Brawley strictly impersonal, so why did she wish to appear attractive for him? Habit, that was all, she decided, the habit of preening for a male.

The day was fine, with just a touch of chill in the air, and the horses seemed eager to stretch out. Stuart had some difficulty in holding them to a sedate trot and laughed as he sawed back on the reins. "Whoa there, you frisky devils! We have a lady with us. Restrain yourselves!"

Marianna, enlivened by the sun and the wind created by their speed, laughed aloud. "You needn't restrain them on my account, Mr. Brawley."

Stuart looked over at her; then with a glint in his eye, he loosened his hold on the reins, letting the horses set their own pace.

Soon they were racketing down the narrow dirt road at a speed that made it necessary for Marianna to cling to her bonnet with one hand and to the side rail with the other. It was grand, wild, and exciting, and perhaps a touch dangerous, and she felt more alive than she had in weeks.

The trees and bushes whipped by in a blur of brown and green, and Marianna forgot herself and whooped with delight. They sped past a two-storied brown house, and she caught a glimpse of white faces, two women, she thought, as they thundered by.

And then, with terrifying suddenness, the horses veered as a frightened animal scooted across the road. The buggy lurched sideways, tilting up on two wheels.

Marianna was aware of being propelled out of her seat, of flying through the air like a projectile, and of great fear as she began to fall toward the earth.

It was the last thing she remembered.

At a soft knock on his office door Ezekial Throag leaned back from his desk and called, "Come in!"

The door opened, and Benton, the counter clerk from downstairs, sidled in. Approaching Throag with a deferential air, he placed an envelope on the desk. "The mail just came, Mr. Throag. This is addressed to you, personal."

"Thank you, Benton." Throag dismissed him with a wave of his hand. "That will be all."

Benton bobbed his head and scurried out of the office. Throag did not open the envelope at once, but sat bouncing the envelope on the desk and reflecting on the status that had become his these six months past.

There had been one attempt to kill him, his first week in Southampton. A thug had rushed at him out of an alley while he was wending his way home from a tavern one night. A knife had glittered in the moonlight, as it arched in toward his guts. Even though slightly woozy from ale, Throag had reacted instantly. He seized the thug's wrist, twisted to one side, at the same time bent his attacker's arm up and in. Using his great strength to an advantage, he had buried the knife in the thug's belly, then brought it up, ripping brutally. The man screamed once, shrilly, and then Throag pushed him away. He strode on, leaving the man dying, his lifeblood staining the cobblestones.

The next morning Southampton seethed with rumors. There was never the slightest suspicion attached to Throag, and he never mentioned the incident to the Barths. Yet he let them know, in a subtle way, that *he* knew who had been responsible for the attempt on his life. They took the hint and did not initiate another attempt.

Shortly thereafter, the name of Ezekial Throag appeared on the sign out front—Barth, Barth & Throag, Shipping— and an office had been made available to him.

He had attacked his job with considerable enthusiasm, and through schemes devised by his ingenious mind, the firm's income had increased by thirty percent, and a substantial portion of that increase was pure profit.

Some of Throag's innovations were ethical, some were not, but whereas many of the brothers' shady schemes involved out-and-out criminality, Throag got around the law by using it to his advantage. He had long been familiar with maritime law, and he had applied himself to it assiduously since joining the firm; now he knew it as intimately as any maritime lawyer. After all, much of such law, in that particular time, was written for the benefit of shipowners, not the common seaman or the people who used shipping to serve their needs. In short, many of the laws were written with the profit motive in mind—profit to the shipowners—and a mind as clever as Throag's could manipulate it to his, and the Barths', advantage.

Aside from his increasing the company profits, Throag was pleased by another benefit—the employees of the firm knew who was responsible for the brighter profit picture, and they held him in awe because of that. This awe gave him a power akin to what he had wielded on the Outer Banks, and Throag loved power.

One fact about the power he had gained here pleased him immensely. On the Banks he had held sway over the wreckers through intimidation and fear. At the shipping company it had mainly come about through respect for the things he had accomplished. Oh, all the employees feared him to a degree, but lesser men always stood in awe of the powerful. And the fear, he thought, smiling coldly, also extended to the brothers. They, he knew, were absolutely terrified of him.

He had yet to exploit their fear, but he intended to, yes, indeed! In fact, his ultimate aim was somewhat grander than it had been in the beginning. In time, he intended to completely take over the shipping company.

Still smiling, he glanced at the envelope for the first time. His smile died as he saw the name of the sender—Rhys Carlin, the manhunter in his pay.

With trembling fingers he tore open the envelope and eagerly read the letter:

Ezekial Throag, Esquire:

The identity of the Harper woman's cohort was gratefully received. It at least gives me a starting point. My investigation has disclosed, through an eyewitness on the Boston docks, that one Phillip Courtwright was shanghaied on board the brig, Serena, nigh onto a year past. The brig's destination was the Orient. There is naught that I can do until she returns. Since the last known location of both Phillip Courtwright and the girl is Boston, I am at present residing here and will continue my investigation from this base.

As to the girl, Marianna Harper, the tidings are not cheerful. At present, I am at a dead end. I have spent these past weeks talking to everyone who had the least contact with the girl. Not a single person knows where she might have gone. There was a drayman, a man by the name of Thornton, who took the girl and her trunks to the Boston docks. I am confident that he knew of her destination, or at least what vessel she took from Boston. Unfortunately, by the time I had learned of this, the man had died, and if he knew, he failed to pass his knowledge on to anyone.

I have talked with crew members from a great many ships, but none would admit to seeing the Harper girl. As you are aware, a great many vessels come and go from Boston, to all points of the globe. I shall, of course, continue to question all ships and their crews. Hopefully, in time I shall come across the one that took the girl from Boston. At least, we do know that she took a ship, and did not leave by carriage or stage.

I will, of course, continue to pursue my investigation diligently. I am not a man to give up easily. Hope-

*fully, my next message to you, sir, will contain better
tidings.*

Yrs. sincerely, Rhys Carlin.

Muttering an oath, Throag crumpled the letter up and
sent it sailing across the room. Goddamn the girl! She was
more elusive than an eel. Already he had spent a small
fortune in search for her, and with scant results. Briefly he
toyed with the idea of giving up the hunt and devoting his
time to his business here. Also, he had a strong feeling that
Rose Lake was with child, *his* child. . . .

Knuckles rapped on the door. Throag leaned back, arranging his face in a stern expression. "Come in!"

It was Enoch Barth, carrying a letter in his hand. He
looked agitated. He waved the letter excitedly. "This just
came in the morning post! It's a letter from Peters, down on
the Banks. The scoundrel is demanding more of a cut of the
salvage for himself. Says if we don't agree, he'll just cut
himself loose from us and keep it all for himself."

Throag shrugged. "I fail to see much of a problem. Send
one of your bully boys down to reason with him. Break an
arm or a leg and tell him that's only a sample. If he kicks up
his heels again, he'll end up dead. That'll bring him around."

"I was thinking—" Enoch Barth coughed and averted his
gaze. "We were thinking, my brother and me, that perhaps
you'd like to go down there and take over again."

Throag laughed harshly. "You were thinking that, were
you? Don't tell me you don't like all that extra profit I'm
bringing to the company?"

"Well, of course we do, Ezekial, but—"

"No buts, Enoch. Now you listen to me." Throag leaned
forward, his hard gaze pinning the man. "So far as I'm
concerned, the Ezekial Throag of the Outer Banks never
existed. I'm quite content where I am, and if the pair of you
think I'm about to leave, disabuse yourselves. I can't stop
you from hoping, but if you ever broach the subject again,
you'll rue the day. Do I make myself clear?"

Enoch Barth backed a step, eyes darting about wildly.
"Yes, yes, I understand. Don't get angry, Ezekial. I didn't
mean anything."

Throag leaned back, his expression smoothing out. "Angry? Why, I'm not angry, Enoch. When I become angry, you will know it without a shadow of a doubt. Now, about Peters. Can you handle the problem, or shall I do it for you?"

The man bobbed his head, still pale of countenance. "I will handle it, be assured."

"Good," Throag said calmly. "If there is nothing else, Enoch, I am quite busy this morning."

Enoch Barth nodded and started to sidle out.

Throag let him get as far as the door before saying, "Enoch?"

Enoch Barth gulped. "Yes, Ezekial?"

"There is something else you should warn Peters about. There was never anything on paper between us, if you recall. You inform this fellow that if he ever again puts anything on paper to this firm, I will personally wring his neck. And destroy his letter, on the instant. Is that clear?"

"Clear, Ezekial." For a moment the man's gaze rested on Throag, and naked hate was apparent in the muddy eyes. Then, as if realizing he was giving himself away, a film seemed to snap down over his eyes, masking his expression, and he quickly scuttled out of the room.

Throag gave way to a rolling laugh, loud enough, he was sure, to be heard clearly by the departing Enoch Barth.

Still rumbling with laughter, he bent to his tasks. During the course of the day, several problems needing his personal attention cropped up. For supper he went up the street to the tavern, then returned to his office to finish his work.

Consequently, it was quite late when he returned to the Inn of the Rose. The windows were dark, with the exception of Rose's bedroom. As always, after besting one or the other of the Barth brothers, his lust was strong. At the top of the stairs he pushed open Rose's door without knocking. He was surprised to find her undressed and in bed.

He removed his coat and shirt as he crossed to the bed. Rose muttered and raised her head. Her face was pale, seemingly drained of blood, and her eyes were enormous.

She held up a hand, as if to fend him off. "No, please, Ezekial. I'm not well this night."

He was already out of his breeches, and he came down

on the bed on his knees. "You'll feel better, after," he said grinning cruelly. He reached for her.

She scooted across the bed, avoiding him. He started to reach for her again, but in moving she had thrown the covers back, and he saw blood spotting the sheets.

He stared at the blood spots, then up at her face. "What's wrong with you?"

Fear leaped into her eyes. "I'd rather not talk about it. I'll be fine in a few days."

He seized her arm and twisted it up behind her back. "You'll talk about it! Tell me, woman!"

"You're hurting me, Ezekial!" Her face contorted with pain. "All right, I'll tell you. I was with child."

He started to inform her that he already knew that, but he kept his lips sealed and tightened his grip. "What do you mean, *was?*"

"I went to a midwife! I couldn't bear a child, I'm not wed to you. The disgrace—"

"I would have wed you," he snarled, "if you had told me you were carrying my son."

She shook her head, tears leaking from her eyes now. "It's not only that. I'm too old to bear a child, especially for the first time. I could have died!"

A fury was building in Throag; so great was it that he was having trouble controlling it. Through gritted teeth he said, "How far along were you? How long, damn you!"

She wailed, "Going on three months."

"The sex of the child—what was it?"

She stared at him in bewilderment. "I don't understand."

"Don't be dense, woman! A boy or a girl?"

"It was a boy."

His son, the son to take Jude's place, was dead, and this bitch had murdered him! The rage exploded. He saw everything through a red mist, and the only thing he could really see was the exposed neck of the woman on the bed. Operating as though through a will of their own, his hands flew up and fastened like a vise around her throat. Her eyes glared with terror, and her body convulsed under him. Throag ground his thumbs into her neck, shutting off the scream about to erupt from her.

He squeezed and squeezed, until the thrashing of her body grew less and less, until finally she was still, blood suffusing her face, her tongue protruding. Still, Throag continued to squeeze. Finally the strength gave out in his hands, and he let go, sitting back.

For a long while he sat with his head hanging, his breath coming in gasps. Gradually sanity returned to him, and he raised his head, staring about, listening intently. He could remember very little about the time he was strangling her, but he was confident that she had made no outcry. He could hear nothing, no sounds of alarm, only the creakings of the old house.

He looked down into her contorted face. In a gloating whisper, he said, "You'll kill no more sons of mine, bitch! Would that it had been the Harper girl's neck between my hands as well, and I would have sent you both to hell!"

Over the past two weeks, Throag knew, his resolve to track down the killers of Jude had weakened somewhat, especially after he had begun to suspect that Rose was with child.

But now, with a second son murdered, he knew that he would never rest until Jude's killers were no more.

The question now was, how to deal with this situation? There was no thought of fleeing. He was solidly entrenched with the Barth firm, and a respected citizen of Southampton. ton. The hard-won respectability was now in jeopardy, and he would have to dispose of Rose's body so that not a breath of suspicion would come his way. His thoughts darted back to that other time, when his fury had gotten the better of him, and he had killed Anne Roberts; that time he had taken flight, but never again.

He forced himself to wait, sitting patiently on the edge of the bed, like a silent Buddha. He waited an hour, two hours, until after midnight. The town should be asleep, even the taverns were closed. Finally he stirred and crossed to the window to peer out.

A thick fog had rolled in. Good! He should be able to lug Rose's body to the sea and throw it in. Hopefully the tide would carry her body far out to sea, and she might never be found. Even if she was, the likelihood of suspicion falling on him was small.

Moving to the bed, he wrapped her body in the sheet she had blood-spotted, then lifted it easily to his shoulder. He made his way quietly down the stairs and out the door, into the white fog. There was no one in sight.

He moved down the walk and through the gate, then turned toward the waterfront.

Throag did not see the man across the street, hidden behind a tree. The man waited until Throag was almost swallowed up by the fog, then fell in behind, always staying far enough back not to be seen.

Chapter Thirteen

As consciousness returned, it brought pain; and Marianna longed to remain in the darkness, out of which she was rapidly ascending.

However, someone was speaking to her, nagging at her, attempting to get her to relinquish the pleasant state of unawareness; and she heard herself cry out petulantly, her voice sounding thin and childish in her ears.

"Come now, Mrs. Street! Open your eyes. That's a good girl. Wake up now. You have survived your fall."

The voice exhorting her was masculine and scratchy, and she slowly opened her eyes to see the whiskery face of Dr. Isaac White bending over her. Oh, dear! She had fallen into his hands, after all; and then the word, "fall," triggered her memory, and she cried out, this time in earnest, and tried to rise.

Dr. White's wrinkled hands held her down, and his usually dour face framed a meager smile. "There, there, my girl. Don't struggle now. Everything is all right. You are going to be just fine."

When Marianna had attempted to rise, a sharp pain had stabbed her stomach, causing her to gasp. If she was fine, why did she hurt so?

"I hurt!" she said accusingly.

The doctor made a clucking sound with his tongue against the roof of his mouth. "Why, I suppose you do, my girl," he said almost jovially. "You took a nasty spill, and you are rather badly bruised. But as I said, you will be all right.

There was nothing broken, and you should recover within a week or ten days. There is another thing, though—"

His countenance softened even more, and Marianna, in her pain and confusion, found his words incomprehensible. "What? What thing?"

"The baby," he said softly. "I could not save the baby, I'm sorry. You have miscarried."

As Marianna tried to absorb this bewildering piece of information, he went on, "But you will have other children. You are a healthy, strong young woman, built for childbearing. You will have another, I wager, within the year. Now, I want you to—"

Marianna heard no more. Her mind was on the phrase, "But you will have other children." *Children?* What on earth was he trying to say?

She stared up at him. "Doctor, what do you mean, you couldn't save the baby? What baby?"

He stopped in mid-sentence and stared down at her in astonishment. "You mean you didn't know?"

"Didn't know *what?*" she demanded. "Talk plain for once, will you? What are you talking about?"

The doctor looked nonplused. "Why, I am sorry, Mrs. Street. I naturally assumed that you knew. You were pregnant. With child. About three months into your term."

Marianna sank back against the pillows, trying to understand. She had been pregnant? She had been carrying a child?

"You really didn't know, did you?" Dr. White made the clucking sound again. "Well, I suppose it is not that unusual, a first child, and an inexperienced girl. Tell me, Mrs. Street, didn't you notice anything unusual about your, uh— your health? Didn't you notice that your, uh, cycle was not regular? Had you noticed no physical changes?"

Marianna's head was whirling. Physical changes? Cycle? And then suddenly she realized what he meant. Her monthly cycle had always been irregular, and so she had thought little of the fact that she had not been cursed for some time. And her sickness, the nausea; and yes, her breasts had been tender.

"I just didn't put it together," she said apologetically. "I thought it was something I ate, or a touch of the colic. . . ." She spread her hands. "I'm sorry."

Dr. White's stern face actually showed a genuine smile. "No need to apologize, my girl. It's the fault of our culture. No one bothers to prepare a young woman. No one tells her what to expect. They seem to believe that ignorance is the best policy. There was nothing you could have done, in any case. You would have no doubt gone for a buggy ride, even if your condition had been known to you. At three months it would still have been quite proper, so don't blame yourself. As I said, there will be other children."

Marianna nodded and placed her hand upon her stomach, which felt bruised and tender. There had been a child there—or the start of a child. Her child, and Adam's. All at once, she experienced an acute sense of loss, and tears came to her eyes.

The doctor appeared upset. "Now, now. It will be all right, I tell you. You will be fine. In a few weeks your spirits will revive. You will see. You will recover nicely."

In that particular moment Marianna wondered if she would ever feel normal again.

For almost three weeks, Marianna languished in her room, remaining in bed for the most of every day, needlessly pampering her body and spirits. She actually felt fine physically. Her bruises had stopped hurting within a few days, her black and blue spots were almost gone, and the bleeding had stopped. It was only in her mind that she felt unwell, missing the child that she had not known she carried, and blaming herself for its death. If she had not gone with Stuart . . . if she had not encouraged him to let the horses run . . .

Stuart called regularly, as did Lavinia, and even Mrs. Brawley came to call one afternoon. They were all very solicitous, seeming to believe that Stuart was in some way to blame. Marianna had to wonder how they would have felt if they had known about the baby. But of course they did not; that was something only she and Dr. White knew about. Strangely, Marianna had now come to like and trust the elderly physician, finding him truthful and outspoken, as she was herself. She had a suspicion that Mrs. Horner realized the truth, but it was a subject they never discussed.

Suddenly, one afternoon, she had had enough of mooning about. It was a fine day, and her body felt the need of some exercise. She had lost a baby, true, but there was no reason for her to spend the rest of her life drooping about. She must take up life where she had left off; make friends with the women of the island; involve herself in useful activities.

And from that day she put the tragedy behind her. She joined the Columbian Temperance Society and the Ladies Poetry Society. She even joined a group that met once a week to help one another make the complicated quilts that seemed to be the island women's pride—and Marianna hated sewing with an abiding passion.

She continued to see Stuart, Lavinia, and occasionally Mrs. Brawley, as she was invited to all the social functions at the Brawley house.

All in all, the time passed—not quickly, but it did pass. Soon it had been close to a year since Adam had sailed the *Viking Queen* out of Sag Harbor.

There had been one letter, delivered by a ship returning to Sag Harbor, a letter that spoke of a good catch, a profitable voyage, and of how much Adam missed her and longed to be with her.

The letter both comforted Marianna and made her unhappy. She of course treasured the words that Adam had written, and she slept with the letter beneath her pillow; but it also made her long for him and rekindled in her body the passions she had been keeping so carefully under control.

It was shortly after the letter arrived that she and Stuart had a disagreement, although that was probably not quite the word to use to describe it, she concluded.

Stuart had been a good friend to her; and without him, she was certain, the year of Adam's absence would have been indeed miserable. It hurt her that they now could no longer be quite the friends they had been.

It was not wholly Stuart's fault, Marianna fully realized. She was to blame as much as he, for she had allowed him to keep seeing her, using him in a way, wanting his company and his friendship, but not wanting to give him what he wanted in return. For in her heart she had known all along that he wanted much more from her than the platonic friendship she was prepared to give.

It was late afternoon, and Marianna and Stuart were returning from tea with Mrs. Timber, the wife of a prominent shipowner. The afternoon was hot, and Marianna was very much out of temper, for she had overheard something at the tea that made her furious.

She had been standing behind two women who were deep in conversation and unaware of her. Mrs. Clements, the elder of the two, was leaning toward the other woman and speaking very softly, but she had a nasal voice that carried, and Marianna could hear her words perfectly: "I wonder what Captain Street, poor man, will think when he returns home. She is in Mr. Brawley's company constantly, I understand. It's shameful, is what I say. A shame and a disgrace. Sets a bad example for the younger women."

The other woman, Mrs. Higgins, nodded eagerly. "Yes, shameful indeed. I've seen them often together, myself. But then, she's an outsider, and they never seem to know what's proper. Perhaps someone should speak to her, let her know that people are talking. Perhaps they are just friends, and she doesn't realize how it looks, them being together all the time, and her husband away, and all."

Mrs. Clements sniffed. "Oh, I dare say she knows what she's doing, right enough. *That* kind usually does! She was a tavern wench, didn't you know?"

Marianna hurried on, trembling with outrage. How *dare* they? How dare they speak of her in that fashion? And they said "everyone" was talking, so they evidently weren't the only ones. Hellfire and spit! They had a nerve!

She went in search of Stuart and demanded that he take her home at once.

And now, as they arrived at the house, after a silent ride during which Stuart gave her many quizzical glances but remained quiet, he asked if he might come in for a moment.

Marianna glared at him, and he answered her look with raised eyebrows. "Why the baleful glance, Marianna? What have I done? No man deserves the 'look that kills' without *some* explanation."

"Hellfire and spit!" she said under her breath, but apparently loud enough for Stuart to hear her.

He burst into laughter. "What did you say? You, Marianna, the perfect lady?"

"Not such a lady, according to some," she muttered. Then she gestured angrily. "Oh, come in! You might as well, the damage is already done."

"What in heaven's name are you talking about?" he asked, as he helped her down from the buggy seat.

"I'll tell you inside, after you've had a drink," she said briskly. "The gossiping old biddies!"

When they were inside and Mrs. Horner had served Stuart a glass of brandy and left them alone, he turned to Marianna. "Now, would you mind telling me what this is all about, Marianna? Why are you so upset?"

She studied him, trying to think how best to say what she had to say. "Pour me a brandy," she said harshly. "I need one as well."

Stuart raised his eyebrows but complied, pouring a finger of brandy into a small snifter and handing it to her.

Marianna took the glass and swirled the amber liquor around in the bottom, looking at the glass rather than meeting Stuart's gaze. She felt strangely reluctant to put it into words.

"Stuart?"

"Yes, Marianna?"

"Did you know that there is gossip going around about us, about you and me?"

She glanced up quickly, and he looked away and sighed. "Yes, I have heard a few remarks. But it doesn't mean anything. There are always those who take delight in gossiping about their neighbors."

Marianna slammed her glass down. "Well then, damnit, why didn't you tell me?"

Stuart, she saw, was startled by her vehemence and strong language, but she was past caring. "If you knew people were talking, why did you continue to see me? I'm a married woman!"

Stuart swallowed the remaining brandy in a gulp and moved to take her hands in his. "Because I wanted to keep seeing you, my dear, to be with you. You must know how important you are to me."

Marianna tore her hands away. "You've been a good friend, Stuart, and I value your friendship. I can't deny that, but they are hinting that we've been more than that to each other, more than friends. When Adam returns, what if he should hear the gossip? What will he think?"

She raised her glass and drained the contents, almost choking on the sudden jolt of strong liquor.

"Marianna," Stuart said softly. "You must know how I feel about you. You must know in your heart that those words they speak are true. I want you, my dear. I have since that very first moment on the Long Wharf."

In a single step he was next to her, and his arms were around her. She could smell the good male scent of him, the tobacco, bay rum, and brandy scent of him; and then his mouth was on hers, with a fierce demand that for a moment took her breath away. She did care for him and she was attracted to him. Being in his arms was pleasant and frightening, all at the same time. If it were not for Adam, she thought, she would be pleased at his embrace. But there *was* Adam; Adam, her husband, whom she loved with all her heart.

Placing her hands against Stuart's chest, she pushed him away far enough so that his mouth was torn from hers. But with his greater strength, he pulled her to him again and murmured above her ear. "Oh, Marianna, you don't know how long I've wanted to do this, how long I've wanted to hold you like this, to kiss you. My dearest Marianna."

Frightened now at his growing passion, she pushed against him again and pulled loose from his embrace. "Stuart, no! Please, you must stop this. It's wrong, wrong!"

Blind and deaf, he endeavored to embrace her once more. She did the only thing she could think to do. She slapped his face sharply.

The sound of the slap was loud in the sudden stillness. and Stuart stopped as if once again aware of himself. His hand came up, his fingers caressing the redness on his cheek where she had slapped him. His lips tightened, and his eyes were both angry and sad.

"So that's the way it is," he said slowly.

Marianna was immediately contrite, all her anger gone. What had she done to this man, this good, decent man? Belatedly, she realized that she had led him on, unwittingly leading him to believe that she would give to him something she had no intention of giving.

"Oh, Stuart," she said brokenly, "I am *so* sorry! I never meant to hurt you. I care for you, I really do, and in any other circumstances, things might be different. But I *am* married, Stuart. I made a marriage vow, and I take it seriously. I could not betray Adam. If I've led you to believe otherwise, I'm dreadfully sorry. You must understand that."

Anxiously she studied his face, trying to gauge his reaction. "You do understand?"

Slowly the look of anger left his face, leaving only the pain. "Yes, I understand. I suppose that I just didn't want to recognize the truth." He sighed. "And it's I who should beg forgiveness. It won't happen again."

He turned to go, and Marianna, realizing that things between them would never be the same, felt tears burn her eyes. "Goodbye, Stuart," she said softly.

He picked his hat up from the table. "Goodbye, Marianna."

When he was gone, she let the tears come. Where was Adam now, now that she needed him? Where was her husband, for whom she had just driven away her best friend?

She could not know that at that very moment Adam's ship was approaching Sag Harbor and that in the town the cry of "Ship in the bay!" had already gone up.

Two hours later, an out-of-breath youngster came knocking at her door to tell her excitedly that her husband's ship had come home.

Marianna felt as nervous as a new bride. It had been fourteen months since she had seen Adam; and although many of the wives would consider such a voyage a short one, to her the time had seemed endless.

Following the youngster knocking at her door, there had been another message, sent by Adam's signalman to the harbor at Shelter Island, that Adam would be home by nightfall, and now Marianna awaited his arrival in an extreme state of anxiety and longing.

Mrs. Horner had prepared a fine supper, which was keeping warm in the kitchen, and Marianna was dressed in her most attractive home wear—a pale, pink peignoir over a lacy camisole and petticoat, trimmed in pink ribbon. A pink ribbon also tied back her dark curls and heightened the color of her cheeks.

She had planned to wait for him in their bedroom, posed invitingly in the large upholstered chair; but when Adam finally arrived, when she heard his footsteps on the walk and heard the sound of his voice greeting Mrs. Horner, she could not contain herself and came flying down the stairs to greet him.

"Adam!" she shouted, as she raced down the stairs, holding her skirts up with one hand, so she would not fall. "Oh, darling!"

She could see him looking up at her, face gray and slack with fatigue; and then his eyes lit up, and he held out his arms, a blaze of great pleasure transforming his features. "Marianna!"

Almost crying, she threw herself into his arms, clutching the warm solidity of him, burying her face in his waistcoat as he squeezed her mightily and murmured her name over and over.

He held her close, her feet off the floor, and swung her once around. "My love, I am so glad to be home. I've missed you so."

Their joyous reunion was interrupted by Mrs. Horner's loud cough. "Welcome home, Captain. Will you be wanting your supper served now, madam?"

Marianna turned to her, smiling brilliantly, eyes misted with tears of pure happiness. "Oh, yes, please. In our room, as I requested."

"Very well, madam." Mrs. Horner's own face held a benign smile.

But Adam and Marianna did not hear her, for they were too taken up with themselves, with each other. Marianna felt as if her hands must again memorize the shape and size of him, the feel of him; and Adam embraced her as if he must make up in one moment the deprivation he had experienced for those long months.

Her arms around his neck, he put his arm under her, scooped her up, and began to mount the stairs.

In the privacy of their bedroom, he began to pluck at her clothing, but she demurred, laughing. "Not yet, my darling. I am as eager as you, but Mrs. Horner will be bringing us supper in a moment. I thought you would be hungry."

Shaking his head, he pulled her close again. "And so I am," he murmured into her hair, "but not just for food."

At that moment Mrs. Horner knocked on the door, and Marianna stepped back demurely, trying unsuccessfully to straighten her clothing. "Come in," she called.

A blushing Mrs. Horner, eyes lowered, bustled in with a huge tray, covered with a large white napkin. "Shall I set it out, sir?"

"No, thank you, Mrs. Horner," Adam replied. "We will serve ourselves when we're ready. You may have the rest of the evening free. We will have no further need of you this night."

As soon as the door had closed behind the housekeeper and the sound of her footsteps could be heard going down the stairs, Adam again swept Marianna into his arms and drew her with him toward the bed.

"Godalmighty, sweet, how I've dreamed of this moment! You have no idea. Out there alone at sea, alone in my bunk, thinking of you here. . . ."

For the first time Marianna knew true pride in her womanhood; his confession that he had missed her and longed for her gave her spirits a tremendous lift.

Adam groaned and bent his head, his lips fastening upon hers with a demanding hunger that she could feel clear down to her soul. Eagerly she rose to meet him with her own hunger.

His hands were on her body, touching, demanding, pulling away the clothing, baring her satiny skin to his sea-roughened hands.

The touch of those hands on her flesh sent a blaze of desire through her, and her own hands became busy with the large buttons and rougher fabric of his sea clothing. Grunting impatiently, Adam helped her, quickly divesting himself of his garments, and then coming to her with his hot, hard-muscled body, his organ already upright and amazingly rigid.

As she had on their first encounter, Marianna wondered if she could accommodate him, and the thought excited her even further. As he moved to enter her, she opened fully, surging to meet him, relishing the pleasure and the pain as he penetrated her.

And then all thought and reason fled, as they moved in unison and cried out in that loving struggle that binds a man and a woman together.

Because of his long abstinence, Adam climaxed too quickly for Marianna to do the same; but in a very short time he was fully aroused again, and this time a slower, sweeter coupling brought Marianna to that delicious peak of pleasure, that spasm of bliss that left her weak and gasping, completely fulfilled.

It was very late when Mrs. Horner's excellent supper was remembered, and then they fell upon it with ravenous appetite.

In the days that followed Marianna thought of almost nothing but her husband.

After the long separation, they could not get enough of each other, and Marianna was sure that they shocked the faithful Horners with their constant touching, kissing, and other, more intimate liberties they took with one another. They were like newlyweds, and Marianna wondered if that was one of the attractions of being a sea captain's wife. Would they always experience a renewal of their love after one of Adam's lengthy voyages?

Two weeks passed before Marianna would accept any social invitations; and even then she did so reluctantly and only because Adam insisted that they must be polite.

Since men were always in short supply on Shelter Island, the invitations were many, and Marianna and Adam attended many luncheons, teas, and suppers at various homes on the island, as well as Sag Harbor, during the next few weeks.

Captain Jack Hammond was also in port, and he and his wife sent over an invitation to supper at their home on a Sunday. This was one invitation Marianna was delighted to accept, as she was fond of both Captain and Cora Hammond and looked forward to seeing them.

The evening started out well enough, with pleasant conversation and a fine supper. It was after they had eaten that the conversation turned inevitably to the sea, and whales, and thus to the men's next voyages.

Marianna, when the conversation took a sea turn, felt her nerves begin to tighten. The past few weeks had been so perfect. She had been so involved with Adam's loving presence that she had not even allowed herself to contemplate the future, and certainly not Adam's next voyage.

"Your last trip was short, Adam," Captain Hammond remarked as they sat on the porch enjoying the breeze and a cooling drink.

"Aye," Adam agreed. "Dame Fortune smiled again. For several voyages now, I have filled my hold in little more than a year. The next journey will probably be a long one."

"What do you men consider a long voyage?" Marianna inquired. Her voice was tart, she noticed, and she attempted to relax and speak in a normal voice.

"Oh, two years, maybe even more, Marianna," Captain Hammond replied, lighting his heavy briar pipe. "You can be out for months, you know, without sighting whales. It's a strange, chancy business."

Marianna turned to the captain's wife. "Mrs. Hammond, tell me, in all of your married life, how much of the time has your husband been home?"

Cora Hammond sighed wistfully. "My dear, I hesitate to tell you, for fear it will dishearten you, but the captain and I have been married for fifteen years, and he has spent with me approximately three years of that time. I sat down one day and figured it up."

Marianna swallowed hard. Cora Hammond sounded sad but resigned. How had she managed? How had she coped? Marianna had to know. "How did you—? I mean, how did you keep from going—" She stopped, too embarrassed to continue.

Cora Hammond laughed. "How did I keep from going mad or from leaving my husband and running off with the first man who would have me? I don't know, child. I honestly don't know."

Marianna suddenly found that she was the focus of all eyes: Captain Hammond's quizzical and wise, Adam's questioning, and Cora Hammond's sympathetic.

This scrutiny upset her, but she was doggedly resolved that she would have her say. Something had been in her mind for some time now—the fact that some wives of whaling captains sailed with their men, or so she had heard.

She tried to appear unconcerned. "I have heard that, sometimes, wives go with their captain husbands on whaling expeditions, even wives with children. Is that true?"

Captain Hammond exchanged a quick look with his wife. "Yes, Marianna, that is true," Cora Hammond said slowly, "but it is a hard life, and one for which few women are suited. I, myself, tried once to sail with Jack, but I proved to be a very bad sailor and was always seasick. I was miserable the whole time. By the time we reached the islands, I weighed only seventy pounds, and it was necessary to put me ashore. Jack sailed on without me, and it took me more than a month to recuperate before I was up to returning home on another ship."

"But I don't suffer from seasickness," Marianna said defiantly. "I never have."

Adam was staring at her, face creased in a scowl. "Do you mean that you wish to sail with me?"

"Yes," she said, lowering her gaze. "I suppose that is just what I *do* mean." She looked up into his eyes. "Adam, I can't bear it when you're away! You say that this last one was a short voyage, but it seemed like an eternity to me. I don't think I can abide being married to you for only part of the time, and such a small part it is. I'll die, I know it!"

Captain Hammond and his wife looked away in embarrassment, and Adam shifted uncomfortably. He said distantly, "Marianna, I hardly think this is the time to discuss the subject."

"Of course," she said quickly, suddenly conscious of how emotional she had become, yet feeling relief that she had brought it out into the open. She turned to the Hammonds. "Please forgive me for bringing it up now. It is not your problem."

Cora Hammond placed her hand on Marianna's. "Don't be silly, child. It's a problem that all of us who are married to seafaring men have, although admittedly we each must find our own solution to it. May you do so as well."

Marianna smiled and said no more, but she had made up her mind. She was going with Adam when next he sailed, and nothing was going to change her decision.

On the way home Adam was strangely quiet and cool toward her, and this annoyed her more than a little.

True, she had dared to discuss a personal matter in front of friends, yet they were good friends and had not appeared to be in the least shocked or disturbed. Was it that Adam did not want her on his ship, did not want her to go with him? She had to know.

They were in their room preparing for bed when she turned to him from the dressing table where she was brushing her hair. "Adam, you seem out of sorts with me. Is it because I want to sail with you?"

He shook his head, but did not answer. He was seated in the upholstered chair, with the reading lamp burning, and the lamp highlighted the planes and angles of his face, showing his strong good looks to advantage.

Marianna felt her heart swell with love. "Darling, please answer me. If you *are* angry, tell me what it is. I can't do anything about it if you won't tell me what it is."

"I told you, I am not angry," he said, but his voice was distant.

This was enough to arouse Marianna's temper, and she slammed down the brush, glaring at him in the mirror. "Hellfire and spit, Adam! What kind of an answer is that? You say one thing, and your attitude says another. Can't you at least be honest with me?"

He looked at her severely, which made her apprehensive, for usually when she used profanity, he was merely amused.

"All right, Marianna, I'll tell you, since you keep on about it. I am not angry, but I am upset over something I have heard, in fact over several things that I have heard, the last from Jack Hammond, just today."

He paused, and Marianna said impatiently, "Well? Pray continue. What did you hear?"

Adam spoke slowly and did not look at her. "I told Jack that I had been hearing talk, certain rumors going round since my return, and I asked him if he thought they were true."

Marianna felt a chill spread through her. She faced him, trying to hide her dismay. She knew the substance of the rumors. Still, she managed to keep her voice steady. "What are the rumors you've heard?"

He fixed his gaze upon her. "Several people have told me that, in my absence, you have been seeing a great deal of a certain Stuart Brawley. In fact, I was told that you were frequently in his company and that he showed every sign of being taken with you."

Marianna kept her face expressionless. "And what did Captain Hammond tell you?"

"Jack told me that it was true, that you had been in Brawley's company, but it is his opinion, and his wife's, that you and Brawley are friends, nothing more."

"And did you believe him?"

"I'm not sure what I believe, but it's sure as hell not a thing a man likes to hear about his wife, when he has been away for over a year."

"That year was hard on me, too, you know," she said tartly. "Why didn't you come directly to me when you first heard these—rumors? Why didn't you ask me if they were true?"

He looked down at his hands. "Perhaps I was afraid," he said in a soft voice. "Afraid of what you'd say."

Marianna ached to go to him, to take him in her arms, but she made herself sit quietly. There was one more thing she had to know. "Will you believe me when I tell you that there was nothing between us but friendship, at least as far as I was concerned?"

Now Adam looked up, his gaze searching. "Yes, I believe you, Marianna."

Marianna let her breath go with a sigh. "Well, that is

very wise of you, for it is the truth. And while we are speaking truth, I am honor bound to tell you something else, something I have not wanted to mention since it might have spoiled your homecoming. When you left, I was with child."

Adam started and looked at her in disbelief. "With child?"

"Yes. I miscarried, due to an accident, at three months."

Adam was still staring at her blankly, and then one expression after another washed across his face, with sympathy winning out. "You poor girl! And you had to bear it all alone."

"Dr. White tended me, and did it very well, but I must tell you one more thing so that there may be no secrets between us." She drew a deep breath. "The accident that brought about the miscarriage was in Stuart Brawley's buggy." She held up her hand. "It was no fault of his. Foolishly, I encouraged him to let the horses run, but I had no idea I was carrying a baby, Adam. I swear!"

She watched his face closely as she spoke. Adam was a fair man, but she knew enough about men to realize that all this might be hard for him to accept.

For an extended time an inner struggle was mirrored on his face, but in the end he nodded and looked up at her. "I believe you. You are my wife, my one and only love, and I love and trust you with my life. And because I do, I will take you with me when I go to sea again. There will be problems, and perhaps trouble with the men, but I can see that it is cruel, and perhaps foolish of me, to leave you alone for all those long months. At least at sea we will be together. You are not as docile and accepting as the other wives." He smiled with an effort. "But then I knew that when I married you. I dare say it's a part of your charm."

Marianna felt her face break wide in a smile. Thank God! Was there ever such an understanding man? She was the most fortunate of women.

Uttering a glad cry, she hurried to him, and Adam enfolded her in a bone-crushing hug. When he took her a few minutes later, he did so as if to possess her utterly, as if he wanted her to know that she was his forever.

Part Three

1845:

At Sea

Chapter Fourteen

MARIANNA'S journal:

Sept. 25, 1845: On this day, my husband, Captain Adam Street, sailed from Sag Harbor on a whaling voyage. However, this time there will be no tears from me, for I am sailing with him.

Although I well realize that life at sea will have its difficulties and discomforts, none, I am certain, could compare with the torture of being left alone for months and even years, wondering how my husband is faring, and praying for his safe return.

The day began early, and we sailed with the morning tide. It has been a full and exciting day, and now, as darkness falls, I take pen in hand to write this journal so that I may have a permanent record of this voyage and all that occurs.

The voyage began not entirely happily, for early in the day, when my husband called the crew together so that he might lay down the rules and regulations of the ship, he used that opportunity to introduce the men to me.

Some of the men were polite enough; but it was clear, at least to me, that many of them were displeased by the presence of a woman aboard ship. Adam had warned me that this might be so, for many of the men are superstitious and cling to the old myth that it is bad luck to have a female on board a ship; but despite this warning, I must admit that I found it hurtful when some of the men looked away from me and muttered what surely must have been disparaging remarks beneath their breaths.

Adam has told me to take no heed of it, and that they will eventually become used to having a woman aboard. I am sure he is right. Still, it was a jarring note in an otherwise perfect day.

Our quarters, which I recall from my previous short trip on the *Viking Queen,* are quite comfortable. In addition to the captain's cabin, there is another smaller cabin, which my darling Adam says that I may use for my own and arrange it as I see fit.

I have brought with me a potted geranium, a gift from Mrs. Horner, and a kitten, given me by Lavinia Brawley. The kitten is dark, with a white mask and boots, and I shall call her Bandit, as she shows signs of a temperament not unsuited to such a calling.

At supper, my first meal on the voyage, I was somewhat surprised to find that we were served much the same food that we might have supped on at home. Adam warns me that such will not always be the case; but I did notice that aboard ship there are several pigs and a number of chickens, all surely destined for our table.

At Mrs. Horner's behest, I have taken along a large chest filled with tinned delicacies, to eke out our rations, should they become low.

I am looking forward to our first night on board, for as I recall, the cabin bed is suspended upon some kind of device that lets it swing free of the pitching of the ship.

My husband calls to me now that it is time to retire, and so I close this willingly, until tomorrow.

Sept. 28, 1845: Have had three very rugged days. I did not think I would, but I succumbed to seasickness, a dreadful ailment that makes you unwilling to live and too miserable to die.

But today has dawned clear and fair, a pleasant breeze and just warm enough to be comfortable. I went on deck early, to take the air and to view the sea in another aspect. One would never suspect, seeing her so sparkling and calm, the treachery that lurks in her bosom. Everything is clean and fresh, and the vista is unmatched. No wonder so many choose a sailor's life! Although it is a life of hardship, there is also romance and adventure.

Oct. 5, 1845: Flying fish were all about the ship this morning, and the steward prepared one for my breakfast. Very nice, rather like a fresh herring. We have a very good steward, but have had rather bad luck with the cooks, of which we have had two in almost as many weeks. The first did not like being in the galley, as he claimed it made his head ache; and the present one has a hurt arm, which makes it difficult to perform his duties. Still, I suppose I am fortunate, since I dislike all household tasks, particularly cooking, that they do not call upon me, for no woman is allowed in the galley. I count my blessings!

This afternoon we sighted a school of porpoises, and several were taken. The meat looks much like beef. Oil is contained in the skin, which the men will boil out, they say, tomorrow. I must confess that I was somewhat upset at seeing the porpoises killed, as they are such attractive creatures. Animals, Adam assures me they are. They have such intelligent eyes and a perpetual smile upon their faces. Some of the meat is to be fried for supper, but I do not know if I shall be able to partake of it.

Oct. 10, 1845: Spoke the ship today, which proved to be the *Eagle*, commanded by Captain Elias Barlowe, bound from Philadelphia for Buenos Aires. She is a clipper ship, and very beautiful. Adam tells me of the custom called "gamming," which is visiting between ships, or rather between the captains of the ships, and their families, if these be aboard. We did not have time for a visit with the *Eagle*, but Adam has promised me that later there will be other ships and that we will indulge in this pastime. Truly, I was not disappointed, as I am still very pleased to have my husband to myself. After being without him for so long, it is pure pleasure to have him with me each night. His days, of course, must be shared with his work, but since we have not yet sighted whales, he still has considerable time for me.

The men caught another porpoise yesterday, and some of

its meat was cooked for supper and some made into sausages. I ate some of the fried meat at supper but kept thinking of the porpose's smiling face, and could not down more than a mouthful. The sausages, however, tasted much like pork sausages, and I was able to forget their derivation. Also at supper was a delicacy that I found quite tasty; a large pumpkin with a round piece cut out of the top, through which to remove the seeds and the insides, then filled with stuffing, the cap put on again, and stewed. It was served whole, with the stem in the center of the little cap.

Oct. 15, 1845: This morning we sighted whales! My husband went aloft with his glass to determine what kind they were. He thought they were sperm, but they were too far away to be certain, and they soon went down—sounding, it is called—staying down a good while, during which we had breakfast, keeping a man on the masthead, which they always do during the day.

When breakfast was just finished, we heard the cry, "There blows!", and all rushed above decks. Now the whales were very close, and Adam said there was no mistake. They were sperm whales.

Immediately the boats were lowered, and the men rowed strongly toward the whales. The creatures were enormous, and I must confess that the sight of them filled me with awe and fear. Even so, it is a thrilling sight. The boats, and the men, looked so small and helpless arrayed against them. Adam was in the front of one of the boats, and his first and second mates in the front of the others. The sea was growing somewhat rough, and I watched the scene with my heart in my throat, as they say.

Adam's boat was heading toward one of the monsters, the largest, and as the whale turned, I saw his huge flukes. He was a formidable sight, indeed!

The whales then moved away, slowly, with our boats following them. Sometimes the huge beasts would sound, going down and staying down a considerable amount of time, and then surfacing in another place entirely. The sun was very hot, and much time passed, but I called for my parasol and stood watching, for I wanted to see everything there was to see.

Aboard ship they placed signals on the masthead so that the men in the boats might know where the whales were, for many times they lie very low in the water and are not able to be seen from the small boats.

After a considerable time, the first mate's boat rowed very near the biggest whale, and the harpooner sank his weapon into the whale's back, after which the first mate, Mr. Karnes, set his own lance. The whale turned and heaved, in apparent pain, and I found it a disturbing sight.

Even at a distance, I could see the water stain red as the creature's huge bulk rolled in the roughening sea. I felt a great feeling of sadness that something so huge and grand should have to die to allow us to earn our livelihood, yet I must tell myself that it is the way of the world and is necessary.

After the whale was dead, the other boats joined Mr. Karnes's in towing the creature to the ship. It was a strange sight, those three small boats, strung together with rope, pulling that great bulk through the sea.

I hurried to the side of the ship to see him when he was made fast, and he looked gigantic to me. They say he will make abut sixty barrels of oil, which they tell me is good, as the sperm whale is not so large as a right whale, which will often yield as much as two hundred barrels. I am determined to watch the entire process by which the creature is rendered into oil and whalebone.

When my husband came aboard, he set me in his boat so that I might have a good view of all that transpired.

When they had secured the whale to the side of the *Viking Queen*, I could see the whale very well. It was long, shiny, and mouse-colored, with white spots on the belly. There are ridges and scars all over its back, which Adam tells me is caused by fighting.

Although the creature is not especially good to look upon, lacking beauty in shape, its tail and flukes are handsome. There does not seem to be much form to the head, which is large, rather flat, with a very large mouth and small eyes. I saw no ears, but Adam assures me that there are such. He says that their hearing is very acute, for they can hear the boats before they get to them. The jaw, actually, is frightful, for it looks capable of taking in a complete whaleboat, men and all. Adam asked me if I wished to stand in the mouth, but I shuddered and refused. I was as close today as I care to be.

Watching the cutting in, it seemed to me that this takes as much courage as did going after the whale in the boats. The sea was growing quite rough, but a young man with a safety rope tied about his middle, went right over the side and onto the body of the whale, where he hooked a stout rope that was made fast to the whale's jaw. This then was made fast up above by means of ropes and tackles.

Then two stages, being platforms of planks, were lowered so that they hung just above the whale's body, and men went down with spades and other cutting implements to slice away the blubber in long strips, which were then lifted by use of the hook, to the deck. These strips are huge, weighing, Adam tells me, as much as 2,300 pounds. These strips are drawn up by the tackle, as the whale turns, much like you would peel an enormous fruit.

It is an awesome and somewhat upsetting spectacle, as there is much blood and stench, and the water below swarms with sharks. The air above is filled with shrieking gulls, and the men work furiously, covered with blood and grease. It is, I think, much like a scene from hell, and not a pretty sight to watch.

I found a handkerchief, soaked it in cologne, and held it over my mouth and nose. I continued to watch until the last strip of blubber had been peeled from the giant carcass and taken to the try works, where it will be boiled out tomorrow. I have resolved that I will watch this also, no matter how unpleasant it may be, for I wish to know all the facets of my husband's trade.

Oct. 16, 1845: Today I watched as they minced the huge strips of blubber, first cutting them into what they refer to as "horses," and then into smaller pieces, called "Bible leaves," although I cannot think why.

These pieces are put into the try pots, huge iron kettles, where they are boiled until the oil is rendered out. The oil is then put into a cooking pot and, finally, into barrels.

The heat is intense, and the smell fearsome, in the try works. I am much amazed at the attitude of the men, which seems cheerful enough, even though they are soaked with oil and blood and must work like madmen. I am also impressed by my husband. On shipboard I see him in a different light. Here he is the utmost authority, Godlike in his position. Each day brings grave decisions, which may involve life or death, and in addition, he must mediate arguments and differences between the men. It would seem to me a very difficult task, but he does it with seeming ease and authority. He is a good captain, and the men appear to respect him. I do believe that they are even getting used to me!

Oct. 23, 1845: We sighted whales again today, right whales, and have taken two, despite a rough sea and two stoven boats. We almost lost the second mate, as well, but he is recovering now, with naught but a broken arm.

Adam says that we are very fortunate, for we have taken so many whales that the men have been kept busy cutting in, or trying, for many days in a row.

I no longer watch the bloody process, although I do watch the hunt because I fear for Adam and cannot abide being below with the knowledge of what is going on.

As I have set down earlier, I have a greater respect for my husband, after watching him command his ship and crew; yet I must confess that I find his trade a bloody business, and cannot help but wish that he were in another profession.

Oct. 30, 1845: Spoke the ship today, which proved to be the *Reliance*, out of New Bedford. Her captain, Amos Carter, is well-known to my husband, and both of our ships lay to so that we might have a gam.

Adam said that she was a lady ship, meaning that the captain's wife is on board, which was happy tidings to me, as I have not seen another woman since our voyage began.

I was lifted aboard the *Reliance* in a gamming chair, which is a kind of armchair suspended upon ropes. The chair is used because they say that a woman could not possibly climb the ladder with skirts, for she might show her ankle. Hellfire and spit! I could hardly keep my laughter inside, thinking of the days when I could have scrambled up that ladder with the best of them. I wonder if I still could, or if the ladylike life I have been leading has softened me.

At any rate, being a lady now, I rode the chair cheerfully and came on board the *Reliance*, where I met Mrs. Carter and her two children, a boy of five and a girl of two years, as well as a lady companion. This is their second season out from home on this voyage. Mrs. Carter told me that she loves the life at sea and has been sailing with her husband for some ten years. She seems not to mind the killing and the processing of the whales, and is very knowledgeable on the subject.

We had a nice visit, and it was very pleasant talking to another woman. The children were well-behaved, and the little one, in particular, is enchanting, with huge blue eyes and round pink cheeks. The sight of her made me miss the child that I lost. I really think that I would like to have another. It is quite common, I gather, for women to take their children to sea with them. They usually go ashore to bear them but are soon back aboard the ship again, and they seem to fare quite well.

When we left the *Reliance*, we did so bearing gifts, for Captain Carter presented me with a small pot of honey-comb, and Mrs. Carter gave me a dozen oranges, which they had taken aboard on the islands. We had taken them a paper of almonds and raisins from my own stores.

Nov. 3, 1845: A terrible thing happened today; or I should say, two things, actually. The day began with the first mate awakening my husband just after dawn and telling him that there was a large whale in sight. Adam went on deck and had the boats lowered, while I returned to sleep for a short while.

By the time I was up and dressed, I heard the first mate's

voice on deck, talking to my husband. I had been told earlier by the steward that the mate's boat was fast to the whale, and so I was alarmed, for I knew that something must have happened.

I was just about to go above decks when Mr. Karnes came into the cabin. He was soaking wet, and his face was very pale. He told me that Joseph, his harpooner, was gone. Adam had come into the cabin behind him and now gave him some brandy to warm him. Mr. Karnes was very upset and told us that when they had hauled up to the whale, after making fast to it, and when the mate had gone forward to kill it, the whale had come under the boat, tipping it to one side until it half filled with water. It righted again, but several of the men, out of fear, had jumped into the water, then turned, catching onto the side of the boat, causing her to capsize. One of the other boats was near and picked up the men, except for Joseph, who got fouled in the line and went down with the whale. A few minutes later the whale surfaced, dead, and the men got him, but found poor Joseph fast in the line, it being wound around him several times. He was very bruised, the first mate said, and they buried him in the sea.

I could not keep the tears from my eyes. I knew of Joseph, and he was much respected as an excellent steerer and harpooner, albeit he was not much more than a lad. He was a happy young man, always with a ready smile, and it is a wrench to think of him now cold and dead in the sea and to imagine how his poor mother will feel when she hears the sad news. It seems a rough and lonely way to die, and yet I cannot find it in me to blame the great whale, who only fought for his life, a thing we will all do when in danger.

But this was not the only sad occurrence this day, for later, another whale was sighted, a large cow in company with her calf. When she was sighted, I asked Adam what would happen to the baby when the mother whale was killed. He looked at me kindly but told me that the calf would be killed also, although it would not bring in much oil. I am afraid that I was short with him, for I was still considerably upset by the other events of the morning. I asked him to spare the mother and calf, or at least the calf, but Adam refused. Without the mother the baby would die, he said, and that, after all, our business here was taking whales.

I left him and went below decks, and as I write this, my temper is not much improved. Today, I have seen the harsh and ugly side of life at sea, and I find that it has shattered some cherished illusions.

Nov. 26, 1845: This morning dawned cold, stormy, and rough. I have had a recurrence of seasickness and kept to my bunk. The sea is so wild that nothing in the cabin is safe, and our belongings, those that are not tied or bolted down, are thrown about, willy-nilly.

Adam is above decks, working with the men, to get us round Cape Horn. I cannot say that I like the weather in this part of the world.

Dec. 3, 1845: Have had a continuation of the bad weather and are still in the same position we were in five days ago. It seems impossible to me that it is summer here now. I should hate to have to experience their winters! Also, the days are very long, and growing longer. It is odd to be able to read late into the evening without lamplight. Adam is somewhat discouraged by our lack of progress, and the men are unhappy as well. I hope that soon the weather will break and allow us to get round this devilish point of land, with its wicked seas and strange, light nights.

Dec. 10, 1845: Since Thanksgiving was spent attempting to make our way around the Horn, today we celebrate it belatedly. We have much to be grateful for. Yesterday we finally rounded Cape Horn and entered the broad Pacific; and this morning the weather has calmed, and we again make good speed.

The cook (our third, the one with the hurt arm being replaced by still another, one who finally seems to know something of his craft) has prepared an excellent supper, one which would not suffer by comparison with any table at home. We had no turkey, but did not miss it for the abundance of other good victuals. There was stuffed roast chicken, potatoes, turnips, onions, stewed cranberries, pickled cucumbers and beets, and a fine plum duff with brandy sauce. For tea, I prepared a tin of preserved strawberries and cut a fruitcake from my store in the cabin. We all are very thankful to be past the Cape and heading into calmer waters. I have even forgiven Adam, although I still feel some annoyance over his behavior.

Dec. 11, 1845: Saw a ship today, which we passed, but did not speak her. We are still traveling slowly, as there is a calm. There was a fair wind for a few hours, but it faded. Adam is very anxious to be on our way, for he says this is only wasted time.

Saw a school of porpoises this afternoon, and as the crew hurried forward preparing to strike them, one of the men frightened the chickens, which were loose on deck. One of the chickens, the big brown one, flew overboard. As soon as the chicken touched the water, the sea birds (goonies and mallemucks) dove down at her and killed her. Despite the fact that she was just a chicken, the incident depressed me.

Dec. 20, 1845: Saw Maus Afuera this morning, and Adam decided not to touch, as the wind was not fair, and he said that it would take more time than we could afford to lose.

The sight of land was very welcome, and as I gazed at those tall mountains, so beautiful from the ship, I longed to be ashore, if only for an hour. They say the island abounds with goats and that fresh fish is plentiful. The men say that they would welcome such fare, for our supplies are growing less diversified the longer we are at sea.

The sunsets are amazing here, and at night I have never seen a sky so studded with stars. What Adam tells me are the Magellanic clouds, are also to be seen, two clusters of stars that resemble two white clouds. It is as if nature spreads all her wonders here for us to enjoy.

Dec. 22, 1845: Saw a ship today, off the weather beam. The crew lowered for blackfish, without success.

This afternoon we spoke the ship *Bridgit,* and her master, a Captain Howland, and his first mate, Mr. Bruther, came aboard. They brought a large turtle to be killed for meat. They say it is very tasty, and it is true that we could do with some fresh meat. They also brought me a small basket of feather flowers, which are most attractive.

Later this afternoon we sighted whales, but were not able to make contact. I did not admit it, but was secretly glad. I am growing to hate the bloody process of whale killing. It is foolish of me, I know, for it is the way my husband makes his living, and mine, but although my mind may agree with his point of view, my heart, and my stomach, have another viewpoint entirely.

Dec. 23, 1845: Sighted sperm whales this morning and took two, at the cost of two stoven boats. I stayed below most of the day to avoid the sights and smells of processing. I used the opportunity to do some ironing, which I find an unpleasant chore, but at least it passes the time. The new cook, a black man of some years, has made me some excellent starch, which I have long needed. At least our clothing will be crisp and fresh, although I confess that I wish there were someone else aboard to see to the doing of it.

In two days it will be Christmas, but I feel little joy or anticipation. I have brought with me some presents for Adam and the mates, so there will be something under the tree. But that is foolish, for there will be no tree! Still, it is something to look forward to, for I am growing more and more bored with each passing day. Adam is busy now above decks much of the time, and when he is in the cabin, he is often occupied with his papers, books, and charts.

At times like that, I think I would be better off back in Sag Harbor!

Dec. 25, 1845: Christmas! Yet it seems to me that it might as well have come in July, for Christmas to me means cold weather.

The steward has made a colorful stocking for both Adam and myself to hang tonight, and I was extremely touched by his thoughtfulness. He said he wished to "remind us of childhood Christmases," and it is a kind thought, although my own childhood Christmases on the Outer Banks were little different than any other day of the year. Still, observing Christmas is a custom I have grown to cherish, and I find that now the day is here, I am filled with kind thoughts and good cheer. The steward and I have decorated the cabin with ribbons and bits of jewelry, and in the evening the mates will join Adam and me for an exchange of gifts and a rich tea.

Strangely, a melancholy thought has nibbled at me all day, and that is the thought of my lost child. If I had not lost it, he (I somehow think of it as he) would be with us on this special day, laughing at the singing and trying to catch the ribbon with his tiny hands. I must confess, the thought of my lost babe comes to me often, and I find it a saddening thing.

Dec. 26, 1845: We had a fine Christmas, after all, and we all seem much improved in spirit by our celebration.

From Adam, I received a beautiful piece of scrimshaw, a spool holder, carved with ivory hearts, diamonds, and rings. It was made by his own hand, and it is a lovely, darling thing, and useful as well. I shall treasure it always.

He also presented me with a bottle of my favorite scent, Violet, which he brought with him from Sag Harbor and saved for this occasion; also a lovely mantilla, which I shall get more use of at home than here, I am sure.

My sweet, thoughtful Adam!

From the first mate, Mr. Karnes, I received a finely carved ivory box and from the second mate, a carved wooden candlestick.

They all professed to like their gifts from me, and a fine time was had by all, as we partook of a rich plum cake, several bottles of port, nuts, and one of my tins of grape preserves. At times like this, being at sea seems a fine thing.

Jan. 2, 1846: Saw a strange-looking fish in the water early this afternoon. Mr. Karnes lowered his boat and caught it, and it proved to be what they call a diamond fish. They tell me this fish is seldom caught, and it was considered a great curiosity on board, no one having seen one dead before.

There are some marvelous sunsets in this region. I often wish that I were a painter so that I might capture these views to show my friends back home. I am certain that those who have not been to sea will never believe my description of them.

We are now in sight of Albemarle Island (one of the Galapagos), and Adam tells me that this is our last sight of land until we reach the Sandwich Islands. I must confess that I will be glad to see them, for more and more I long for the feel of real land under my feet.

Feb. 19, 1846: Saw land today for the first time since Albemarle. It is the island of Hawaii, of the Sandwich Islands. It delights me very much to have a view of land, when for so many weeks nothing was visible from east, west, north, or south, except the endless ocean.

Feb. 20, 1846: Land was in sight all day, but Adam thought it prudent to keep off as the weather is very rough, dark, and stormy. If the weather clears tomorrow, we will approach the island.

Feb. 22, 1846: Maui is now in sight, and the town of Lahaina is exposed to our delighted gaze. I am struck by how different and strange it is, compared to my native land. The mountains loom up in the distance, sharp and high, surrounded by a crown of clouds. The sky is intensely blue, and the water, as we near the island, changes shades, from dark blue to blue green, and is very clear.

There are clumps and patches of greenery on the mountainsides and along the white beaches. It is very beautiful, but it is a strange and unusual beauty. Very exotic. The air carries the scent of flowers.

As soon as we were at anchor, the customs officer came on board with a crew of natives; and when he returned to shore, Adam went with him, to arrange a boarding place for us for the time we will be on shore.

I am most excited and full of anticipation. I have packed

what belongings we shall need and am all prepared for going ashore. I can hardly wait to put my feet upon land once more, and I am most anxious to see at close hand this vivid and exotic land.

Chapter Fifteen

As the small boat made its way through the many canoes filled with natives, Marianna could scarcely control her excitement.

The air was pleasantly warm, and a soft breeze carried the scent of growing things, mixed with exotic port odors. The natives fascinated her—laughing brown men and women, some of them naked to the waist and apparently unashamed. The sight of them did not shock her, but seemed natural in this place.

She had seen many *Kanakas* in Sag Harbor and Boston, for they comprised a large part of many whaling crews; but she had never seen them in their natural habitat. Tall and brown-skinned, white-toothed, and black-haired, vivid and vital, they were at home with the sea in a way that even the whalers could not rival.

She turned to Adam seated beside her in the boat and squeezed his arm. "It's beautiful!" she whispered.

He smiled down at her. "It is that, but I must caution you, be prepared to see some things that you may not like."

His warning could not dampen her pleasure. What could she possibly witness in this paradise that she would not like?

The cottage they were to use was constructed of dried grass but was still a most handsome edifice, surrounded by trees, with walks laid out neatly and bordered with bright flowers. The house came complete with a native cook and a native woman to take care of them.

The cook was a huge woman, nearly as tall as Adam, and

much heavier. Marianna had never seen a woman so large. She was wearing a rather comical garment, constructed like a nightgown, full-sleeved and gathered from the shoulder to fall in deep folds to her feet. The material was rather bright and patterned with flowers.

The housekeeper was quite a different matter—a slender young woman with full breasts and shining, dark hair that fell to below her hips. Her body was covered with what appeared to be a long strip of bright, colored cloth, which was wound around her figure and fastened in a drape at her side. It came from just over her breasts to below her knees, but left her magnificent shoulders bare.

She would have been beautiful, Marianna thought, except for her rather flat nose and thick, rather odd-shaped lips.

The cottage contained four rooms: a sitting room, two bedrooms, and a dining room. The sittin iroom extended the whole length of the house, a feature that Marianna found was usual on the island. There was a door at either end of the sitting room, to allow the breezes to blow through, and there were four windows. It was furnished in an Oriental style, with Chinese chairs and lounges and a curio cabinet filled with Japanese curiosities. The walls were hung with spare, lovely Oriental paintings. The furnishings suited the house, she concluded, providing a graceful and comfortable appearance.

From the front door, Marianna could see the ocean and the white beach. She thought it exceedingly lovely, though different from anything she had ever known.

They were sharing the house with another couple, Captain and Mrs. Whipple, but after confinement for so long on the *Viking Queen*, it seemed like almost complete privacy to Marianna.

She arranged their clothing in the tall dresser in their bedroom and gazed with delight upon the large, comfortable bed. It was going to feel strange to be sleeping upon a surface that was not in constant motion. She was finding it difficult enough just finding her "land legs" after so many months at sea.

That night she and Adam came together with no reservations, and as the odor of damp flowers permeated their bedroom, carried in on the warm breeze that seemed as soft and caressing as the touch of fine silk upon the skin, Marianna thought that she had never been so happy.

The next morning was Sunday, and she and Adam, at the invitation of the Bigelows, attended services at the native church. Lawrence Bigelow, a local merchant, owned the cottage where they were staying.

Marianna thought that the services were both unusual and touching, and she found herself much entertained and distracted by the parishioners, who were dressed in as gaudy a collection of garments as she had ever seen.

The women were dressed in a wide range of materials, from coarse calico to the richest silk, all made into strange, nightgownlike dresses, such as their cook wore. Most of them wore a shawl or handkerchief, worn not cornerwise, as Marianna was accustomed to seeing them worn, but square, with the two corners tied around the neck.

The final touches were the bonnets. Marianna had to exert considerable control to keep from laughing at the sight of them. The bonnets encompassed every style imaginable, including fashions of many years gone by, and were worn untied and simply set upon the top of the head. The bonnets, the first she had seen on the native women, were evidently worn only at church, as were their shoes, which they wore only until they were seated in the pews.

The men made an equally strange appearance, being clothed, those of them who *were* clothed, in a miscellany of articles that looked as if they had come from a jumble sale: work breeches, matched with cutaway coats, and top hats; breeches, showing much wear, with gold braid down the sides, partnered with tailored jackets, worn with bone and shell necklaces. Many of the men wore only a piece of cloth wound around the hips, a sight that Marianna might have found disconcerting if she had not already seen many males completely nude, going about their work the day before.

The ceremony was in Hawaiian, but the minister utilized many gestures, which made his message at least partially understandable, and Marianna much enjoyed the sound of the language, which was full of vowels, and soft and flowing, with few harsh sounds.

After the service Mr. Bigelow and his wife took Adam and Marianna for a buggy ride to show them more of the island.

The roads were rough, but the beauty of the trees and flowers was breathtaking, and quite made up for the bumpy ride. Marianna exclaimed over the sight of breadfruit, coconut trees, and marveled aloud at the pineapples growing in the center of their crown of leaves.

And as they rode, she saw some of the things of which Adam had warned her. The nude, communal bathing practice of the islanders did not make her blush, as it did Mrs. Bigelow, but the sight of the drunken, pox-ridden native men lounging before the taverns and near the waterfront saddened her; and the gaggle of small boys, some only knee high, who ran after the carriage, begging for money and occasionally swearing in vivid English, caused her to shake her head in distress.

"I told you, my love, that there would be things that would upset you," Adam said, taking her hand when she turned her face away from the sight of a drunken islander vomiting in the street in the main part of town.

"What upsets me," said Marianna, swallowing hard, "is that it appears to me that the bad things we see were all brought here by us, by the white man. I can't help but think that these people, if left to themselves, would live quite differently, natural and free and happy."

Mr. Bigelow raised his eyebrows, and Mrs. Bigelow looked disapproving. "Admittedly we have affected their lives," Lawrence Bigelow said thoughtfully, "but we have brought progress here. They can't remain savages forever, you know. And whenever there is change, some harm is done in the process, I suppose. But we have brought them Christianity, and we are winning them away from their pagan ways. They will be the better for it in the end, Mrs. Street."

Marianna did not answer, but she wondered if this was really so.

That evening they were invited to a real native feast, a

luau, given by Kualu, the islander from whom Adam purchased his fresh fruits and vegetables for the *Viking Queen* and, Marianna gathered, an old and dear friend of her husband's.

Kualu had sent to the house a fine necklace made of large, shiny, polished beads, as a gift for Marianna. It was very handsome, and Adam told her that the beads were made from *kukui* nuts, and that such a gift bestowed much prestige, as the nuts were extremely hard, and difficult to process. Also the nuts were held in high esteem by the islanders, who burned the fatty, odoriferous oil for light, calling them "candlenuts."

Marianna was looking forward to the evening with much anticipation. Her bright, inquisitive mind found the natives and their customs fascinating, and this would be an excellent opportunity to see both at first hand.

She prepared for the occasion by wearing her least formal dress, a cotton print, and by letting her hair fall loose, in the native fashion. She wore no jewelry other than the kukui nut necklace.

The luau was being held on the beach, and when Adam and Marianna arrived, the festivities were already underway.

A large pit had been dug in the sand and lined with plantain and banana leaves. Heated rocks were being placed in the body cavities of a large pig, which had been cleaned and gutted.

Marianna watched with interest as the pig was wrapped in leaves, placed in the pit, and surrounded by the heated rocks. Then everything was covered with seaweed, and finally the pit was mounded with sand.

Marianna found it a curious way to cook, and she asked Adam how long the process would take.

He laughed heartily. "Several hours, my love, and you will be surprised when you taste it. Delicious, aye, that it is."

Marianna was astonished. "Several hours? However will it be done in time for us to eat?"

He laughed again. "Oh, this one is for later eating. They

started one cooking much earlier, and that one should be done soon. This kind of celebration goes on all night, and by the time the first pig is eaten, the second one will be ready."

Marianna could only shake her head in wonder.

"Captain Adam! Old friend!"

The voice was almost as big as the man, Marianna found, when she turned to see who was hailing her husband.

At least six feet, six inches, brown as mahogany, muscled like a wrestler, Kualu was a formidable sight. Wearing only a length of brightly colored cloth around his broad hips, a garment that Adam had told her was a *lava-lava*, and a necklace of shark's teeth, he looked primitive and somehow frightening; still, his English was fair, and his white-toothed grin was disarming.

Marianna gingerly accepted the hand he offered her and looked up into his brown visage with something approaching awe. He was the first man she had ever met who was taller than her husband.

She noticed that his thick, almost kinky black hair was speckled with gray; he must be a good deal older than she had thought at first.

"Welcome!" he boomed in his deep voice. "Welcome, dear Mr. and Mrs. Captain."

He motioned with his arm, and a slender, dark girl came running up, her arms heaped with flowers. Kualu, smiling broadly, placed a garland around Marianna's head. The sweet-smelling flowers, white and soft as baby skin, felt cool and refreshing as they caressed the skin of Marianna's neck.

Then Kualu leaned down and kissed Marianna on first one cheek, then the other. Marianna, a bit disconcerted, quickly glanced at Adam, to see how he was taking this liberty; but Adam, she saw, was paying no attention, for he was also being given a flower necklace, and a kiss, by the slender, brown-skinned girl.

When the presentation was completed, Adam looked at her. He read the question in her eyes and laughed. Moving close to her, he whispered into her ear, tickling it with his breath. "It's all right, my love. They mean nothing forward. It is only their way, their custom. They are a very friendly people."

"I would call that an understatement," Marianna said, a bit tartly. She was not certain that she liked this young woman kissing her husband, and could not help but wonder about the other times Adam had been in the islands, before he married her; or, for that matter, on his last trip, without her.

But she was given little time for pondering, for Kualu had taken both her and Adam by the arm and was leading them toward a strip of woven cloth spread upon the sand. The cloth was crowded with bowls and baskets of food, little of which Marianna recognized, all piled in colorful and artistic abandon. On both sides of the cloth, just as if it were a table, were the guests, seated cross-legged on the sand.

It was a strange but beautiful company to Marianna's eyes. The older women were dressed in either the long, full, nightgownlike garments, or in the ubiquitous lengths of cloth, wrapped around their bodies from below the waist to mid-calf. Some of the younger women also wore fabric from armpit to calf; but a number of them wore it draped only over the hips, leaving their well-shaped breasts exposed.

The men wore their lengths of cloth rather like a diaper—the fabric brought between their legs and then wound around the hips, with a flap hanging down in front. All of the guests wore wreaths of flowers around their necks and in their hair, and they all seemed to be pleasantly intoxicated from the native beverage they were drinking from coconut shells.

Marianna found the scene exotic and exciting, although she was somewhat embarrassed by the amount of flesh exposed, and could not help but keep glancing furtively at Adam from time to time to see if he was looking at the younger women's bared breasts.

"Here, drink!" Kualu thrust a half-filled coconut shell into her hands.

Startled, she looked at the milky, slightly acrid-smelling contents of the shell.

"You have to take some, my love, or he will be insulted and hurt," Adam whispered into her ear. "It is the custom here."

Trying to keep her face expressionless, Marianna took a sip of the liquid, and almost gagged. Quickly she handed the shell to Adam, who, smiling, took a deep draft. Marianna shuddered, closing her eyes.

However, once the liquid had spread in her stomach, it began to produce a pleasant glow, and when the shell was passed again, Marianna held her breath and took a deeper drink. Looking up, she saw Adam's smile of approval.

"Good girl!" He touched the flowers around her neck. "Isn't that a beautiful lei? It takes hundreds of flowers to make them, you know."

She gazed down at the necklace of blossoms and inhaled their sweet, rather powerful scent. "Is that what they are called? A—how did you say it?"

"Lei," Adam said, and she repeated the word after him.

Then Kualu asked for silence, and all conversation suddenly ceased. Into the abrupt silence intruded the dry, rhythmic sound of gourd rattles, hissing and thumping as they were first shaken, then thumped into the palms of a trio of women who stood at Kualu's side. And then Kualu's voice began to chant, steadily, in the soft, vowel-filled language of the islanders.

Marianna, of course, did not know the words, but she sensed that the chant must be something like the grace that Prudence Courtwright had spoken before their daily meals in Boston.

The sing-song chant, with the sounds of the gourd rattles and the surf a counterpoint to it, suddenly made Marianna aware of just how alien and unusual was the place she was in, and she marveled at the combination of circumstances that had brought her here.

Just as suddenly the chant was over, and with shouts and cries of pleasure, the eating began.

The islanders, it seemed, took a serious interest in eating and were able to put away huge amounts of food. Personally, Marianna was almost overwhelmed by the variety and quantity of food offered her. Remembering what Adam had said about the drink, she tried to sample all the dishes, finding some delicious, and some unpalatable.

The roast pork was wonderful, so tender that it shredded, and she liked the roast plantains and sweet potatoes. However, she found the staple food of the islands, poi, similar to library paste, with a flavor that she supposed might be much the same.

For a period of time the islanders devoted themselves wholly to eating and drinking; and then, operating evidently on some mysterious timetable, the entertainment began.

Replete with food, Marianna leaned against Adam's shoulder and listened raptly to the primitive sound of the drums and rattles, accompanied from time to time by the sound of chanting voices. She found the sounds very compelling, as primal as a heartbeat, and extremely stirring to the senses.

In the flickering light of tall torches placed at intervals in the sand, dancers, supple and uninhibited, moved in patterns both forceful and graceful. At first, only the men danced, and Marianna, watching their muscular brown bodies, found herself thinking thoughts that made her blush. She glanced quickly at Adam to see if he had divined what she was thinking. but Adam, relaxed and as caught up in the dancing as she, did not notice, and she gratefully turned her own gaze back to the dancers.

More food followed, more music, and more dancing, until the night became a blur of color and sound, and time ceased to have meaning.

Marianna did not know just when the women began to dance, but when she looked up from the cup of *okolehau*, which she was now drinking without hesitation, she saw that the men had been replaced by wahines, six young women, bare to the waist, their long dark hair swinging free to their hips, their high, firm breasts catching the firelight.

The male dancers had been bold, full of aggressive motions and strange, guttural grunts, but the women danced in a different manner, with a fluid, gentle movement. The swaying of their hips, the movements of their skirts, was clearly designed to be provocative, and Marianna looked sidelong at Adam, to gauge his reaction. He appeared to be quite pleased to see the girls and with frank delight was watching them dance.

The girls moved as one, sinuously, always smiling, moving first near, then away, from the guests. The drums throbbed, the gourds rattled, and the torchlight flickered in fantastic patterns over the scene.

Marianna began to feel dizzy, drowsy, and somewhat annoyed with Adam's obvious pleasure, all at the same time.

The beat of the drums was growing faster now, and the girls moved with more abandon, their movements now frankly lascivious, or so it seemed to Marianna.

One of the girls—Marianna thought it was Kualu's daughter—was staring boldly at Adam, dancing toward him, her arms outstretched, her graceful hands in constant motion.

Marianna felt a quick surge of annoyance. What was going on here? She noticed that the other girls were doing the same, each of them selecting one particular man, and the men were getting to their feet and going to the girls, joining them in the dance.

Her gaze went back to Adam and caught him with an embarrassed expression on his face. She looked again at the dancers. The men chosen by the dancers were dancing with them in what appeared to be a mating dance of some kind, and the girl who had chosen Adam was still dancing in front of him, holding out her hands invitingly, beckoning him to her.

Outrage rose in Marianna like a hot tide. How dare this native wench act so to *her* Adam?

Adam's face was red, and he was motioning the girl back, making gestures as if to push her away; but the girl simply shook her dark head, smiled, and danced closer still, twisting her pelvis in the most seductive manner.

"Just what does she think she's doing?" Marianna said explosively.

"It's only a dance, a custom with these people," Adam muttered, firmly taking her arm and pulling her against him, as if to indicate to the native girl that he was already spoken for.

"But why did she choose *you?*" Marianna knew that her

voice was rising, but she did not care. "Do you know her from another time?"

The girl finally moved away, shrugging her shoulders, going on to another man, an islander this time, who jumped up eagerly to join her in the dance.

"I said, did you know her before?" Marianna demanded, unwilling to drop the subject until she found out what she wanted to know.

Adam shifted uncomfortably. "Aye, I knew her," he said, sighing. "She's Kualu's daughter, Hina. Now let's just drop the subject and enjoy the luau, shall we?"

Marianna tore her arm from his. So he wanted to drop the subject, did he? That had to mean that he knew the girl, all right. Knew her *very* well, in fact!

She looked back to the dancers and saw that they had dwindled in number; and even as she looked, she saw one of the few couples left run together, laughing, holding hands, into the darkness beyond the torches.

"Did you ever perform that dance with her?" she asked sharply.

He said in a soft voice, "I said, let's drop the subject, Marianna."

A burst of anger made Marianna's voice strident. "Oh, *you* do not want to discuss it! How convenient. Well, it so happens that *I* want to discuss it!"

Adam, his own temper ignited by hers, turned on her and said in a low, angry voice, "All right, Marianna! You want to hear about it, I'll tell you. Yes, I've done the dance with Hina. But it was before I met you, and had nothing to do with you. I don't badger you about Phillip Courtwright, do I?"

"That's different!"

"Is it?" He shrugged. "I fail to see the difference."

"What about your last voyage, after we were married?"

Adam's face was flushed with anger and drink. "Godalmighty, Marianna, if you don't trust me, there is nothing I can do about it! My friendship with Hina was before I met you, and you can believe that or not."

"Friendship! Is that the word for it in these pagan islands?"

"*Pagan* islands? I should think those islands you came from are more pagan than these."

Marianna sniffed. "I don't understand what you see in her, anyway. Her nose is too flat, and her lips are thick. Her ankles, too!"

Kualu chose that moment to come up, squatting down behind them, placing a large hand upon each of their shoulders. "Are you having a good time? Are you enjoying the dancing?"

Marianna forced herself to smile as Adam assured his old friend that they were indeed having a wonderful time.

A new troop of dancers had taken up the beat, which was slowly changing to a slow, hypnotic rhythm, and Marianna fixed her attention on them. They were all male dancers this time, and she wondered how Adam would feel if one of them approached her, as the girl, Hina, had approached him.

Later that night, or rather morning, since the luau went on until dawn, she and Adam went unspeaking to their big double bed.

When the oil lamp had been extinguished, Adam turned to her, and Marianna knew that he wanted to make love.

Men were strange creatures, she thought. He was still angry, she knew, as was she; and yet he wanted to make love. She could not understand this, for she felt tight with anger and unresolved resentment. If he cherished her, if he apologized, assured her, convinced her of his devotion and love, then, and only then, could she think of love-making.

"No!" she said icily, knocking his hand away from her breast. "I don't want to." Wasn't he perceptive enough to see that she was angry and hurt?

"Godalmighty, Marianna, what's wrong with you this night? I'm your husband!"

"So you are, but that does not give you the right to do as you please with me. I have some rights, too!"

She turned on her side away from him, her body stiff and unyielding.

She felt his hand grasp her shoulder, turning her back

toward him, and suddenly she thought of Jude Throag and his brutal, heedless violations of her body. Revulsion filled her, and she pulled away, springing out of bed. "I said I don't want to!"

She stood rubbing the shoulder where he had touched her, and in the faint moonlight she could see his face darken and his lips thin.

"Marianna, what's come over you? You've never acted this way before."

"And you've never behaved like you did tonight!"

He sat up in bed. "And what's that supposed to mean?"

"If you don't know, it wouldn't do any good to tell you."

Giving an angry snarl, Adam got out of the bed and began putting on his clothes. She watched him in silence, aching to ask him where he was going, yet too proud and angry to give him the satisfaction of doing so.

When he was dressed, he set his cap on his head, and throwing her a dark glance, strode toward the door. She jumped as the door slammed violently behind him, belatedly wondering what the Captain and Mrs. Whipple must be thinking of all the noise.

After Adam had gone, Marianna stood for a long time, staring at the closed door, her thoughts turned inward. He was a beast! Like all men. He was probably going to Hina, to be soothed and made over. Hina seemed eager enough, at any rate. Unbidden images tumbled through Marianna's mind of the shapely, brown-skinned girl writhing in passion in Adam's embrace.

Marianna shivered, hugging herself, suddenly cold despite the balmy breeze.

All men were beasts!

Except for Phillip, who had never used her roughly. Oh, why had she married Adam? Why hadn't she waited for Phillip? Where was he now, sweet, gentle Phillip, who would never have treated her in such a fashion?

Phillip Courtwright rested the oars, letting the small dinghy glide to a stop. Leaning on the oars, he stared across the channel at the low-lying Outer Banks. It was twilight, and he could barely make out the white blur of the sand dunes. He wanted to wait until full dark before he landed, since he had no idea as to what kind of a reception he would receive.

He felt a tug of longing; here, near the Banks where he had first met Marianna, her presence was almost tangible. It was a poignant moment for him. She had scarcely been out of his thoughts since the last time he had seen her in Boston, but now the memory of her surged back full force. The pain of his longing was so powerful that he felt the hot sting of tears in his eyes.

Where was she? What had happened to her? Would he ever see her again?

Suddenly he was struck by a startling thought. Could she possibly have returned here, to the Outer Banks? Almost before the thought was complete, he dismissed it. The Marianna of Boston was a totally different person than the half-savage he had met here. She had nothing in common with the girl she had been on the Banks.

Phillip sighed and began thinking about what might await him here. Over the years since he had fled from here with Marianna, he had been relentless in his single-minded purpose—the unmasking of the Barth brothers for the villains they were. He had partially succeeded in doing this, but he well realized that he did not have enough solid evidence to convict them. He might be able to discredit them, but that was not enough. They had to be made to pay for their crimes; only then would his thirst for revenge be sated, and he could be at peace with himself.

Phillip had known all along, far back in his mind, that he would have to return to the Outer Banks in the end. A connection between the Barths and the wreckers had to be firmly established, and to make that connection he had to get sworn testimony from the wreckers.

He had postponed it as long as he could, knowing full well that to return to the Banks and confront the wreckers could well mean his death. Now he was willing to face that fate, if it had to be. There was no other way.

On the face of it, getting the wreckers to give testimony that could place themselves in jeopardy of criminal prosecution seemed an impossible task. Yet he had to try.

He sighed again, rousing from his reverie. It was full dark now. He could not postpone it any longer.

Wrapping his hands around the oars, he began to row. He was drenched in a cold sweat from fear of what might happen. He gritted his teeth and rowed on.

Chapter Sixteen

THE *Viking Queen* was three weeks out of Lahaina when the lookout spotted whales, a large school of them. Adam welcomed the call with a feeling of great relief.

Full of hurt and anger at Marianna's incomprehensible behavior, he looked forward to the impending action, knowing that the danger and excitement of the chase and the kill would help purge his mind of some of his darker feelings.

At the moment the sun was out, and the sea was relatively calm, but it was one of those variable days, when the weather seems undecided as to what it shall be, and Adam knew that the situation could change at a moment's notice.

He called for the boats to be lowered and took his place in the bow of the first boat, watching as Karnes, his first mate, and Rollins, his second mate, took their places in the other two whaleboats.

The whales, sperms, seemed placidly unaware of the ship and the men upon her. Floating on the surface like small islands, they rolled lazily, the mist of their blowings making fountains against the sky.

A hail from the lookout aloft caused Adam to glance up just as his boat was pulling away from the ship.

"Captain! Captain! To starboard! A sperm whale as big as a mountain!"

Adam, his adrenalin racing, exhorted his rowers to greater effort. As the whaleboat rounded the bow of the *Viking Queen*, he stood up, the better to see.

At first he saw nothing out of the ordinary, just the rounded backs of several whales as they lay quietly, filling their

267

lungs with air for the next dive; and then he saw, among the smaller backs, a great, gray expanse that might have belonged to Mocha Dick[1] himself. Adam estimated, from the exposed area, that the creature must be a good seventy feet long. What a prize he would make!

"Row hard, men!" he shouted. "Put your backs into it!"

He could see that the other two boats had also sighted the giant and were coming in on either side of him, for a whale of this size would need more than one harpoon in him to make him fast.

As the boats bore down on the basking whale, all thoughts except those of the hunt were driven from Adam's mind. This was the moment of truth, the test, the battle of six men in a small boat against a leviathan of the deep. Abruptly the huge back heaved and raised in the water, affording Adam and his men a terrifying view of the great gray shape just beneath the water.

As the mammoth rolled, Adam felt his enthusiasm wane into a cold awareness of danger, for the creature was moving with increasing speed, gathering momentum, and heading directly toward them.

"Godalmighty!" he muttered under his breath, realizing that the animal was one of the "knowing ones," those rare whales who had encountered men and his harpoons before and had learned how to fight them. The great back was scarred and studded with broken harpoon shafts.

Before Adam had time to call out the command to change direction, the beast was upon them, his head rearing out of the water like a gray mountain.

Through a wave of water, Adam caught a glimpse of his huge, gaping mouth and teeth. At the same instant he realized that there was nothing under his feet, that his boat was gone, and that he was in the sea, which surged and boiled around him like water in a cauldron. As he fought to find the surface, and light and air, he did not even see the huge fluke that struck him, knocking him senseless and sending him spinning, like a floating toy, through the dark water.

[1]Mocha Dick—A real whale, known to whalers of this era. Probably the prototype for Melville's Moby Dick.

When they brought Adam aboard the *Viking Queen*, unconscious and dripping blood, Marianna at first thought that he was dead.

She rushed to his side, peering anxiously down into his face for signs of life, and was rewarded by seeing his eyelids flicker. The relief that filled her made her aware of just how much she loved him, and the sight of his pale face, so vulnerable in his unconscious state, made her cry out.

His left leg was twisted at an impossible angle, and the flesh showed red and bloody through his torn trousers. He was not the only man injured by the great whale; several other crew members were being placed beside him on the blood-slippery deck.

Marianna raised terrified eyes to Rollins, who had come to kneel beside her. "What can we do?" she cried wildly. "There is no doctor. Who will set the bone?"

"I don't know," he mumbled. "The captain usually does the mending. I just don't know."

Sudden anger blazed in her. The man was useless. "Where's the first mate? Where's Mr. Karnes? He must know something about doctoring."

Rollins only shook his head, the stunned look still on his face. "He's dead, Mrs. Street. Went overboard and never came up."

Marianna shuddered, thinking of the first mate's terrible death in the cruel sea. But it was Adam who mattered now. Adam was still alive.

"You!" she said to another seaman—the ship's carpenter, she thought. "What about you? You must be able to do something!"

The man shook his head briskly, as if to deny any responsibility. "I know a bit, mam. But small things only. I never tended to nothing like that." Grimacing, he gestured to Adam's broken and bleeding leg. "Why, I'd be afraid to touch it, that I would. Afraid I'd do the captain more harm than good."

Marianna took her gaze from his face and looked around the deck, seeking *someone* who could help.

The men were all back on board now, including all the injured, and everyone was gathered around, examining their wounds and offering crude first aid to each other. They seemed to assume that Marianna and the second mate were attending their captain, so the men concentrated on the other injured.

Marianna stood up awkwardly. The wind had risen, and clouds now obscured the sun. She shivered, but not entirely from the cold. She raised her voice. "Do any of you men have any experience with broken limbs?"

The men looked at her and then down at the still form of their captain. They stood mute.

"The captain needs help," Marianna said. "Hellfire and spit, one of you must know how to set a broken leg!"

Finally, a rough-looking, bandy-legged man shuffled forward. "I 'ave some experience," he said in a Cockney accent. "Got it in Her Majesty's service. But I never 'andled nothing like this! The bone is gone plumb through the flesh, it 'as. Don't know as how I could 'andle that kind o' thing."

Marianna said firmly, "You must try."

The man shifted his feet, his expression worried. " 'Ow about the second? Can't 'e 'elp?"

"He has no experience in such matters, so he claims." She glared at Rollins, and the second mate looked away shamefacedly.

The Cockney shrugged. "You see, 'tis usually the captain what 'andles such things. 'E's the only one wot really knows 'ow."

"You have to try," Marianna said forcefully. "There is no one else. I'll help you all I can."

"If you say so," the man said dubiously. "But you got to promise me I won't be 'eld responsible for wot 'appens."

"Yes, yes, I promise! Now, tell me what to do."

The process of setting Adam's shattered leg was a long and messy business, and took the bandy-legged Cockney, Marianna, and another seaman over an hour.

Marianna thanked God that Adam remained unconscious during the setting; otherwise, the pain would have been unbearable.

Finally the bone was set, with a whalebone splint, and

the torn flesh cleaned as well as possible and wrapped in clean bandages. Adam lay white and still as death in the bunk in his cabin. He had lost a lot of blood. The Cockney had shown Marianna how to take Adam's pulse, and now she checked it, finding it weak but steady.

After the chill of the deck, the cabin was warm, and Marianna, as tired as she had ever been, almost nodded off in the chair beside the bunk. A soft cough roused her. Looking up, she saw the second mate standing over her.

"What is it, Mr. Rollins?" she said drowsily, wishing he would go away.

He coughed again, and Marianna saw that his eyes were vague, and he was twisting his cap in his hands, as if it were an animal he was attempting to strangle.

"The first mate is gone," he said tentatively, "and the captain is unconscious, and I was wondering—"

"Yes?" Marianna said impatiently. What was wrong with the man?

"Well, I guess that leaves me in command." He stared down at his feet.

Marianna, too exhausted to think coherently, tried to get the drift of what he was saying. "Yes. But then I suppose you know more about that than I do. But what is it you want of me?"

His narrow face flushed. "Well, I was just wondering if the captain had come to or had said anything. I mean, about where to go next. What course to set."

Even through her weariness, Marianna felt the hot prick of anger. "We must head for the nearest port, of course. The captain sorely needs medical attention, and so do some of the other men. We must get them to where they can get medical care."

Rollins swallowed, bobbing his head. "That sounds sensible. Yes. Very wise."

Marianna, watching him through fatigue-dimmed eyes, saw that this man—hardly more than a boy, really—had reached and gone beyond his ability to cope. Yet, he was the only one left who could command the ship, the only man left who had the authority to command.

"What is the nearest port?" she asked.

Rollins thought for a moment. "There's a Spanish settle-ment, San Diego, in California."

"Then we must go there," she said firmly. "As quickly as possible. How far is it? How many days?"

He thought again. "Not overly far, a three-day sail, may-be." He looked at her as if he feared her disapproval.

"Set our course then," she said crossly, and then fell asleep, even as he left the cabin.

The next three days were what Marianna imagined Hell must be like.

Adam alternated between periods of merciful uncon-sciousness and grinding pain. Although the makeshift splint seemed to hold his broken bones together well enough, the wound quickly became infected, sending Adam into bouts of fever and delirium. At times it was necessary to lash him to the bunk frame to prevent him from further injuring himself.

The second mate, after setting the course, was found standing placidly on deck, withdrawn into himself and help-less as a baby.

With no officer left to assume command, Marianna did the only thing she could think to do. She combed her hair, washed her face, and calling the crew together, informed them that she was acting as captain, in behalf of her hus-band, who had given her instructions to do so.

The men first appeared skeptical, and then rebellious, so she told them that Adam was conscious and lucid, but un-able to walk about as he was still too weak, and was relaying his commands through her. She also reminded them that their captain's life, and the lives of several of their com-rades, was at risk if they did not reach land quickly.

After that, the sailors, encouraged by the bandy-legged Cockney, who had formed a strong admiration for Marianna, set about getting the ship to San Diego as soon as possible, and Marianna had only Adam and the other injured hands to worry about and to tend.

When they reached San Diego, Adam and the other injured men were put under the care of a local doctor, a peppery ancient, one of the few non-Spanish men in the port. He quickly set about doing what he could for them. Although he clucked over Adam's condition, he finally succeeded in conquering the infection without having to amputate, an operation that had been a distinct possibility.

The ship lay at anchor in the harbor at San Diego for two weeks, and at the end of that time, Adam was conscious and lucid, although much thinner and very pale. All of the injured hands were also recovering.

Adam, now that he was on the mend, became restless and short of temper. Marianna spent every minute possible with him, and he was grateful for her company; but after two weeks of inactivity, he began to snap at her.

When she chided him for it, he apologized. Taking her hands in his, he said, "It's the passing of time, my love. If we don't get to sea again soon, they'll ship aboard another vessel or jump ship and remain behind here. We've got to get to sea again."

She tried to calm him. "But, darling, you're too weak yet, the doctor said so. It would be different if you had a good first mate, or even a second, but you have no one." She smiled impishly. "Except me."

"I'll find another!" he snapped. Then he fell back against the pillows, exhausted. He said disgustedly, "What's the use of fooling myself? I'll never find another first here. Not one I could really trust. But I *am* strong enough. Aye, I don't have to be up and about to give orders. I can do it from my bunk."

Marianna said quickly, "You'll make yourself ill again, Adam. You're still very weak. The doctor said you need to rest if that bone is to heal properly, and your wounds are still raw."

"The men will desert! If they do, I'll have to ship a crew of brigands and thieves and risk losing the cargo we've already taken."

Finally Marianna discussed it with the doctor, who bluntly told Adam that if he sailed, it must be for home. It would be weeks, perhaps months, the doctor told him, before the leg would be completely mended. Even then he would probably always walk with a limp. Adam cursed him, but at last a compromise was reached. They would sail, but for

Sag Harbor, and Marianna was going to continue to act as first mate, overseeing the ship and its workings. She would represent Adam and relay his commands to the crew. It was certainly not a usual situation, but then they were not *in* a usual situation.

The crew took the news well, quite happily in fact, since they too wanted to get their cargo back to Sag Harbor, where they would share in the lay. Also, over the past few weeks, they had developed a new respect for their captain's lady, and all vowed, to a man, to support her and follow her directions to the end of the earth, if necessary.

The return voyage to Sag Harbor seemed to take forever. For Marianna, the days seemed to run together into a repetitious series of incidents and activities, one much the same as another.

Some of the crew had elected to remain behind in San Diego, but the majority returned to Sag Harbor with the *Viking Queen,* in order to claim their share of what profits there were and perhaps ship out on another whaler.

Adam was still quite weak, and unable to walk; he slept a great deal of the time, which Marianna found a blessing; for when awake, he chafed at being confined to his bunk and fretted that she would not be able to oversee the ship properly.

Actually, she was performing the duties of a first mate quite efficiently. Her insatiable curiosity about the ship and its workings now stood her in good stead, and since she had the liking and respect of the men now, there were no real problems.

Within a few weeks, Adam felt well enough to be lifted into a chair beside his bunk; and a few weeks later, he talked Marianna into letting him be carried above decks where he might get some sun. Still, it was Marianna who ran the ship, albeit with his consent and advice, and she found that she was enjoying the experience.

Although their main concern was to get to Sag Harbor as soon as possible, they now and again sighted spouts, and twice, when the opportunity and circumstances were too much to pass up, they stopped long enough to kill and process whales, while Adam supervised from the deck.

There were still enough hands to man the whaleboats, and there were some good harpooners among them. The taking of the whales did not delay them longer than a few days, and added to the store of oil and whalebone below decks.

Still, Adam worried over the poor showing they would make on this voyage, for the oil they had taken, before his accident, was barely enough to make expenses of the trip, and he had been counting on a good profit.

"I'll have to sail again as soon as I can provision the ship and collect a full crew," he said more than once.

To which, Marianna always replied, "Hellfire and spit, you can't even walk, and you're talking about going out again!"

"Be that as it may, I'm going!"

At last, they sighted the steeple of the Whaler's Church piercing the sky, and they sailed into Sag Harbor. Marianna felt a great relief at being home again. Perhaps they had not made a great profit, but Adam was alive and almost well, and during his long convalescence they had managed to put behind them the bad feeling that had begun at Lahaina.

The return of the *Viking Queen* to Sag Harbor was greeted with considerable fanfare. News of their plight, and of the fact that Marianna had, in effect, been captaining the ship, had preceded them, brought in by ships that had returned before them.

The townspeople, always hungry for news and for any excitement that could break the monotony of their usually placid lives, took to the story with enthusiasm and some embellishment. Marianna was surprised and somewhat dismayed to find herself the local heroine, besieged on all sides by friends and acquaintances, and literally overwhelmed by invitations to suppers and socials in all the better homes in town.

Adam, walking now, but with a painful limp, and using his whalebone stick for more than an ornament, seemed rather disgruntled by all the attention she was receiving. It was not, as he hastened to assure her, that he disliked the fact that she was receiving so much attention, but that somehow all this talk of her accomplishment in some way diminished him, as a captain and as a man.

However, he stood for "all this nonsense," as he termed it, with good enough grace and always appeared reasonably pleasant and smiling, holding Marianna's arm, at all the social events.

The climax of the affair was that a newspaperman came from New York to interview "The Brave and Beautiful Heroine of Sag Harbor." He promised Marianna and Adam that "All the world will know your heroism, Mrs. Street. I shall make your name a byword across the land!"

Marianna could see that Adam's patience was at an end. He was a social man, one who liked good company. However, he still had trouble with his leg and at times suffered considerable discomfort; also, he was beginning to weary of the round of parties and suppers. And, Marianna thought, the constant focusing of attention on her did little for his peace of mind.

Yet, she was enjoying the attention and the parties—life at Sag Harbor and on Shelter Island had never been so exciting—and when Adam wanted to beg off attending a party given by Mrs. Brawley, she accused him angrily of being jealous.

"Jealous!" he snorted. "And why should I be jealous because a pack of gossiping idiots chooses to make you into some kind of a heroine? It's just that I can't abide one more of these suppers, with everyone simpering over you and telling you how 'wonderful and brave' you are!"

Marianna threw down the brush with which she had been taming her hair. "Hellfire and spit, Adam, you *are* jealous, you just as much as admitted it! You don't really mind all the fuss, you're just upset because it's being made over *me*."

He glared at her from where he was seated on the bed. "That's utter nonsense, and you know it, Marianna. I suppose you think that I'm jealous over that wet-behind-the-

ears lawyer, too. Next you'll be accusing me of not wanting
to go tonight because the party is at his house!"

Marianna stared at him thoughtfully. "Well, now that you
bring up the subject. . . . At least Stuart Brawley is a gentleman. I'm sure he would be big enough to be pleased if
his wife was so well thought of."

Adam's laughter was harsh. "But he hasn't got a wife, has
he? He's too busy courting the wives of other men."

Marianna could feel heat rise to her face. "That's unfair,
Adam! At any rate, he doesn't pursue native girls. If he *was*
married, I'll wager that he wouldn't stay out all night, doing
heaven knows what, with some half-naked, fat-bottomed—"

The sound of the door slamming cut off the end of her
sentence. Walk out on her, would he? Well, she would go
to the party alone. She did not need Adam Street!

Dropping down onto the bench before her dressing table, Marianna briskly set about making herself beautiful for
the Brawleys and their guests, her mind set against any
thoughts of Adam whatsoever.

That night at the Brawleys, Marianna scintillated, flirted
outrageously, and graciously accepted all the compliments
offered her. By any standard, the evening had undoubtedly
been a great success. So why, she wondered as she drove
the buggy home, did she feel so depressed?

The house was dark when she reached home, and she had
to wake Mrs. Horner to gain entrance.

When she got to her and Adam's bedroom, he was not
there, and she felt herself tighten with anger and hurt. She
would not wonder where he was. She would not! She would
go quickly to sleep, for it had been a long day.

Too tired to remove all her garments or take down her
hair, Marianna lay down in her petticoats, convinced that
she would go to sleep immediately; but sleep was a long
time coming, and it was near dawn before she finally drifted
off.

Adam still had not returned.

When Adam did come home about noon of the following
day, his manner toward Marianna was cool and distant. He

did not speak of where he had been, nor did he ask her about the gathering at the Brawleys'. He could have been a polite stranger.

Marianna, more hurt than ever, stubbornly decided that she could play at that game as well as he and adopted the same tactics. Supper that evening was a formal and chilly affair, and Mrs. Horner, nervously serving the meal, stared at both of them in puzzlement.

It was after supper, over sherry in the parlor, that Adam made his pronouncement. He put it very bluntly, and his tone brooked no argument. "I am going back to sea, madam, as soon as the *Viking Queen* can be outfitted and a full crew recruited."

Marianna felt as if an iron hand had squeezed her vitals. She well recognized that his use of the pronoun "I," and not "we," meant that he intended to sail alone. This knowledge hurt her deeply, and she found that she had to swallow before she could find her voice.

"So soon?" she said plaintively. "Your leg still pains you, and we have only been home a few weeks."

He nodded formally. "That is true, madam, but the leg, I fear, will always pain me. And, as you well know, my last voyage was cut short, and I was forced to return to port without a full load of oil. I have therefore decided that it is necessary that I return to sea as quickly as possible. I have already made some preparations."

Although she already knew the answer, Marianna felt compelled to ask the question: "You intend to sail alone this time? Without me?"

"Aye. In my judgment, that would be best."

"But I created no problems on the ship! You have told me as much."

"Aye, that is quite true. However, on this voyage, I intend to drive the ship and the men very hard, for we must take on a full load. It will be easier without a woman's welfare to consider. I shall let you know when we are ready to sail."

Marianna wanted to run into his arms, she wanted to plead with him to take her with him, but her pride would not let her. She said coldly, "Very well, sir. If that is your decision."

"Aye, it is."

Adam did not inform her of when he was to sail.

After two weeks of sleeping in the guest room, and with only a minimum of communication, he was gone. Marianna awoke one morning to find the bed in the guest room empty, and not even so much as a note biding her farewell.

She cried in her room for an hour and then soaked her eyes so that she might go down to breakfast and pretend to Mrs. Horner that she knew where her husband had gone.

Part Four

1846:

Sag Harbor

Chapter Seventeen

EZEKIAL Throag leaned back and sighed. It was late afternoon, and for the first time in weeks, it seemed, his desk was cleared of paper work. He reached across to the cabinet behind him, pulled open a drawer, and took out a bottle of brandy. He poured a glass and drank it down in a couple of swallows, then sat rubbing the glass back and forth between his huge hands, feeling the bite of brandy in his belly.

His thoughts roamed back over the past year. It had been a good year. He had solidified his position with the shipping company; almost every scheme that he had devised reaped good profits, and the Barths' animosity had diminished considerably. He grinned savagely. They might still hate him underneath, but so greedy were they that they were careful to keep any such hatred well hidden.

Also, his position within the community was assured; he was well respected in Southampton nowadays, as well as within the shipping community. He was so gratified by this climb to respectability that he had all but forgotten the days on the Outer Banks and his life as a wrecker. He knew that the brothers were still having trouble with the man Peters on the Banks and several times they had hinted that he, Throag, should take matters in his own hand. He had finally done just that, over their protests. He had reached the conclusion that it was past time to sever all connections with the wreckers. The company was so prosperous that the wreckers were no longer needed, and any connection with them only posed a threat. The last time an emissary from Peters had visited the shipping company, Throag had sent back a message—Barth, Barth & Throag no longer required the unique services of Peters and his cohorts. Peters was no doubt incensed, but what could he do, without incriminating himself?

Throag thought of Rose Lake. It had been several days after he dumped her body into the ocean before her disappearance was thought serious. There had been a great hue and cry, and Throag had been questioned, since the other tenants of the Inn of the Rose knew of, or suspected, his intimacy with their landlady; but Throag denied any knowledge of her whereabouts, and the hubbub eventually died down, especially after it became known that Rose's moral values had not been of the highest—she had been intimate with a number of drummers staying at the inn over the years since her husband had passed on. The conclusion was finally reached, by the authorities, that she had run off with one of them. It had been fortunate for Throag that her body had never washed ashore, leaving her demise a secret forever.

He laughed aloud and splashed more brandy into his glass. He turned to replace the bottle in the open drawer, then paused as he started to knee it shut. There were several newspapers in the drawer; he had been so busy of late that he had put them away until he had time to peruse them.

Now he took out the stack of papers and thumbed through them idly. On the front page of a month-old Sag Harbor newspaper was a single column, with the heading: "Injured Captain's Wife Brings Ship Home."

Marianna Street, spouse of whaling Captain Adam Street, of the Viking Queen, *was interviewed yesterday in her gracious home on Shelter Island.*

Mrs. Street, a mere 22 years old, recently survived an experience that few young women would attempt. When her husband, Captain Street, was badly injured in an accident that killed his first mate, Mrs. Street stepped in and captained the Viking Queen *during the ship's return to Sag Harbor.*

Throag stopped reading in mid-sentence, his gaze darting back to the first line of the headline. Marianna Street? *Marianna?* Was it possible? It was not an unusual name, yet it was not all that common, either.

Quickly he scanned the rest of the article and in the last column found confirmation of what he sought:

Mrs. Street tells us that this was her first whaling voyage, and she does not come from a seafaring family. Married to Captain Street for more than two years, she came to us from Boston, and before that the Carolinas. A Southern belle, no less!

Throag had stopped breathing, and a black rage rose up to almost choke him. It *was* her! It was Marianna Harper!

And all this time, for at least two years, she had been abiding in Sag Harbor, only a short journey from Southampton.

The long passage of time, plus the failure of his manhunter to locate Marianna, had dulled much of Throag's raging thirst for vengeance. Now it returned full force, and it was only with a great effort that he did not rush from the building and to Sag Harbor on the instant.

He reached for the brandy bottle again and took a drink right out of the bottle. It cleared some of the rage from his mind, and he was able to think more calmly.

She was going to pay, there was no doubt in his mind about that, but he would have to proceed cautiously.

He gave a bark of harsh laughter as he realized the reason for caution. Once he would not have hesitated a moment, but things had changed. Now he had respectability, and he had to be careful that whatever course of action he took was done in secret.

But the wench would pay for murdering his son, and it would be done soon.

Marianna picked at the food on her plate. She was despondent and had little appetite. Adam had been gone only a week, and already she missed him terribly. Her loneliness might have been easier to bear if they had not parted in anger.

She knew now that she had made a mistake; she should have insisted that she accompany him. She could well remember the incident in Lahaina, and Hina, the native girl. If not Hina, there would be other girls along Adam's sea route; and in the mood in which he sailed, he might well console himself with them.

Marianna sighed heavily and got up from the table. Carrying a demitasse of coffee, she wandered into the parlor. The evening was chilly, and she could see the grayness of fog as thick as cotton through the parlor window. There was a fire burning in the fireplace. She placed the tiny cup on the mantelpiece and poked up the flames. Then she leaned the heavy poker against the wall and retrieved her coffee, sipping as she dreamed into the flames.

It was snug here, warm and safe, none of the hardships and dangers of life at sea, and she knew that most captains' wives would be content. Yet, she had had a taste of the sea now, and she could well understand how it could get into a person's blood—

Her head came up as she heard a knock on the front door. She drained the cup and waited, wondering who could be paying her a visit. Stuart Brawley, she knew, was away for a few days.

She heard Mrs. Horner's voice, and then the deep rumble of a male voice, which sounded hauntingly familiar. Frowning, she waited, as she heard footsteps along the corridor.

Mrs. Horner stood in the doorway. "Madam, there is a man here who insists on—"

A large figure loomed behind her, then stepped forward, shouldering Mrs. Horner aside.

Marianna gasped in shock. Even without the beard, she would have known him anywhere, this incarnation of evil who still, on occasion, haunted her dreams. "Master Throag," she said faintly, instantly despising herself for the subservient form of address.

Throag said to Mrs. Horner, "You may go. I wish a private audience with your mistress."

Mrs. Horner stared at Marianna in question. The last thing Marianna wanted was to be left alone with this man, and yet she did not want the housekeeper to overhear what he might have to say. In as steady a voice as she could muster, she said, "Yes, Mrs. Horner, leave us alone, please."

Throag carefully closed the door after the housekeeper and then turned to Marianna and grinned mockingly. "What, no glad welcome for an old friend?"

"You have never been a friend of mine, Ezekial Throag."

"Ah, the wench has gained some spirit, I see. Perhaps it comes of being such a fine lady now. A captain's wife, no less!" Throag's smile faded away, and he stared at her with a raw and hungry look. "Strange, the ways of ironic fate. All this time I have been searching for you, and here you are, only a short journey from where I have lived for so long. And I, too, have become respectable."

"Then why are you here?"

"Because I have unfinished business with you, girl."

Marianna's heart began to beat wildly. "What business can you possibly have with me?"

"You know very well. You murdered my son!" He took a step toward her, his face working. "And I'm here to see that you pay for that crime."

"It wasn't a crime, it was self-defense!" she cried. "Jude had a great club and was going to kill Phillip, so Phillip had to kill him in—" She broke off, refusing to place the blame on Phillip. She stood with her head thrown back, staring at Throag defiantly.

"Oh, I know all about your Phillip Courtwright, girl." He sneered. "He will pay as well, when I get my hands on him. And your plea of self-defense matters not a whit to me. You were the instrument of my son's death, my only son, and I've lived only for this moment."

Marianna backed a step, her heart thudding with terror. "You can't harm me and hope to escape. Mrs. Horner knows who you are, and her husband is about."

"I care little for them." He shrugged massive shoulders. "When I leave this house, nothing will be alive, no one to point a finger at Ezekial Throag."

His eyes were glazed with a killing rage, and he continued his slow, shuffling, inexorable advance. Marianna retreated until she felt her back against the mantelpiece. Her eyes darted to the left, and she started to move around him, but he was far too quick for her. He was on her in an instant, those terrible hands fastening around her throat. He began to squeeze, and his mouth was open in what seemed a soundless shout of joy.

The strength of his hands was incredible. Marianna could not breathe, and black spots began to dance before her eyes. She knew that she had only a few seconds of consciousness left. Groping behind her, her right hand closed around the poker. With a small prayer she lifted the poker and brought it around with all the strength she could manage. It struck him alongside the head, and he grunted explosively, his grip loosening slightly, enough for Marianna to gulp at sweet, precious air.

Again she struck. Throag's face now wore a look of astonishment, and his grip loosened further. Shaking his head like a gored bull, he backed a step, allowing Marianna to move out of his grasp.

She then gripped the poker in both hands, raised it high, and, standing on her toes, she brought it whistling down on top of Throag's skull. His face went slack, and he stood with his body slumped; a trickle of blood flowed down across his forehead. He began to fall, slowly, seeming to fall in sections, like lumps of clay dissolving. He hit the floor with a great thump.

Marianna stood over him, breathing heavily, the poker poised to strike again. His head was twisted sideways, and she could see that his eyes were open and staring.

Ezekial Throag was dead.

A gasp from the doorway brought Marianna's head up.

"Madam!" Mrs. Horner was staring saucer-eyed at the body on the floor.

Marianna slowly roused from her state of anger. She began to tremble violently. She saw the blood on the poker and in a convulsive motion threw it from her, across the room. She closed her eyes, swaying, afraid that she might be ill.

"Madam?"

Marianna opened her eyes. "Yes, Mrs. Horner," she said in a dead voice. "You had better send your husband for the local constable."

Constable Dawes was a middle-aged, slow-talking man, raw-boned and melancholy of countenance. He had been Shelter Island's constable for several years, and clearly he was out of his depth. This was the first time he had ever been involved in a crime as shocking as murder.

Clucking and shaking his head, he walked around Throag's body a number of times. Marianna, pale and shaking, huddled on the sofa in the corner, sipping at the glass of brandy provided by Mrs. Horner, who sat beside her, trying vainly to comfort her.

Finally Constable Dawes came over to stand before her. "Mrs. Street, I know you're terribly upset, but it is my sad duty to question you." At Marianna's mute nod, he pulled up a footstool and perched his ungainly bulk on it gingerly. "First off, did you kill this man here?"

"Yes, yes, I did," she said in a barely audible voice.

"Must be a stranger hereabouts, since I've never seen him before." The faded brown eyes gleamed hopefully. "He broke into your house and tried to, uh, attack you, did he? Is that the truth of it, Mrs. Street? And you had to defend your life?"

"I had to defend myself, yes," Marianna said in a stronger voice. "But that is not the reason Ezekial Throag was here, not to abuse me sexually."

"Ezekial Throag?" Constable Dawes sighed. "You knew him, then?"

"Yes, from several years ago."

"Ayuh. I guess you'd better tell me the whole story, madam."

Marianna finished the brandy, using the time to arrange her thoughts. What would the truth, when it came out, do to her reputation in Sag Harbor? Thank God, Adam already knew about her life on the Outer Banks, about the death of Jude Throag. . . .

289

She had no choice, of course, but to tell the truth, to convince the constable that she had killed Throag in self-defense.

Taking a deep breath, she told her story. Mrs. Horner refilled the brandy glass once during the telling. Constable Dawes listened intently, and it was clear, even to Marianna's unpracticed eye, that she had his sympathy.

When she was finally done, he cleared his throat. "Well! You've had a time, Mrs. Street, that I must say." He got to his feet and walked over to stare down at Throag's body. "A proper villain, this one, it would appear." The constable stood for a moment in thought, chin cupped in his hand. Then his head came up at the creak of wagon wheels outside. "Ah, that'll be the man I sent for. We can move the—uh, body, out of your house now, Mrs. Street."

Marianna sighed in relief. Despite her deep-seated fury at Throag and her relief that she had managed to escape death at his hands, the fact of his death had been on her mind all the while she had talked, and she was glad the body was to be removed.

Constable Dawes left the parlor for the front door, and at the sound of voices in the entryway, Marianna got up and went out into the hall. "Constable? I shall be in the sitting room, should you need me."

The constable came toward her. He looked uneasy. "Mrs. Street, everything seems clear cut, but I will have to leave a man here to guard the house until my investigation is completed."

"Does that mean that I am under arrest?"

He looked shocked. "My land, no! It's just that it is the required procedure. And I should think that you'd feel safer with a man around for a day or so, after what happened here."

"Perhaps you're right," she said in a subdued voice.

After the constable's man came and was posted outside the house, Constable Dawes took his leave, with the promise to conclude his investigation as quickly as possible.

Mrs. Horner parted the curtains to peer at the man pacing outside the house. She said apprehensively, "Perhaps I should send Mr. Horner to fetch Lawyer Brawley, madam?"

"Of course not," Marianna said sharply. "I have no need of a lawyer, Mrs. Horner. Besides, it's my understanding that Stuart—Mr. Brawley—is away at the moment."

The next three days passed slowly, and Marianna found she was glad that the constable's man was present. She had no wish to leave the house, knowing that everyone on the island, and likely in Sag Harbor as well, knew of her predicament; and she dreaded having to face them. The man's presence gave her an excuse not to be about, and also kept visitors away. She told Mrs. Horner to feed him, and she allowed him to sleep in the spare bedroom downstairs.

But by the afternoon of the third day, she was growing restless and concerned. It should not have taken Constable Dawes this long to learn all there was to learn. Consequently, when she heard the sounds of a buggy driving up, Marianna rushed to the window, expecting it to be the constable with good tidings.

Instead of Constable Dawes, it was Meg Mundy. For an instant Marianna thought of having Mrs. Horner turn Meg away, then a wave of gratitude, and self-pity, swept over her, bringing a mist of tears to her eyes. She realized how much she had missed the comforting words of a good friend.

Hurrying to the door, she threw it open, as Meg puffed up the walk. "Oh, Meg, I'm so glad to see you!"

Without a word Meg opened her arms. Marianna wept on her broad shoulder for a minute. Meg patted her head with affection. "I'm sorry, lovey, that I haven't made it over sooner, but I just heard last night. What a terrible time you've had of it, child!"

"It was horrible," Marianna said, stepping back to dash tears from her eyes. "Come in, Meg. I'll have Mrs. Horner made a pot of tea. Her tarts aren't quite as good as your favorites, but they're tasty."

A short time later they were in the front parlor, with a teapot steaming before them and a platter of Mrs. Horner's tarts. Meg swallowed a large bite, took a sip of tea, and then, an avid gleam in her eye, glanced at Marianna. "Now, lovey, tell me all about it." She laughed wryly. "Just listen to me! I'm as eager for the lurid details as any old gossip!"

"It's all right, Meg. I *want* to tell somebody about it, aside from Constable Dawes, that is," Marianna said bitterly. "I had to tell him, but I need somebody who'll listen with an understanding heart."

"My heart is always open to you, lovey, you know that."

Marianna took a deep breath, and the tale poured out of her. She held nothing back. Tears stood in Meg's eyes when she heard about Marianna's life with the wreckers.

She exclaimed, "You poor child. What an awful life that must have been."

And when Marianna had related Throag's villainy and his attempt in this very house to kill her, Meg was indignant. "The blackguard got his just desserts!"

"But will other people think so?"

"I'm sure they will, lovey, when they learn the truth of how it happened."

"Yet they may turn away from me when they learn that I was once a wrecker."

"That was through no fault of yours. And if they speak ill of you"—Meg made a fist and thumped her knee—"they'll dare not speak so in my presence!"

Marianna laughed weakly. "Oh, Meg, you are a true friend."

Her head swung around as she heard a horse outside. She ran to the window and looked out. It was Constable Dawes. At the parlor door she called out, "Mrs. Horner, Constable Dawes is here. Will you show him into the parlor?"

She and Meg were composed, the perfect picture of two ladies having a friendly tea chat, when the constable was ushered in.

One look at his grim visage sent a ping of alarm through Marianna's mind. She came to her feet. "Will you join us for a cup of tea and a tart, constable? Do you know Meg Mundy?"

The constable tipped his hat and said, "How do, Mrs. Mundy?"

Marianna, her apprehension growing, said, "And will you have tea and a cake, Constable Dawes?"

"No, I don't believe it proper under the circumstances. I am here to do my duty."

Meg spoke up. "And what does that mean, pray?"

Constable Dawes did not look at her, but stared at Marianna instead. "Mrs. Street, it appears that you told me many falsehoods in relating to me what occurred here."

Marianna sat down weakly. "What falsehoods, sir? I do not understand!"

"About the murdered man, Ezekial Throag, madam. My inquiries disclose that he was much respected in Southampton, a man held in great esteem by his fellows. He was one-third owner of the Barth shipping firm. He was a man of some worth, not at all the villain you made him out to be."

Meg interjected, "He was a villain of the worst stripe!"

Marianna said bewilderedly, "I still do not understand, Constable Dawes. Everything I told you is the truth, I swear! What has happened to him since I knew him on the Outer Banks I have no way of knowing, but he came here intent on killing me. If I had not defended myself, I would be dead now, instead of he."

"That is not the way it was told to me," the constable said doggedly. "Furthermore, folks are demanding that you be bound over for trial. They are clamoring for justice, madam."

"Folks!" Meg Mundy snorted indelicately. "Busybodies, nosing into something not their business!"

The constable's gaze shifted to her. "They are respectable folks, Mrs. Mundy, demanding that justice be done."

"Justice has been done, you ninny," Meg said. "This poor girl was defending her life, hasn't she told you as much?"

Constable Dawes looked again at Marianna and shifted his feet uncomfortably. "And that's the nub of it, you see? Who's to be believed, respected citizens of the community or a woman who was a former tavern wench? The dead man had a fine reputation, which some think Mrs. Street is trying to blacken to save herself."

Marianna felt despair well up in her. "But if I didn't kill

Throag to defend myself, for what earthly reason *did* I kill him?"

"Your motive, madam, is not my concern. That will likely come out at your trial."

"Trial?" Meg was indignant and went to put her arm around Marianna's shoulders. "You mean that this poor girl is to be placed on public trial?"

"That is the way of it, Mrs. Mundy." The constable looked miserable. "Now it is my sworn duty to place you under arrest, Mrs. Street, and take you into custody."

"Surely you're not going to place her in jail, with common criminals?" Meg demanded, appalled.

"We have no jail, Mrs. Mundy, seldom having need of one. I shall have to keep her on board the ship—"

"Not the Hell Ship!" Meg clapped a hand to her mouth in horror. "Dear God, how could you dream of such a thing, sir!"

"I have no choice, Mrs. Mundy. The ship is the only facility available for holding prisoners."

Marianna had been too stunned by the very fact of her arrest to pay much heed to Meg's horror at the mention of the Hell Ship, but when she saw the ship, she realized the reason for Meg's concern.

The Hell Ship was an abandoned hulk offshore of Sag Harbor. The ship had run aground years ago on a foggy night, staving in its hull and settling to the harbor bottom in shallow water. There were a number of such ships throughout the harbor; it was not deemed profitable to salvage them, and they had been left to rot, a constant hazard to shipping. Most of the damaged vessels were left to disintegrate, but the one designated the Hell Ship had been maintained to a degree, and a number of cabins above the water line were kept in a livable condition. The term, livable, was debatable, Marianna found, when she was left locked into one of the cabins.

There was a bunk of sorts, a slop jar, one chair and a rough table, and a porthole that admitted light, but since the glass had long since been shattered, it also admitted

294

wharf rats and an icy wind. The cabin, indeed the whole ship, stank of decay and a rank mixture of other odors.

Marianna at first thought she would be unable to sleep in such surroundings, yet she slept like one dead, for sleep offered the only escape from her dreadful predicament. She spent the days either lying on the uncomfortable bunk or staring out the porthole, gazing with longing at the distant shore, abundant with its new spring greenery, or looking with envy at the ships sailing past. How she wished she was on one of those ships, putting this nightmare behind her!

An apologetic Constable Dawes came twice a day, in the mornings and late afternoons, bringing food and other necessities.

Meg Mundy also came almost every day, bringing cheer and news of Sag Harbor. "It will turn out all right, lovey. They will never in this world convict a woman for defending herself."

Marianna shook her head drearily, pushing her lank hair out of her eyes. Although the constable provided water, soap, and towels, the facilities were not good for washing her hair, and it was growing filthy. She had a dread of lice or other vermin infesting her hair and person.

To Meg's comment she responded, "But what you don't seem to understand, Meg, is that the constable, and apparently most others as well, don't see it as self-defense. They think I killed a respected citizen for dark reasons of my own."

"Nonsense!" Meg said briskly. "Give it time, child. They'll come to realize the truth."

"I only wish I could believe that." Marianna gave a hopeless shrug, and for just a moment her face convulsed, as despair threatened to overwhelm her. Then she straightened up, throwing back her shoulders. "Stuart—Mr. Brawley. Have you gotten in touch with him, like I asked you to?"

Meg shook her head dolefully. "I'm sorry, lovey. The whole Brawley family is away, in New York, I've been told. Perhaps I should try and get another legal man for you?"

"No, Meg. He's the only one I know and trust." But even as she spoke the words, Marianna had to wonder if she

could rely on Stuart for legal assistance. What assurance
did she have that he would not believe, along with everyone else, that she was a murderess?

Stuart Brawley was deeply angry and outraged when he
learned what had happened to Marianna. He did not for a
moment believe that she was guilty of the crime she had
been accused of. He had taken his mother and sister to
New York for a few days' outing, and knew nothing of what
had happened until he returned to Shelter Island.

In a fury he went to Constable Dawes immediately.

"Mr. Brawley, I was given no choice," the constable said
defensively. "I had to charge her."

"Constable, it is unconscionable to confine Mrs. Street
to that damnable ship!" Stuart raged. "I dread thinking of
what such confinement there will do to her spirit. Now,
take me to her at once!"

On the way out to the Hell Ship in Constable Dawes's
dinghy, Stuart was of two minds about seeing Marianna. He
loved her, God, how he loved her! But he had seen very
little of her since Adam Street's last visit home, and Stuart
had reconciled himself to the glum knowledge that he would
never possess her. In the beginning his only goal had been
seduction, and he believed that he could still succeed in
that if he went about it the right way—Stuart was confident
of his ability with women—yet he no longer wanted merely
that. He wanted Marianna for his wife, and to try again to
seduce her would only soil their relationship, at least in his
mind.

A flare of hope arrowed into his thoughts. When Captain
Street learned of Marianna's predicament, would he turn
away from her? No matter whether she was guilty or innocent, her reputation would be tarnished. Might that be
more than the much-respected captain could endure? It
would certainly be a true test of his love.

Stuart shrugged the thought away as unworthy of him. If
he could not win Marianna's love through his own worth,
he did not deserve it.

As for her innocence, he had not the least doubt of that,
but whether he would be able to prove her innocent was

another matter entirely. It looked black for her, if all he had heard was true. Also, his experience at law was still limited. He had never handled a murder trial, which he knew that this would turn out to be. Perhaps he should advise her to employ another lawyer, one with more skill and experience.

When Constable Dawes unlocked the door to the cabin where Marianna was confined and ushered Stuart in, Stuart was appalled at her appearance. Her once beautiful hair was a tangle, her clothes were wrinkled, and her face was pale, without her usual high color.

"Marianna! Dear God, what have they done to you!" he exclaimed.

From the bunk where she sat, Marianna looked at him with dull eyes. Then a spark of recognition brought life to her features, and she sprang to her feet. "Stuart! Oh, thank God!"

She ran to him, burying her face against his chest, her thin shoulders heaving with sobs. Stuart glanced at Constable Dawes over her head. "Would you leave us alone, please?"

After the constable had departed, Stuart held her away from him, gazing down into her tear-filled eyes. He said soothingly, "It's all right, dear Marianna. We'll soon have this straightened out." But even as he spoke the words of reassurance, he felt a tremor of uncertainty pass through him.

"It's been horrible, Stuart, like some terrible nightmare!"

"I can well understand, and this"—he raked the cabin with a glance—"damnable place didn't help, I'm sure. Now, you must tell me every single thing that happened." He led her to the bunk and sat down beside her, both her hands cupped in his. "I've heard it, of course, but no version is the same. I must hear it all from you, just the way it really happened."

Haltingly, Marianna told him her story, beginning with her life on the Outer Banks and bringing it up to that fateful moment when she brought the poker down across Ezekial Throag's skull.

Marianna was drained and pale when she had finished, and she drooped against his shoulder. Stuart's mind was racing, assessing her story and trying to see ahead to what sort of defense he could construct for her.

He became aware that she was speaking. "What, Marianna? I'm sorry, I was thinking."

"I said—do you believe me?"

He said instantly, "Of course I believe you."

"Thank you for that." She tried to smile. "Few other people seem to."

"People always tend to believe the worst. Now, I have one question for you, Marianna. Do you wish me to handle your defense, or would you prefer another, more experienced lawyer?"

"Oh, yes, I want you to defend me!" She clutched his hand fiercely. "I don't know another lawyer, and even if I did, he probably wouldn't believe my side of it."

"Then I have much work to do," he said briskly. "But first, we have to get you out of this hellhole." He stood up and called, "Constable Dawes!"

After a moment the cabin door opened, and the constable stepped in. "Yes, Mr. Brawley?"

"Mrs. Street cannot remain confined here. Not in this place, fit only for sots and rowdy seamen. It's shameful, man!"

"I'm sorry, Mr. Brawley," Constable Dawes said stubbornly. "I have no choice. She is charged with a capital offense."

Stuart took a step forward. "Where do you think she might flee to? She has every intention of fighting against this absurd charge, until she is proclaimed innocent. I shall vouch for her. I should think that would be sufficient, since I am a citizen of some standing in the community."

The constable hesitated. "You will be responsible for her, sir?"

"Of course I will! You have my word of honor that she will be available at all times and will most certainly appear for trial—if this calumny continues that long."

The constable's gaze moved to Marianna. "Well, sir, that does put matters into a different light. I well know that this is no place for a woman, but as I saw it, it was my duty. However, if you will stand responsible—" He looked again at Stuart. "But you do understand that I will keep her house under close watch. I still have my duties to discharge."

Stuart gestured. "If you feel you must, just so long as she is removed from this hellish ship."

An hour later Marianna was welcomed with open arms, and copious tears, by Mrs. Horner. "Oh, madam! I am so relieved to have you home again. But goodness me!" She stepped back and surveyed her mistress. "You do look a sight!" She became brisk. "Come, we must have a bath and get you out of those clothes."

Marianna turned a pale face to Stuart. "When shall I see you again?"

"I'll drop by at every opportunity, Marianna. But you must remember, I am going to be quite busy preparing for your trial." At her look of concern, he added quickly, "Now don't be upset, my dear. I am confident that I shall be able to easily establish that yours was an act of self-defense."

Brave words, Stuart thought a week later; brave words indeed.

Inquiries at Southampton had disclosed that Ezekial Throag had indeed been a man of substance, a respected shipper, his business acumen highly regarded. True, there were a few who did not like the man, including several of the company employees, but that opinion, Stuart was forced to conclude, was due to the fact that Throag had been a hard taskmaster.

Stuart did not like the Barth brothers—they struck him as sly, furtive individuals—but they gave their dead partner high marks as well. The fact that they seemed secretly pleased at his demise, Stuart put down to envy and greed on their part.

The few times that he obliquely hinted at Throag being in command of a crew of wreckers on the Outer Banks, he was greeted by incredulity.

And in all fairness to the dead man, how could such a capable businessman have risen from being a wrecker to the position of owner of one-third of a prosperous shipping firm?

Possibly an answer would be forthcoming from the Outer Banks. Stuart could not spare the time necessary for a trip of that distance, so he had sent an investigator down, while he went ahead with preparations for the trial.

Despite all his efforts, Marianna was doomed to be tried on the murder charge, and in New York, not in Sag Harbor or Shelter Island. "All my talks with the people on the prosecutor's staff in New York have been fruitless," he explained glumly to Marianna. "They adamantly refuse to accept a plea of self-defense, maintaining that there is no evidence showing that you acted in self-defense." He added hastily, "I shall prove them wrong, Marianna, never fear."

Marianna seemed resigned to being placed on public trial, and did not show any reaction to his words. She was of course well-groomed now, a marked contrast to her appearance on the Hell Ship, but her spirits were low, and she seemed always in a lethargic state. She said listlessly, "But why New York? Why not here?"

"There are no facilities for a trial in this area. Except for an instance of a drunken sailor killing another, there has never been a murder committed in Sag Harbor, hard as that is to believe."

"But for what reason do they believe I killed Throag?"

"They cannot ascribe a motive to you, as I have pointed out repeatedly. But they claim that you killed a respected citizen and that your motive will become clear during the trial."

A week later he came to her again, wearing a glum face. "I have upsetting news, Marianna. The man I employed to go down to the Outer Banks and talk to the band of wreckers returned this morning. They did not deny knowing Throag, all admitted that he had lived among them. But they deny that he was their leader or that they ever had anything to do with wrecking ships. Naturally, they would not admit to being wreckers by trade, but as for Throag. . . . Evidently he had instilled such fear in them that they are still in terror of him, dead."

Marianna had been listening intently, dismay growing on

her face. "But can't you legally bind them to come to New York and testify at my trial?"

Stuart nodded. "I could, yes, but I think it would do you more harm than good. If they testified one after the other that they were not wreckers and that Ezekial Throag was not only not their leader, but was never engaged in nefarious activities, what would that do to your story?" He took her hand and felt a tremor go through her. "It would not help you, making them testify. Believe me, Marianna."

"I see," she said dully, sinking back into her lethargy. Then suddenly, in an outpouring of emotion, she pounded her fist on her knee. "Dear God, how I wish Adam were here!"

Chapter Eighteen

ONCE again Adam was in Charleston. The *Viking Queen* had encountered a violent storm off the Carolina coast, and a mast had sheared off, killing two men in the process. Adam had brought the crippled ship into the port of Charleston and learned, to his dismay, that it would be at least two weeks before a new mast could be installed.

It was a galling two weeks for him, not only because of the boring delay and the costly repairs, but also because this was the first time he had been in Charleston since that night he had rescued Marianna and Phillip Courtwright from their attackers, and everything reminded him of Marianna.

The fact that they had parted unhappily only made matters worse. Adam had regretted his cold behavior toward Marianna almost before Sag Harbor was out of sight, and he felt guilty. He had been unjust to her, and could not ask her forgiveness for God only knew how long—except by post, and that was not the same thing. He was almost tempted to turn about and beat his way back up the coast when the repairs were finished. But that would be a costly maneuver and would result in a very disgruntled crew.

Finally the repairs were made, and the *Viking Queen* was in readiness to resume the voyage. During the two-week delay, Adam had remained close to the vessel, overseeing the repairs, and on the last day he was busy seeing to fresh stores and all the other chores necessary on the eve of sailing. Now, he concluded, he was entitled to an evening of relaxation.

Leaving the ship, he limped along the cobbled streets of the tavern where he had fed a hungry Marianna and Phillip Courtwright on that long-ago evening. He had to stop now and then to ease his leg, leaning on the whalebone stick.

When he finally made it to the tavern, Adam soon realized that his choice of inns was a mistake. The memories of Marianna were too sharp. But be damned if he was going to let those memories have that much sway over him!

So he sat alone at a table, hunched over a mug of ale, brooding down into it. The good spirits he had courted never came, and his mood grew blacker and blacker.

Consequently, he glanced up and snarled angrily when a heavy hand clapped him on the shoulder. "Godalmighty, can't a man drink in peace? Can't you see I'm alone and like it that way. . . ." His voice died, as he saw Captain Jack Hammond staring gravely down at him.

Adam came to his feet. "Jack! Godalmighty, it's grand to see a familiar face!" He gestured. "Sit down and join me in a glass, man."

Captain Hammond sat down, and Adam motioned a serving girl over and ordered two more mugs of ale.

When the girl left, Hammond said, "I didn't expect to come across you here, Adam. You sailed two weeks ahead of me."

"Ran into some foul weather and had a mast snapped clean off, but it's fine now, and I sail with the morning tide."

Hammond's gaze had never left his face. "You don't know, then?"

Adam felt a shiver of apprehension. "Know what, Jack?"

"About Marianna."

Adam said tightly, "What about Marianna? Damnit, Jack!"

"I'm sorry, Adam. I didn't mean to—" Hammond scrubbed a hand down across his face. "She's been charged with murder and is about to go on trial." Tersely, Hammond related what he knew of Marianna's plight. When he mentioned Throag's name, Adam grunted.

"You knew this Throag, then?"

"Aye. Or rather, I knew *of* him. He came from close by, a wrecker off the Outer Banks."

Hammond raised an eyebrow. "It's true then, that the man was a villain?"

"Of course it's true! In fact, Marianna told me about him in this very room, the very first time I saw her. Shortly thereafter, anyway."

"Then you never met the man? You have only her word that he was a wrecker?"

"Now what does that mean?"

Hammond spread his hands. "It's just that this Throag appears to have been a respected citizen in Southampton, and most people are skeptical about her story, that she killed in self-defense. Now wait—I'm not saying I don't believe her story. But that is the atmosphere in which she is being tried, my friend."

"Marianna's word is good enough for me, Jack. Look—" he leaned forward—"if you had seen her, and the boy with her that night, you would have believed them, too. They were frightened out of their wits. They had barely escaped with their lives. In getting away they had killed Throag's son, but that was necessary, they told me. Marianna was sure that Throag would pursue them to the ends of the earth to avenge his son's death, and I am convinced that is what must have happened."

Hammond was nodding. "I believe you, Adam, but I'm not the one to convince."

"Godalmighty!" Adam slammed his mug down. "I've got to get back to her. I can only hope that I'm not too late."

The *Viking Queen* sailed for Sag Harbor the next morning. She sailed with a skeleton crew. Many of the hands elected to remain behind in the hope of signing on with other whalers. Adam did not blame them for leaving him. At least he was left with enough men to sail the ship. If need be, he would have sailed her himself.

It seemed to take forever, but in reality the ship, with a favoring wind, made better time than on the way down. They dropped anchor off the Long Wharf close to noon, and Adam had a dinghy lowered at once, leaving his new first mate in charge until his return. He did not row for the Long Wharf, but headed straight for Shelter Island.

After tying up the dinghy, he ran most of the way home, cursing his lame leg. He clattered up on the veranda, and, finding the door locked, he thumped on it. "Marianna! It's me, Adam!"

A curtain stirred at the window beside the door, and he caught a glimpse of Mrs. Horner's white face. There was the sound of a bolt rattling, and the door was flung open.

"Oh, sir! Thank the good Lord you're here, captain!"

"Where's Marianna? Where's my wife?"

"Oh!" Her hand flew to her mouth, and Mrs. Horner backed a step. "You don't know, do you, sir? Oh, the poor child!"

"I know," he said grimly. "Where is she, Mrs. Horner?"

"She's not here, captain."

"Where, damnit?"

"In New York, sir. That's where the trial is taking place."

Late that afternoon, Adam left Sag Harbor in a rented rig, bound for New York.

Even in her inexperience, Marianna knew that the trial was going against her. It had gone badly from the first, despite everything that Stuart could do. Marianna did not blame him; he was doing as well, or better, than most lawyers could have done under the circumstances.

The trouble was, the whole outcome of the trial rested on Ezekial Throag's character. Marianna could not deny that she had killed Throag, but since her plea was self-defense, Throag's true character had to be brought to light; and witness after witness testified that he had been a fine, upstanding citizen of Southampton for a considerable time. Every time words of praise came from a witness, the all-male jury's collective gaze, it seemed to Marianna, came to rest on her accusingly, and it took all her willpower to keep her head high. The magistrate, a scowling figure all in black, seemed to Marianna to be the executioner, impatient for the trial to get over with so that he could get on with the business of seeing her properly punished for her crime.

There was an additional, upsetting factor that she had not counted on. Due to the unusual aspect of the case—a pretty woman on trial for murder—the courtroom was packed every day.

When they learned that the trial would be held in New York, Stuart had said to her, "That may be all to the good, Marianna. If you were on public trial in Sag Harbor, the atmosphere would probably be hostile. But since you are not known in New York, and the crime did not occur here, the interest should be minimal."

On the second day of the trial, watching people fight to get into the courtroom, he had observed sadly, "It would appear that I was mistaken, my dear. In fact, it would appear that I am wrong about many things. You likely would have been better off with another lawyer."

Now, into the fourth day of the trial, Stuart was cross-examining yet another character witness the prosecution had put on the stand, this time the owner of a tavern Throag had frequented.

"Now, Mr. Rawlins, you have testified that Ezekial Throag patronized your establishment?"

"Yup, that he did," the witness said proudly.

"How often would you estimate? Once a week? Twice a week?"

"More'n that. Hardly a day passed that Squire Throag didn't drop in for a mug."

"A mug? Every day, you say?"

"Near about, yup."

"Did he ever drink more than one mug? Two, perhaps more?"

"Yup, times he would."

"A toper then, was he?"

"A toper now, is it?" The tavern keeper, middle-aged, plump, and red of face from liberal use of his own product, scowled. "That depends on how you look at it, I'd say. I wouldn't call a man a toper 'cause he has a glass or two at the end of a hard day. Leastways," the man grinned, "if'n it's my ale he's drinking."

A titter of laughter swept the courtroom.

Flushing, Stuart said in a tight voice, "This is not a matter for humor, sir. A woman is on trial here."

The witness's gaze darted to Marianna. "It seems to me

the woman you're talking about should know about a man and his ale, being she's a tavern wench."

"Your Honor, this is unpardonable!" Stuart said angrily. "Will you instruct the witness to confine his remarks to a simple response to my questions?"

The magistrate rapped his gavel languidly. "The witness is so instructed. Members of the jury will disregard the remark."

The man in the witness chair looked at the jury, his eyebrow arched.

Stuart said in a hard voice, "Let me put it to you this way, sir. Did you ever see Ezekial Throag intoxicated?"

Rawlins shrugged. "Nope, never did. Always a perfect gentleman, was Squire Throag."

The testimony had been so similar, so damning for Marianna, that her attention had long since dulled. What was the use of this charade, she thought despairingly. She was doomed. It might save her a lot of personal agony if she just told Stuart to give up his efforts, then threw herself on the mercy of the court. However, her glance came to rest on the man in the black robes, and she knew that she would receive no mercy at his hands. This knowledge stiffened her resolve, and she sat up straight, chin jutting forward. Hellfire and spit! Hopeless as it might seem, she was determined to fight on to the bitter end.

She concentrated her attention anew on Stuart and the witness. Stuart turned in disgust and gestured wearily. "No more questions, Mr. Rawlins."

Just before Stuart reached the table, he paused in midstride, staring in astonishment toward the back of the courtroom. Marianna turned, following his gaze. She went rigid with amazement. It was Adam, striding purposefully toward them, his face grave. Marianna could not move. Her heart began to beat erratically, and she opened her mouth to cry out, but no words came. For a moment she feared that she would faint.

Then Adam was there, leaning down, his big hands engulfing hers. "Marianna! Godalmighty, my love, what are they trying to do to you?"

Unsteadily, she got to her feet and leaned into him, her

nostrils gratefully inhaling the male odor of him. "Adam, I was never so glad to see anyone!"

Dimly, she heard the buzz of voices, the banging of the gavel, and the magistrate's annoyed voice. "Mr. Brawley, what is the meaning of this disturbance? Sir, if you do not—"

"Your Honor, the hour is growing late, and I would like to petition the court for a recess until tomorrow morning. The man just arriving is the defendant's husband. He is a whaling captain and has been out to sea. He knows nothing of the circumstances of his wife's situation, and I would plead time to acquaint him with it."

"Very well, Mr. Brawley," the magistrate said grumpily. "I shall be lenient in this instance, but I must warn you that I do not like my court disrupted in such a fashion!"

Stuart had found quarters in a private home for Marianna, not far from the courtroom, and he was staying in a hotel farther uptown. The three of them walked over after leaving the courtroom, Marianna plying Adam with questions about how he had heard about the trial. When he had explained everything to her satisfaction, he queried her about Throag's death and all else that had transpired.

By the time the explanations were all made, they were at the house where Marianna was staying. They sat on the porch, and the discussion grew more serious, as Adam said, "Brawley, how is the trial going?"

Try as he would, Adam could not keep the hostility out of his voice, as he well remembered the gossip about Marianna and this man. He had no doubt that Brawley was capable, yet he did wish that Marianna had employed someone else. However, he knew that it was too late now for that.

Stuart said glumly, "Not at all well, Captain Street. No matter how hard I go at them, I can't seem to shake the character testimony of the witnesses. Unfortunately, the dead man appears to have been the most respectable man on Long Island."

"Then let me testify," Adam said heatedly. "I can tell them what a bastard he was!"

Marianna brightened. "That's right, Stuart, I told him about Throag."

Stuart sighed. "That's the difficulty, Marianna. You *told* him about Throag. Captain Street never clapped eyes on the man. Did he?"

"Well, no," she admitted. "But Phillip and I both told him about Throag, about what a terrible man he was. That should count for something."

Stuart sighed again. "I fear not, Marianna. Aside from the fact that Captain Street's testimony would all be hearsay, any evidence he gave would be given little credence by the members of the jury."

Adam was indignant. "Why would that be?"

"Simply because you are her husband, captain. Naturally, out of your concern and love for your wife, you would lie to protect her good name."

"I am not a liar, sir, and it would not be necessary to lie. I need only tell the truth."

Stuart was shaking his head. "No, no, you misunderstand me, sir. I am not calling you a liar, I am merely stating what the members of the jury will believe. No, in my most earnest opinion, placing you on the witness stand would only do your wife grave harm. I shudder to think what the prosecutor would do to you, should I permit you to testify."

"But I must be able to do something!" Adam said. "I feel so damned helpless."

"Adam—darling, you *are* doing something." Marianna placed her hand on his arm. "You can't know what your just being here, by my side, means to me. I felt so alone before. Now I can face anything."

Stuart got to his feet. "Well, it has been a long, trying day, and you must be exhausted, Marianna. You as well, Captain Street. Do you have accommodations?"

Adam stared at him in surprise. "No, of course not. I came directly to the courtroom the instant I arrived in New York."

"I'm sure I can get you a room in the hotel where I am staying."

Marianna stirred in protest. "But why can't Adam stay here, with me?"

Stuart was shaking his head. "I'm afraid that is out of the question. Even if it wasn't, it might not be advisable."

"Why not, for heaven's sake?" she demanded.

"Because you are in my care, in my custody, Marianna. I arranged that, back on Shelter Island, to keep you off that Hell Ship. Well, the same holds true here, you see. If I had not made myself responsible for you, Marianna, you would be held in prison here."

"I still fail to see—Adam is my husband!"

"And that is the problem, you see. I can imagine the uproar should it be learned that you are—uh,"—Stuart turned red, his gaze sliding away—"being permitted conjugal rights. Not only would it be frowned upon by the court, but it might even result in your being placed under lock and key. I'm sorry, Captain Street," Stuart said more firmly, "but it will only be for a short time. The trial will be over shortly."

Adam got to his feet, accepting it with as much grace as possible. "It's all right, my love. We have to think first and foremost of winning your freedom." He framed her face with his hands and kissed her gently.

Marianna clung to him fiercely. "Darling, I want you with me!"

"I know, but it cannot be. Be brave, Marianna. You've borne up well this far. You can survive a few more days."

He disengaged her hands, nodded curtly to Stuart, and limped away without looking at her again.

Stuart gave Marianna an apologetic shrug and followed Adam down the steps. As Marianna went slowly into the house, she was wondering if Stuart had an ulterior motive in keeping her apart from her husband. Did he still harbor hopes of taking her away from Adam? During the days of the trial, Marianna had grown to respect Stuart more and more. Even though the trial was not going well, she had come to know how intelligent he was, how well-versed in the law, and she realized that if he was able to somehow extricate her from the situation she was in, she would be eternally grateful to him.

And now, it dawned on her just how dependent she had become on him. She knew that if her blind faith in him wavered for an instant, she would be lost to despair.

However, that did not mean that she loved him or that he should expect any reward beyond a lawyer's fee.

But *did* he expect more?

And perhaps more important, what did Adam think of it? If she became too emotionally dependent on Stuart Brawley, it could well destroy her marriage.

Chapter Nineteen

IT was the Barth brothers' turn to testify. Marianna had disliked them on sight. They struck her as slimy and sly; one of them would have been enough; the pair together were almost too much.

But no matter what Marianna's impression of them might be, they were highly thought of in Southampton, as the prosecutor managed to bring out in their testimony.

Now it was Stuart's turn at the second Barth brother, Enoch.

Frustrated by his efforts to shake the first brother's testimony, Stuart took up a belligerent stance before the witness. "Mr. Barth, I find myself puzzled by one aspect of your testimony, as well as that of your brother's. Your shipping firm is a prosperous concern, is it not? Wait. Allow me to rephrase the question. Before you made the deceased a partner, it was doing very well, was it not?"

"It was, indeed," said Enoch Barth.

"Then, as you have testified, Mr. Throag came along, and you allowed him to purchase a third interest in the company. Is that not correct?"

"Yes."

"Is that not unusual?"

Enoch Barth frowned. "I don't catch your meaning."

"Well, you were doing very well, not in the need of fresh investment capital, which is usually the case when a third interest in a company is sold. Why then did you sell to him?"

"Ezekial was an old friend," Enoch Barth said through

pursed lips. "He has—had a vast experience in shipping, and he had the money to invest."

"Ah, an old friend, an experienced shipper. Where exactly was he involved in shipping?"

"Oh, somewhere in the south, I believe," Enoch Barth said vaguely.

"That is where you and your brother became acquainted with the deceased?"

"Uh, yes. In Charleston."

"Charleston?" Stuart pounced. "Would it not be more accurate to say that you met Ezekial Throag on the Outer Banks, where he was the leader of a band of wreckers?"

Only Stuart, from his position directly in front of the witness, saw Barth's faint start, the slight widening of his eyes. But he recovered nicely and said bewilderedly, "I don't catch your meaning, sir."

"Oh, I think you do. Ezekial Throag's experience in shipping was limited to the criminal business of wrecking ships by luring them to their deaths by false signals and then looting them of their cargoes, is that not true?"

Belatedly, the prosecutor leaped to his feet and shouted indignantly, "I object most strenuously, Your Honor! Not only is Mr. Brawley attempting to blacken the name of a dead man, but he is also attempting to impugn the good name of this witness!"

"Your Honor, this man is the prosecution's witness," Stuart said, "and as such I have the right to examine him as to his character and veracity. And the character of the deceased goes to the heart of the case for the defense."

The magistrate glowered down at Stuart, but finally he said grudgingly, "Very well, Mr. Brawley, but the court hopes that you prove the relevancy of this line of questioning. If you do not, you shall incur the court's displeasure."

"It is relevant, Your Honor, and I shall prove it so," Stuart said with far more confidence than he felt. "Now, Mr. Barth, is it not true that the dead man was a wrecker by profession?"

Enoch Barth had been given time to recover his aplomb. "If that is so, sir, it was never revealed to me—"

"And that, Enoch Barth, is a falsehood!" cried a voice from the rear of the courtroom.

The courtroom broke into an uproar, and the gavel banged repeatedly. Marianna whirled around in her seat and froze in astonishment at the sight of a slim figure in the doorway. In the front row directly behind her, Adam had also turned around, his face registering disbelief.

Marianna rose unsteadily to her feet. Then Stuart was at her side, staying her. In a fierce whisper he said, "Marianna, do you know that man?"

"Yes! It's Phillip! Phillip Courtwright!"

It was indeed Phillip—an older, obviously more mature Phillip, gaunt, and with lines in his face. He was leaner, harder, and he made Marianna think of a honed razor as he stood without moving, his burning gaze fixed on the man in the witness chair.

The repeated pounding of the gavel was gradually quieting the courtroom, and the magistrate finally made himself heard. "Order in the court! I will have order and quiet in my court, or I will clear the room!" A stillness fell. "Now, who are you, sir, and how dare you interrupt this court proceedings?"

Stuart faced around. "This man is Phillip Courtwright, Your Honor, and he is a missing witness the defense has sought desperately. He has testimony pertinent, nay, vital, to these proceedings. If I may have a few words with him, Your Honor?"

The man on the bench scowled blackly. "Very well, Mr. Brawley, but I must caution you, sir, that you are sorely trying the court's patience."

Phillip was already making his way to the table where Marianna was standing. He was smiling in delight as he searched her face with his gaze.

"Phillip! I'm so happy to see you!" She kissed him full on the mouth. "I haven't heard a word from you, and I feared that you were dead."

He held her off to look at her. "You look wonderful, Marianna, considering the circumstances. As for my getting word to you, how could I? I arrived in Boston only a short while after Aunt Prudence's passing, and you were gone, with absolutely no word as to your destination."

"How did you find me, Phillip?"

"I read the newspaper article in a New York newspaper about Marianna Street, the captain's wife, who brought his ship home after the captain had been so badly injured that he could not command her. I knew it had to be you. I hastened to Sag Harbor at once, and what did I find? I found that you were being tried for the murder of Ezekial Throag, and I came here as quickly as I could." His smile died, and pain was mirrored in his eyes. "It was a blow to me, Marianna, learning that you were wed to another. You promised to wait for me."

"But you were gone so long, Phillip, and I—" She broke off as she saw Adam making his way toward them, frowning at Phillip. "Here's Adam now. You remember him, don't you?"

Phillip turned slowly, his expression guarded. "Yes, I remember Captain Street very well. How are you, captain?"

He held out his hand, and after a brief hesitation, Adam took it. "I'm fine, Mr. Courtwright, except for Marianna's plight."

"And speaking of that," Stuart interrupted, "can we not leave the greetings until later? I must have a few words with you in private, Mr. Courtwright, if you please."

"This is my attorney, Phillip. Stuart Brawley," Marianna said.

The two men shook hands, and then Stuart guided Phillip to the table and sat down with him. Heads together, they conversed in whispers. Marianna stood with Adam. Neither could find anything to say. Marianna felt strangely shy toward her husband after Phillip's sudden appearance. Not only that, but she was swept by a turmoil of emotions, old feelings reawakened by Phillip's return to her life.

On his part Adam, with his usual perceptiveness, realized what Phillip's startling appearance, as if from the dead, must mean to her, what a rage of emotions it must have set up in her breast. This aroused a certain feeling of jealousy in him, and he wanted to tell her, sternly, that he was her husband, that they loved one another, that she was promised to him forever. Yet, he did not speak, feeling that it was neither the time nor the place.

The rap of the gavel had an angry sound. "Mr. Brawley, the court's patience is about at an end. I wish to get on with the progress of the trial."

Stuart bobbed to his feet. "And I as well, Your Honor. And in that respect, toward that goal, to expedite justice, I have a proposal to make to the court. Mr. Courtwright has vital testimony to lay before the court, and in the interest of speeding up the proceedings, I ask leave to place him on the witness stand out of turn. He is, of course, a witness for the defense, and the prosecution has yet to complete its case, but it is my belief that when this witness's testimony is heard, this trial will reach a speedy conclusion."

The magistrate glanced over at the other table. "Does the prosecution have any objections?"

The prosecutor, young, eager with ambition, got to his feet and said cautiously, "This is highly unusual, Your Honor, but the prosecution has no objection if it is in the interest of justice."

Stuart said gravely, "The court has my assurance that the testimony of this witness is definitely in the interest of justice."

The magistrate sighed. "Very well, Mr. Brawley, you may proceed."

Phillip was sworn in, and Stuart led him adroitly into his background, establishing him as a young man from a respected family, and a man of substance. Phillip's sincerity was evident, and Marianna saw that the jury was impressed. She had to admire Stuart's skill at questioning him. When Phillip related the events that occurred on the Outer Banks, how they had come to kill Jude Throag, the courtroom was quiet as a grave, the audience hanging on every word. The prosecutor objected a few times, but he soon desisted, evidently realizing that he was doing more harm than good and antagonizing the members of the jury. The picture of Ezekial Throag that now emerged was totally different from the one the other witnesses had painted.

During the earlier part of his testimony, Stuart was quick to restrain Phillip when he touched on the Barths, but even so, they began to emerge as villains.

When Phillip had told of his being shanghaied and his eventual return to Boston, to find Marianna vanished without a trace, Stuart said, "All right, Mr. Courtwright, now tell the court what transpired after that."

"I decided that I would go to Southampton, to investigate the Barth brothers. I had collected some evidence connecting them with illegal activities in the shipping industry, nefarious schemes such as the one that bankrupted my poor father, but I had as yet no connection between them and the wreckers on the Outer Banks."

"Your Honor," the prosecutor snarled, "the Barth brothers are not on trial here, and since they have no legal representation, I must protest in their behalf."

"I fully intend, Your Honor," Stuart retorted, "to impeach the testimony of the Barths through this witness. Mr. Courtwright has documents attesting to his testimony, and I can enter them into evidence now, but it would expedite matters considerably if I could finish my examination first."

"You may continue, Mr. Brawley."

"Now, Mr. Courtwright, you went to Southampton. What, if anything, transpired there?"

"I discovered, to my astonishment and consternation, that Ezekial Throag had somehow become a third owner of the Barth Shipping Company. I began to observe him closely, and late one evening I saw him come from his rooming house, the Inn of the Rose, with a body on his back." A gasp swept the courtroom, and Phillip waited until the magistrate had gaveled the audience into silence. "I followed him at a discreet distance and saw him drop the body into the ocean off the wharf. I continued to watch Throag. He went about his normal activities after that, but I soon came to know that the body he was carrying was that of Rose Lake, his landlady, the owner of the inn where he was staying."

"The inference being that Ezekial Throag murdered his landlady."

"That is true."

"Your Honor, I must object!" The prosecutor was on his

feet. "Counsel for the defense himself states that it is only inference on the part of the witness that Ezekial Throag committed murder, or even that murder was committed! This is calumny, defaming a dead man who is not here to defend himself!"

"Your objection is well taken," the magistrate said. "Mr. Brawley, what your witness believes is not evidence, you well know that. Objection sustained. Members of the jury will disregard the charge of murder, and consider the words of the witness as only what he *believes* to be true."

Stuart stood with his head bowed meekly during the reprimand, but his gaze was on the jury, and he was pleased at their reaction. They believed that Throag had been a murderer, and that was the important thing.

"Mr. Courtwright, you state that it is your—uh, belief that Ezekial Throag committed murder, yet you did not report what you observed to the authorities. Why is that? It was your duty to do so."

"That is true, I well realized that at the time, and I debated with myself about doing so. But it would have given my presence away and would have interfered with my primary purpose there, that of connecting the Barth brothers with criminal activities. I didn't consider Throag a threat to me, and since I did not know where Marianna was, I figured that he did not, either, and therefore was no threat to her."

"Then you did not notify the authorities of your suspicions?"

"No, sir, I did not. I can see now that I was wrong."

"We all suffer from hindsight. We would be less than human if we did not. Please go on, Mr. Courtwright. What happened next?"

"Well, I had a stroke of good fortune. I became friendly with a clerk employed by the Barths, a man by the name of Benton." Phillip smiled. "We became drinking companions, you might say. One evening, over a mug of ale, Benton told me something of much interest."

"And what was that?"

"He informed me that a letter had come to the Barths, from the Outer Banks, off the Carolina coast. The sender of

the letter was a man named Peters, and the substance of
the letter was to the effect that this Peters was in cahoots
with the Barth brothers. He was the man in charge of the
wreckers on the Outer—"

The prosecutor was up. "Objection, Your Honor! This is
all pure hearsay! Direct the witness to produce this letter."
He sneered. "If such a letter exists."

"Mr. Brawley?"

"The letter is not in our possession, Your Honor. But if
the court will bear with us, we shall shortly produce documents that will establish without a shadow of a doubt that a
connection did exist between the Barth Shipping Company, Ezekial Throag, and the ship wreckers on the Outer
Banks."

"Very well, Mr. Brawley, you may continue."

"Thank you, Your Honor. Now, Mr. Courtwright, what
transpired next?"

"I journeyed down to the Outer Banks and talked to the
man, Peters, not knowing what to expect. To my surprise, I
found him most cooperative. He is bitter, it seems. In his
words, 'The bloody brothers have been rooking us, not
giving me and my men my fair share. When I charged
them with this, they sent down two bullies to break my legs
for me. Well, they forgot one thing. The men here are loyal
to me, and they stood the bullies off. You see, bloody Throag
was their leader afore me, and he was cheating them as
well, keeping the big share of the loot for him and his son.
Then I came along and shared and shared alike with them,
and they stand by me. Now I hear the brothers want nothing more to do with us. Well, we don't need the bloody
brothers, you see. We do just fine on our own.' "

The prosecutor was on his feet again. "Hearsay, Your
Honor! Rank hearsay!"

"If it please the court," Stuart said quietly, but with an
edge of triumph, "we have documents to confirm the testimony. Mr. Courtwright has in his possession affidavits,
signed and sworn to by the man Peters. Everything that
the witness has testified to here is included, and much
more. Also in his possession are more affidavits, signed by
other wreckers, swearing that Ezekial Throag was their

leader for some twenty years and participated personally in the crimes, that he, in fact, planned them. Altogether, documents damning Ezekial Throag and the Barth brothers for the criminals that they are—"

"It's all lies, damned lies!" Enoch Barth was standing up in the back of the courtroom, along with his brother.

The gavel banged, and the magistrate leaned forward, his stern gaze on the Barth brothers. "Bailiff, arrest those men at once!"

The brothers, who had been seated about halfway back in the courtroom, turned in unison and broke for the door. But the crowd was on its feet by this time, and they swarmed into the aisle, making it impossible for the Barths to make headway. The bailiff soon had them by the arms.

The next afternoon, the jury, after deliberating for only a half hour, delivered its verdict—not guilty!

The courtroom broke into an uproar of applause and cheers. Adam, standing in the front row directly behind the table where Marianna, Phillip, and Stuart Brawley were, felt a wry sense of amusement. Where before the crowd had been a mob, thirsting for Marianna's blood, now they were all on her side, seeing her as the victim of the villainous Ezekial Throag, believing as one that she had killed him in defense of her life.

Then Adam sobered as his glance rested on Marianna. Her face was aglow with happiness. Expecting her to turn to him, he felt a stab of dismay as she threw her arms around Phillip and kissed him soundly.

"Phillip, you saved me! You saved my life!"

An embarrassed Phillip smiled shyly. "It was your due, little one, since you once saved mine."

Stuart gripped Phillip's hand and wrung it, while Marianna clung to Phillip's other hand. The lawyer said, "But we are grateful, Marianna and I. You certainly arrived in the nick of time. But I am puzzled by one thing, sir. I sent a man down to the Outer Banks, and everyone there denied any knowledge of criminal activities, their own *or* Throag's."

Phillip smiled sheepishly. "Your man represented a threat to them, to their way of life. I did not. After Throag deserted them, or so they considered it, and Peters took command, they learned how much Throag had cheated them all those years, and they hated him for that and thus were willing to incriminate him, so long as their own livelihood was not threatened, and I promised them that it wouldn't be. Of course," he laughed, "I have no power to keep that promise, so I don't know what will happen to them now. Also, I am afraid that I boasted a trifle. I told them that I had taken care of Jude Throag, had I not? Therefore, I would also take care of his father. It was foolish of them to believe that, but then perhaps they wanted to."

Marianna was gazing at Phillip admiringly, and Adam experienced a sinking feeling. He well remembered how Marianna had been enamored of the youth before, and apparently she still was. His mind was a battleground of conflicting thoughts. Marrying Marianna could have been a mistake. The life of a sea captain was rough on a woman. She was an impatient person, and his long absences did not set well with her. And although her accompanying him on the one voyage had turned out well enough, under the circumstances Adam had to wonder if she would be content with spending most of her life at sea.

On the other hand, Phillip Courtwright was a gentleman born, at ease with the gentry; and the life he would be able to offer her, now that his thirst for vengeance was sated, would be a life of ease, fine clothing, grand balls, and social affairs—none of which Captain Adam Street would ever be able to give her. He loved Marianna with all his heart and being, but not even for his love of her would he forsake his life at sea. He snorted at the concept of living on shore, performing for her like a tame seal. Perhaps he was being unfair to her, yet it could not be denied that she yearned for a more cultured life than that of a sea captain's wife.

For a moment he contemplated stepping forward, seizing her by the arm, and hauling her bodily away from here and back to Shelter Island.

No. Godalmighty, he wanted no wife he had to force to remain by his side.

He wheeled and strode away, leaving Marianna to her milksop and her fancy lawyer.

"Adam?" Turning about, Marianna was just in time to see Adam's broad back going out the courtroom door.

Where was he going? Why had he not shown his pleasure at the jury's verdict?

She had been so caught up in delight at her sudden freedom and her gratitude to Phillip for being the means of saving her that she had momentarily forgotten everything else.

And now, now that she had turned to share her happiness with Adam, he was walking away without a word. It was inexplicable and brought to her a sudden wrench of sadness.

She took two steps after him, then Phillip called, "Marianna?"

She turned back. "Yes?"

"I want to buy you supper, in celebration. You and Mr. Brawley. And your husband, of course." He glanced about the now-empty courtroom in surprise. "Where *is* Captain Street?"

To the devil with Adam, she thought, her dismay now replaced by a thrust of anger. "He had something better to do, it seems," she said bitterly. She linked her arm with Phillip's. "Yes, I would dearly love to go to supper with you."

Adam was supervising the fitting of a new sail; one had been seriously weakened by the rough weather off the Carolina coast, and he wanted it replaced before sailing again. He intended to sail on the morrow.

It had been five days since the end of the trial, and he had not seen Marianna. Returning from New York without her, he had stopped off at the house on Shelter Island for his trunk, avoiding Mrs. Horner's questions as to the whereabouts of Marianna; and since then he had spent the days and nights on the *Viking Queen*, lying sleepless in his lonely cabin. The only times he had been ashore were to order supplies for the coming voyage and to recruit seamen to replace those who had left the ship in Charleston. The supplies had been loaded, and he had a full crew.

Now, the new sail was in place, and Adam dismissed the

men for the noon mess, after which he stood alone on the captain's bridge, staring toward Shelter Island.

For the hundredth time he wondered if he should at least make a quick trip home to see if Marianna had returned. Perhaps he was wronging her. Viewed in retrospect, he realized that he had behaved churlishly by allowing jealousy to drive him away from her, turning away without even a word about how happy he was that she was a free woman again.

But Godalmighty, she had had plenty of time to return from New York—*if* she had returned at all. So why had she not come to him? Of course, Marianna was stiff-necked with pride, he had observed this quality in her any number of times.

A small voice hooted in his mind: And you, Captain Adam Street, how about your own stubborn pride?

He made an impatient sound deep in his throat. And yet, he was honest enough with himself to admit that he might well have lost the love of his life through foolish pride, for he knew that he would never love another woman, not in the way he loved Marianna.

For some minutes he had been aware of a dinghy rowing toward the *Viking Queen.* Now he focused on the boat and saw two figures in it. He squinted against the afternoon sun's glare, and his heart gave a great leap as he recognized Mr. Horner at the oars and Marianna sitting primly in the bow, hands folded in her lap.

He turned his head and bellowed for a seaman. As the man hurried up, skidding to a stop, Adam said gruffly, "A boat is coming alongside, seaman. Throw down a rope and lower the Jacob's ladder."

With alacrity the man obeyed, and within a few minutes the dinghy was lashed to the ship, and Marianna was clambering up the rope ladder. Adam limped down to the main deck but stood well back, arms crossed over his chest, his expression giving away none of the turbulent feelings in his breast. His heart was thudding with hope, but he would be damned if he would give her the satisfaction of . . .

Marianna's face appeared above the rail. She gave him a single flashing glance, then turned her head to shout down to the dinghy, "Wait for me, Mr. Horner. I may well be returning shortly!"

She came on up the ladder, the sailor giving her a hand up onto the deck. She took a few steps toward Adam, then stopped, her hands on her hips. Her eyes threw off sparks. "Well?"

"Well what?"

"Hellfire and spit, Adam Street! You owe me some sort of explanation!"

He said tightly, "Do you think so?"

"Yes, I think so! You walked off without a word to me, as if you didn't care whether or not I was found innocent."

"I care."

"Then why didn't you say something? It's been five whole days, and I've been home waiting for you. I just found out today that you're sailing. You were going to sail away without a word to me!"

"The last time I saw you, you were rather busy," he said in a dry voice.

"You were jealous!" She began to smile. "Captain Adam Street, jealous."

"It seemed to me that I had reason to be. After all, you were quite enamored of young Courtwright at one time, as I recall, and I thought that perhaps your old love had been rekindled on seeing him again."

"Men! Adam, for a knowledgeable man, you can be so foolish at times." She shook her head. "If I had not met you, I probably would still be in love with Phillip, or think that I was. But I fell in love with a boy. I was a child, Adam, and Phillip little more than that. But I am no longer that child. I shall always care for Phillip, and I am eternally grateful for what he has done for me, but he and I are both different people now. What I once felt for him now seems a dream."

A slow smile illuminated Adam's face. "You're no longer a child, Marianna, that is for certain. You've grown into a perceptive woman, my love."

She stepped to him, her eyes and face luminous. "Am I, Adam? Am I your love?"

"Yes, Marianna," he said tenderly. "For now, and always.

And now"—he became brisk—"we'd better accompany Mr. Horner back to the house and pack your trunk, if you're to sail with me."

"There's no need for that." She reached up to touch his face. "I packed my trunks before I left the house. I would rather—" A faint color touched her cheeks. "I would rather spend the night in the captain's cabin."

"You've become not only a grown woman, but a bold one, as well."

"I trust you'll not mind a wanton, as well, sir, because that is certainly what I intend to be this night," she said in a soft voice.

He gave a shout of laughter, then limped to the rail and called down, "Mr. Horner, will you be so kind as to return home and fetch Mrs. Street's trunks to the ship?"

Returning to Marianna's side, he gave her his arm. He said gravely, "It is yet early, but perhaps you would care to retire to the captain's cabin?"

"I can think of nothing that would pleasure me more, sir," she said demurely.

As Adam opened the door to his cabin and started to usher her inside, Marianna held back. "Adam?"

"Yes, my love?"

"Would you really have sailed without me, without even a word of farewell? If I had not come to you?"

"Some day I may see fit to answer that question, but not now."

He picked her up by the elbows, swung her around into the cabin, and closed the door firmly.

News item: November 8, 1848:

> The ship, Viking Queen, *owned by Captain Adam Street, of Shelter Island, New York, left Sag Harbor yesterday with a load of passengers bound for the gold fields of California. Captain Street, a well-known figure in Sag Harbor, spoke with this reporter of his decision to convert his ship, a whaler, into a passenger vessel. The* Viking Queen *was one of the last whaling*

ships operating out of our harbor to make such a change, and her departure sadly marks the end of an era.

Accompanying Captain Street was his wife, Marianna, and their two-year-old son, Phillip.

ABOUT THE AUTHOR

A few years ago Patricia Matthews was just another housewife and working mother. An office manager, she lived in a middle class home with her husband and two children. Like thousands of other women around the country she was writing in her spare time. However, unlike many other writers Patricia Matthews' own true life story has proven to have a Cinderella ending. Today she is "America's leading lady of historical romance" with ten consecutive best-selling novels to her credit and millions of fans all over the world.

Along with her husband, Clayton, who is a very successful writer himself, Patricia travels over 20,000 miles a year researching her books. She likes to know each place she writes about, and her exotic locales have ranged from the Alaska wilds to southern plantations. The Matthews, who say they have a "paperback perfect" marriage, live in Los Angeles.

Dear Reader:

I should like to take this opportunity to tell you about a soon to be published book that is rather special to me, for it is a book that I wrote in collaboration with my husband, Clayton Matthews.

Many of you are familiar with his work, and have enjoyed his many novels and short stories, and I believe that you will enjoy this work we have created together.

The book is titled *Midnight Whispers,* and it is a romantic suspense novel. The story is contemporary, not historical; yet it has, I believe, the same qualities which many of my fans have written to tell me they look for in my historical romances: romance, adventure, intriguing plot, and characters that you can identify with, and care for.

Both Matt and I thoroughly enjoyed writing this novel—we traveled to Ireland, England, Austria and Switzerland, doing the research—and we both hope that this enjoyment will be passed on to you, our readers, through this book.

Midnight Whispers will be published by Bantam, and will be available wherever paperback books are sold in mid-September 1981. Both Matt and I hope that you will read it, and enjoy it.

Love,

Patricia Matthews